THE
SILVERED
SERPENTS

Also by Roshani Chokshi

For Young Readers
Aru Shah and the End of Time
Aru Shah and the Song of Death

For Older Readers
The Star-Touched Queen
A Crown of Wishes
Star-Touched Stories
The Gilded Wolves

THE
SILVERED
SERPENTS

Roshani Chokshi

Wednesday Books
New York

First published in the United States by Wednesday Books, an imprint of
St. Martin's Publishing Group

THE SILVERED SERPENTS. Copyright © 2020 by Roshani Chokshi. All rights reserved.
Printed in the United States of America. For information, address
St. Martin's Publishing Group, 120 Broadway, New York, NY 10271.

www.wednesdaybooks.com

The Library of Congress Cataloging-in-Publication Data is available upon request.

ISBN 978-1-250-14457-7(hardcover)
ISBN 978-1-250-75992-4 (international,
sold outside the U.S., subject to rights availability)
ISBN 978-1-250-14459-1 (ebook)

Our books may be purchased in bulk for promotional, educational, or business use. Please contact your local bookseller or the Macmillan Corporate and Premium Sales Department at 1-800-221-7945, extension 5442, or by email at MacmillanSpecialMarkets@macmillan.com.

First U.S. Edition: 2020
First International Edition: 2020

10 9 8 7 6 5 4 3 2 1

To Nicolas Cage, the muse I didn't ask for

Oh Faustus, lay that damned book aside,
And gaze not on it lest it tempt thy soul
And heap God's heavy wrath upon thy head.

— FAUSTUS

PROLOGUE

Thirteen years ago . . .

The matriarch of House Kore adjusted the Christmas present in her arms. It was a portable little theatre, full of brightly painted figurines and miniature objects—swords and capes, whirring carousels, and even a rich velvet curtain controlled by a small draw-string mechanism. Séverin would love it. She had planned the surprise after last week, when she had taken him to the theatre. Most six-year-olds would have looked at the stage, but Séverin had spent the whole time watching the audience.

"You're missing the show, my dear," she'd said.

Séverin looked up at her, large violet eyes questioning.

"Am I?"

She'd let him be after that, and afterwards he'd told her in a rush how peoples' faces changed when something happened on the stage. It seemed the magic of the performance had somehow been both entirely lost on and entirely understood by him.

The matriarch smiled to herself as she walked up the stone steps of the House Vanth manor where the bright lights of the Winter Conclave beckoned. Although this year's Winter Conclave took place in the cold shadow of the Rhône-Alpes Mountains, the itinerary had not changed in centuries. Each House of the Order of Babel would bring new and unmarked Forged treasures from their colonies to be redistributed in the Midnight Auction. It was a test for the many Houses, and a representation of their country's wealth and imperialism if they could bring in not only their own treasures, but purchase new ones. All Houses had a specific interest, but some had enough resources to diversify their interests.

House Kore had an eye toward botanical advancements, but her illustrious wealth and coffers brimmed with as much varied treasure as there were languages in the world. Others, like House Dazbog of Russia, drew little income from their colonies and could trade only in secrets and parchment. Regardless of the differences between the Order's attending Houses, the purpose of the Winter Conclave never changed: to renew their pledge to safeguard Western civilization and its treasures, to keep safe the Babel Fragments, and thus preserve the divine art of Forging.

But as lofty as it sounded, it was, essentially, a festivity.

The manor of House Vanth drank in the early winter sunlight, chimney smoke curling catlike along the roof. She could almost sense the fête inside: cinnamon sticks soaking in goblets of mulled wine, pine wreaths and ornamental snow Forged to spangle in the air like caught stars . . . and Séverin. Sweet and earnest and observant. The child she would have chosen for herself.

The matriarch moved her hand across her flat belly. Sometimes when she walked, she thought she could feel the hollow parts of herself jangling together. But when she looked down, she caught sight of her Babel Ring, and she held her chin higher. Power liked irony, she thought. She had been denied a woman's power to give birth, but granted the power her birth as a woman should have denied. Her family still bristled at how *she* had become matriarch of House Kore.

But they didn't have to like it.

They just had to obey it.

Flanking the wrought iron manor door stood two large pine trees decorated with dripping candles. The House Vanth butler greeted her at the top of the steps.

"Welcome, Madame, please allow me to assist—" he said, taking the gift.

"Careful with that," she said sternly.

She rolled her shoulders, curiously missing the weight of the box, which, for a moment, had reminded her of what it felt like to carry Séverin . . . warm and sleepy in her arms as she had returned him to his home after the theatre.

"Pardon, Madame," said the butler guiltily. "Though I do not wish to detain you from the festivities . . . *she*, ah, wished to speak with you."

She.

The pine tree on her left rustled slightly as a woman stepped out from behind it.

"Leave us," said the woman to the butler.

The butler promptly did as she asked. The matriarch felt a stab of reluctant admiration for the woman who held neither power nor status in House Vanth, but commanded it anyway. Lucien Montagnet-Alarie had brought her back with him after an artifact excursion to Algeria, and six months later she gave birth to their child, Séverin. There were plenty of women like her, women carried into another country while carrying a white man's child. Not quite wife or lover, but an exotic ghost haunting the halls and edges of society.

But the matriarch had never met a woman with those eyes.

Séverin could pass for a boy of France, but his eyes belonged to his mother: dusky and violet, the night sky veiled in smoke.

The Order of Babel had ignored this woman just as soundly as they had ignored the Haitian mother of the House Nyx heir . . . but there was something about the Algerian woman that demanded noticing. Maybe it was because she flaunted protocol, wearing her absurd tunics and scarves. Or maybe it was due to the rumors she cast before her, vast as her own shadow. That she had powers that didn't even look like any Forging affinity. That the patriarch of House Vanth had found her in an enchanted cave, a dark-eyed mirage who appeared as if from nowhere.

That she had secrets.

"You have no right to corner me like this," said the matriarch.

Kahina ignored this.

"You brought something for him," she said.

Not a question.

"What of it?" the matriarch shot back.

Guilt flickered through her when she caught Kahina's gaze: hungry. Hungry for all that the matriarch could do that was denied to her. Kahina had the power to give birth to him, but not the privilege to call him her son.

Power liked irony.

"Why did you choose that present?" Kahina asked.

The question threw the matriarch. What did it matter? She

simply thought he'd like it. She could already imagine him crouched behind the toy theatre, moving the puppets, his face not on the wooden stage but the imagined audience. He had a knack for under-standing how things fit together. How to draw the eye. Perhaps he would grow up to be an artist, she mused.

"Do you love him?" asked Kahina.

"What—"

"Do you love my son?"

My son. The words felt like a slap. The matriarch of House Kore could take him to the theatre, shower him with gifts, but he was not hers. And yet, her heart did not notice.

"Yes," she said.

Kahina nodded once, as if steeling herself, and then said: "Then, please . . . you must promise to protect him."

PART I

From the archival records of the Order of Babel

Master Boris Goryunov, House Dazbog of the Order's Russian faction 1868, reign of Czar Nicholas II

On this day, I took my men to Lake Baikal. We waited until night fell. The men were scared and spoke of restless spirits in the water, but they are simple-minded and perhaps overly swayed by the reports of screaming girls. It is possible some Forged object of the mind has driven the locals insane, and for that reason I have investigated but found nothing. I have dutifully requested the assistance of the Order, but I doubt we shall find anything. I heard no haunting calls of dying women, which means they either never existed or are already beyond my help.

I

SÉVERIN

Three weeks before Winter Conclave . . .

Séverin Montagnet-Alarie looked out over what had once been the Seven Sins Garden. Rare, coveted blossoms once coated the grounds—milk-petaled aureum and chartreuse golden moss, skeleton hyacinths and night-blooming cereus. And yet, it was the roses that his brother, Tristan, loved most. They were the first seeds planted, and he'd fussed over them until their petals ripened red and their fragrance bloomed to create something that looked and smelled like melted sin.

Now, in late December, the grounds appeared stripped and barren. When Séverin breathed deep, cold seared through his lungs.

The grounds were almost scentless.

If he wanted, he could have asked his factotum to hire a gardener with a Forging affinity for plant matter, someone who could maintain the garden's splendor, but he didn't want a gardener. He wanted Tristan.

But Tristan was dead, and the Seven Sins Garden had died with him.

In its place lay a hundred Forged reflection pools. Their mirror-still surfaces held images of desert landscapes or skies quilted with dawn light when nighttime had already stolen across the grounds. The guests of L'Eden Hotel applauded his artistry, not knowing that it was shame, not artistry, that had guided Séverin. When he looked in those pools, he didn't want to catch sight of his own face staring back at him.

"Monsieur?"

Séverin turned to see one of his guards striding toward him.

"Is he ready?" asked Séverin.

"Yes, Monsieur. We arranged the room precisely as you requested. Your . . . *guest* . . . is inside the office outside the stables, just as you asked."

"And do we have tea to serve our guest?"

"*Oui.*"

"*Très bon.*"

Séverin took a deep breath, his nose wrinkling. The rose canes had been burned and yanked out at the root. The grounds had been salted. And yet, even months later, he still caught the phantom scent of roses.

SÉVERIN HEADED TOWARD a small building near the horse stables. As he walked, he touched Tristan's old penknife, now tucked into his jacket pocket. No matter how many times he washed the blade, he still imagined he could feel the small bird feathers and bone splin-

ters that had once clung to the metal, remnants of Tristan's kills . . .
proof of the twisted violence his brother had tried so hard to hide.

Sometimes he wished he'd never known. Maybe then he would
have never gone to Laila's room. All he'd wanted was to dissolve
her ludicrous oath to act as his mistress during the Winter Conclave.

But he didn't find her. Instead, he had found letters addressed
to Tristan, and his brother's gardening satchel—the same one Laila
swore had gone missing—untied beside them.

I had thought not reading your objects was for the best, my
dearest Tristan. But every day I ask myself if I might've caught
the darkness inside you earlier. Perhaps, then, you might not
have turned to those poor birds. I see it in the blade. All those
kills. All your tears. I may not have understood all of you, but
I love you wholeheartedly and pray you might forgive me—

Even before this, Séverin knew he'd failed in his only promise to Tristan: to protect him. Now he saw how deep that failure
stretched. All he saw were paths not taken. Every time Tristan
wept, and he'd left the room to give him privacy. Every time
Tristan had furiously stomped into his greenhouse and stayed
there for days. He should've gone. Instead, he let his brother's demons feed on him.

When he read those letters, it wasn't just Tristan's dead stare
that swam before his eyes but everyone's gazes—Enrique, Zofia,
Hypnos. *Laila*. He saw their eyes milky with death, death that he'd
let happen because he hadn't been enough to protect them. Hadn't
known how.

Eventually, Laila caught him in her rooms. He'd never quite

remembered all that she'd said to him, except for her last words: "You cannot protect everyone from everything. You're only human, Séverin."

Séverin closed his eyes, his hand on the doorknob of the office.

"Then that must change."

SÉVERIN CONSIDERED HIMSELF something of an artist when it came to interrogation.

It came down to the details, all of which needed to look coincidental rather than controlled: the chair with uneven legs; the room's cloying scent of too-sweet flowers; the too-salty snacks provided earlier. Even the lighting. Concealed glass shards refracted the sunlight, casting glares on everything from the walls to the ceiling, so that only the wooden table laden with a warm and fragrant tea service earned notice.

"Comfortable?" asked Séverin, taking a seat across from the man.

The man flinched. "Yes."

Séverin smiled, pouring himself tea. The man before him was thin and pale, with a hunted look to his face. He eyed the tea warily until Séverin took a long sip.

"Would you like some?" asked Séverin.

The man hesitated, then nodded.

"Why . . . why am I here? Are you . . ." his voice dropped to a whisper, ". . . are you with the Order of Babel?"

"In a fashion."

Months after they broke into House Kore's home, the Order of Babel had hired Séverin's crew to find the Fallen House's hidden treasure, rumored to be in an estate called the Sleeping Palace, though no one knew where that was. In exchange, Séverin would be allowed to catalogue and analyze these treasures for himself, a privilege unheard of outside the Order. Then again, he *should* have been one of them, but he no longer wanted that mantle. Not after Tristan.

The Order claimed they wanted the treasure to gut whatever power the Fallen House still had left . . . but Séverin knew better. The Fallen House had shown their cards. They were snakes that cast large shadows. Without their treasure, they would be irredeemably weakened, true, but the real reason behind the Order's search was simple. The colonies brimmed with treasure—rubber in the Congo, silver in the Potosi Mines, spices in Asia. The lost wonders inside the Fallen House's hoard were too tantalizing not to pursue, and Séverin knew the members of the Order would fall upon it like wolves. Which meant he had to get to it first. He didn't care for its gold or silver, he wanted something far more precious:

The Divine Lyrics.

A treasure the Order would not even notice had gone missing, for it had always been considered lost. The lore of the Order of Babel held that *The Divine Lyrics* contained the secret for joining the world's Babel Fragments. Once joined, the book could rebuild the Tower of Babel and thus access the power of God. It was an effort that had gotten the Fallen House exiled fifty years ago. And yet, the book had long been missing, or that was what everyone had thought . . .

Until Roux-Joubert's tongue slipped.

After the battle in the catacombs, the captured Fallen House members proved to be useless informants. Each had not only taken their lives, but also burned off their faces and fingertips, thus escaping recognition. Only Roux-Joubert had failed. After he killed Tristan, he bit down instead of swallowing the suicide pill required to take his secrets to the grave. He had died slowly over weeks, and in a fit of madness began to speak.

"The doctor's papa is a bad man," he said, laughing hysterically. "You know all about bad fathers, Monsieur, you sympathize I am sure . . . oh how unkind . . . he will not let the doctor into the Sleeping Palace . . . but the book is there, waiting for him. He will find it. He will give us life after death . . ."

He? The question haunted Séverin, but there was no surviving record of the last Fallen House patriarch, and though the Order seemed disappointed the Sleeping Palace could not be found . . . at least they felt reassurance in the knowledge the Fallen House could not find it either.

Only he and Hypnos, the patriarch of House Nyx, had continued searching, scouring records and receipts, hunting for any inconsistencies which eventually led them to the man who sat in front of Séverin. An old, shriveled man who had managed to hide for a very long time.

"I have paid my dues," said the man. "I was not even part of the Fallen House, merely one of its many solicitors. And I told the Order before that when the House fell, they gave me a draught, and I remember *nothing* of its secrets. Why drag me here? I have no information worth knowing."

Séverin set down his teacup. "I believe you can lead me to the Sleeping Palace."

The man scoffed. "No one has seen it in—"

"Fifty years, I know," said Séverin. "It's well hidden, I understand. But my contacts tell me the Fallen House created a special pair of lenses. Tezcat spectacles, to be precise, which reveal the location of the Sleeping Palace and all its *delicious* treasures." Séverin smiled. "However, they entrusted these spectacles to a unique person, someone who does not know what they guard."

The man gaped at him.

"H-how—" He caught himself, then cleared his throat. "The Tezcat spectacles are mere rumor. I certainly don't possess them. I know nothing, Monsieur. I swear on my *life*."

"Poor choice of words," said Séverin.

He removed Tristan's penknife from his pocket, tracing the initials on it: *T.M.A.* Tristan had lost his surname, and so Séverin had shared his. At the base of the knife was an ouroboros, a snake biting its tail. It was once the symbol of House Vanth, the House he might have been patriarch of—if things had gone according to plan . . . if that dream of inheritance had not killed the person closest to him. Now it was a symbol of all he would change.

He knew that even if they found *The Divine Lyrics*, it would not be enough to protect the others . . . They'd wear targets on their backs for the rest of their lives, and that was unacceptable. And so, Séverin had nurtured a new dream. He dreamt of that night in the catacombs, when Roux-Joubert had smeared golden blood over his mouth; the sensation of his spine elongating, making room for sudden wings. He dreamt of the pressure in his forehead, the horns that bloomed and arced, lacquered tips brushing the tops of his ears.

We could be gods.

That was what *The Divine Lyrics* promised. If he had the book, he could be a god. A god did not know human pain or loss or guilt. A god could *resurrect*. He could share the book's powers with the others, turn them invincible . . . protect them forever. And when they left him—as he knew they'd always planned to—he wouldn't feel a thing.

For he would not be human.

"Are you going to stab me with that?" demanded the man,

pushing back violently from the table. "How old are you, Monsieur? In your twenties? Don't you think think that is too young to have such blood on your hands?"

"I've never known blood to discriminate between ages," said Séverin, tilting the blade. "But I won't stab you. What's the point when I've already poisoned you?"

The man's eyes flew to the tea. Sweat beaded on his brow. "You're lying. If you poisoned the tea, then you'd be poisoned too."

"Most assuredly," said Séverin. "But the poison wasn't the tea. It was your cup's porcelain coating. Now." From his pocket, he withdrew a clear vial and placed it on the table. "The antidote is right here. Is there really nothing you wish to tell me?"

TWO HOURS LATER, Séverin poured sealing wax onto several envelopes—one to be sent out immediately, the others to be sent out in two days. A small part of him hesitated, but he steeled himself. He was doing this for them. For his friends. The more he cared about their feelings, the harder his task became. And so he endeavored to feel nothing at all.

2

LAILA

Laila stared at the letter her maid had just delivered. When she took the envelope, she thought it would be a note from Zofia that she'd returned from her visit to Poland. Or Enrique, letting her know how his meeting with the Ilustrados had gone. Or Hypnos, wondering when they could dine together. But instead, it was from the last person . . . and held the last *words* . . . she ever expected:

> *I know how to find The Divine Lyrics.*
> *Meeting at 12 o'clock.*
> —SÉVERIN

The sound of rustling sheets in her bedroom startled her.

"Come back to bed," said a groggy voice.

Cold December light streamed through the bay windows of her suite in the Palais des Rêves, the cabaret where she performed as the dancer L'Énigme. With the light trickled in the memories of last night. She had brought someone to her suite, which was not unusual lately. Last night was a diplomat's son who had bought her champagne and strawberries after her performance. She had liked him on the spot. His body was not sleek, but broad; his eyes not deep violet, but pale as a young wine; his hair not plum-black, but golden.

She liked who he wasn't.

Because of that, she could tell him the secret that ate her alive every day. The secret that had made her own father call her an abomination. The secret she couldn't bear to tell her closest friends.

"I'm dying," she'd whispered when she drew him down to her.

"You're dying?" The diplomat's son had grinned. "That eager, are we?"

Every time she uttered those words to a lover, the truth felt smaller, as if she might someday wrangle it down to a manageable size and hold it in the palm of her hand rather than let it swallow her up entirely. The *jaadugar* had said her body—built rather than born—would not last past her twentieth birthday. *She* would not last, which left her with little over a month of life. Her only hope of survival was *The Divine Lyrics*, a book that held the secret to the power of Forging, the art of controlling mind or matter depending on one's affinity. With it, her own Forged body might find a way to hold itself together for longer. But months had passed, and the trail to find it had gone cold despite everyone's efforts. There was no option but to savor the time she had left . . . and so she had.

Now, a sharp pang bloomed in her chest. She placed the letter on her vanity. Her fingers trembled from reading it. *Truly* reading it. The object's memories flooded her head: Séverin pouring black sealing wax onto the paper, his violet eyes aglow.

Laila looked over her shoulder to the boy in her bed. "I'm afraid you have to leave."

A FEW HOURS LATER, Laila walked onto the frigid streets of Montmartre. Christmas had passed, but winter was not yet robbed of its holiday magic. Colorful lights winked behind frosted panes. Warm steam drifted from the bakeries, carrying the aroma of *pain d'épices*, deep golden spice bread glossed over with amber honey. The world leaned hungrily over the cusp of a new year, and every moment, Laila wondered how much of it she would live to see.

In the morning light, her scarlet gown with its beaded neckline of onyx and carmine looked garish. Blood-soaked, even. It felt like necessary armor for what awaited her in Hotel L'Eden.

Laila had not seen Séverin since he'd entered her room without permission and read a letter not meant for him. How different would her life be if he'd never found it? If she'd never *written* it?

At the time, she had not known how to reconcile how she felt about Tristan. She mourned the violence of his death as much as she mourned the hidden darkness in his life. His secret felt too huge to bear alone, and so she had written to her lost friend, informing him of what she'd found and how she still loved him. It was something she did from time to time—address those who couldn't answer, and hope that it granted her some peace.

She'd only left her suite for a few minutes, and when she returned, her heart jolted at the sight of Séverin. But then her gaze had fallen to the letter in his clenched hand, the bloodless white of his knuckles, his eyes black as a hellscape, unearthly and huge in their shock.

"How long did you think you could hide this from me?"

"Séverin—"

"I let this happen to him," he'd murmured.

"No, you didn't," she'd said, stepping toward him. "How could you have known? He kept it from all of us—"

But he recoiled from her, his hands shaking.

"Majnun," she'd said, her voice breaking on the name she hadn't uttered in months. "Don't let this ghost haunt you. He is at rest, free of his demons. You can do the same and still live."

Laila grabbed his wrist, where her fingers brushed against the oath bracelet. She'd extracted his promise on the night of his birthday. That night, she'd wanted him to take her on as his mistress so she could track his progress in finding *The Divine Lyrics*. But there was another reason too. She wanted him to want something more than numbness . . . and she thought, for a moment, that it could be her. She hadn't forgotten the cruel words he'd uttered, but she could forgive cruelty stemming from guilt as long as he could forgive himself.

"Choose life," she'd begged.

Choose me.

He looked at her. *Through* her. Laila could not bear to watch him retreat into himself, and so she'd grabbed his face, turning it toward her.

"You cannot protect everyone from everything," she said. "You're only human, Séverin."

Something had kindled in his eyes at that. Hope flickered inside her, only for it to dim as he pulled back. Without a word, he left her room. The last she'd heard, he had thrown himself back into the search for *The Divine Lyrics*, as if by finding it, he might avenge

Tristan and absolve himself of the guilt that he had lived while his brother had died.

Laila pulled her coat tighter around her. Her garnet ring caught the light. She had asked Zofia to make it for her not long ago. The stone looked violent and wet, as if it were not a jewel at all, but a bird's ripped-out heart set in gold. In its face read the number *21*. Twenty-one days to live.

Today was the first time she let herself doubt that number.

Until now, she'd made peace with small dreams . . . more afternoons with Zofia, Hypnos, and Enrique. Perhaps one last winter evening where fresh snow sugared the streets of Paris and her breath plumed gently before her. Sometimes, she imagined it looked like death, as if she were watching her own soul unspool from her lungs. She could tell herself that yes, death was cold, but at least it didn't hurt.

Séverin's letter changed everything.

The Order had hired them to find the Fallen House's treasures, but to do that required finding the Sleeping Palace . . . and it had thwarted all attempts at discovery. Once Séverin's steady stream of reports dried up, the Order said they would find the Fallen House's treasure on their own. There would be no Winter Conclave for her or the others, and the only relief was that she would no longer have to play Séverin's mistress.

Now, it seemed, she would.

Slowly, Laila became aware of a sound following her. The steady *clip-clop* of hooves. She stopped, turning slowly as an indigo carriage ornamented in chased silver stopped a mere five feet from her. A familiar symbol—a wide crescent moon like a sly grin— gleamed on the carriage door as it swung open.

"I'm hurt you didn't invite me on your adventure last night," pouted a familiar voice.

Hypnos leaned through the open door and blew her a kiss. Laila smiled, caught the kiss, and made her way to him.

"The bed was too small," she said.

"I hope its owner wasn't," he said. From his jacket, he pulled out a letter with Séverin's seal. "I imagine you were also summoned."

Laila answered by holding up her own letter. Hypnos grinned, then made room for her in the carriage.

"Ride with me, *ma chère*. There's no time to waste."

A pang dug into Laila's chest.

"How well I know it," she said, and stepped into the carriage.

3

ENRIQUE

For the fifth time in the past minute, Enrique Mercado-Lopez smoothed his hair and patted his immaculate shirtfront. Then, he cleared his throat. "Gentlemen of the Ilustrados, I thank you for joining me today for my presentation on ancient world powers. For this afternoon, I have assembled a selection of Forged artifacts from around the globe. I believe that as we advance the sovereignty of the Philippines, we should look for guidance in history. Our *past* can reshape our *future*!"

He paused, blinking. Then he muttered, "Wait, *our* past . . . or *the* past?"

He looked down at his notepad where he'd crossed and re-crossed, underlined and blotted out nearly half of his original presentation that had taken weeks to prepare.

"*The* past," he said, making another note.

He looked out over the reading room of the *Bibliothèque nationale de France*. It was one of the most beautiful libraries he had ever seen, the ceilings vaulted like the rib cage of a slain monster out of myth, and full of stained glass windows, book-lined walls, and Forged reference books that perched on slender golden racks, preening and flapping their covers.

It was also completely empty.

Enrique glanced at the center of the room. In place of a chandelier rotated a great, glowing orb displaying the time: *half past eleven.*

The Ilustrados were late. *Too* late. The meeting was to start at ten. Perhaps they had gotten the time wrong. Or had they lost the invitations? No, that couldn't be it. He'd double-checked the addresses and confirmed their receipt. They wouldn't ignore him like this . . . would they? Surely, he had proven his worth as a curator and historian. He'd written articles for *La Solidaridad* and eloquently—or so he thought—argued his case for the equality of colonized civilizations to its colonizers. Besides, he had the backing of Hypnos, a patriarch in the Order of Babel and Séverin Montagnet-Alarie, Paris's most influential investor and owner of the grandest hotel in France.

Enrique put down his notebook and stepped from his podium to the dining table arranged in the middle of the room and set for the nine members of the Ilustrados inner circle . . . soon to be ten. He hoped. The hot ginger *salabat* tea had begun to cool. Soon, he'd have to cover up the *afritada* and *pancit* on their heating platters. The bucket holding champagne was more water than ice.

Enrique looked at the spread. Perhaps it would not have been so bad if non-Ilustrados members had come. He thought about Hypnos, and warmth pleasantly curled through his body. He'd wanted to invite him, but the other boy tended to balk at any sign of too much commitment and preferred their casual not-quite-friend and not-quite-lover territory. Gracing the end table was a beautiful bouquet of flowers from Laila, who he knew wouldn't attend. Once, he'd woken her up before ten o'clock in the morning and was met with a wrathful growl, a red-eyed glare, and a vase flung at his head. When she eventually stumbled downstairs closer to noon, she had no recollection of the incident. Enrique had decided never to meet pre-noon Laila again. Then there was Zofia. Zofia would've attended and sat straight-backed in her chair, her blue-as-candle-hearts eyes alive with curiosity. But she was returning from a family visit in Poland.

In a moment of desperation, he'd considered inviting Séverin, but that felt callous. Half the reason he had arranged this presentation was because he couldn't stay as Séverin's historian and curator forever. Besides, Séverin wasn't . . . the same. Enrique didn't blame him, but there were only so many times he could accept a shut door in his face. He told himself he wasn't leaving Séverin, but choosing life.

"I tried," he said aloud for the hundredth time. ". . . I really tried."

He wondered how many times he'd have to say it, for guilt not to creep into his veins. Despite all his research, they'd found nothing that could lead them to the Sleeping Palace, the place full of the Fallen House's treasure and the one object within that Séverin was determined to find: *The Divine Lyrics*. Taking back *The Divine Lyrics* would be the final blow to the Fallen House. Without it, their plans to rejoin the Babel Fragments would crumble. They needed *The Divine Lyrics*, and perhaps then, Séverin would feel as though Tristan had truly been avenged.

But it was not to be.

When the Order said they would take over the mission, Enrique had felt nothing but relief. Tristan's death haunted him. He'd never forget that first breath he took after he knew Tristan was dead—jagged and harsh, as if he'd fought the world for the privilege to draw air into his lungs. That's what life was. A privilege. He wouldn't waste it chasing vengeance. He would do something vastly more meaningful, more important.

After Tristan died, Laila had left L'Eden entirely. Séverin became as cold and unreachable as the stars. Zofia had stayed more or less the same, but she'd gone to Poland . . . which left Hypnos. Hypnos who understood his past enough, perhaps, to want to be part of his future.

Behind him, a voice called out, "Hello?"

Enrique leapt to attention, straightening his jacket and fixing a bright smile on his face. Maybe all his worry was for nothing. Maybe everyone really *had* been running late . . . but as the figure walked toward him, Enrique deflated. It wasn't a member of the Ilustrados at all, but a courier holding out two envelopes.

"Are you Monsieur Mercado-Lopez?"

"Unfortunately," said Enrique.

"These are for you," he said.

One letter was addressed from Séverin. The other from the Ilustrados. Heart racing, he opened the latter, skimming it as a knot of hot shame coiled in his gut.

. . . we feel as though this position is outside the realm of your skills, Kuya Enrique. Age gives us wisdom, and we have the wisdom to push against sovereignty, to know where to look. You are only recently a man of twenty. How do you know what you want? Perhaps when a time of peace comes, we will turn to you and your interests. But for now, support us from where you stand. Enjoy your youth. Write your inspiring articles on history. It is what you do best . . .

Enrique felt oddly light. He pulled out one of the seats from the dining table and slumped into it. He'd spent half his savings renting the library's reading room, arranging the food and drink, scheduling for the transportation of several artifacts on loan from the Louvre . . . and for what?

The door slammed open. Enrique looked up, wondering what else the courier had to deliver, but it wasn't the courier at all but Hypnos striding toward him. His pulse kicked up at the sight of the other boy, with his mouth made for grinning and frosted eyes the color of fairy pools.

"Hello, *mon cher*," he said, swooping to kiss his cheeks.

Warmth shivered through Enrique. Perhaps not all his daydreams were foolish after all. For once, he wanted to be sought after, picked first. Wanted. And now here was Hypnos.

"If you thought to attend the presentation to surprise me, I appreciate it . . . but you seem to be the only one."

Hypnos blinked. "Attend? *Non.* It's before noon. I hardly exist before noon. I'm only here to fetch you."

Cold crept through Enrique, and he folded away his daydreams and shoved them in the dark.

"Didn't you get the letter?" asked Hypnos.

"I got several letters," said Enrique sullenly.

Hypnos opened the one from Séverin and held it out to Enrique.

A FEW MOMENTS LATER, Enrique joined Laila in Hypnos's carriage. Laila smiled warmly, and he immediately curled against her. Hypnos held his hand lightly and caressed his thumb against Enrique's knuckles.

"How did it go?" she asked. "Did you get my flowers?"

He nodded, his stomach still tight with shame. The Ilustrados had told him plainly enough that what he had to say was not worth hearing. But this, finding the treasures of the Fallen House, returning *The Divine Lyrics* to the Order of Babel . . . this could change everything. Besides, one last acquisition felt right somehow. Like he was not only honoring Tristan's legacy, but also laying rest to this chapter of his life as the historian of L'Eden . . . as a part of Séverin's team.

"No one came," he said, but his words were drowned out by the sound of the carriage lurching onto the gravelly streets.

In the end, no one heard him.

4

ZOFIA

Over the past months, Zofia Boguska had learned how to lie. In December, she told the others she was celebrating Chanukah in Glowno, Poland, where her sister, Hela, worked as a governess to their uncle's family. But that was not the truth. The truth was that Hela was dying.

Zofia stood outside Séverin's study in Hotel L'Eden. She still had her travel bag at her side, and she had not removed her outer coat or the violet hat that Laila said "brought out her eyes"—a statement that horrified Zofia and made her anxiously touch her eyelids. She had not meant to return so soon. There was no point when Séverin had not accepted any acquisition assignments, and her skill set had gotten them no closer to finding *The Divine Lyrics*. But two days ago, she had received an urgent letter from Séverin, instructing her to return to L'Eden, though he did not say why.

"Go, Zosia, I will be well," Hela had insisted, pressing her lips to Zofia's hand. "And what about your studies? Won't you be in trouble for taking off so much time from university?"

Zofia had lost count of how many lies she'd told. In the end, she had no choice but to return. She was out of money. And Hela was right about one thing—she *did* seem better. Just days ago, Hela's fever raged through her body. Once she slipped into unconsciousness, her uncle had sent word to a rabbi for burial rituals. But then a new doctor visited her uncle's home. The man insisted Zofia had paid for his services, and though she did not remember doing so, she admitted him anyway. Hope provided flimsy statistics, but it was better than nothing. That night, he injected Hela with a pharmaceutical compound he claimed was available nowhere else, and promised she would live.

And so she had.

The next morning, Séverin's letter arrived. Even though Hela might be recovering, Zofia had decided not to stay in Paris. She would return to Poland, to take care of her sister . . . but she needed more money. Her savings had gone to Hela's care and her uncle's charges—compensation he demanded for the time Hela had not been able to instruct his children. Though if she died, of course, he would "generously" forgive the debt.

After all, they were family.

Zofia needed to go back to Paris. She needed to say goodbye. And she needed to sell her laboratory for parts. What money she received would go to Hela's care.

In L'Eden, Zofia rapped on the door to Séverin's study. Behind her, she could hear the hurried footsteps of Séverin's butler. He hissed under his breath, "Mademoiselle Boguska, are you sure this cannot wait? Monsieur Montagnet-Alarie has been very—"

The door swung open, and Séverin stood in the doorway. He

glanced wordlessly at his butler, and the man quickly fled down the hall. Distantly, Zofia wondered how Séverin could do such things, command without articulating. She would never have that kind of power. But at least, she thought, holding her resignation letter tightly . . . at least she might save someone she loved.

"How was your journey?" asked Séverin, stepping aside to admit her.

"Long."

But not as bad as it might have been. When Séverin sent for her, he had included a first-class train ticket with a compartment to herself so that she need never speak to another person. She liked that the compartment had lamps with many tassels, and a rug that was one color, and she'd spent the whole trip counting things aloud . . . calming herself for what she had to do.

Zofia thrust the resignation letter to him.

"I have to go back," she said. "My sister needs me. I'm resigning. I came back to say goodbye to everyone."

Séverin stared at the paper without taking it.

"My understanding upon your employment was that you were building an income to supplement your sister's tuition at a medical university. Is that no longer your wish?"

"It . . . it still is, but—"

"Then why would you need to leave?"

Zofia searched for the right words. When she had reviewed the order of events, she had not anticipated an outcome of him not accepting her resignation on the spot. After all, it was not as though she had any work to do in L'Eden. He had ceased pursuing all acquisitions when the hunt for the Sleeping Palace had failed. Zofia had no work.

"My sister is dying."

Séverin's expression did not change.

"And that is the reason you returned to Glowno?"

She nodded.

"Why did you lie to me?"

Zofia hesitated. She thought of Tristan's last laugh, and Hela's fevered murmurings of how their family used to spend Chanukah, crowded around the table as their mother ladled out stew and the smell of candle wax burning in the chanukia.

"Because I did not want it to be true."

There was another reason, though. When Zofia had started writing a letter to Enrique and Laila, Hela had told her to stop: "Oh, don't make them worry, Zosia. They might start fretting over who would have to take care of you when I'm gone." What if her sister was right? The shame of not knowing whether she was an imposition or not stayed her hand.

Zofia watched as a small muscle twitched in Séverin's jaw. Still, he did not take the letter. New words found Zofia, plucked from every time she had watched Séverin turn Tristan's old penknife over and over in his hands, or stand at the door to his room and never open it, or stare out the window to what had once been the Seven Sins Garden.

"You understand," she said.

Séverin flinched. He turned sharply from her.

"Your sister will not die," he said. "And though she might need you, I need you more. There's work to be done."

Zofia frowned. One moment she was wondering how Séverin could be so sure about Hela's recovery, the next moment, the thought of work jolted her with a small rush of joy. Without work, she had felt restless. And she was not cut out to take Hela's place in their uncle's home, where all her wages would go toward Hela's remaining debt.

"I checked your savings this morning. You have no money left, Zofia."

Zofia opened her mouth. Closed it. Anger warmed her cheeks.

"That . . . that is not for you to see. That is private."

"Not to me," he said. "Stay until this next job is done, and I will double your income. Your sister will not have to work as a governess. You could provide comfortably enough for the two of you for years to come. I will start sending her portions of your income now . . . but you cannot go back to Poland. And any doubled income will be given to you upon completion of the job."

"And I . . . I am to keep none of my earnings in the meantime?" asked Zofia.

She did not like that. Already, she had to rely so much on others.

"I will take care of your living and laboratory expenses."

"What about Goliath?"

Séverin turned around sharply, his mouth a flat line. "What about him?"

Zofia raised her chin. Ever since Tristan's death, she had kept his venomous tarantula warm and safe in her lab. The only time she hadn't watched the animal was during her trip away when she had asked Enrique. At the time, Enrique declared, "I would rather set myself on fire." This turned out to be an exaggeration for he eventually, despite grudgingly, agreed. She imagined it would have made Tristan happy.

"He needs money for food and bedding."

Séverin looked away. "I will take care of it. Do you accept the terms?"

Zofia searched his face, looking for the familiar patterns in his expression. She used to be able to decipher him, but perhaps he had only let her. Now, he was a stranger. Zofia wondered if this was the effect of death, but that could not be true. She and Hela had seen their parents' death. They had watched their home and all of their possessions burn. But they had not become strangers. Zofia closed her eyes. *They*. They had each other. Séverin—for all that he could command men without words—had no one. Her anger faded.

When she opened her eyes, she thought of Hela's weak smile. Because of her, her sister would survive. For the first time, Zofia felt a touch of pride. She had always relied on Hela and so many others. This time, she was repaying that debt. Maybe one day, she would not need to rely on anyone.

"Every week, I will personally send for two letters of health written in your sister's hand," added Séverin. "At *my own* expense."

Zofia remembered her sister's kiss on her hand. *Go, Zosia.*

"I accept," she said.

Séverin nodded, then glanced at the clock. "Then head downstairs. The others will be here any minute now."

5

SÉVERIN

Séverin knew that to become a god required divorcing oneself from all the elements that made one human. When he looked at Zofia, he extinguished whatever kernel of warmth lay inside him, and he felt a little less human. He could have given her the money to go home, and he hadn't. He'd thought, briefly, that if she had no sister, then she'd have no reason to return to Poland . . . but some vestige of himself recoiled. Instead, he'd sent a physician to her uncle's home. He told himself it was smarter, colder. That it meant nothing. And yet, even as he repeated this to himself he remembered their first meeting.

Two years ago, he had heard rumors of a brilliant Jewish student, expelled and imprisoned for arson and abusing her Forging affinity. The story hadn't sat right with him, so he'd taken his carriage to the women's prison. Zofia was skittish as a colt, her striking blue eyes more creature than girl. He couldn't bring himself to leave her there, so he took her to L'Eden. Days later, his staff reported that every night she slept on the floor with blankets rather than in the swansdown bed.

When he heard that, something in him warmed.

He'd done the same thing at every foster father's home. He and Tristan never stayed with one father for long, and so it was too dangerous to get attached to anything. Even to a bed. Séverin removed every object from Zofia's room, gave her a catalogue, and told her to select what she wanted, informing her that each item she picked would be deducted from her salary, but at least every item would be hers.

"I understand," he'd said quietly.

That was the first time Zofia smiled at him.

THE FIRST THING he heard when he approached the stargazing room was piano music. Soaring notes rich with hope sank through him, freezing him into place. The music overwhelmed his senses, and for one bright moment of wonder, it seemed as if the sounds drifted down from the stars themselves, like the mythical Music of the Spheres that moved the planets in a solemn rhythm. When the music stopped, he let out his breath, his lungs aching from holding it too long.

"Again, Hypnos!" said Laila.

Séverin knew her well enough to hear the smile in her voice. The sound of his pulse drowned out the memory of music. How easy it was for her to smile. After all, she'd lost nothing. She might have been disappointed they could not find *The Divine Lyrics*, but she merely wanted the book to satisfy a curiosity of her own past.

"Since when do you play the piano so well?" asked Laila.

"He's not *that* good," grumbled Enrique.

Two years ago, Enrique had tried—much to everyone's chagrin—

to learn the piano. Soon, his "playing" infected the hallways. Tristan declared his music was killing the plants, and afterwards Zofia had "accidentally" spilled a wood-decaying solvent on the instrument, thus ending his lessons for good.

Once more, the music swelled and with it, his memories. Séverin dug his nails into his palms. *Leave me*, he begged of his ghosts. The recollections faded. But in their wake, he caught the scent of Tristan's roses.

The phantom perfume made him stumble. Séverin flung out a hand to steady himself, only to catch the heavy doorframe. Abruptly, the music stopped.

When he looked up, Hypnos was crouched over the piano, hands hovering above the keys. Laila sat stiff-backed on her favorite green couch. Zofia perched on her stool, an unopened matchbox in her lap. Enrique halted in his pacing, right in front of his research on *The Divine Lyrics* that hung against the bookshelves.

Two images superimposed onto his vision.

Before. After.

Before, there would have been tea and sugar cookies. Laughter.

Slowly, Séverin righted himself. He released his grip on the doorframe and straightened his cuffs, daring all of them to meet his gaze.

None of them did except Hypnos.

Hypnos lowered his hands from the piano.

"I hear you have good news for us, *mon cher.*"

Séverin forced himself to nod, and then he gestured to the research hanging against the bookshelves.

"Before I begin, let's review what we know—"

Hypnos sighed. "*Must* we?"

"It's been some time," said Séverin.

"Two months, I believe," said Laila sharply.

Séverin didn't look at her. Instead, he gestured to Enrique. For a moment, Enrique stared blankly at him, and then he seemed to remember himself. Enrique cleared his throat, then pointed to the sketch behind him showing the hexagram symbol of the Fallen House, a golden honeybee, and the Biblical Tower of Babel.

"These past few months, we've been trying to locate *The Divine Lyrics*, the ancient book that holds the secret of Forging, the knowledge of how to rejoin the Babel Fragments and—in the eyes of the Fallen House—how to access the power of God," said Enrique. His eyes darted to Séverin, as if checking to see if that was correct. Séverin raised his eyebrows.

"Um, there's very little information existing on the book itself," said Enrique hurriedly. "Most of it is legend. Our only known record of the book is a faded inscription from one of the original Knights Templar, written on a piece of vellum where the letters have been cut off—"

Enrique held up an illustration of the vellum:

THE DIVINE LYR

"As far as the lore of the book is concerned, it dates back to the fall of the Babel Tower," he said. A familiar excited shine crept into Enrique's eyes. "Supposedly, there was a group of women near the original site who had touched the topmost bricks of the Tower, and thus absorbed some of the divine language. They wrote down their knowledge in a book. From there, they tasked the women of their lineage to guard the book's secrets so that no one could use the language to rebuild the Babel Tower. Isn't that amazing?"

Grinning, Enrique flailed a hand to a different sketch, this one showing an illustration of nine women.

"They were called the Lost Muses, which, presumably, is a nod to the Greek goddesses of divine arts and inspiration. Seems fitting since Forging itself is considered a divine art. There used to be sites all over the ancient world dedicated to them," said Enrique, staring wistfully at the images. "It was said that *The Divine Lyrics* was not just a book anyone could pick up and read, but required a skill inherited through the bloodline of the original Lost Muses."

"What a silly myth," scoffed Hypnos, plinking one of the piano keys. "The ability to read a book based on a bloodline? Forging doesn't work that way. It's not passed down through the blood, or *I* would possess Forging affinity of the mind."

"I wouldn't dismiss myths," said Enrique quietly. "Most myths are just truths covered in cobwebs."

Hypnos's face softened. "Ah, but of course, *mon cher*. I did not mean to insult your craft."

He blew him a kiss, and Enrique . . . blushed? Séverin scowled, looking between the two of them. Hypnos caught his eye, and a corner of his mouth lifted.

When did this happen?

But Séverin's attention quickly returned to Enrique, who had pulled down a yellowing map showing the southern tip of the Indian subcontinent. Out the corner of his eye, he saw Laila lean forward as if in longing, and Séverin tasted bitterness on his tongue.

"The last known location of *The Divine Lyrics* was Pondicherry, India," said Enrique. "According to the Order of Babel documents, the Order went to retrieve it, but by the time they arrived, they discovered that someone had already taken the artifact in their name—"

"—and then kept quiet about the theft for nearly twenty years, claiming it was lost," added Hypnos.

Enrique nodded. "Thanks to Roux-Joubert, our best lead for finding *The Divine Lyrics* is inside the Sleeping Palace . . . which is where our search ended." He looked up at Séverin. "Unless . . . unless you really do know how to find the Palace?"

Séverin used to love this moment—the moment where he could reveal something new and watch wonder transfix their expressions. He used to love hiding hints about their future acquisitions . . . like asking Laila to bake a cake full of golden roses for the time they went after the Midas's Hand in Greece. This time, he didn't look at their faces.

"Yes," he said, not moving from the doorway. "The coordinates to the Sleeping Palace are concealed by a pair of Tezcat spectacles, and I know where they can be found."

Zofia leaned forward, interested. "Spectacles?"

Laila's voice cut through the air: "How do you know this?" she asked, her voice cold.

She didn't look at him, and he didn't look at her.

"An informant," said Séverin, with equal coldness. "He also told me the Sleeping Palace is somewhere in Siberia."

"Siberia?" repeated Hypnos. "That place . . . it's full of ghosts."

Hypnos looked around the room, perhaps expecting someone to agree with him. The others stared at him blankly.

He pressed on. "Well, it was before my time . . . but my father once told me about something strange that happened there years ago. There were stories of terrible sounds near Lake Baikal, like girls screaming for their lives. It terrified the locals, and got to be so bad that the Russian faction, House Dazbog, asked the Order to intervene. My father sent a small unit of mind Forging artists to detect if anyone was being controlled. But no one ever found anything."

"And it just stopped?" asked Laila.

Hypnos nodded. "Eventually. The locals claimed girls were being murdered, but they never found any bodies." In a smaller voice, he added: "I hope the Sleeping Palace isn't in Siberia."

Enrique winced. "I think the name alone confirms it . . . The etymology of the word 'Siberia' isn't exactly clear, but it does sound remarkably close to the Siberian Tatar word for *sleeping land*, which would be *sib ir*. Hence, *Sleeping Palace*. But maybe I'm wrong," he added quickly when he saw the panic on Hypnos's face. "Where are the Tezcat spectacles anyway? A bank? A museum?"

"A mansion," said Séverin.

He tapped the Mnemo bug pinned to his lapel. The Forged creature shivered to life, its jewel-colored wings whirring and its pincers clicking as it opened its jaws and projected an image onto the bookshelf showing a huge waterfront mansion overlooking the Neva River. He'd written the street name in the margins: *Angliskaya Naberezhnava*. The English Embankment of St. Petersburg, Russia.

"That's . . . a big house," said Enrique.

"It's in Russia?" asked Zofia, her eyes narrowing.

Séverin switched the image to another external shot of the waterfront mansion. "The Tezcat spectacles are concealed in a private collection in the home of an art dealer. The room itself is called the Chamber of Goddesses, but I could find no information—"

Enrique squeaked. "I've heard of that installation! It's hundreds of years old . . . No one knows the original sculptor. If it *is* sculpture. At least, that's my guess. I've been dying to see it!" He beamed at the room, sighing. "Can you *imagine* what's in the Chamber of Goddesses?"

Zofia raised an eyebrow. "Goddesses?"

"Well, that's just the title of the room," sniffed Enrique.

"The title is lying?"

"No, the title is *evocative* of the art, but it could be something else."

Zofia frowned. "Sometimes I don't understand art."

Hypnos raised a glass. "Hear, hear."

"So, we have to go into the Chamber, find the Tezcat spectacles, get out," said Zofia.

"Not quite," said Séverin. "The Tezcat spectacles are like ornamented glasses, and one critical piece . . . the lens . . . is kept around the neck of the art dealer." He paused to consult his notes: "A Monsieur Mikhail Vasiliev."

"Why do I know that name . . . ," said Hypnos, rubbing his jaw. "He owns the Chamber of Goddesses?"

Séverin nodded.

"But why would the Fallen House entrust him with the key to finding their ancient estate and its treasure vaults?" asked Hypnos. "What does he know?"

"And why would he wear something like that around his *neck*?"

"He knows nothing, apparently," said Séverin. "According to my informant, the lens is disguised as a nostalgic keepsake, shaped like the old key that had once unlocked his lover's bedroom."

Laila looked down at her lap, pulling at a tassel on her dress. It was a shade of blood red that unnerved him. He didn't want to look at it.

"But why him?" pressed Enrique.

"He's important enough to keep his objects safe and insignificant enough that he draws no eyes," said Séverin. "He's not related to the Order, so he wouldn't be brought in for questioning. The most scandalous piece of his past is an affair with a prima ballerina that soured. He got her pregnant, refused to marry her, the baby was stillborn, and she killed herself." Enrique shuddered and crossed himself. "As a result, Vasiliev went into hiding for a few years, and that's when he purchased the Chamber of Goddesses. He wears his guilt over the whole affair around his neck."

"Now I remember his name . . . the Russian Recluse," said Hypnos. He shook his head. "I don't know how you'll make him leave home. I haven't brushed up on my gossip of St. Petersburg in some time, but the only thing he leaves his house for is—"

"The Imperial Russian Ballet," finished Séverin, changing the image to the stately Mariinsky Theatre, shining and extravagant with its decoration of Forged smoke ballerinas that pirouetted on the outside balconies and unraveled in the moonlight. "Their next performance is in three days, and he'll be there. What I need is the box next to his."

Hypnos snapped his fingers. "Consider it done. The Order keeps a standing box, and I can secure you a ticket."

"How?" asked Enrique.

"The usual route." Hypnos shrugged. "Money, charm, etcetera . . ."

"I'll need more than one. Two or three tickets," said Séverin, risking a glance at Laila. "Laila will be posing as my mistress for the duration of this acquisition. Another person should join us."

Silence.

Séverin raised an eyebrow. "I believe two people should be enough for the job inside Vasiliev's home. A third can go with us."

More silence.

Enrique seemed extraordinarily preoccupied with something under his nail. Zofia scowled. Séverin looked to Hypnos, who *tsked*.

"You could not pay me to be in that guest box between the two of you."

Beside him, Enrique reached for a glass of water, drank it too quickly, and started choking. Zofia slapped his back. Séverin tried not to look at Laila, but it was like ignoring the sun. He didn't have to see it to feel its glare.

"There's still several other issues to consider," said Séverin brusquely. "Vasiliev has a special salon within the Theatre that he frequents with his bodyguards. Admittance depends on a special blood Forging tattoo—"

"Blood Forging?" repeated Zofia, paling.

Hypnos whistled. "Certainly a rather expensive indulgence."

"What's blood Forging?" asked Enrique. "I've never seen that."

"A talent for a mixed set of affinities," said Zofia. "Mind and matter, liquid and solid metal."

"It's very rare to find someone who can manipulate both the mind and the presence of iron in the bloodstream," said Hypnos, before smiling slyly. "And also *very* pleasurable."

Séverin had seen such artists a couple times in L'Eden. Many of them chose to hone their craft in ice affinity rather than blood, but the ones who specialized in blood were often brought along with a patron who either required numbing during painful medical procedures, or for recreation, to heighten one's senses before certain . . . activities.

"We need to separate Vasiliev from his bodyguards," said Séverin. "Something that can pull men apart—"

"Money?" asked Enrique.

"Love!" said Hypnos.

"Magnets," said Zofia.

Laila, Enrique, and Hypnos turned to stare at her.

"Powerful magnets," Zofia amended.

"Can you do that?" asked Séverin.

Zofia nodded.

"That does not solve how we would enter his salon," said Enrique.

"I have an idea around that," said Laila. "I am L'Énigme after all. I can bring a certain notoriety when I wish."

Despite himself, Séverin looked at her. A thousand moments converged and fell apart. He saw her hair spangled with sugar. He saw the blur of her body when he'd thrown her to the ground, thinking she was Roux-Joubert's target that night in the Palais des Rêves. He remembered the painful words he'd uttered and how he wished, now, that they were true. If only she weren't real.

Laila raised an eyebrow.

"I am assisting you, am I not?" she asked frostily.

"Yes." Séverin pretended to adjust his sleeves. "We leave for St. Petersburg the day after tomorrow. We have much to do."

"What about after we get the Tezcat spectacles?" asked Hypnos. "Will we tell the Order—"

"No," said Séverin sharply. "I don't want their interference until we know what we're working with. Winter Conclave is in three weeks' time in Moscow. If we have something by then, we'll share."

Hypnos frowned at this, but Séverin ignored him. He was not letting the Order take this from him. Not after so much had changed. As Séverin turned to leave, he caught sight of evening falling outside the stargazing room.

Once, this meeting room had served as a reminder that the

stars themselves were within reach. Once, they could tip back their heads and dare to gaze at the heavens. Now, the stars seemed a mockery: teeth-white snarls of destiny and constellations, spun out into a celestial calligraphy that spelled unshakable fates for all mortals. That would change, thought Séverin. Soon . . . they would find that book.

Then, not even the stars could touch them.

6

LAILA

Laila watched Séverin leave the stargazing room, a tilted emptiness settling inside her.

On the one hand, she let herself hope for the first time in ages. If Séverin's informant proved right, then perhaps she had more left of life than she imagined. On the other hand, Séverin stained all that fresh hope with hate. She hated the cold light in his eyes and the frigid tug of his smile. She hated that the sight of him twisted something inside her, forcing her to remember that, once, he had made her feel wonder.

Worse, she hated hoping that the moment he found *The Divine Lyrics* would be the moment he would return to who he had once been. As if some spell might be broken. Laila tried to push out that dream, but it was stubborn and stuck fast to her heart.

"My laboratory—" started Zofia, at the same time Enrique muttered about the library. Hypnos shushed them violently.

"*Non*," he said. He pointed at the floor. "Stay here. I will be *right* back. I have a surprise."

He fled the room, leaving the three of them alone. Laila cast a sidelong glance at Zofia. She'd hardly had a chance to speak to her before the meeting. Now that she looked at her, new details leapt to her attention . . . Zofia had not changed out of her traveling clothes. Violet circles haunted her eyes. There was a thinness to her face that spoke of worry. That was not how she should look after spending Chanukah with her family.

"Are you well? Are you eating enough?"

Before Laila had moved out of L'Eden, she'd written explicit instructions to the cooks on how to serve Zofia. Zofia hated when her food touched; didn't like overly bright or patterned plates; and her favorite dessert was a perfectly pale and perfectly round sugar cookie. Laila used to do those things for her. But that was before. And the moment the question left her mouth, the more guilt sharpened in her heart. What right did she have to ask after Zofia when *she* had left? When *she* had put distance between them?

Laila turned the garnet ring on her hand. Sometimes she felt her secret like a poison slowly leeching into her bloodstream. More than anything, she wanted to tell them, to free herself from this burden . . . but what if the truth repulsed them? Her own father could barely look at her. She couldn't lose the only family she had left.

Zofia shrugged. "Goliath is losing his appetite."

"Considering Goliath eats crickets, I'm not sure I blame him," said Laila teasingly.

"He's not eating as many crickets as he should," said Zofia, plucking a matchstick and chewing it. "I made a chart documenting the volume of crickets consumed, and the trajectory is descending. I could show it to you if you'd like—"

"I'm fine without," said Laila. "But thank you."

Zofia stared at her lap. "I don't know what's wrong with him."

Laila almost reached out to hold Zofia's hand before pausing. What looked like love to her did not always look like that to Zofia. Zofia's gaze lifted to the black cushion Tristan used to sit on, now shoved under the coffee table.

"Perhaps Goliath is grieving," said Laila softly.

Zofia met her gaze. "Perhaps."

Zofia looked like she would say more, but Enrique wandered over to Laila.

"We need to talk later," he murmured before he sat in front of her.

"There's little to say," said Laila.

Enrique fixed her with his you-reek-of-lies face, but he didn't press her. Laila had told him about the *jaadugar* in her town, who had once guarded *The Divine Lyrics* . . . but that was all. Enrique and Zofia knew she had been trying to find the book, but they didn't know why. And she could not bear to tell them.

Sighing, Enrique angled his back just so, and Laila, recognizing what he was doing, sighed and started to scratch between his shoulder blades.

"I miss back scratches," said Enrique sadly.

"There was a dog in Poland who used to do something similar," observed Zofia.

"I don't have the energy to unpack that insult," said Enrique, sounding at once amused and bruised.

"It's not an insult."

"You basically called me a dog—"

"—I said your actions paralleled that of a dog."

"That's not exactly complimentary."

"Is it complimentary if I tell you he was an exemplary dog?"

"*No*—"

Laila ignored them, basking in the fragile whir of their bicker-ing. This felt like an echo of how they used to be. She had tried, from a distance, to stay close after Tristan had died. But the mo-ment she saw Séverin, she was reminded of how impossible that would be. If she'd stayed in L'Eden, she could not have survived the constant reminder of this unhealed and unclosed wound. Even now, he haunted her. Though he'd stopped eating cloves altogether, she still imagined the scent of them. When he left the room, un-wanted ghosts of memories snuck up on her. Memories he didn't know she had, like when they had been attacked by a Forged crea-ture inside House Kore's underground library. When she regained consciousness, the first sound she remembered was Séverin's voice at her ear: *Laila, this is your Majnun. And you will drive me well and truly mad if you do not wake up this instant.*

"Voila!" called Hypnos from the doorway.

He was pushing a cart laden with treats. They were colorful cookies—which disgusted Zofia—and ham sandwiches—which turned Enrique's stomach—and . . . a steaming samovar of hot co-coa. Which only Tristan drank.

Hypnos's smile wasn't his usual catlike grin. Now it looked shy and quick. Hopeful.

"I thought, perhaps, before all the planning . . . we might re-fresh ourselves?"

Enrique stared at the cart, finally managing a bemused "Oh."

Laila wished she hadn't seen the way Zofia leaned forward

eagerly, only to snap back in a recoil. And now Hypnos stood before them, his smile stretched a second too long . . . his shoulders falling a fraction.

"Well, if you're not hungry, *I* will eat," he said, a touch too brightly.

This used to be Laila's responsibility. In that second, the room felt cloying and too tight, brimming with so many old memories that there was hardly enough air to draw into her lungs.

"Excuse me," she said, standing.

Zofia frowned. "You're leaving?"

"I'm sorry," said Laila.

"Cookie?" asked Hypnos hopefully, holding one up to her as she passed.

Laila kissed him on the cheek and plucked it from his hand.

"I think the others just ate, unfortunately," she whispered.

"Oh," said Hypnos, his hands dropping from the cart. "Of course."

Laila left the room quickly, tossing the cookie in a potted plant at the entrance. All she wanted was to leave and run out into the streets. She wanted to be free of her secret and scream it to Paris . . . but then she turned the corner.

And there he was.

Séverin. A silhouette of silk and night, a boy with a mouth made for kisses and cruelty. A boy who had once conjured wonder and came too close to touching her heart. Laila reached for her hate like armor, but he was too fast.

"Laila," he said slowly, like her name was something to savor. "I was about to look for you."

Laila's heart didn't know how to hate. Not *truly*. And a small part of her wished never to learn. She could only stand there, staring at him. She remembered his face as he read the letter meant for Tristan . . . the pain when he'd discovered how many demons his brother had hidden from him. Maybe it was that which finally let her speak.

"I am sorry you found out the truth about Tristan the way you did, but I—"

"I'm not," he said. He tilted his head slightly, and dark curls swept across his forehead. His lips curved to a cold grin. "In fact, you deserve my thanks. And since you'll be acting as my mistress, I have a present for you. I can't have L'Énigme on my arm with a bare throat."

Until that moment, Laila hadn't noticed the velvet box under his arm. A jewelry box. He opened it, revealing a diamond choker that looked like snapped icicles. Just the thought of putting it against her skin made her shiver.

"They're real," he said, holding them out for her to touch.

Laila traced one jewel, only to feel a slight *resistance* in her thoughts. That only happened when she touched a Forged object. Séverin's shadow fell over her.

"When I have need of you, this diamond necklace will turn warm and tighten ever so slightly," he said. "Then you will report to me and tell me of any findings. Likewise, I will inform you of my progress with securing *The Divine Lyrics*."

Laila jerked back.

"You wish to *collar* me?"

Séverin raised his wrist, where her own oath bracelet caught the light.

"I wish to return the favor. Are we not equals in all things? Was that not what we promised each other?"

His words were a twisted echo of their first meeting. Fury stole Laila's voice just as Séverin stepped closer.

"Let's not forget that it was you who came to my chambers and demanded to act as my mistress, to be in *my* bed."

The Forged diamonds seemed to glint knowingly, as if sneering to her: *What did you expect?*

He lifted the choker, letting it dangle from his fingers. "I assume you have no objections."

Ice snuck up her veins. Objections? No. She wanted to live, to savor existence. And so all she felt was disbelief at this stranger before her. The longer she stared at him, the more it felt like watching night creep toward her, her eyes adjusting to the dark.

"None whatsoever," she said, swiping the diamond necklace from him. She nearly closed the distance between them, and felt a sharp stab of pleasure when he flinched from her. "The difference between a diamond necklace and a diamond dog collar depends on the bitch. And they both have teeth, Monsieur."

7

ENRIQUE

St. Petersburg, Russia

Enrique pulled his scarf tighter, as if it might keep out the Russian winter. Snowflakes whipped around his steps, pressing cold kisses to his neck. St. Petersburg was a city suspended between old and new magic—electric streetlamps cast wide pools of golden light and bridges arched like the outspread wings of angels, and yet the shadows looked too sharp and the winter air smelled of warm copper, like old blood.

Beside Enrique and Zofia, the Neva River gleamed like a black mirror. The lights of palatial homes along the English Embankment—one of the grandest streets of St. Petersburg—had abandoned their windows for the lustrous water. Unstirred by the wind, the Neva's reflection looked as if a different, parallel St. Petersburg had been poured into the water.

Enrique believed in it sometimes—other worlds crafted from

the choices he had not made, paths he had not followed. He stared at the water, at the wavering image of the other icy St. Petersburg. Maybe in that world, Tristan was alive. Maybe they were drinking cocoa, and making an ugly tinsel crown for Séverin, and thinking of how to make off with a barrel of imported champagne for the annual New Year's party at L'Eden. Maybe Laila hadn't given up baking, and L'Eden still always smelled of sugar, and he and Zofia would fight over cake slices. Maybe Séverin had accepted his inheritance, instead of throwing it away, and maybe that other Enrique was not only a member of the Ilustrados but the toast of Paris, surrounded by a gaggle of wide-eyed admirers hanging on his every word.

Maybe.

Not far off, the heavy clang of the clocks of St. Petersburg marked the eighth hour of the night. Enrique paused, and then heard it: silvery wedding bells in the distance. In two hours, the couple newly wed at Our Lady of Kazan Cathedral would hold their wedding procession down these streets in a flurry of wintry, horse-drawn carriages. Which meant they were still on time. They weren't expected at the art dealer's waterfront mansion until a quarter after eight, and the walk was long. At the second chime of the clocks, Enrique shuddered. Only one hour until Séverin and Laila would meet at the Mariinsky Theatre, laying a trap for the art dealer to secure the lens of the Tezcat spectacles. God could've promised Enrique salvation on the spot and there was still no way he'd want to be there, stuck in the middle of Laila and Séverin. Vaguely concerned that he'd just committed blasphemy with this thought, Enrique crossed himself.

Beside him, Zofia matched him stride for stride.

For tonight, she'd disguised herself as a slight, young man. Her candlelight hair was tucked into a broad hat, her lithe frame hidden by a padded coat, and her diminutive height bolstered by a pair of clever shoes. Her design, naturally. A fake beard stuck out the front pocket of her greatcoat on account of Zofia declaring it far too itchy to wear until necessary. She didn't shiver as she walked. If anything, she seemed to luxuriate in the cold, as if it ran through her blood.

"Why are you looking at me like that?" asked Zofia.

"I like looking at you," he said. Horrified at how that came out, he quickly added, "I mean, you look almost convincing, and I appreciate it merely on an aesthetic level."

"Almost convincing," repeated Zofia. "What's lacking?"

Enrique pointed at his mouth. Her voice gave her away entirely.

Zofia scowled. "I knew it. It must be a genetic predisposition from my mother." She pursed her mouth. "I thought the cold would help, but my lips always look too red."

Enrique opened and closed his mouth, struggling to find his next words.

"Was that what you meant?" she asked.

"I . . . yes. Of course."

Now that she'd mentioned her mouth, of course he had to look at it. Now he was thinking of how red her lips were, like a winter apple, and what they might taste like. And then he realized what he'd just thought and shook himself. Zofia *disquieted* him. It had snuck up on him unawares, and now made its presence known at the damndest of times. Enrique forced his thoughts to Hypnos. Hypnos understood him. The other boy knew from experience what it was like to live with a fissure in one's soul, never quite knowing which side of oneself would reign sovereign—Spanish or Filipino, the son of the colonized or the son of the colonizer. For

THE SILVERED SERPENTS   Ֆ   57

now, their arrangement was casual, which suited Enrique just fine, but he wanted more. He wanted someone who would enter a room and look for him first, to behold him as though the secrets of the world lay somewhere in his gaze, to finish his sentences. Someone to share cake with.

Maybe he could find that with Hypnos.

To live a full life would have made Tristan happy. Lightly, Enrique touched the flower peeking out of his lapel and murmured a prayer. It was a dried moonlight flower, one of the last ones Tristan had ever Forged. When the flowers were fresh, they could absorb moonlight and hold on to its glow for several hours. Dried, it was nothing but a ghost of its former luster.

"That's Tristan's," said Zofia.

Enrique dropped his hand from the flower. He didn't think she'd seen him. When he glanced down at her, he saw that her hand was in her pocket . . . an identical Forged flower stem poking out . . . and he knew Tristan was with them.

THE WATERFRONT MANSION ROSE like a moon before them. Snow caught in the ribbons of tinsel wrapped around hundreds of stately pillars. Delicate bells hidden in the Christmas pines lining the entryway chimed as they walked past. The mansion itself looked like a child's dollhouse brought to life—candy-colored mosaics beveled its domes, and the frosted panes looked more like sugar than glass.

"Remember our roles?" asked Enrique.

"You're playing an eccentric and easily distracted human—"

"—A writer, yes," said Enrique.

"And I'm the photographer."

"The very *silent* photographer."

Zofia nodded.

"Only distract the butler for a few minutes," said Enrique. "That should give me enough time to scope for any recording devices before we enter the Chamber of Goddesses."

He adjusted the lapels of the bright emerald velvet jacket that he'd borrowed from Hypnos, and then pulled the enormous door knocker shaped like a roaring lion. The Forged knocker narrowed its eyes, feigned a yawn, and then let out a huge, metallic roar that shook the small icicles from the threshold. Enrique screamed.

Zofia did not, and merely raised one eyebrow once he regained composure.

"What?" said Enrique.

"That was loud."

"I *know*. That Forged lion—"

"I meant you," said Zofia.

Enrique scowled, just as the butler opened the door and greeted them with a broad grin. He was light-skinned, with a trim black beard, and wore a heavily embroidered blue-and-silver coat over billowing pants.

"*Dobriy vyecher,*" he said warmly. "Mister Vasiliev sends his apologies for being unable to join you, but he is most delighted by the coverage on his collection, especially by such an esteemed art critic as yourself."

Enrique puffed out his chest and smiled. The fake documents he'd cobbled together *had* seemed remarkably impressive. He and Zofia stepped into the wide vestibule of the mansion. So far, the blueprints matched. Crisscrossing star-and-lozenge patterns formed the mahogany floor. Floating lanterns lit the halls, and all along were portraits of women in movement—some mythological, some modern. Enrique recognized Salomé's Dance of the Seven Veils, and a depiction of the Indian nymph, Urvashi, performing before the Hindu gods. But the painting that dominated the wall was that of a beautiful woman he didn't recognize. Her bloodred hair curled down her white neck. Judging by the slippers in her hand, she was a ballerina.

The butler extended his hand in greeting. "We are most—"

Enrique flourished his hand, then yanked it back before the butler could attempt to shake it. "I do not . . . savor the touch of flesh. It reminds me of my mortality."

The butler looked faintly disturbed. "My deepest apologies."

"I prefer shallow ones." Enrique sniffed, examining his fingernails. "Now—"

"—did our photography equipment arrive?" cut in Zofia.

Enrique had a split second to hide his frown. Zofia must have been distracted because she'd never once messed up her lines in the past. Now that he looked at her, he noticed her mustache lifting slightly at the edges.

"Yes, it did," said the butler. A slight furrow appeared between his eyebrows. "They were locked inside a massive traveling cabinet." He paused, and Enrique watched his eyes flick to Zofia's lifting mustache. ". . . I must inquire, is everything quite all right—"

Enrique let out a loud, hysterical laugh.

"Ah, my dear man! So thoughtful, is he not?" he said, grabbing Zofia's face and pressing his thumb over the lifting mustache. "What a piece of work is man! How noble in reason, how infinite in faculty . . . uh . . ."

Enrique stalled. That was about all he knew of *Hamlet*, honestly, but then Zofia spoke.

"—In form and moving how express and admirable," she said, her voice pitched low.

Enrique stared at her.

"You must forgive the eccentricities of my friend," she said smoothly to the butler, remembering her lines. "Would you be so good as to show me some of the rooms? A short tour is all that is necessary, but I want to ascertain whether any other photographs will be required for the article."

The butler, still wide-eyed, nodded slowly. "Right this way . . ."

"I will stay here," said Enrique, turning in a slow circle. He tapped his temples and took a loud, deep breath. "I want to soak in the art. *Feel* it, before I may be so bold as to write about it. You understand."

The butler flashed a strained smile. "I leave you to what you do best."

And with that, he led Zofia to a different part of the house.

Once they were out of sight, Enrique drew a Forged sphere from his pocket and threw it into the air, watching as it slowly scanned the room for any detection devices. The butler's words curdled in his gut. *What you do best.* He thought of standing in the atrium of the National Library, his damp fingerprints smudging his notes for the presentation that no one attended . . . and, later, the letter from the Ilustrados.

. . . Write your inspiring articles on history. It is what you do best . . .

It still stung. Enrique's references hadn't mattered at all. He had expected the weight of his professors' and advisor's words might not mean much to them, but he was shocked Séverin's influence had done nothing. Séverin's public support meant a universally appreciated influence: money. But maybe his ideas were so foolish that no amount of money made them worth listening to. Maybe he simply wasn't enough.

What you do best.

Enrique clenched his jaw. By now the spherical detection device had settled on the floor. The room was safe. Footsteps resounded on the other side of the hall. Zofia and the butler were returning. In a moment, they'd enter the Chamber of Goddesses where they would find the Tezcat spectacles and with it, *The Divine Lyrics*. The Ilustrados thought he did nothing but master dead languages and pore over dusty books, that his ideas were worthless, but there was so much more to him. Getting *The Divine Lyrics* was all the proof he needed. They wouldn't be able to deny, then, that his skills could procure power.

Now all he had to do was get it.

THE CHAMBER OF GODDESSES nearly brought Enrique to his knees.

It was like the foyer of some forgotten temple. Life-size goddesses leaned forward from recessed niches. Above stretched an elaborate cerulean ceiling, mechanized so the stars rotated slowly, and the planets spun as if on an invisible axis. The artwork made him feel small, but gloriously so, as if he were part of something greater than himself. It was how he used to feel every Sunday when he went to mass, drinking up the reminder that he was surrounded by a divine love. This room was the first time he had felt like this in years.

"The chamber is truly overwhelming," said the butler in reverent tones. "Though it does not last."

That sharpened Enrique's attention. "What? What do you mean?"

"The Chamber of Goddesses has a unique function, one that we don't fully understand but that we hope will become more clear once your article publishes. You see, the Chamber of Goddesses . . . disappears."

"Excuse me?"

"Every hour," said the butler. "The goddesses sink into the walls, and all these gilded trappings turn white." He consulted his watch. "By my estimate, you have about twenty minutes left of this before it disappears and returns at the next hour. But I figured that would be sufficient time to take your photos and take notes. Besides, it becomes nearly freezing in here once the door is shut. We believe the original artist installed a Forged temperature-control mechanism, perhaps for the preservation of the stone and paint. Anyway, do let me know if I can be of any assistance."

And with that, the butler left, shutting the door behind him. Enrique suspected his heartbeat had changed to: *Oh no oh no oh no.*

"Where's Hypnos?" asked Zofia.

A muffled sound caught his attention. Nearly hidden by a pillar and propped against one of the gilded chamber walls stood a large, black luggage piece marked: *photography equipment.* Zofia quickly unlocked the cabinet hinges. The door swung open and a very annoyed-looking Hypnos stepped out and shook himself.

"That was . . . awful," he said, heaving a dramatic sigh. He blinked against the sudden light and beauty of the room. A naked wonder lit up his face, but it faded when he turned to the two of them. " Zofia, you're a charming man, but I much prefer you without a beard . . . and why is it *so cold in here*? What did I miss?"

"We only have twenty minutes before this whole art installation of goddesses disappears," said Zofia.

"*What?*"

While Zofia explained the situation, Enrique focused on the actual statues inside the room. There was something strangely unifying about the goddess statues around them. He thought the goddesses would be from different pantheons around the world . . . and yet all ten of them wore the same flowing, marble tunics common to Hellenic-era deities . . . except for *one*. They looked almost identical, save for a distinguishing object here and there: a lyre or a mask, an astronomical device or a sprig of herbs.

"These goddesses strike me as odd," said Enrique. "I thought they'd be varied. I thought we'd see Parvati and Ishtar, Freya and Isis . . . but they're all so similar?"

"Spare us the art lecture for now, *mon cher*," said Hypnos, reaching out to touch his cheek. "Focus only on where the Tezcat spectacles might be."

"In a goddess?" asked Zofia.

"No," said Enrique, eyeing the collection. "I know how Fallen House safety boxes work . . . they always hide a riddle. And they wouldn't have done anything that required destruction of the property itself."

"Cold is the baseline temperature," said Zofia, almost to herself.

"I think we know that, *ma ch-chère*," said Hypnos, shivering.

"So change the factor. Add heat."

Zofia pulled off her jacket, and, with one smooth move, she ripped out the lining. Hypnos shrieked. "That's silk!"

"It's *soie de Chardonnet*," said Zofia. She reached for a match behind her ear. "A highly flammable silk substitute that was displayed at the Exhibition in May. Not good for mass production. But excellent for a torch."

Zofia struck the match and dropped it, then held up the flaming cloth, warming the air in a bright rush. She cast the flame around, but nothing on the walls or the faces of the statues changed. The Chardonnet silk burned fast. In a minute, it would hit her hands, and she'd have no choice but to drop it to the floor.

"Zofia, I think you were wrong," said Enrique. "Maybe heat doesn't work—"

"Or . . ." said Hypnos, grabbing his chin and pointing it to the floor. The thin layer of frost on the marble floor began to melt. When Enrique leaned closer, a mirror-bright shape caught his eye, like the outline of a letter. "Perhaps you have not debased yourself enough to a room full of goddesses."

"Of course," said Enrique, sinking to his knees. "The *floor*."

Zofia drew her torch closer. There, a riddle took shape:

THE NOSE KNOWS NOT THE SCENT OF SECRETS

BUT HOLDS THE SHAPE.

8

SÉVERIN

Séverin had seven fathers, but only one brother.

His seventh father—his favorite father—was Gluttony. Gluttony was a kind man, with many debts, and that made him dangerous to love. Tristan used to count the minutes he left them alone, terrified Gluttony would abandon them, no matter what Séverin said to calm him. After Gluttony's funeral, Séverin found a letter shoved under his desk and streaked with dirt:

My dear boys, I am so sorry, but I must relinquish my role as your guardian. I have offered my hand in marriage to a rich and lovely widow with no desire for children.

Séverin held the letter tightly. If Gluttony was to marry, then why had he taken his life with rat poison? A poison that was only kept in the greenhouse to ward off pests, a greenhouse that Gluttony never entered, but that Tristan loved.

You will always have me, Tristan had said at the funeral.

Yes, thought Séverin now. He would always have him. But would he always know him?

AS THE *TROIKA* rumbled over the streets of St. Petersburg, Séverin drew out Tristan's penknife. A shimmering vein of Goliath's paralyzing venom ran down its edge. When he touched the blade, he imagined the soft brush of ghostly feathers, remnants of Tristan's kills. And then he'd remember Tristan's wide grin and sly jokes, and he couldn't reconcile this blade with his brother. How could someone hold so much love and so many demons in one heart?

The *troika* pulled to a stop. Through the pulled velvet curtains, Séverin heard laughter and violin music, the bell-like chime of glasses clinking together.

"We've arrived at the Mariinsky Theatre, Monsieur Montagnet-Alarie," called his driver from the front.

Séverin hid the blade behind a steel-lined pocket of his jacket where it couldn't hurt him. Before he stepped outside, Séverin closed his eyes and pictured Roux-Joubert in the catacombs, his mouth dripping with golden ichor, that shining blood of the gods. Phantom sensations crawled over his skin—black feathers shooting from his spine, wings draping around his shoulders, horns unraveling from his head, and that unmistakable rush of invincibility. Of *godhood*. Bad or benevolent, he didn't care. He just wanted more of it.

Inside the Mariinsky Theatre, the glittering elite of St. Petersburg glided about before the ballet performance. At the entrance, a Forged ice sculpture of Snegurochka—the snow maiden from Russian fairy tales—twirled slowly, her gown of ice stars and crystal pearls catching the light and spreading nets of frost over the red carpet floors. Women wearing *kokoshniks* of golden appliqué and swan feathers laughed behind pale hands. The air smelled of ambergris perfume and tobacco smoke, salt and the occasional metallic tang of snow. A couple of women draped in ermine and sable fur walked past him, trailing gossip in their wake.

"Is that the hotelier from Paris?" whispered one. "Where's he sitting?"

"Don't look at him like that, Ekaterina," snapped the other. "Rumor has it he's got a cabaret star or courtesan warming his bed tonight."

"Well, *I* don't see her on his arm," she said with a sniff.

Séverin ignored them, turning instead toward the ivory-and-gilt doors of the entrance. The minutes ticked slowly past. Séverin twisted the diamond signet ring around his pinky. Laila would hate him for summoning her like that, but it's not as though she'd given him a choice. She was supposed to meet him here fifteen minutes ago. Séverin turned about the room. A server in a crisp silver jacket balanced a platter of etched glasses carved from ice and filled with black peppercorn vodka beside *zakuski* on small porcelain dishes: pickled cucumber and glossy roe, bits of meat suspended in aspic, and thick slabs of rye.

A man wearing an ermine ruff caught his eye and followed his gaze to the door. He flashed a knowing smile, then picked up two glasses, handing one to Séverin.

"*Za lyubov!*" he said, and cheerfully knocked back the glass. The man lowered his voice. "It means 'to love,' my friend." He winked and looked back to the door. "May she not keep you waiting for long."

Séverin drained his vodka in one swallow. It smoldered down his throat. "Or may she never find me at all."

The man looked confused, but before he could say anything, an announcer from the top of the golden, spiraled staircase called out: "Ladies and gentlemen, please take your seats!"

The crowd moved toward the staircase. Séverin hung back. Laila still wasn't here, and yet even in her absence, she'd managed to drive him mad. He heard her in the chime of another woman's too-throaty laugh, the whip of a fan she'd never bother to carry. He thought he saw her through the golden haze of a floating candelabra, trailing a bronze hand down someone else's jacket. But it was never her.

Inside the auditorium, golden champagne chandeliers drifted over the guests, who waved down flutes with a sharp flick of their hand. An artist with an affinity for silk matter had Forged the embroidery of the stage's scarlet curtains, so the threads moved fluidly into the shape of swimming koi fish. The stirring of a long-ago childhood impulse flickered inside his chest . . . to watch the audience, to follow the paths of their gaze. To make *wonders*. But he shoved it down.

Séverin snuck a glance at the empty box beside his. The art dealer, Mikhail Vasiliev, was due to arrive any minute now. Impatiently, he tapped his foot against the ground, and then let out a small curse. Some of the anti-magnetic dust Zofia had coated their shoes with left a fine grit along the wooden floor. He looked down at his hand, to the diamond signet ring that was bonded to Laila's choker. He scowled at it. Either it wasn't working, or she'd chosen to ignore him entirely.

At the sound of the door opening, Séverin sat up straight. He expected Laila, but it wasn't his door that had opened—it was Vasiliev's. Two armed guards entered the booth beside his. Their cuffs were rolled, and the blood Forged tattoo that allowed them entrance into the downstairs' private lobby salon cast a scarlet glow beneath the gas lamps. Séverin could just make out a small symbol . . . an apple . . . before the guards turned, scanning the box.

"This isn't the usual," murmured one of the guards.

"The other was under construction," said the second. "Even Vasiliev's salon is under construction. They had to add new metal beams or something in the corners."

The other guard nodded and then made a sound of disgust as he scraped his feet on the floor. "Do they no longer clean this establishment? Look at all this dust. Disgusting."

"Vasiliev won't like all these changes . . . he's nervous tonight."

"Well, he *should* be. Someone stole the verit stone lion at the entrance. Not that he knows, so don't tell him." The man shuddered. "He's hard enough to be around these days."

Séverin smiled into his champagne flute.

The first guard picked up the bottle of champagne sweating in its ice bucket.

"At least the Mariinsky Theatre saw fit to send a bubbly apology."

The second one only grunted.

The two guards headed back outside, no doubt to assure Vasiliev that everything was safe. On the curtain, the embroidered koi fish swam into an elaborate number 5.

Five minutes until curtain.

Vasiliev's door opened once more, and Séverin dug his nails into the armrest. It was only when the door shut that he realized it was not Vasiliev's box entrance. But his. The scent of roses and sugar filled the air.

"You're late," he said.

"I'm sorry I kept you pining, Séverin," she said smoothly.

Before, she would have called him *Majnun*, but that was life-times ago.

He turned his head and saw Laila. Tonight, she wore a mag-nificent golden gown. A thousand tempting bows embellished her waist. Her hair was pulled up, and an artful gold-feathered fasci-nator sat in her curls like a small sun. His eyes went to her neck—her throat was bare.

"Where's your necklace?"

"A diamond choker with a metallic gown looks rather tacky," she said, making a *tsk* sound. "Our arrangement allows you to—supposedly—lay claim to my bed, not my sense of taste. Besides, this is our first public appearance together. A gaudy diamond necklace loudly proclaims I do your bidding for money, when the world already knows that a woman like me can't possibly exist out-side the cabaret without the excuse of a wealthy lover. Your *collar* would have been an exaggeration for tonight."

She added this last part bitterly, for it was true. Women like Laila could not move freely through the world, and the world was only poorer for it.

"Unless you believe my outfit is overplaying my role?" she asked, raising her eyebrow. "Would you have preferred the dia-mond necklace with a less eye-catching gown?"

"It's not about the outfit. It's about the appearance," he said tightly. "I expected you to enter with me, and I expected you to wear that necklace as I wear my oath to you."

Just then, the curtain was called, and ballerinas in delicate white tulle twirled across the stage. The Forged lights caught the edge of Laila's dress, turning her molten. Séverin scanned the au-dience's expressions, annoyed to see several of them had turned in his direction, though their eyes were fixated on Laila. Too late, he realized Laila's fingers had crossed the barrier of their shared armrest until her hand rested on his sleeve. He jerked back.

"Is that any way to treat the girl you love?" she asked. "Surely, you can endure my touch."

Laila leaned in closer, and Séverin had no choice but to look at her: at the sleek line of her neck, her full lips, and cygnet eyes. Once, when they had trusted each other, she told him she had been cobbled together like a doll. As if it made her less real. Those parts—those lips he'd traced, neck he'd kissed, scar he'd touched—were exquisite. But that wasn't the essence of her. The essence of her was walking into a room, and all eyes pinned to her, as if she were the performance of a lifetime. The essence of her was a smile full of forgiveness, the warmth in her hands, sugar in her hair.

Just as quickly as the thought rose to his head, it disappeared, swallowed up by the memory of torn-up bird wings and ichor, Tristan's gray eyes dulling and Laila's rapid pulse. Numbness rose, icing him over until he felt nothing.

"I don't love you," he said flatly.

"Then pretend," she whispered, her fingers trailing up his jaw now, turning his face to hers.

She moved so close, he thought she'd actually—

"I read the coats of Vasiliev's security detail in the main foyer," she whispered. "Vasiliev leaves two guards outside the private salon. One with a weapon, and one who has blood Forged access to open the room. The one with the tattoo is . . . an admirer . . . of mine." Séverin didn't miss the way her lip curled in distaste at this. "Hypnos has several House Nyx guards placed to redirect the crowd. A couple are disguised as Vasiliev's guards."

Séverin nodded and started to pull away from her. He hated being this close to her.

"I am not finished," she hissed.

"We're drawing too much attention. Tell me later."

Laila tightened her grip on his hand, and Séverin felt scalded. This had gone far enough. He reached out, cupping the back of Laila's head, feeling the hot pulse of her skin as he bent to the hollow of her neck. Her breath hitched.

"Now you're overplaying your part," he said and then released her.

THIRTY MINUTES LATER came the call for intermission.

The stage curtains drew tight. Séverin listened for the sound of Vasiliev rising from his chair in the box beside them.

"I've had enough of this," he said.

That was the first time Séverin heard his voice. It wasn't what he expected. Vasiliev was a broad man, with a shock of dark hair and silver at his temples. He looked full of strength, and yet his voice was almost thin and wispy. Around his neck shone a gold chain. At the end of it twirled the lens piece of the Tezcat spectacles.

Laila rose, her hand resting on his shoulder. She touched her throat, and her L'Énigme headdress unfurled around her face, concealing her eyes and nose, leaving only her mouth which curved in a sensuous suggestion. Her coy smile acted as its own camouflage as they slipped away from the crowd, down the servants' service halls and into a darkened hallway that shot off from the main lobby.

The entrance to Vasiliev's private salon was designed as two, twelve-foot high marble hands cupped in prayer. When someone was granted entrance, the palm doors swung open. Séverin studied the threshold. Every acquisition was the same in the sense that every hiding place contained a message that someone hoped would outlive them. The trick lay in understanding the context. Vasiliev's salon was no different. Someone might think the hands pressed together were a sign of a guest humbling himself before Vasiliev . . . but Séverin suspected it was the opposite. The doors loomed huge, rendering whoever stood before them—regardless of their stature—small. There was something apoolgetic about the de-sign. To Séverin, it was a loud, public expression of guilt. The same guilt that perhaps convinced Vasiliev to wear the Fallen House's Tezcat lens necklace in the first place, thinking it was a nod to his dead ballerina lover.

Séverin judged the distance between the two men stationed at the entrance. One was a guard with a bayonet across his back. The way he stood, tilted to one side, suggested a bad leg. The other guard had his hands clasped before him. When he saw Laila, he flashed an oily smile.

"Mademoiselle L'Énigme!" he said, bowing his head. "I heard the rumors that you would be here this evening."

He barely registered Séverin walking behind her.

"To what do we owe the pleasure?"

Laila laughed. It was a high, false sound.

"I am told I have an admirer inside who wishes to greet me personally."

"Ah, Mademoiselle, if only . . ." The first guard leered. "But, one cannot enter without one of these." He raised his wrist, displaying the apple-shaped blood Forged tattoo. "Unless Mademoiselle has one hidden somewhere secret on her person?"

His eyes roved down the length of her, and Séverin had a great urge to snap the man's neck.

"You're welcome to check," she said silkily.

The guard's eyes widened. He straightened his lapel, then walked over to her. Laila stretched out her bronze leg for inspection. Séverin counted down from ten.

9...

The man reached for her thigh.

7...

Laila feigned a laugh as his other hand went to her waist.

4...

The second the man touched her, Laila drew out a knife and pressed it against his neck, leaving Séverin standing there uselessly holding a knife in his hand.

"Guard!" shouted the first.

But the man with the bayonet didn't move.

"Get this bitch off me," he said.

Séverin raised his knife and walked forward. "I'm afraid he doesn't work for you. He works for us."

Laila pressed the knife tighter to his throat.

"If you kill me, you can't get inside," said the man, starting to sweat. "You need me."

"On the contrary," said Laila. "We only need your hand."

The man's eyes widened. "Please—"

Laila looked at Séverin. Séverin raised his knife higher.

"No—" started the guard.

Séverin brought it down, switching his grip at the last second, so the heavy hilt slammed into the back of the man's skull. He slumped forward, unconscious.

"Repulsive," hissed Laila, pocketing her knife. When she saw Séverin looking at it, she shrugged. "I was *going* to tell you I could render him immobile on my own. You were the one who chose not to listen."

Séverin shut his mouth.

With the help of the disguised House Nyx guard, they dragged the guard forward, placing his wrist with the blood Forged tattoo on an access point in the middle of the pressed-palm marble doors. The marble shuddered open at the touch, and Séverin dropped the man to the floor.

Séverin glanced at the guard. "Get the wedding carriage ready."

The other man nodded and left.

Inside the salon, rich curtains and portraits of a ballerina with red hair adorned the licorice-black walls. Vasiliev sat at a desk, sketching. At the sight of Laila and Séverin, his guards leapt forward.

"Rather dusty inside here, isn't it?" asked Séverin.

He pushed down on Zofia's magnetic signet ring, and the guards zoomed backwards into the four corners of the room where, earlier today, a false construction team had erected several powerful magnetic beams, to Zofia's specific instructions.

Vasiliev stared at them, his face pale.

"How?"

"Adhesive magnets," said Séverin, with a grim smile. "Fascinating, aren't they? Even small particles that can coat a man's shoes might retain their strong polarity. Now, the chain and lens pendant around your neck, if you please."

He expected Vasiliev to frown in confusion . . . but instead, the other man just bowed his head. Guilt scrawled across his features. The same guilt Séverin detected in the design of his salon's entrance.

"I knew this was coming."

Séverin frowned, on the verge of speaking when Vasiliev grabbed a champagne flute, knocked back the drink and then shuddered as he wiped his mouth with his sleeve.

"A truly blessed man is one who knows his burdens," said Vasiliev. His gaze slid to the champagne. "It was kind of you to provide mind Forged champagne. It absolves one of guilt, though I have few people left in my life to answer to these days."

Vasiliev unwrapped the chain from around his neck, already starting to sway on his feet. The Tezcat spectacle lens glittered in the dark room. It was the size of an ordinary monocle and set into a structure that resembled a key. He placed it on his desk, his eyes slowly closing.

"She's not safe, you know," he said wearily. "She'll find you. And then she will see reason."

His chin dropped to his chest as unconsciousness overtook him. Laila looked at Séverin, horror on her face.

"Who is he talking about?"

But Séverin had no answer.

9

ZOFIA

Zofia pulled her now flameless jacket back on and tore off one of her Tezcat-detecting pendants.

Over the past few months, she had perfected the formula, so all she had to do was hold the pendant to an object and it would reveal whether there was a concealed Tezcat door. One by one, she held the pendant to the statues, but her pendant never changed color.

Whatever lay hidden here had taken different precautions. Zofia frowned, shivering. Arctic air filled the Chamber of Goddesses. A white tinge spread from the door, erasing the gold filigree on the tile and creeping up the walls. Where the white touched the statues, their shapes began to dissolve back into their wall niches. In a matter of minutes, they would disappear entirely. Even the riddle had begun to disappear from the floor:

THE NOSE KNOWS NOT THE SCENT OF SECRETS

BUT HOLDS THE SHAPE.

It meant nothing to her, but when she looked at Enrique, his eyes seemed alight. Hypnos stood on his right, patting his own nose and then sniffing his hand.

"I've drawn zero conclusions," announced Hypnos.

"Then keep an eye on the time and guard the door," said Enrique, walking toward the statues. "The butler said we have twenty minutes. Zofia?"

Zofia rehooked her pendant.

"No Tezcat presence detected," she said. "If there is one here, it must have several security layers."

Enrique paced the room slowly. Zofia rummaged through the rest of her jacket pockets, pulling out more flammable Chardonnet silk, a box of matches, a small set of chiseling tools, and a Forged ice pen that drew water from the air and froze it. Zofia analyzed the room, but none of the tools she brought were helpful.

"I thought . . . I thought there'd be a sign or something to the treasure," said Hypnos, blowing into his cupped palms for warmth.

"Like an 'X marks the spot'?" asked Enrique.

"That would've been helpful, yes," said Hypnos. "Someone should inform this treasure that I find it unbecomingly teasing. I thought it was supposed to be hiding in one of the goddesses? But then the riddle is talking about noses?"

"Zofia, any luck with the tools?"

"Luck is useless," she said.

"Fine, any success?"

"No."

"Mythologically speaking, we're talking about something that is thought to guard or hide things," he said. "There are ten goddesses here, maybe one of them has a story about hiding something?"

"How can you tell which goddess each is?" asked Hypnos.

"Iconography," said Enrique. He stared at the ten statues, all of whom looked the same to Zofia except for whatever object they might be carrying. And then, Enrique snapped his fingers. "I get it now . . . these are the nine *muses* from Greek mythology, goddesses of the arts. See that lyre?" He pointed at one of the blank-faced statues clutching a golden harp. "That's for Calliope, the muse of epic poetry. Beside her is Erato, the muse of love poetry with her cithara instrument, and then Thalia, the muse of comedy, with her theatre masks."

Zofia watched, rapt. To her, these statues were feats of Forging technology. They were marble and affinity. But that was all their shapes told her. When she listened to Enrique, though, it was like a new light turning on in her mind, and she wanted to hear more. Enrique paused in front of a statue with outspread wings.

"Strange," said Enrique. "There's a tenth statue . . . This one doesn't fit. But why *muses*? It might be a nod to the Order's lore of the Lost Muses who guard *The Divine Lyrics*?"

"The Order didn't construct this art, though," pointed out Zofia.

"True," said Enrique, nodding. "And then there's this tenth statue, which doesn't fit at all. It's strange, honestly, look at the shape of—"

"This isn't the time to ponder!" said Hypnos, gesturing at the floor. "We've got about fifteen minutes left by my count."

By now, the white tinge had spread across nearly half of the room and had begun to creep up the legs of half the goddess statues.

"I don't think this one is a goddess," said Enrique. "No distinguishing iconographic aspects. There's some gold leaf on the wings, but that doesn't tell us much. And the face is devoid of expression."

Zofia didn't move, but there was something familiar about the statue . . . something that made her think of her sister.

"I want to see too," grumbled Hypnos, walking over to the statue. He eyed it, then scowled. "If *I* looked like that, I wouldn't demand worship either. None of that outfit says 'pay me obeisance, mortals.'"

"It's not a muse . . . it's a seraph, an *angel*," said Enrique.

He took a step closer, then ran his hands along its face, across the shoulders, and down the body of the statue.

Hypnos whistled. "Rather forward of you . . ."

"I'm trying to see if there's any depressed spots," said Enrique, "some sort of release mechanism to get at whatever might be hiding inside here."

By now, the white tinge had gotten to the statue of the angel. It started at its feet, slowly pulling the marble back into the walls. Zofia's breath plumed in front of her. The longer she stared at it, the more an old story and game that she and Hela used to play came to mind. She remembered her sister whispering, *Can you keep a secret, Zosia?*

"Hypnos? Zofia? Any ideas?" called Enrique.

"The nose knows not the scent of secrets, but holds the shape," Zofia repeated, touching her mouth. Zofia started to cross the room to them. "Hela and I used to play a game from a story our mother told us about angels and children . . . Before you are born, you know all the secrets of the world. But an angel locked them up by pressing his thumb right above your lips. That's why everyone has a dent right above their mouth."

Hypnos frowned. "That's a pretty tale—"

But Enrique grinned. "It fits . . . it's demonstrating the concept of *anamnesis*!"

Zofia blinked at him.

"Is that a disease?" asked Hypnos.

"It's this idea of a cosmic loss of innocence. The thumb print of a seraph right below your nose fits with the riddle because the nose would not know the scent of secrets, but *holds the shape*. It's the phil-trum! Or the Cupid's bow! That dip right above one's mouth—below one's nose. In fact, in Filipino mythology, there are *diwatas* who—"

"Stop lecturing us and get on with it, Enrique!" said Hypnos.

"Sorry, sorry!"

The white tinge had crept up the seraph's waist now, and the hands had begun to lose their shape. Quickly, Enrique reached up. He pressed his thumb to the angel's upper lip. A sound like rushing water emanated from inside the seraph statue. Immediately, it split down the center, the two halves swinging open like a hidden door. Inside the hollow angel stood a slender onyx pedestal, and on that sat a small, shining metal box no bigger than the span of Zofia's hand. Slender cracks networked across its surface, as if it had been fused together long ago.

"We found it," said Hypnos, awed.

Enrique reached in, pulling on the box . . . It didn't budge.

"Wait," said Zofia. She held up a pendulum light, shining it on the metal. Small finger indents appeared where Enrique had tried to pull away the box. When she touched it, her Forging affinity for solid matter prickled through her fingertips. "That box is made of Forged tin, reinforced with steel."

"Is that bad?" asked Enrique.

Zofia nodded, grimacing. "It means my incendiary devices won't work on it. It's flame-retardant." She looked at the interior of the hollow angel and frowned. "And the inside of this statue is a sound barrier . . ." She touched the layers of sponge, cloth, and cork. Why would a device need to be silent?

A small chime sounded on Hypnos's watch. He looked up at them.

"Five minutes."

Zofia felt her throat tightening. The room felt too small, too bright, too much like the laboratory in her old university where they'd locked her inside and—

"Phoenix," said Enrique softly. "Stay with me. What do we have? You always have something."

Chardonnet silk was useless here. Beyond her regular tools and matches, all that was left was a controlled incendiary device, which wouldn't help, and the ice pen in case they needed to freeze the hinges off doors.

"An ice pen," said Zofia.

"In an already freezing room?" wailed Hypnos. "So, fire is useless . . . ice is useless . . . for that matter, *I* am useless."

"We can't even pry it off the stand, so how will we crack it—" started Zofia, but suddenly Enrique paused, something lighting up behind his eyes.

"Crack," he repeated.

"Aaaand there goes his sanity," said Hypnos.

"Zofia, hand me that ice pen. It draws water out of the air, yes?" asked Enrique.

Zofia nodded and handed it over, watching as Enrique began to trace every single one of the cracks in the tin box. "Did you know—"

"Here we go," muttered Hypnos.

"—In 218 BC, the Carthaginian general Hannibal made his way through the Alps with his huge army and forty elephants intent on destroying the heart of the Roman Empire," said Enrique. He poured out the water the pen had collected from the air. The liquid disappeared into the cracks of tin. "Back then, the standard for removing rock obstacles was fairly torturous. Rocks were heated by bonfires, then doused with cold water . . ."

He touched the ice pen to the box, and a glittering and crackling sound echoed in the silent chamber. Ice spidered out from the fissures. A snapping sound rattled from deep within the box.

". . . which would make them crack apart," said Enrique, grinning.

The box split open, the edges of the metal gleaming damply.

Enrique reached into the box, pulling out the delicate Tezcat spectacles. They were the size of ordinary glasses . . . albeit more elaborate. The gunmetal-gray frames formed an ivy-and-flower pattern of wrought iron that could be wrapped around the head like a diadem. A pair of square lens frames jutted out, but only one of them held a piece of prismatic glass.

Hypnos clapped slowly, grinning. "Well done! Although, I do find it strange that this time the engineer used a story and the storyteller used engineering."

"I'm a *historian*," said Enrique, tucking the Tezcat spectacles into his jacket. "Not a storyteller."

"History, storytelling," said Hypnos, waving his hand and smiling at Zofia. "*Quelle est la différence?*"

Another chime sounded. Soundlessly, the angel statue was swallowed into the wall, leaving them in a pristine marble room. Zofia turned around, but the walls were smooth, no sign whatsoever of the muse statues that had once been here.

"Time's up," said Hypnos. "And it's rude to be late to weddings."

"You're going to have to get back into that cabinet—"

"—*Ugh.*"

"It's either that or—"

Just then, the door to the chamber opened. The butler walked inside, carrying a tray of refreshments.

"I thought you might like—" He stopped abruptly when he saw Hypnos and the broken traveling cabinet.

"I told you to watch the door!" said Enrique.

"I forgot!"

"*Who the hell is this?*" demanded the butler. "*Guards!*"

"*Run!*" shouted Enrique.

Zofia, Enrique, and Hypnos bolted out of the Chamber of God-desses. Behind her, Zofia heard the clatter of a tray crashing onto the ground, and the butler hollering. They flew through the exquisite manor. For a fleeting moment, Zofia felt a rush of adrenaline, the kind of energy that made her feel as if anything were possible.

Enrique glanced at her, his cheeks flushed, one corner of his mouth curved slyly even as he ran. Zofia recognized that expression from Laila each time she used to sneak her an extra cookie. It was conspiratorial, like being let into a secret. It made her feel grateful . . . and confused, because she wasn't sure what secret he was offering.

At the end of the hall, the wide front door glowed bright in warning. Hypnos reached it first, pulling the handle. On the other side of the door, Zofia could hear wedding bells clanging loudly, and the *clip-clop* of horse hooves and carriage wheels shattering the ice-crusted streets.

Behind Zofia came the sound of heavy scratching and thudding. Enrique looked over her shoulder, his face paling.

"*Damn,*" hissed Hypnos, tugging at the handle.

"Dogs!" said Enrique.

"Not quite the blasphemy I'd use to articulate the situation, but—"

"No," said Enrique. "*Dogs!* Move faster!"

Zofia looked behind her, her mind processing the sight before fear caught up: four massive white dogs bounded toward them.

"Got it!" yelled Hypnos.

The door flung wide open. Dimly, she felt Hypnos's hand wrapping around her wrist. He tugged hard, pulling her into the icy night of St. Petersburg as the door slammed shut behind them, and frigid air hit her like a punch.

Up ahead, wedding bells chimed from a slew of *troikas* storming the street of *Angliskaya Naberezhnaya*. A team of three dappled draft horses pulled each of the fifteen white carriages. Forged firecrackers whizzed into the air, exploding into silhouetted images of the bride and groom, roaring bears and soaring swans that dissolved into the night.

"There!" said Enrique.

One of the carriages sported a black stripe down the middle. It turned the corner toward them just as the front door swung open once more. Enrique cursed loudly from the end of the sidewalk. He waved wildly at the carriage with the black stripe, but the carriage never slowed. Growls erupted behind Zofia.

"We won't make it in time!" said Hypnos, his face shining with sweat.

With a twist of her wrist, Zofia tore one of the fire pendants from her necklace, throwing it at the dogs. At the same time she pushed her *will* into the metal object: *Ignite.*

She heard the crackling rip of flames catching one upon one another, followed by indignant yelping and the sound of paws skittering backward. A column of flame shot up from the sidewalk, forcing back the guard animals.

The carriage with the black stripe skidded to a halt at the end of the manor entrance. The other *troikas* wound past it just as the door opened from the inside . . . Hypnos and Enrique clambered into the dark of the carriage. Zofia grasped the rails, then felt Laila's warm hands pull her onto the seat.

On the far side of the carriage sat Séverin. He didn't glance at any of them as he rapped his knuckles twice on the roof. As they sped away, Zofia peered out the window. The column of fire had died down. The butler and a slew of guards had run outside . . . but their *troika* had already fallen into line with the rest of the wedding procession.

Hypnos flung himself across the seat, his head resting in Laila's lap, his legs sprawled over Enrique. Without quite knowing why, Zofia glanced at Enrique. She wanted to know what his expression looked like with Hypnos's body against his. She had not forgotten Enrique and Hypnos's kiss from months ago. The memory startled her. She didn't know why that image drifted to her right then, but it did—the slowness of it, like a wick burning to some explosion she couldn't comprehend. Couldn't create. Thinking about it summoned a painful weight against her chest, but she didn't know why.

"Zofia nearly got eaten by dogs," announced Hypnos. "I mean, she did basically figure out how to get to the spectacles, but *I* did some rescuing too! Honestly, phoenix, what would you do without us?"

He grinned widely, but Zofia could not smile. She thought of Hela crumpling the letter she had tried writing to them when she was in Poland. *Don't make them worry, Zosia. They might start fretting over who would have to take care of you when I'm gone.* Even if the money from her work had saved Hela's life; even if the team would fail without her inventions, she did not like feeling as though the way she functioned somehow made her a burden. And yet, she knew sometimes she needed help when other people didn't. That knowledge sat inside her like an ill-fitting puzzle piece.

"I don't know," she said softly.

10

LAILA

Laila stepped out of the wedding carriage and looked up at the yawning dark of the shopfront nestled on a sleepy corner of St. Petersburg. The snow fell like sugar—softly and sweetly, gently brushing the wooden eaves of the storefront. But while the city looked sugared with snow, the cold of Russia tasted of bitterness. It snuck behind coat collars, stained fingers blue, and scorched the inside of her nose simply because she dared to breathe.

"Come along!" said Hypnos, practically skipping ahead of them. "And you—"

He paused to look at the person who had stepped out of the carriage behind them. Laila bit back a shudder. She still hadn't grown accustomed to the sight of a Sphinx, the guard members of the Order of Babel who wore grotesque crocodile masks and who always faintly reeked of blood.

"You know how and where to meet us. Get the carriage ready."

The Sphinx did not speak. Perhaps they couldn't, thought Laila with a pang of pity. Behind the Sphinx stood four other guards of House Nyx, men who still wore the uniform of Vasiliev's men. Though they had the pendant with the missing Tezcat lens, the job in the Mariinsky Theatre disturbed her. She couldn't stop thinking about Vasiliev's last words before he slipped into unconsciousness. *She'll find you.* Who was she? Séverin had no idea and dismissed it as the words of a man on the brink of nervous exhaustion. But Laila felt the echo of those words shadowing her thoughts.

Inside the shop, strange objects lined the walls. Glossy gourd-shaped dolls no taller than the span of her hand covered shelves like a small army. Delicate blue ceramic pitchers and teacups, sterling silver samovars and boxes of imported tea and tobacco lay half unpacked from wooden crates packed with straw. Along one of the walls hung pelts of expensive furs—spotted lynx and velveteen sable, frost-colored mink and fox fur the rich orange and scarlet of a sunset ripped off the sky. And at the far end of the room, Laila could just make out a pair of glass doors against a wall. Frost spidered against the glass, but through the door on the left, Laila could just make out the silhouette of a city . . . and it wasn't St. Petersburg.

Hypnos followed her gaze, grinning.

"One of the Order of Babel's better secrets," he said. "Those are ancient Tezcat portals that use technology from the Fallen House to cross huge distances. That door on the left leads straight to Moscow."

"And the one on the right?" asked Zofia.

Hypnos frowned. "I never opened it after that one time I saw a puddle of blood seeping through from the other side."

"Excuse me, what?" demanded Enrique. "Also why do you have so many portals in Russia?"

"It's the capital of the Order of Babel's learning, *mon cher*," said Hypnos, as he walked to the back of the room. "There's only one House in Russia, House Dazbog. Imagine that! *One* House to throw all your parties? It boggles the mind. Anyway, Russia does not have nearly as many colonies beyond some fur-trapping what-nots. Maybe it's too distracted from its constant skirmishes with China and the like, so House Dazbog specialized in its own currency: *knowledge*. As for the portals, there needed to be secure ways for each House to get information or meet in secret, so Russia has the highest concentration."

Laila half listened as she made her way to one of the shelves lined with the painted dolls. A lump stuck in her throat. Growing up, she'd only ever owned one doll. And she didn't like to remember what had become of it.

"Those are *matryoshka* dolls," said Hypnos, taking one down from the shelf.

He twisted the doll's top and bottom torso and it broke apart, revealing a smaller set. Then he did the same thing to that set . . . on and on, until there was a perfect, descending order of miniatures.

"Beautiful," said Laila.

"They're the latest design from Vasily Zvyozdochkin," said Hypnos.

Laila traced the doll's design—the ice-blue coat and shell-colored skin, the painted snowflake over the doll's heart.

"Who is she?" asked Laila.

Hypnos shrugged. By then, Enrique had made his way to them and peered over her shoulder.

"Snegurochka," he said.

"Bless you," said Hypnos solemnly.

Enrique rolled his eyes, even as a small smile touched his mouth.

"The snow maiden from Russian fairy tales," explained Enrique. "Legend goes that she was made of snow, and though she was warned all her life not to fall in love, she couldn't help herself. The moment she did, she melted."

Laila's palms felt prickly with annoyance. She wanted to shake this Snegurochka for breaking so easily. After all, they were hardly different from each other. Laila was salvaged bones, and the snow maiden was only gathered snow. Love didn't deserve to thaw their wits and turn their hearts to dust.

"Is everything in order?" asked a familiar dark voice.

A flash of heat wound through Laila's traitorous body, and she turned sharply from the snow maiden dolls.

"Yes, yes, everything is ready," said Hypnos, looping his arm through Enrique's and walking to a wooden crate heaped in hay.

Beyond him, Séverin caught her eye and his gaze moved slowly to the dolls behind her. Laila stalked off toward Zofia, who was sitting at a low table and playing with her box of matches.

"Shots?" asked Hypnos, pulling out a bottle of vodka netted in ice.

"Spectacles," said Zofia.

"Never heard of that drinking game."

"I thought we were putting together the Tezcat spectacles," said Enrique.

"Not here," said Séverin, casting an eye to the door. "Too noticeable. Vasiliev's men could still be out there. We're going to take the portal to Moscow first."

"And it's bad luck to start a journey sober," added Hypnos. He lifted up the vodka bottle. "Now. To Lady Luck?"

"I don't see the point of toasting to an anthropomorphization of chance," said Zofia. "It doesn't increase the frequency of its occurrence."

"And for that, you're getting *two* shots," he said. "Also, do be careful sitting on those wooden crates. They're old and have a fair number of treacherous splinters."

Laila sat. She forced herself to smile, but those dolls had shaken her. She turned the garnet ring on her hand: *18 days*.

We have the Tezcat spectacles, she reminded herself. But her doubts snapped through her hope: What if it didn't work? How did she know for certain that the secret to life lay in the pages of *The Divine Lyrics*? What if the book had been moved from the Sleeping Palace?

"Laila?" asked Hypnos.

She looked up. She hadn't been listening.

"We were going to go in order of birthdays. When's yours?"

"Eighteen days," she said.

Her stomach turned to say it aloud.

"So soon, *ma chère*! You should have told me! Will you have a party?"

Or a funeral? she thought. She shook her head as Hypnos put a cold glass in her hand, then handed one to Enrique and—though she scowled—Zofia. Séverin refused. He stood by the hearth, away from the rest of them. Shadows and firelight licked over him, rendering him almost inhuman. The curve of her neck prickled, remembering the near brush of his lips against her skin. *Now you're overselling your part.* Séverin's gaze lifted sharply to hers. A second too late, she turned her head.

"May our ends justify our means," intoned Hypnos.

Any time she thought of ends, Tristan's quicksilver smile twisted through her heart. Laila murmured his name under her breath, then knocked back the icy vodka in one swallow. It tasted like ghosts, she thought, for even after she'd finished her drink, the alcohol lingered bitterly on her tongue.

"*L'Chaim*," said Zofia softly, throwing back the vodka.

Enrique drank his, then sputtered, clutching his throat. "That's *disgusting*."

"Here, have more," said Hypnos, holding out the bottle. "Enough shots and you won't taste a thing."

"I'd like a word alone with my team," said Séverin quietly. "Go check on the portal, Hypnos."

Hypnos slowly put the bottle on the ground. The smile slipped off his face.

"Of course," he said.

When he stood, Enrique caught his hand, squeezing it for a moment before letting go. Laila recognized that longing expression on his face, and it made her pause . . . It was the same expression he wore when he had become enamored with an idea. Like with his piano playing or his short-lived obsession with bonsai trees that annoyed Tristan to no end. Laila watched as Hypnos absentmindedly smiled at Enrique before turning to his guard and heading to the portal. She was happy for them, of course, but that didn't stop the pang of misgiving in her heart. Hypnos enjoyed falling in and out of love as if it were a hobby. If someone fell too hard along the way, Laila wasn't sure he'd stop to care.

Enrique turned to Séverin, his eyes cold. "I think he's earned his place here by now."

"He's earned a place in your bed," said Séverin. "Not at my table."

Splotches of red appeared on Enrique's cheeks. If Séverin noticed this, he ignored it.

"Besides, he's still part of the Order."

Laila thought of Hypnos carefully assembling snacks for them in the stargazing room, the sheen of his eyes when he surprised them with everything he'd made and the fall in his shoulders when he realized it wasn't the surprise he'd intended. She glared up at Séverin.

"Hypnos is every bit as trustworthy as any of us," she said, slamming her hand down.

All she'd wanted was to make a point. Instead, white-hot pain flooded her senses. Too late, Hypnos's warning sounded in her mind: *Do be careful.* Blood welled onto her palm from the puncture of a loose nail.

"Gods, Laila, are you all right?" asked Enrique, rushing to her.

Laila's hand pulsed as she pressed it to her dress, heedless that it destroyed the golden fabric. She was so careful not to cut herself. The last time she'd been twelve. The monsoon rains had swept through their village, and the bark of the lime tree she usually climbed was rain-slicked. When she fell and cut her hand, she'd run to her father, her ego bruised and her hand bloodied. She just wanted him to fuss over her, to tell her she would be fine. But instead, he'd recoiled.

Get away from me. I don't want to look at whose blood the jaaduagar *filled you with.*

Whose blood was on her hands?

It made her sick.

"Excuse me," she said, pushing away Enrique's hand. "I need some air."

Her breath felt tight in her lungs as she ran outside. The Sphinx merely turned his head, but otherwise didn't acknowledge her. Too late, Laila realized she'd left her coat on the wooden crate. She thought she knew what winter was, but the cold of Russia felt . . . vindictive.

"Laila?"

She turned and saw Enrique and Zofia standing at the door. Enrique held out her coat.

Zofia held up a lit match. "Fire cauterizes wounds."

Enrique was appalled. "It's a tiny cut! Put that flame away!"

Zofia blew it out, looking mildly annoyed. In one of his hands, Enrique balanced a roll of bandages and a tiny shot glass full of vodka. He poured it over her hand. It stung so sharply that Laila couldn't breathe.

Zofia took the bandage from him and started wrapping her hand. It was such a small thing. To be fussed over. To be the one treated tenderly. When she'd last cut herself, she'd merely stood in the rain, her hand throbbing as she let the water rush over her palms until there was no trace of someone else's blood on her skin. Tears started running down her cheeks.

"Laila . . . Laila, what's wrong?" asked Enrique. His eyes were wide with alarm. "Tell us."

Tell us. Maybe it was the pain in her hand or the pained note in his voice, but Laila felt her secret slip out of her control.

"I'm dying," she said softly.

She looked into Enrique's face, but he only shook his head with a small smile. Zofia, however, looked shocked.

"It's just a cut, Laila—" said Enrique.

"No," she said sharply. She looked at them, memorizing their features. Maybe this would be the last time they would ever look at her like this—like they cared.

"There's something you don't know about me," she said, looking away from them. "It's easier if I show you."

Laila's heart leapt as she reached out, touching the rosary that Enrique wore around his neck.

"Your father gave this to you when you left the Philippines," she said.

"That's not exactly a secret," said Enrique gently.

"He told you that he too once dreamt of running away . . . on the night before he married your mother. He thought of giving it all up, the Mercado-Lopez Mercantile Enterprise, everything . . . for the love of a woman in Cavite. But he chose to see his duty through, and he has never once resented it . . . He gave you his rosary and told you he hoped it would guide you on the right paths . . ."

Enrique looked stunned. He opened his mouth, then closed it.

"I can read the memories of objects," said Laila, drawing back her hand. "Not all of them, of course. But strong emotions or recent ones. It's because I . . . I'm Forged."

Without looking at them, she told them the story of her making. Not her birth. Because she'd never really been born. She'd died inside her mother's womb, and the rest of her was cobbled together.

"It's why I need to find *The Divine Lyrics*," she said. "The *jaadugar* who made me said I wouldn't live past my nineteenth birthday without the secrets inside that book."

The seconds of silence stretched into a full minute. Laila thought they'd turn around or step away, or do *something*, but instead, they just stared, and all she wanted was to run. Zofia's blue eyes sharpened with a new light, and Laila nearly winced from the resolve she saw there.

"I will not let you die," said Zofia.

Enrique gripped her hand, his touch full of warmth.

"*We* won't let anything happen to you."

You.

No conditions. No change in how they referred to her. No change, even, in how they looked at her. Laila held back, and it took a moment to realize that her whole body had seized up, ready to flinch. To flee. Knowing, for the first time, that she didn't have to run made her stare at her hands, utterly lost. And then, as if he knew what ran through her thoughts, Enrique reached out. That touch shocked through her, and a second later, Laila threw her arms around Zofia and Enrique. Miraculously—more miraculous than a girl brought back from the dead or the terrible wonders of the Catacombs—they held her tight. When she finally let go, Enrique's eyes were full of question.

". . . So you could do that the whole time?" he asked, turning a little red. "Because if so, I know it may have looked like I stole that feathered boa from the cabaret, but I swear it—"

"I don't need to know, Enrique," said Laila, laughing despite herself. "Your secrets are still yours. I never read the objects of my friends."

Unbidden came the memory of Tristan and all his hidden darkness, all the ways he'd needed help and all the missed times she could've figured out how to give him that. Maybe she should change that policy.

"Does Séverin know?" asked Zofia.

Laila clenched her jaw.

"Séverin knows that I was . . . made. And that I can read objects. But he doesn't know why I need *The Divine Lyrics,*" she said, adding in a colder voice, "He doesn't need to know. I don't owe him my secrets."

If he knew and it made no difference, she would be no wiser than Snegurochka whose thawed heart turned her to nothing more than a gathering of lacy snowflakes. Laila wouldn't do that to herself. Maybe for girls made of snow, love was worth the melt. But she was made of stolen bones and sleek fur, grave dirt and strange blood—her heart wasn't even hers to give. Her soul was all she had, and no love was worth losing it.

Enrique squeezed Laila's shoulder, then walked ahead of them. Laila swiped at the last of her tears and lifted her chin. She was nearly through the door when the light touch of Zofia's hand made her turn.

"Thank you," she said.

"For what?" asked Laila.

Zofia hesitated. "For the truth."

"I should be thanking you," said Laila. "Secrets are heavy burdens."

Zofia's expression shuttered. "I know all about burdens."

ON THE OTHER SIDE of the door and in an alleyway of Moscow, a *troika* stood waiting to take them to House Nyx's secure location. In the distance, she caught the sound of the second carriage laden with their belongings heading to their new hideout. A bright lamppost illuminated the falling snow, and the alchemy of its light seemed to turn the snow to gold coins. The air smelled of distant woodsmoke and tin, and the shards of ice on the deserted sidewalk snapped like bones beneath their boots. Wooden shutters cloaked the storefronts in shadows and silence. From the *troika*, three inky horses tossed and turned their heads. Two of the House Nyx guards waited to take them, but as they started walking toward the *troika*, Zofia reached out, grabbing Laila's wrist.

"Do you smell that?" she asked.

Hypnos wrinkled his nose.

"Wasn't me," said Enrique quickly.

There was a slight . . . burn to the air.

"That's saltpeter," said Zofia. Her eyes widened as she looked at them. "It's an explosive—"

She hardly got the word out before something behind the *troika* exploded into flames. The horses shrieked, jetting off into the darkness as huge flames rolled toward them.

II

SÉVERIN

Séverin stumbled backwards. The horses reared, snapping free of their tethers and fleeing into the night just before tall flames swallowed up the *troika*, and choked off their exit. He slammed his hand against the brick wall behind him, scrabbling for any sign of a dent, any sign of escape. But the brick was slicked over with ice. Whatever stronghold he managed slipped out from under his fingers. Not like this, he thought, staring at Hypnos, Laila, Zofia, and Enrique . . . *Not like this.*

"I don't understand . . . I don't understand . . ." whispered Hypnos over and over, staring at the slowly blackening *troika*. Screams erupted from within the carriage. Two of the House Nyx guards were burning alive.

Hypnos tried to run to the carriage, but Zofia held him back.

"Water!" shouted Enrique. "We need water to put out the flames!"

Enrique grabbed handfuls of the dirty city snow, stuffing them in his hat and tossing them on the encroaching flames. Dimly, Séverin realized Enrique was trying to put out the fire. It was useless and stupid and . . . brave. Séverin could only stare at him. Enrique looked over his shoulder and called out over the sound of the flames, "Don't look at me like that!" He glowered. "Trust me, I know how it looks!"

Séverin dropped to his knees and started gathering the snow, pushing it between the flames and the others. His hands froze, and the long scar down his palm burned. Zofia moved beside him, filling his hat with snow, melting it with a touch of her fire pendant, and flinging it—uselessly—against the flames. He looked at her, at their hands working side by side. He heard the others beside them, and he turned on impulse, his eyes filling with the sight of all of them.

I wanted to make you gods.

I wanted to protect you.

Séverin felt like he was watching Tristan die all over again, only this time his failure had become a living thing, snapping at the heels of everyone who got too close. He saw his hands not moving fast enough, his legs frozen, a terrible consequence slipping past outstretched fingers. It was the same and it was different. No one in gilded wolf masks, no heads thrown back and throats bared and stars peeling off the ceiling. Just snow and fire and screaming. Flames rolled toward them, and Séverin's breath ached in his lungs. He would choke on the smoke before the fire got to him, but at least he could go before them. At least he wouldn't have to see. Someone drew him back sharply. Even in the reek of sulfurous flames, he caught the fairy-tale scent of sugar and rosewater.

"*Majnun,*" said Laila.

He had to be hallucinating. She no longer called him that.

Séverin jerked his shoulder out of her grasp, refusing to look at her. He could not watch her die. He could barely handle the sight of pain on her face. Heat seared his face, and Séverin forced his gaze to the flames rolling toward them. He could hear Hypnos, Enrique, Zofia, and Laila shouting for him to move away. He took one step forward and stretched out his hands, his palms turned toward them as if he could hold them back from death or offer himself to the world's twisted sense of mercy that he might not see how he'd failed them one last time.

He closed his eyes, readying himself for the stinging heat—

But the flames stilled.

Séverin's eyes flew open. Blue light knifed through the flames. Their once intense scarlet hue dimmed as more and more shards of blue light shredded them. Séverin blinked, his hands falling a fraction. Great waves of smoke poured into the air. Where the flames had burned red, now they flushed blue at the roots, as if an infection of ice had grabbed hold of their heat. The blue spread upwards, swallowing the flames whole before cascading back down to the ground and leaving nothing but veils of indigo mist. Beneath his feet, the stones hissed and steamed. Slowly, the world gained clarity as the smoke dissolved into the air, revealing the cold night and its colder stars. When he looked to his left, he saw that the brick-walled alley once choked off by the troika fire now presented a clear—albeit charred—escape.

"We're *alive!*" whooped Enrique happily.

He looked at Séverin, grinning and hopeful, and Séverin almost—*almost*—grinned back. But in the abrupt departure of the flames, Séverin remembered that he still had his arms raised. As if that could've saved them. Shamed, he lowered his hands. His chest heaved, sweat slicked down his spine, and his mouth tasted of smoke. He was so . . . uselessly human.

But that could change.

Enrique kneeled in the snow, his face still joyful, still hopeful. "Séverin?"

Séverin remembered the first time he met his historian. Back then, Enrique was merely a sharply dressed university graduate. A boy with a book tucked under his arm as he paused to study a statue in L'Eden's museum gallery.

"THIS DESCRIPTION IS ALL WRONG," Enrique said.

Séverin felt taken aback by this boy who spoke to him like an equal. No one spoke to him like that in L'Eden, and the effect was . . . refreshing.

"Excuse me?"

"That's not a death deity. It's the sun god. Surya." Enrique pointed out the breastplate and dagger. "Those markings on the statue's shin represent the markings of boots."

"Hindu gods wear boots?" asked Séverin.

"Well, Hindu gods who might not have originated in India," said Enrique, shrugging. "It's believed that the sun god Surya originated in Persia, hence his depiction as a Central Asian warrior." He shook his head. "Whoever bought this was a fool in need of a real historian."

Séverin grinned, then held out his hand: "My name is Séverin, and I am a fool in need of a real historian."

Séverin turned away from Enrique and the hope in his eyes. The cold reasserted itself in the alley and the stinging winter air slashed against Séverin's skin. His hand went to the Tezcat spectacles buried deep inside the pocket of his jacket.

He could no longer afford to be a fool.

Up ahead, his gaze went to the cleared exit.

"What are we waiting for?" demanded Hypnos. "Let's go!" His voice rose as he stared at the smoldering *troika* where the House Nyx members had fought to escape.

It looked too still, too empty.

"Wait," said Séverin, holding up his hand.

Someone had rescued them. Someone had also set a trap for them. Someone was now waiting to see their next move.

His mind whirred with names and faces and threats, but no one rose to the front of his thoughts. At the end of the alley came the sharp snap of boots against the concrete. The person's gait was measured. Purposeful.

Séverin reached for the blade concealed in the heel of his shoe. He snuck a glance at them all—Zofia's snow-damp hair clung to her face, her blue eyes huge. Enrique crouched in the snow. Hypnos clung to Laila, staring unblinkingly at the *troika*. And Laila— Laila looked only at him. Séverin turned from her, dread cold in his heart. They were in no shape to fight. They had nothing but hats full of melted snow and a handful of weapons that slipped in their damp grasps. Still, he drew himself up, tense and waiting until the figure finally stepped into the light.

Séverin thought he had to be mistaken. But the moonlight didn't lie. His scar pulsed, and the briefest memory—of being held close and kept safe—disappeared in a flash of blue light.

"Now . . . who do we have here?" said Delphine Desrosiers, the matriarch of House Kore. She lazily stroked the sable ruff of her coat. "Why, there's the engineer with the arson charge."

Zofia's eyes flashed.

"A historian in need of a haircut."

Enrique scowled and flattened his hair.

"A courtesan."

Laila raised her chin.

Hypnos coughed loudly.

"And *you*," said the matriarch, in an affectionately loathing voice. "And, finally, Monsieur Montagnet-Alarie . . . the Order's favorite treasure hunter. Whatever are you doing so far from home?"

She smiled, and her teeth caught the light.

PART II

From the archival records of the Order of Babel

From the Hindu text, *The Book of Dynasty*
written by Vidyapathi Das
1821 translation by Fitzwilliam Ainsworth

Upon coronation, the new king makes offerings to the gods with bowls of spiced milk and honeycombs, gold coins wrapped in rose petals and the choicest of sweets. He must make particular obeisance to the various avatars of Saraswati, goddess of knowledge, music, art and [translator's note: the writer of this text refers to Forging as "chhota saans," or "the small breath" as it mimics the art of gods to breathe life into creations. Hereinafter, I shall refer to this by its proper name, Forging] Forging.*

*Archivist note:

It is most curious to see a reference to the avatars of the goddess Saraswati, whose religious purview seems most similar to the nine Muses of ancient

Greece, and who is responsible for the ancient (or apocryphal, depending on one's intellectual bias) guardian group, the Lost Muses. Perhaps an Indian trader brought back news of these Hellenistic deities and thus introduced it to the Indian continent's consciousness? How else would they make such a connection?

12

SÉVERIN

Séverin had seven fathers, but only one brother.

His fourth father was Envy. Envy had a beautiful wife and two beautiful children, and a beautiful home with a window that looked out over a patch of violets and a murmuring creek. The first day, Envy's wife said that he and Tristan could call her "Mother," and Séverin wondered if he might be happy.

But it was not to be.

"I wish they had some other family!" Clotilde—who no longer wished to be called Mother—despaired.

I did, thought Séverin. Once, he had Tante FeeFee, who loved him and held him close, up until the day she told him they were no longer family. After that, she became Delphine Desrosiers, matriarch of House Kore. He said he did not love her, but every night when Tristan had gone to bed, Séverin knelt beside his mattress and prayed. He prayed that she would come. He prayed that she would love him again. He prayed and prayed, until his eyes drooped and he could no longer hold up his chin.

One day, Delphine arrived at Envy's home. Clotilde simpered and flattered. He and Tristan were dragged from the gardening shed where they lived and brought to the main foyer. A phantom twinge ran through Séverin's hands, and he forced himself not to reach for her.

Delphine took one look at him and left without a word.

That night, Tristan sat beside him, their hands clasped like in prayer.

"I will always be your family."

SÉVERIN STOOD BEFORE a teahouse in Khamovniki District. Tinsel and Forged lights twinkled along the snow-dusted eaves. The air carried a faint whiff of steeped tea and the chime of demitasse spoons hitting the sides of porcelain cups. On the streets, bundled-up couples in long, gray coats and fur-lined hats spared them no glance as they disappeared indoors and out of the cold.

Séverin watched, hawkeyed, as Enrique, Zofia, and Laila were led to a different entrance by the matriarch's Sphinx and—at Séverin's demand—the uninjured House Nyx guards.

"No harm will come to them during our private discussion," said the matriarch, eyeing him and Hypnos. "Trust me."

He had, unfortunately, no cause to doubt her. Before they had shoved them into the carriage, the matriarch had stripped his jacket and taken out the Tezcat spectacles. *For safe keeping,* she'd said, smiling. On the carriage ride, he noticed Laila had removed her gloves to touch the House Kore carriage cushion and the matriarch's forgotten fur stole. When he caught Laila's eye, she shook her head. It was a clear signal—the matriarch was not behind the attack.

But that didn't mean he had to trust her.

Hypnos caught his eye and shrugged. "Well, we did get

kidnapped . . . but at least most of our clothes and equipment arrived safely?"

"Small victories," said Séverin darkly.

At the entrance to the teahouse, a woman greeted them in a foyer lined with mirrors on each side.

"Tea for four? And do you prefer black or green leaves?"

"Red leaves," said the matriarch. She held out her hand, where her Babel Ring—a twist of thorns—glinted dully.

"A dragon or a unicorn?" asked the woman.

"Just the horn and the flame," replied the matriarch.

The moment she finished her sentence, one of the mirrors lining the walls glowed a soft green and then parted in the middle, revealing a carmine-red staircase that spiraled up. Annoyingly, Séverin found himself curious.

"Shall we?" asked the matriarch.

Without waiting for them to answer, the matriarch and her guard took to the stairs. The mirror door seamed shut behind Séverin, and the last of the downstairs salon laughter vanished . . . replaced with the rich music of a zither. Hypnos closed his eyes, humming appreciatively. He'd forgotten how much the other boy loved music. When they were young, he remembered that Hypnos possessed a beautiful singing voice. That last year his parents had lived, they'd even put on a Christmas performance, with Séverin controlling the stage and watching as the audience's faces glowed with wonder.

Séverin dug his nails into his palm, willing those recollections to dust. He didn't *want* to remember. He didn't want to see Hypnos as a grinning child, breathless from song. He didn't want to see the matriarch as she had once been to him . . . *Tante FeeFee* . . . whose love, for a moment, had felt unconditional.

At the landing of the stairs, the hallway opened into a wide room. The ceiling was Forged stained glass and appeared like a drop of blood unfurling infinitely into a crystal bowl of water. Private booths of carmine lay behind ivory screens. Red poppy petals carpeted the floor, and the room smelled of musk and smoldering incense.

Masked servers dressed in black moved discreetly through the room, balancing onyx trays holding small, pewter cups while patrons wearing gruesome rabbit masks reached languidly for the cups. It was only when Séverin saw that each of the patrons had a metal claw attached to their pinky finger that he realized what this place was.

"A blood Forging den?" he asked.

"We must have our pleasures one way or the other," said the matriarch.

Séverin had never entered a blood Forging den before . . . but he knew of their reputations. Such a place kept a handful of resident artists who could not only manipulate the presence of iron within one's blood, but also heighten aspects of mind and mood. A drop of blood in the hands of a talented artist could bring dizzying pleasure, erase inhibitions with a single sip, and—it was rumored— even allow someone to wear another's face for an evening, which lasted far longer than the effects of mirror powder.

"Perhaps you imagine that I was behind the attack in the alley," said the matriarch as she slid into a booth.

Thanks to Laila, he didn't, actually, but that didn't explain how she knew where they would be. Vasiliev's last words rang in his head: *She'll find you.*

Was it *her*?

When neither Hypnos nor he said anything, the matriarch continued.

"As you know, the Houses of the Order of Babel are readying themselves for the Winter Conclave in two weeks at a palace in Volgograd," she said, waving a hand. "It's the usual itinerary of posturing and partying before the annual Midnight Auction."

"Then you're in Russia early."

"I had business here," she said, rapping the table with her knuckles.

Hypnos's jaw opened. "Do you *own* this blood Forging den?"

She didn't answer.

"My Sphinx was alerted to the use of one of the Order's inroads when you crossed into Moscow. I grew curious about who else from the Order would be here, and we followed you to the alley in time to save your lives . . . and also with enough time to find this."

She slid something onto the table.

"My men went after someone seen running away from your alley fire, and though they couldn't catch the culprit, they were able to pick this off their clothing."

She removed her hand, revealing a golden honeybee.

"The Fallen House," breathed Hypnos, panic edging into his voice. "We haven't found any traces of their activity since the catacombs attack."

"Well, they're active now," said the matriarch. "I haven't forgotten your last report with the stark mad ravings of Roux-Joubert. He said the Fallen House could not access its own treasures because they could not find the Sleeping Palace. It would seem as though they think you have something worth finding . . . something that might change their situation . . ."

The matriarch examined her fingernails. "I thought the Tezcat spectacles and the lens were mere rumor before I found them on your person. When were you going to tell the Order that you had a lead on the Sleeping Palace? To my knowledge, you're working for us."

Séverin pointed to Hypnos.

"As a member of the Order, the patriarch of House Nyx was present the whole—"

"The patriarch of House Nyx is a puppy within the Order," said the matriarch dismissively.

"I resent that," said Hypnos, muttering, "I am, *at least*, full-grown."

"You should know the rules better, Hypnos," scolded the matriarch. "Any Order activity in Russia must be supervised by two Heads of Houses in addition to representatives from House Dazbog, otherwise you face immediate expulsion from the country. But who knows with the new patriarch? I've never met him, but I've heard he's as reclusive as his father. And he could be five times crueler. Then again, the Order would always help you should you prove that you can find the Sleeping Palace." She raised her eyebrow. "You need us."

Séverin tilted his head, catching a slip in her words.

"Prove?" he repeated. And then he smiled. "You already tried to put the Tezcat spectacles and lens together, didn't you? I wondered why you chose to travel in a separate carriage. I imagine your efforts did not work. And now you try this ploy of benevolence to make sure we don't leave the Order in the dust, scrambling about for their wits."

For a moment, the matriarch looked stunned. Séverin studied her face. She was so much older now. Gray touched her once-blond hair, and hard brackets framed her mouth. In all these years, she hadn't lost that alertness in her blue eyes. It was hard to meet them without thinking about the last time they'd met . . . when he had rejected the inheritance she'd first stolen from him, and relief had filled her whole being. Séverin dropped his gaze, his pulse thudding painfully. How much must she hate him to feel relief that he would never know what should've belonged to him?

"No," she said finally. "It did not work."

"So to amend your statement, it is *you* who needs us."

Her eyes hardened. "You are still vulnerable, Monsieur. If you can determine the coordinates, I will grant you the protection of my House, and make the necessary arrangements with House Dazbog. In return, I want you to find something specifically for me."

Séverin tensed, a part of him knowing what she would say even before she uttered it.

"*The Divine Lyrics,*" she said.

"That book was lost," said Hypnos, a touch too quickly.

"Perhaps," said Delphine. "But if it was not, and if it is there hidden in the Fallen House's treasure hoard, I want it handed over to me directly."

Séverin only smiled. So that was why she wanted it. The Order was still furious with the Houses of France for jeopardizing their secrets. For Hypnos, revealing the location of the Sleeping Palace was enough to win back trust, but the matriarch clearly hungered for the elite status she once held . . . and only a coup like *The Divine Lyrics* would restore it.

Séverin flexed his hand. This arrangement could work quite nicely. More ease of access, more security for the others. And then he could let the matriarch watch as he stole the book right out from underneath her.

"It's a deal," he said.

The matriarch nodded, then signaled to the server who set down a crystal goblet of mint tea and a small crimson vial that looked like blood.

"Wild evening plans?" asked Hypnos, eyeing the vial.

"I don't partake in blood Forging activities," said the matriarch, tossing back the vial. "And I don't trust it."

"Then what was that?"

"My *own* blood, mixed with a connection that repels Forging," she said. "A mithradatic measure, if you will."

"Afraid someone might lure you into a night of debauchery?" asked Hypnos.

The matriarch dabbed at her mouth. "Why not? Skill and experience are always in demand. And I have quite enough of both."

Hypnos spluttered, and before the conversation could take a dismal turn, the server brought out wine and, for Séverin, *mazagran* served in a tall glass. He stared at it. The scent of coffee syrup and ice jolted him to his childhood where Kahina used to drink this every morning in a pale, green glass. When he was little, he remembered Tante—the matriarch—teasing him that if he drank the concoction, he wouldn't get tall. His throat tightened.

"Not thirsty?" asked the matriarch.

His throat felt scorched with smoke, but he shoved aside the glass.

"No," he said, pushing himself from the table and gesturing to Hypnos. "We have work to do."

SÉVERIN HESITATED OUTSIDE the mahogany doors of the music room in the tea salon. Laila, Enrique, and Zofia waited for him inside.

Hypnos had gone before Séverin to tell them of the matriarch's demands, but Séverin hesitated. How would he show his face to them after all his choices had nearly killed them?

Inside, the music room was small and well-lit. In one corner stood a harp. In the other, a piano, where Hypnos sat and plunked at the keys. A handful of couches and satin settees dotted the room, but Zofia and Enrique sat at a table near the entrance. Their heads were bent in conversation. In front of them, the Tezcat spectacles shone brightly beneath the chandelier. Beside the frame, on a square of velvet, sat the lens taken from Vasiliev's chain. Laila walked in from a separate entryway, carrying a tray of tea and biscuits. There was even a cup for him. He didn't know what to make of that.

Enrique saw him first and immediately pointed at Zofia. "Zofia just tried to set fire to the Tezcat spectacles."

Zofia scowled at him. "I tried to see if the lens and the spectacles might be *welded* together."

"And?" asked Laila, setting down the tray.

"And it was unsuccessful."

"House Kore couldn't manage it either," said Laila soothingly.

"The symbology around the instrument is fairly strange too," said Enrique. "A mix of cosmic iconography . . . including, I believe . . . planets."

"Those aren't planets, *mon cher*, those are silver balls," called Hypnos from the piano.

"They're artistic *renderings* of planets."

Séverin bent to examine the Tezcat spectacles. They looked like a strange pair of goggles. The frames were thick and decorated with bulging silver spheres that were indeed planets, judging by the Latin script on each shape. The screws, temples, and hinges each bore decorations of clouds and constellations.

"They're *ugly*," said Hypnos. "And I'm not usually one to judge when—"

"Do not finish that sentence," said Laila.

Hypnos looked over his shoulder, flashing a wicked grin as he played a quick, ominous tune on the piano.

"Wait," said Séverin. "Did you see that?"

On the Tezcat spectacles, he could have sworn he saw the faintest glow around the lens and the empty frame of the spectacles.

"See what?"

"As if . . . as if there was a reaction from the spectacles. From the music."

"Does this make me irresistible to animate and inanimate things?" asked Hypnos. "Because that pleases me."

Laila flexed her fingers and mused, "Interesting that it reacts to music when it seems as though whoever removed the lens did so in utter silence."

Hypnos made a *pah!* sound. "How would you figure that, *ma chère?*"

Laila shrugged. "Let's say I have a knack for it, shall we?"

Zofia sat up a little straighter. "The hollow angel held a sound barrier of cork and wool when we were retrieving the box."

Séverin lifted the Tezcat spectacles and lens, turning them in his hand before raising them eye level. He knew it hid the location of the Sleeping Palace. But what about the instrument itself? Herein lay the secret to unlocking riddles and finding treasure . . . What was the context, what did the maker *want* and *see?* Why all the silent measures taken to protect it?

"This was locked in the Chamber of Goddesses. Part of it hung around someone's neck with the utmost care, and the frame is full of a twisting universe. When lifted to the eye, it was meant to behold the whole world in one glimpse," said Séverin, talking more or less to himself. He ran his thumb along the metal, imagining he was the person who'd first held the object. "No one but a god can create a universe, and the world can be remade through the eyes of God. Whatever key triggers the positioning of the frame, it will relate to movement and planets . . . *sound*. Or, more likely, music, which to some might be considered prayer. In which case, there's only one theory that would fit with unlocking this. *Musica universalis*, or the Music of the Spheres. *That's* the key to opening this."

When he stopped talking and looked up, the others were watching him.

"How did you do that?" demanded Hypnos.

"How else do you think he hunts treasures?" asked Enrique, glancing smugly at Séverin.

Séverin's stomach turned, and he quickly put down the glasses. Each acquisition used to be a symphony of Zofia's engineerings, Enrique's knowledge, and Laila's readings. And then there was his role, a quiet way of slipping behind the eyes of kings and priests, monsters and monks—anyone who had something worth hiding. Whenever his role came into play, those small gestures—Zofia's approving nod, Laila's slow smile, Tristan's trust, and Enrique's pride—used to anchor him. But now it felt thieved. He had no right to find peace in it.

"What, exactly, is the Music of the Spheres?" asked Hypnos. "It sounds like a terribly boring play."

"It's an ancient philosophy that gained a lot of popularity in the fifteenth century," said Enrique, looking bemused as he turned from Séverin. "Theoretically, there's a governing rhythm and movement to celestial bodies, like the sun, moon, and stars."

"Can any kind of music unlock it?"

Hypnos started playing, but the glow around the lens of the spectacles only dimly flickered.

"It would have to be music or rhythm with a universal property," said Zofia. "Try the golden ratio."

"What is *that*?" asked Hypnos, shaking his head. "What I *do* know is that when it comes to tuning a piano, there's an agreed-upon method. One tunes pianos by way of fifths. That's universal enough, I believe. Here. I shall demonstrate with C Major."

Hypnos flexed his fingers and played the scale. At once, the circumference of the lens lit up and so did the frame. The small, silver planets on the outside hummed and spun. Séverin fitted the lens into the empty frame, pressing hard. When Hypnos stopped, the lens had sealed into place. Across the glass, a liquid-silver script appeared:

55.55°N, 108.16°E

Hypnos turned around on his seat. "That's how—" His gaze fell to the Tezcat spectacles and lens, and he fell quiet. Everyone's gaze snapped from Hypnos perched on the piano seat to the Tezcat spectacles in Séverin's hands.

"Those are longitude and latitude coordinates," said Zofia.

Enrique leaned forward, his jaw slack. "An exact map to the Sleeping Palace."

"Am I . . . am I a genius?" asked Hypnos. Without waiting for anyone to answer, he leapt from his seat and bowed.

Enrique clapped indulgently, and Hypnos beamed at him.

"Alert the matriarch," said Séverin. "Let her know we leave at dawn to follow these coordinates."

When he looked at the group, their faces shone with victory, and he wanted to let himself feel it too. But that faint stench of smoke clung to their clothes from the *troika* fire. Beneath it all, he caught a whiff of Tristan's roses left to rot. He nearly gagged.

"*Years* of practice have led to this," said Hypnos proudly, ". . . putting together broken glasses. *Voila!*"

"Years?" repeated Laila. "I can't imagine you working at anything for years."

The light in Hypnos's eyes dimmed a little. He busily straightened his sleeves and lapel.

"Well, one had little choice in these matters," he said brusquely. "I had to entertain myself quite a lot as a child . . . Music helped take away the silence." He cleared his throat. "But enough of that. Let's celebrate before certain doom, shall we?"

Hypnos looped his arm around Enrique's waist, pulling him a little closer. Out the corner of his eye, Séverin caught Hypnos's questioning glance, but he didn't meet it. Let them go, he thought. For the sake of what he needed to do, he had to be apart, not a part. Séverin busied himself with the Tezcat spectacles, ignoring the chatter until the others left the room and he heard the door shut.

But when he looked up, a part of him jolted. Laila hadn't left with the others. She leaned against the doorframe, and he noticed she'd changed out of her golden dress from the opera and now wore a cotton dress and dark blue robe.

"I need something to call you," she said, crossing her arms.

He blinked. "What?"

"As your mistress." Laila crossed her arms. "I need something to call you."

Mistress. The fire and the tea salon had nearly made him forget. But she was right. The charade he thought she wouldn't have to indulge for long had become real in a matter of hours.

"Séverin," he said.

"A *friend* calls you Séverin."

"Monsieur—"

"No. An *employee* calls you Monsieur Montagnet-Alarie. I am your equal. I need a pet name. Something humiliating."

He raised his eyebrow. *"Humiliating?"*

"We debase ourselves for the ones we love."

There was another name that seemed to hang in the space between them. *Majnun.* The name she had given him years ago. The name that had once felt like a talisman in the dark.

"I don't know. Just pair a trait with an article of clothing," said Séverin.

"Stubborn shoe."

He glared.

"Bull-headed glove."

"You can't be serious—"

"Irrational brassiere."

He didn't mean to, and he had no idea how it happened . . . but he laughed. The sound rattled him to the core. Worse, was the softened expression in her eyes. Laila had made a habit of demanding weakness from him. He set his jaw. There would be no softness here.

Séverin's gaze went to her bare throat, and his eyes narrowed.

"Start wearing that diamond necklace."

13

ENRIQUE

Enrique awoke two hours before the morning meeting. As he made his way to the meeting place in the Oriental Room of the tea salon, he clutched his research material. Now that they knew the coordinates of the Sleeping Palace, his research had taken on a new light, and he couldn't stop thinking about it. The coordinates confirmed his suspicions: The Sleeping Palace was somewhere in Siberia.

Today the matriarch of House Kore and the representatives from House Dazbog would be taking them to the Sleeping Palace where his research would either be proven valuable or—he prayed otherwise—worthless. Ever since Laila had told him and Zofia about her beginning and, possibly, her ending, all his knowledge gained a terrible new weight. It wasn't just a career or a future depending on what he knew; it was a member of his family. After Tristan, he couldn't lose Laila too.

To him, Laila was like a fairy tale plucked from the pages of a book—a girl with a curse woven into her heartbeat. In all the time he'd known her, part of her seemed to hum with the force of her secret. Who was she? What could she *do*? Last evening, he'd tried testing her abilities while they waited for Séverin and Hypnos to join the three of them.

"Enrique," Laila had sighed.

"Now read this!" he'd said, pushing another object onto the table.

"Is this your *underwear*?"

"It's freshly laundered! I just fetched it from my suitcase. Were you able to tell by touch? Or was it the shape—"

Laila threw it in his face. "Haven't you had enough? You've already given me a watch, a briefcase, two teacups, and asked me to touch the *couch*, which I am still recovering from." She feigned a shudder. "At least Zofia spared me."

Zofia shrugged. "An object's personal context does not affect its utility."

"Not true!" Enrique had said. "It could be *proof* of something. Laila, you're practically a goddess."

Laila sipped her tea, assuming an expression Enrique had come to recognize as "smug cat."

"I knew I was in the wrong era," she said, before glaring. "But *no more* readings. I'm no instrument."

"What about an instrument of destiny?" he asked, wiggling his fingers.

"No."

"Instrument of—"

"Enrique."

"Instrument of Enrique? Unorthodox, but I like it."

Laila had swatted him, but they'd spoken no more of it once Hypnos had entered the music room.

Ever since, the conversation had lingered with Enrique.

Laila needed *The Divine Lyrics* to live. But did *The Divine Lyrics* need . . . *Laila*? His earlier research about *The Divine Lyrics* suggested that only someone descended of the Lost Muses bloodline could read the book.

What if . . . what if Laila were one of them? It wasn't a thought he wanted to broach with the others. Not yet, at least. If the evidence within the Sleeping Palace fit, then he would tell her. The *troika* fire had unnerved him. He'd thought no one was watching their movements, and now he didn't know who was. The last thing he wanted was to draw their eye to Laila.

By now, he'd made his way to the meeting place in the Oriental Room. The moment he pushed open the door, he grimaced. The Oriental Room was clearly something dreamed up by someone who had never visited the Orient. The room felt like a bone set wrong. On the shelves lining the walls, he recognized a Tibetan prayer wheel placed as a beater for the percussive Chinese gong. Delicate ivory and agate *netsuke*—once used in Japanese menswear—lay scattered across a chessboard as surrogate pieces.

"You have *excellent* hair," said an unfamiliar voice.

Enrique startled, nearly dropping the documents in his arms. A tall, light-skinned man stood from an armchair situated in the shadowed part of the room. He was young, Enrique saw. And bald. When he stepped into the light, Enrique noticed a slight tilt to his eyes that hinted at East Asian descent.

"What do you do? Egg masks? Olive oil?" asked the man. "Can I touch it?"

Enrique stared at this bizarre person. "No?"

The man shrugged. "Very well. Maybe you're born with it." He tapped his bald pate. "My own inheritance is a touch sparser than I'd like."

When he drew closer, Enrique saw the man's arm was in a sling, though it was concealed by the drape of his sable coat.

"Ruslan Goryunov the Bald at your service," said the man, bowing low.

This close, he could see how young the man was . . . no more than in his late twenties.

"Enrique Mercado-Lopez."

"Ah! The historian!" said Ruslan. "A pleasure to meet you."

Enrique's face burned. "You know me?"

He'd never imagined anyone had ever heard of him. It made him wonder if he should've worn something more . . . official-looking . . . more interesting than his usual black suit and simple cravat. Then again he wasn't sure how exemplary it was if the only person who recognized him was someone who went by Ruslan the Bald.

"I know *of* you," said Ruslan. "I know *most* things. Except for how to resurrect a hairline. Alas. I rather enjoyed your article concerning the return of artwork to colonized countries. My understanding is that you've been a historian and linguist to Monsieur Montagnet-Alarie at L'Eden Hotel for quite some time now. Do you like it there?"

Enrique nodded, hating that the first—and probably the *last*—time he was being recognized in public was also the only time he couldn't find the right words. He kept panicking that his voice would come out far deeper than he intended. Or that he might spontaneously belch and therefore destroy all semblance of credibility.

Ruslan grinned, then glanced behind Enrique to the clock above the door threshold. He frowned.

"I've gotten the time wrong," he said. "We will have more time to talk soon, I am sure."

"What are you—" Enrique started, then stopped. He didn't want to seem rude.

"Doing here?" finished Ruslan with a laugh. "I thought I'd be here for a meeting, but then I got distracted by a beetle, then a daydream, and finally that painting." He bowed. "It was an honor to meet you, Monsieur Mercado-Lopez."

He swiftly made his way to the exit, leaving Enrique to ponder what, exactly, just happened. Self-consciously, he reached up and touched his hair. It *was* nice, he had to admit.

Enrique made his way to the back of the room. The mural Ruslan had mentioned lay half in the shadows. At first, the mural was hard to discern amongst the clutter of the room. It merely looked like ugly wallpaper. But the closer he got, the more the images made themselves known. The mural showed dark-skinned villagers holding out a basket of tea leaves, and pale-skinned soldiers, priests, and kings extending their arms to receive the gift. Natives and Europeans. It wasn't an unfamiliar pattern, but as Enrique stared at it, he felt the quiet panic that had haunted him since childhood. Where did he exist in this arrangement? He stared at the empty middle ground of the painting, and a familiar ache settled in his chest.

There was danger in not belonging. He'd learned that at a young age in the fish markets of the Philippines. When his mother had taken him, he'd lost her in the sea of people. He remembered running up and down the market aisle, the smell of fish and vinegar stinging his eyes. Finally, he'd spotted her in her bright pink dress, turning wildly in the market, her basket swinging from her arm as she called his name.

"*Mama*—" he cried, pointing.

A woman grabbed hold of his hand, caught sight of his mother, and laughed. "That can't be your mother, you look nothing alike! Come now, I'll take you to the Civil Guard—"

He howled in terror, and only then did his mother see him and fetch him, folding him against her where he sobbed and refused to be put down. Later, she laughed off the incident, but all he saw was her brown face, and how dark her arms looked next to his. He had the shape of her eyes and the curve of her smile and her habit of hoarding pillows . . . but something about him was not enough to belong to her.

Enrique was still staring at the painting when he heard the door open once more. Hypnos grinned at him as he made a quick scan of the room.

"Is anyone else here?"

"No," said Enrique.

"Good."

Hypnos crossed the room in quick strides and kissed him. The kiss sent a sparkle through his body, and Enrique savored the slow melt of it. It was a welcome distraction, and he leaned into it with the greed of someone starved. Hypnos drew away first, though his thumb rested at the nape of Enrique's neck, tracing small circles against his skin. Enrique didn't know what possessed him that next moment. Perhaps he was still shaken from the *troika* fire, or disturbed by the mural on the wall . . . or maybe drawn in by the other boy's hypnotic touch.

"I don't just want furtive kisses or meetings of convenience," said Enrique in a rush. "The others already know about us . . . What if we made it more public?"

Hypnos's fingers stilled. "Why?"

"Why not?" asked Enrique. And then, feeling foolish, he added,

"If we find what we're looking for, everything could return to normal. Séverin would come back to his senses. You could officially be part of the team, and we could be together too."

He trailed off, staring at the floor until he felt Hypnos's hand tip up his chin.

"That isn't my usual arrangement, you know," said Hypnos gently. "But I could be tempted. Let's see how this job goes first, shall we?"

That was fair enough, thought Enrique. Though he caught something like guilt in Hypnos's eyes, and he couldn't fathom why.

"Would I have to move into L'Eden just to be part of the team?" asked Hypnos. "Because I quite like my living arrangements."

Enrique laughed and shook his head, just as Hypnos's arms tightened around him. Enrique squeezed his eyes shut, imagining what it would be like not to feel this ache in his soul where some part of him always felt wanting. When he lifted his head, he caught a flash of golden hair in the doorway.

"Zofia?"

Hypnos released him, and Zofia stepped inside, looking somewhat stiff as she stared at them.

"I'm here for the meeting," she said tersely.

Hypnos smiled as he flounced into one of the silk chaises, absentmindedly picking up one of the objects on the nearest shelves and jangling it like a toy.

"That's a Tibetan prayer wheel!" said Enrique, snatching it from his hands. "And very old by the looks of it."

"I was merely praying for respite from my impending boredom," said Hypnos.

"How can you possibly be bored?" asked Enrique. "Yesterday, we almost died by fire."

"Not true," said Zofia.

"Not all of us are optimists—"

"Asphyxiation would have killed you first," she said. "Not the flames."

Hypnos snorted. "Ah, *ma chère*, never change."

Zofia perched on a nearby stool, her posture like that of an aerialist.

"Don't say that," said Zofia, sounding rather glum. "Change is the only constant."

"Well—" Hypnos started, and then stopped and stood abruptly. "Madame Desrosiers."

The matriarch of House Kore stood in the doorway, wrapped in her expensive furs. She was someone whose very impression felt *tall*. It reminded him, oddly enough, of his mother. His father teasingly called his mother *Doña* because she could wear a rice sack and still look noble. Even in her letters to him, she managed to sound commanding and intimidating, always ranting about how he was running around Paris for no reason when there were beautiful girls at home waiting for him, and how this behavior was exceedingly disappointing, and also was he eating enough, and do remember evening prayers, Love, *Ma*.

"I don't believe we've formally met," said Enrique. "I'm—"

"The one who posed as a botanist expert and set fire to my garden last spring?"

Enrique gulped and sat.

"And the 'Baronness Sofia Ossokina'?" asked the matriarch, raising an eyebrow at Zofia.

Zofia blew out her match, not bothering to answer to the fake name she'd used when they had stolen into the Château de la Lune last spring.

"I am surrounded by deception," said the matriarch.

"And chairs," pointed out Zofia.

"On that note, won't you have a seat?" asked Hypnos.

"I think not," said the matriarch, examining her fingernails. "I have already summoned the patriarch of House Dazbog and one of his representatives to join us in what might possibly be a fool's errand to the supposed coordinates of the Sleeping Palace. We leave for Irkutsk in two hours. You may have solved the Tezcat spectacles, but that could've been sheer luck. I need to know why I should listen to an impudent girl and"—her gaze cut to Enrique—"a boy *still* in need of a haircut."

One corner of Enrique's heart yelled, *Mother!* The other corner seethed as he flattened down his hair.

". . . I lost my comb," he muttered, self-conscious.

"And I have lost my patience," she said.

"Where's Séverin and Laila?" asked Hypnos.

"Off 'discussing,'" said the matriarch, snorting. "As if I don't know what that means."

Zofia frowned, obviously lost as to what else discussing could have meant.

"You have managed to earn my protection as a matriarch of the Order of Babel. But you have not earned my confidence."

Hypnos cleared his throat. "*I* also have offered protection—"

"Yes, my dear, I noticed with the flaming *troika* the precise range of your protection."

Hypnos's cheeks turned a shade darker.

"What kind of intelligence have you gathered concerning the Sleeping Palace?"

The group looked to one another and said nothing. The truth was that there were no blueprints of the Sleeping Palace. The

Fallen House had managed to destroy the records, which meant that for all intents and purposes, they were going into this excursion blind. Delphine must have caught that from their expressions because her gaze narrowed.

"I see," she said. "And what—besides the ramblings of a dying, broken man—makes you so certain then that there *are* treasures in the Sleeping Palace?"

"It . . ." started Hypnos, before trailing off, ". . . would be a terrible waste of space without . . . treasure?"

Zofia said nothing.

"No historical records of confirmation?" asked Delphine, her gaze zeroing in on Enrique. "Then what do you have?"

Enrique pressed the dossier of papers tighter against him. All he could tell was the truth, so he did. "Ghost stories."

The matriarch raised her eyebrow. *"Ghost stories?"*

Enrique nodded.

"What kind of history or proof is that?" she asked.

Enrique's ears burned, but he heard her curiosity. It was genuine. At the sound of it, a quiet thrill wound through him.

"Madame Delphine, depending on who you ask, sometimes ghost stories are all that is left of history," he said. "History is full of ghosts because it's full of myth, all of it woven together depending on who survived to do the telling."

She raised an eyebrow. "Go on."

"According to the coordinates on the spectacles, we know the Sleeping Palace is somewhere on Lake Baikal."

"There's nothing in Siberia but ice," said the matriarch dismissively. "And murders from the past; that's probably where all ghost stories started."

"Lake Baikal is a sacred place, especially to the Buryats, the indigenous people who live in southeastern Russia near the Mongolian border," said Enrique quickly. "The name itself means 'Sacred Sea.'"

"I'm still not hearing a ghost story," said the matriarch.

"Well, that's the interesting matter," said Enrique. "When you trace the tales surrounding this area of Lake Baikal, what you find is there are a lot of rumors in that area of restless spirits. Women, especially, whose voices are known to cry out to people in the middle of the night, echoing over the ice. There were also stories in the past of . . . of murders in the area. The last of which was committed almost twenty years ago."

Zofia shifted uncomfortably on her stool. Hypnos shuddered.

"And no one was ever captured," said Hypnos, visibly disturbed.

"Supposedly, the murders were committed without motive," said Enrique. "But I don't think that's true."

Enrique walked to the matriarch, holding out one of the papers from his research. It showed an illustration of the Siberian landscape and a huge sepulcher carved from a single slab of black marble, and covered in intricate Forging metalwork of silver vines and looping script.

"In the fourteenth century, a noted traveler named Ibn Battuta observed the burial of a great Mongolian khan. He was placed with his greatest treasures, along with his favorite guards and female slaves. All of them were closed up beneath it."

"The female slaves and guards were killed?" asked Hypnos.

"They died there, eventually," said Enrique.

Hypnos paled.

"Some cultures thought that one could not construct an important building without tithing a human life, and so they buried people in the foundations of buildings." Enrique drew out another paper, this one showing a brick wall. "For example, the Albanian legend of Rozafa where a young woman sacrificed herself so a castle could be built."

"What does that have to do with the ghost stories?"

Enrique swallowed hard. The horror of what he was about to say filmed over his thoughts.

"If you're burying your treasure, you'd need built-in guardians. Guardians who couldn't leave."

There was silence in the room.

"The Fallen House has been known to emulate more ancient practices. I believe that perhaps those missing girls in the area were connected to their effort to conceal treasure. The last murder was twenty years ago, which coincides with the last known documentation of *The Divine Lyrics* before the artifact was lost."

Zofia looked sick now. The matriarch said nothing, but her mouth was drawn. A curious expression passed over her face, as if some terrible idea had only just now made sense to her.

"That," said Enrique, "is why I believe the Sleeping Palace holds the treasure we're looking for."

Delphine did not look at Enrique when he finished. Instead, she turned to face the empty doorway and called out, "Well? Are you convinced or not?"

Someone stepped into the room . . . a stunning redheaded girl that looked about his age. There was something familiar about her, but the thought vanished when another person moved to stand beside the girl: Ruslan.

"As one expected, excellent hair hides an excellent mind!" said Ruslan, clapping. Then, to the matriarch: "Yes, I find myself thoroughly convinced. I was most intrigued by your letter. Admittedly, it's hard to turn down any invitation to eavesdrop on someone else's conversation." He smiled at Delphine. "A pleasure to finally meet you, Matriarch."

"And a pleasure to meet you," said Delphine, extending her hand. "I met your father only the one time, but I am glad to make your acquaintance in person."

She gestured to Ruslan and the red-haired girl. "Zofia, Hypnos, and Enrique . . . may I present to you Eva Yefremovna, a blood Forging artist of impeccable skill and cousin to Ruslan Goryunov, patriarch of House Dazbog."

14

ZOFIA

Dear Zofia,

I am feeling much better. Now, the only ache left is in my
heart because you are no longer here. You work so hard, little
sister. I confess it frightens me. Our uncle told me all the funds
you allotted to my care, and I feel such shame. You're not yet
twenty. You need someone to look after you, Zosia. When I am
better, I shall do so.

Hela

ZOFIA STUDIED THE LETTER. True to his word, Séverin had made sure
she would hear from Hela. Normally, it would have been impossible
to receive mail so quickly, but the Order's portal inroads throughout Russia were numerous, and Poland was not so far. Zofia kept
returning to one sentence: *You need someone to look after you.* It bristled in her thoughts. Perhaps at one point, she had needed her par-

ents to guide her through Glowno, to explain the gaps of meaning between what people did and what people said. And yes, she had needed Hela to guide her after their death. But Paris had changed her. She had the structure of her work, the routine of her laboratory, and everything worked until Tristan had died and Hela had gotten sick. And then, once more, her whole world turned dark and unfamiliar, and sometimes when she was forced to navigate it alone, panic *did* fill her . . . but that did not mean she needed such monitoring. Did she?

"Zofia?"

Zofia looked up from the letter. Laila stood before her, bundled up in a fluffy white coat. A diamond necklace that Zofia did not recognize circled her throat.

"Are you well?" asked Laila, eyeing the letter.

Zofia folded it and shoved it into her pocket. She did not want her friend to see what Hela had written and grow worried for her. Laila was the one fighting to live. Zofia would not add to her burden.

"Are you cold?"

"Yes."

"I thought so." Laila made a *tsk* sound and pulled off her scarf. "You should've told me. Better now?"

Zofia nodded, savoring the scarf's warmth before looking again to the portal entrance at the far end of the deserted train depot. The train depot had been shut down two years ago after riots. There were seven shattered windows which let in broken light. The tiles were uniformly square, but cracked. There were ten benches, but only four could bear the weight of a person. The silence of the place was broken only by the occasional scritching of rats in the walls, and pigeons—exactly fourteen—roosting in the balustrades.

After the attack from the Fallen House, the patriarch of House Dazbog demanded they make separate trips through the portal roads of Russia. They had left Moscow nearly an hour ago and had been waiting for the past hour for House Kore, House Nyx, and House Dazbog to bring the rest of the supplies that could be salvaged from the *troika* fire and whatever else was needed for the expedition—tools, seal-skin gloves, Forging lights, and incendiary strips.

"They didn't forget us, did they?" asked Enrique, pacing. "It's not like they could continue the expedition without us, although if they have the Tezcat spectacles—"

"They don't," said Séverin.

Enrique frowned. "But I saw Ruslan take the box?"

"The patriarch of House Dazbog took *a* box."

Enrique was quiet for a moment. "What do you all think of him?"

Laila sighed. "I think he's *sweet*. Maybe a bit lonely."

"And a bit mad," said Séverin.

"A bit *eccentric*, perhaps," said Laila, frowning. "Zofia, what do you think?"

"He's soft," said Zofia.

And she meant it. After introductions, Ruslan had exclaimed over her blond hair, then patted the top of her head like a dog or a child—which one might consider rude—but then he offered his *own* head, so perhaps this was his normal interaction. Not wanting to be rude, Zofia patted it.

It was soft.

"I think the secret is not to use too much wax," Ruslan had said to her. "If one must look like an egg, then one must aspire to be an erudite egg."

From his pocket, Séverin drew out the Tezcat spectacles, the longitude and latitude coordinates of the Sleeping Palace still gleaming on the glass lenses.

From the opposite end of the train depot came the sound of screeching metal. Zofia winced and covered her ears, turning to the door where people streamed out from the portal. There was the matriarch of House Kore and her Sphinx guard and attendants; Hypnos with his House Nyx attendants and Sphinx; and the patriarch of House Dazbog and his cousin, the blood Forging artist named Eva.

Ruslan gestured to the boxes and equipment they'd carried with them. Zofia recognized her portable laboratory, the Forged suitcase charred. The *troika* explosion had rent a small hole in its side, and saltpeter dribbled out of the crack. Zofia's skin prickled. She needed saltpeter for any demolition required inside the Sleeping Palace. If she didn't have enough, that meant—

"This is the last stop before Lake Baikal," said Ruslan. "If there are any other supplies you require, you have to go into Irkutsk, I'm afraid."

When the House Dazbog couriers brought over her luggage, a pang struck through Zofia. Her storage of saltpeter had definitely been affected. The only question was how much and whether she needed to go into the city. As she started opening the case, a shadow fell over her. Eva walked toward them, and Zofia noticed a slight limp to the other girl's gait.

"I hope I'm not being too forward, but I have to say that I'm a great admirer of you all," said Eva.

Zofia heard her, but it was not a question and did not need an answer. The lock on her luggage had been mangled, requiring a lock and pick from her necklace of pendants. She crouched on the ground, fiddling to open it.

"I've heard of Miss Boguska, of course, a fantastic engineer," said Eva.

Zofia grunted. She had not heard of Eva Yefremovna.

"And, of course, Mr. Mercado-Lopez. Ruslan is quite an avid fan of your articles—"

Enrique let out a laugh, which sounded strangely high-pitched. Zofia frowned and looked at him. He was grinning at Eva. So was Hypnos.

"And I know *all* about you, Mr. Montagnet-Alarie," said Eva.

Zofia detected a slight change in Eva's pitch. It was lower. When she spoke, she fiddled with a silver pendant at her neck, yanking it back and forth.

"The handsome treasure hunter with the opulent hotel," said Eva, smiling. "What a dream. Perhaps you might have need of my services one day. As a blood Forging artist, I'm versed in pain. Or pleasure. Or both, depending on your taste."

Beside Zofia, Laila cleared her throat. Zofia had finally managed to open the luggage. She gazed up triumphantly, but no one was looking at her or the luggage. Everyone's gaze went back and forth between Laila and Eva.

"How rude of me!" said Eva. "I'm Eva Yefremovna, the blood Forging artist of House Dazbog. Are you the cook? Secretary?"

Enrique inhaled sharply. Zofia looked at him, but he didn't seem hurt. When she looked at Laila, her friend seemed to hold herself taller, and she placed her hand gently on Séverin's cheek.

"*Mistress,*" said Laila. "You might know me better by my stage name at the Palais des Rêves in Paris: *L'Énigme.*"

Though Laila had stopped hiding her other job once she left L'Eden, Zofia never remembered her talking about it and sounding quite so chilly. Perhaps she was cold and Zofia should return her scarf.

Eva shrugged. "Never heard of such an establishment. But well done, I suppose?"

Zofia began to lift up the layers of what she'd packed. So far, most of her belongings were intact.

"I've heard all about your exotic tastes, Monsieur," said Eva to Séverin. "Concerning all of your . . . objects. I hope you don't find my question impertinent, but may I ask why you would allow your mistress on such dangerous ordeals? My understanding was that mistresses have a rather distinct place."

Oh no, thought Zofia. Her suspicion was right. She was out of saltpeter. She looked up just as Eva grasped Laila's hand.

"Truly, my dear, this work is dangerous."

Séverin opened his mouth to respond, but Laila lifted her chin and took a step in front of him. Séverin closed his mouth and took one step back.

"My place, Mademoiselle Yefremovna, is wherever I damn well please," said Laila. She flipped her grip, so now it looked as though she was holding Eva's gloved hand with her bare one.

Zofia sank back on her heels. "I'm out of saltpeter."

The rest of them glanced down at her as if they'd only just noticed she was there.

"Peter? Who's Peter?" asked Hypnos, looking interested.

"Potassium nitrate," said Laila. "Not a person."

"How exquisitely boring."

"Surely Irkutsk will have what you're looking for?" asked Eva.

A low frantic buzz started to gather at the base of her skull. Zofia didn't know the Siberian city of Irkutsk. She didn't know how many trees grew next to the sidewalks. She had not prepared for how it would smell, whether there would be crowds or nobody at all.

"I'll come with you," said Enrique. "If that suits you?"

Zofia nodded, grateful. She'd seen Enrique walk into a crowd of strangers and walk out with a group of friends. It was one of the things she liked about him. She also liked how the light played across his skin and seemed, somehow, to get caught in his dark eyes. She liked how the panic in her chest eased when he was near. Although sometimes, in his company, she felt as if she'd been turned around blindfolded in a room. It made her head feel a little light, but it wasn't unpleasant.

Enrique glanced at her quizzically, and she realized she hadn't answered him out loud:

"Yes," she said. "That suits me."

THE CITY OF IRKUTSK was nothing like Paris.

Here, the buildings looked as if they had been cut from lace. Homes painted in shades of cream, blue, and yellow and bearing intricate wooden carvings crowded the wintry streets. Sunlight bounced off the gilded domes of cathedrals, and beyond the city's borders, Zofia caught sight of the snow-dusted taiga with its pine and spruce trees dotting the slopes of the surrounding Ural Mountains. Her footsteps crunched on the ice, and when she breathed deep, the air carried familiar scents—warm honey cake and smoked fish, berries mixed with malt, and even the earthen, sugary scent of borscht, a rich sweet-and-sour soup made from beets that her mother used to serve over mushroom-filled dumplings. There was a bluntness to Irkutsk that reminded Zofia of her home in Glowno.

If she returned home, she would find nothing: no family, friends, job, or even home. Besides, she couldn't leave Goliath behind. It was too cold in Poland for tarantulas.

"Do you think Laila and Eva have killed each other yet?" asked Enrique.

"Why would they do that?"

Enrique made an exasperated sound. "You were *right* there! I could have cut through that tension with a butter knife!"

"That's not physically possible."

"What's going through your head, then, phoenix?"

"Tarantula environmental preferences."

"I regret asking."

"Poland would be too cold for Goliath."

"All of Poland mourns."

Zofia hoped the caretakers at L'Eden were looking after him. Goliath reminded her of different times. Happier times. And even if they no longer existed, she liked the reminders that they had ever been there in the first place.

"I miss him," said Enrique.

Zofia suspected he wasn't talking about Goliath.

"So do I."

Up ahead, Zofia caught sight of an alchemical and pharmacy store painted a pale green. Crouched beside a broken window was a man wearing a *kippah*. Her father, who had not been Jewish, had never worn one, but many of the men and boys in Glowno had. The fabric stretched over the top of the man's skull, a gesture of his faith.

"*Gutn tog*," said Zofia.

The man looked up, startled. His eyes darted across the street before looking at her.

"*Gutn tog.*" He rose to a stand, before pointing at his broken window and saying tiredly, "Third time this year . . . You'd think Alexander II was only just murdered." He sighed. "How may I help you?"

"I need saltpeter," said Zofia.

The man frowned and hesitated, but then he gestured her inside. Enrique, he said, had to wait outside. Alone in the store, Zofia counted the neat wooden rows and the shining, green bottles lined up: *twenty-one, twenty-two, twenty-three.* When the shopkeeper refilled her bag, he lowered his voice as he slid the bag across the counter. "It's not safe for us," he said. "Every year it is getting harder."

"I am safe."

The man shook his head sadly. "We never are, my dear. The pogroms may have stopped for now, but the hate has not. *Kol tuv.*"

Zofia took the package uneasily. *The hate has not.* Her mother had lost family in those pogroms, the anti-Jewish riots that trampled homes and families, blaming them for the assassination of Tsar Alexander II. When she was thirteen years old, she found her mother kneeling in their home before the cold fire, sobbing. Zofia had gone still. Her sister and father always knew how to comfort, but they were asleep. And so, Zofia had done the only thing she could do—make light. She had crouched by the dead fire, reached for some flint, and coaxed the metal to blaze with heat. Only then did her mother look up and smile, before pulling her close and saying: "Be a light in this world, my Zosia, for it can be very dark."

Zofia's throat tightened to think of them now. The world seemed too dark to navigate, no matter what light she tried to bring to it. Outside, Zofia turned slowly on the sidewalk. The city no longer felt familiar like Glowno. Now, her eyes leapt from the shuttered windows and the people in too-bright coats, to the dirty snow trampled by carriage wheels, and the paved streets that seemed to weave together. It was too much—

"Phoenix!"

Enrique rounded the corner, holding up a paper bag and grinning. When he caught sight of her face, his smile dropped and he jogged faster to her side.

"Didn't you see me pointing around the corner before you went inside?"

Zofia shook her head.

"Oh," he said. "Well, I figured what with all the burning carriages, ghost stories, and brooding, we might as well eat cookies."

From the paper bag, he pulled out two, pale sugar cookies covered in a smooth, thick frosting. He handed one to her.

"Took me a bit longer than I thought because originally the cookie had sprinkles, but I know you don't like the texture, so I had them scrape it off and asked the baker to add another layer for smoothness," he said. "I'd savor them because you don't—"

Zofia shoved the entire cookie in her mouth. Enrique stared at her, then laughed and followed suit. On the walk back, Zofia savored the taste of sugar lingering on her tongue. It wasn't until they neared the entrance that Enrique spoke again.

"No thanks for me?" he asked. "I risked my hand giving you a sugar cookie. You ate it so fast, I thought you'd take my hand by accident."

"I wouldn't mistake your hand for a cookie."

Enrique mimicked being wounded. "And here I thought I was sweet."

It was a terrible joke, which Zofia was shocked that she recognized. And yet, she laughed. She laughed until the sides of her stomach hurt, and only then did she realize how she had completely

forgotten about the frigid, unfamiliar city surrounding them. Enrique had brought her a cookie and made her laugh, and it felt like
sitting beside a fire in one's own home, knowing exactly where
everything was and who would come to the door.

"Thank you," she said.

"A laugh from the phoenix herself?" Enrique grinned, pressing
his hand to his heart and saying dramatically, "A man would pit
himself against any challenge to hear such an elusive sound. Worth
a mangled hand. Certainly better than any trite thanks."

Zofia's smile faltered. She knew it was a joke and that he often
said grand things he did not mean. Right before she stepped into
the train depot, she wanted for such a thing to be true.

That the sound of her laugh might someday mean so much to
someone that it was worth any challenge.

THEY HEADED FOR THE lake at dusk, when the world looked blue and
the ice held onto the light. A team of twelve dogsleds fitted with
Forged reins to muffle the sound of their paws awaited them on
the other side of the train station's Tezcat door. There were no direct portal roads to their location. The local Buryats had erected
Forged barriers against such roads long ago. The five of them piled
into a sled, operated by an elderly Buryat man wearing thick boots
lined with fur, and a long sash across his coat strung with small,
copper ornaments. Delphine was already seated in one of the sleds
near the head of the operation, while Ruslan and Eva sat in another sled. Laila sidled in beside Zofia on the sled bench.

"Did you hear the translator?" she asked, shuddering. "He keeps
talking about 'distressed spirits' nearby."

Zofia did not believe in spirits. But the wind made the howling sound that had frightened her as a child, and a small part of her thought of the stories that Hela had whispered in the dark. Tales of *dybbuks* with their disjointed souls and blue lips, of drowned ghost girls forced to guard treasure, of lands between the space of midnight and dawn where the dead walked and the light ran cold and thin. Zofia neither liked nor believed in those tales.

But she did remember them.

"I never had a chance to apologize," said Laila.

Zofia frowned. What did Laila have to apologize for? Laila turned to look at her, and Zofia searched her features.

"I should have told you the truth about me, but I didn't want you to see me any differently. Or, I don't know, not as human anymore."

Anatomically, the body was a machine whether it was born or built. What lay inside was no different, thought Zofia. It was like physics. The transference of energy did not make the energy less real. Therefore, Laila was real, and the chance of her dying was all the more real if they didn't find *The Divine Lyrics* and ensure she could stay this way.

"If there's anything you want to tell me, you can," said Laila. "You don't have to . . . but you can."

Zofia wasn't sure what to say to that. She wanted to tell her about Hela, and the panic she felt at whether or not the way she processed the world made her a burden to others . . . but would such observations then make her a burden?

Laila held out her hand. Zofia caught sight of the garnet ring Laila had asked her to make. She thought the numbered days counted down to the day of Laila's birth. Not her death.

Zofia felt her face heat with fury. She would not be part of her friend's death. She would not let her die.

Zofia reached out, taking Laila's hand, and for a moment, she didn't feel the wind or the ice. Above them, the stars blurred together. The dogsled rumbled over the ice for what felt like hours, even with the Forged runners that allowed them to skid faster over the slick terrain. Just as dawn touched the pale horizon, they came to a stop. Zofia liked it here even though her breath burned in her lungs. She liked how the world looked solemn and cold. She liked the low belt of the Ural Mountains, the way the lake beneath them bore a lacework pattern of ice. She liked that there was nothing here.

But that was the problem.

There was nothing. And yet, according to their compasses, these were the exact coordinates of the Sleeping Palace. Séverin and Ruslan stood apart from the others, with Séverin turning the Tezcat spectacles in his hand. Eva stood between them, peering over Séverin's shoulder, her hand on his back.

"Do you think it's underwater?" she asked.

Séverin didn't answer.

"Did we get the coordinates flipped?" asked Hypnos.

Zofia looked at the spectacles. Then she looked at all the people regarding the instrument without doing the obvious: *using* it.

"They're spectacles," she said loudly.

Séverin glanced up at her, and his mouth curved up. He raised the Tezcat spectacles to his face and held still.

"What is it?" asked Eva. "What do you see?"

Séverin took a few steps to the left, and then he bent toward the ice, reaching for midair while his hand curved as if around a door handle only he could see. Then he pulled. When he did, the light started to waver right in front of him and the air shimmered.

Ruslan laughed and clapped his hands, drawing away Zofia's attention.

"Zofia," gasped Laila beside her.

She looked back to the place where the air had started to shimmer, only now the glittering effect stretched to a distance that seemed to equal the entire length of L'Eden. The Ural Mountains behind the lake blurred away as solid ice appeared midair. With every passing second, the shape of a grand building emerged on the frozen Lake Baikal—frozen cupolas and translucent balconies, crystal spires and thick, ice walls. There was no mistaking what was before them.

The Sleeping Palace of the Fallen House.

15

LAILA

The Sleeping Palace reminded Laila of L'Eden, if it had been dreamed up by winter.

When the door opened, slender icicles shattered on the ground. Her stomach swooped at her first step. Snowflakes dusted the translucent floor, and through the striations of ice, Laila could see the movement of sapphire water . . . as if she might tumble through at any moment. The wide vestibule opened into an expansive, silvery atrium. Forged thuribles of moonstone glided along a vaulted ceiling full of etched crystal and ice. Two snow-bright stairways spiraled up to a balcony that encircled the atrium. The moment they entered the atrium, the Sleeping Palace began to *wake*. Crystalline sculptures of gargoyles untucked their heads from their wings. Designs of closed blossoms and coiled ivy unfurled slowly, snow falling from their shapes like pollen as they opened and arched toward the ceiling. The sounds echoing through the vast halls reminded Laila of crisp snow broken underfoot.

Her breath feathered before her, and not for the first time, she wondered whether she was supposed to be feeling *more* . . . She looked at her hands, flexing her fingers, trying to search her body for some sign that they were closer to *The Divine Lyrics*. But all she felt was the relentless cold, and all she saw was her garnet ring, wet as a heart, with the number *17* leering at her from inside the jewel.

Delphine stayed at the entrance, turning her attention to the guards and the transport, calling for a retinue to examine the rooms, determine their safety, and get them ready for sleeping. Eva had made her way, of course, to Séverin. Laila ignored the sharp twinge in her heart. Perhaps she was being unfair. Eva had not made the most favorable impression, but Laila could let that go.

She forced her eyes to Ruslan, who stared up at the icy vaulted ceiling. Lightly, he cradled his injured hand in its sling. For a moment, something flickered across his face that looked, to Laila, like sorrow.

"Remarkable," he said excitedly, hopping a little on the spot. "This feels like the start of making history, does it not? Can't you *feel* the pulse of the universe speeding up at this discovery? It makes me feel—"

His stomach growled loudly. Ruslan scowled, and whispered *hush!* to his belly. He opened his mouth to speak again, but then Delphine appeared beside him, and Ruslan fell quiet. She surveyed them through narrowed eyes. When she spoke, Laila saw that she only looked at Séverin. "Well, treasure hunters, we have exactly one week before the Winter Conclave and even less time before we have no choice but to reveal this discovery to the Order," she said stonily. "Start hunting."

With that, she and Ruslan left the atrium. Ruslan paused only to glance at Eva with an encouraging smile. Laila thought it was a summons, but Eva did not follow after him. Instead, she walked forward. For the first time, Laila noticed a slight drag to her left leg.

"I wish to stay and help you," announced Eva, crossing her arms. "For one thing, I'm a gifted blood Forging *and* ice artist. As Ruslan's cousin, I've grown up hearing the stories about the Sleeping Palace *and* the Fallen House. You could use me. Finally, I have just as much to offer as anyone else on the team." She shot a scathing glance at Laila. "Perhaps more than some.

"Well?" prompted Eva, when Séverin said nothing.

He looked to Laila. No one joined them without a thorough reading, and what Laila had found of Eva wasn't enough to deem her safe. While the matriarch had called for a morning meeting yesterday, Séverin had summoned her to the luggage room where they had opened the patriarch's and Eva's possessions, and she had read all that she could. There was nothing out of the ordinary in Ruslan's belongings. No memories of import. No emotion except the *pressure* to discover, which she'd felt like a hand pushed on her heart. Eva's objects, however, were sparse. Nothing but a pair of shoes worn through from work at the blood Forging den in Moscow. That was all.

"I'm sorry," said Laila, truly meaning it. "But no."

Eva looked stricken for only a moment, before she glowered and crossed the room to Laila. Hypnos hurriedly scuttled elsewhere.

"Is this because I didn't know who you were?" asked Eva, annoyed.

Laila felt weary.

"I don't particularly care whether you know me or not, Eva. It doesn't change that we follow certain protocols, which you are not familiar with, and so we must decline your well-intentioned offer to provide services."

Eva smirked, tugging at a silver pendant around her neck. "Are you jealous, is that it? I don't blame you." Eva leaned close, lowering her voice. "What artistry do you have to offer other than your body?"

Laila schooled her features blank. She understood how the world cultivated malice between girls, teaching them to bare their teeth when they might have bared their souls. Her own friendships at the Palais des Rêves had started out with cruelty—one girl adding a dye to her face cream and another cutting the heels from her shoes in the hopes that she'd snap her ankle on the stage. *C'est la vie*. It was Paris. It was show business. And they were scared of losing their livelihood. But the difference was that at least the cabaret girls had treated her as a formidable opponent on the same battlefield.

When Eva deigned to speak to her, it was as if she didn't see her at all.

"I see nothing that inspires jealousy," said Laila.

And she meant it. Eva was beautiful, but bodies were just bodies. Easily broken, and unfortunately, not so easily made. Laila had never had control over her physical features, and she never felt it right to hold another's against them.

But at her words, Eva's face turned bloodless.

"You say that because you think you have a protector in Mr. Montagnet-Alarie," she said. "But don't think it will stay that way. Even I noticed he didn't bother defending your honor."

With that, she stalked off.

Laila sank her nails into her palm. Eva was right, but wrong. If

Séverin had wanted to show that she was something he could speak
for or speak over, then he would have. But Laila had watched him
consider speaking before choosing to step back. She wished she'd
never seen that.

For in that second, her mind had conjured up fairy tales and
curses, myths of girls instructed not to behold their lover at midnight lest they glimpse their true form. What Séverin had done
then and how he'd flung out his arms during the *troika* fire were
all cruel glimpses of the boy he had truly been. The boy who had
rescued Zofia and given her a world of comfort, taken a chance
on Enrique and given him a platform to speak, seen Laila for her
soul and not just the flesh that encased it. She hated that glimpse
because it reminded her that he was like a cursed prince, trapped
in the worst version of himself. And nothing she possessed—not
her kiss freely given, nor her heart shyly offered—could break the
thrall that held him because he had done it to himself.

When she turned to Séverin now, he was staring hungrily at the
Sleeping Palace. He swept his dark hair away from his forehead.
The barest smile touched his face. Before, he would have reached
into his coat pocket for his tin of cloves. He once said they helped
him think and remember, but he'd stopped reaching for them after
Tristan had died. Laila wasn't sure why. It wasn't as though not
eating them would help him forget.

Laila returned to the others, and they watched as Séverin
turned around the main atrium. Observation was his domain. She
could hate him all she wanted, but she couldn't deny that when it
came to treasure, Séverin had a knack for understanding its context. Its story, in a way.

"We've been calling it a 'palace,'" he said slowly. "But it's not.
It's like a cathedral . . ."

Séverin made a note in one of his papers.

"What's the holiest part of a cathedral?" he asked, more to himself than to the others.

Laila neither felt particularly qualified for nor interested in answering the question.

"The thing with the wine," said Hypnos.

"How should I know?" shrugged Zofia.

"The altar," said Enrique, shaking his head.

Séverin nodded, his chin turned so the winter light glowed across his face.

"Someone wants to play God."

Laila's mouth twisted into a hollow smile. Sometimes she wondered whether Séverin thought to do the same.

Ahead, four hallways branched out from the main atrium. Rather than risk being separated, they traveled as one unit, documenting things as they went. In the western hall was a library where nine female statues served as pillars. At least, it *should* have been a library . . . but all the shelves were empty of books.

"They might be hidden," said Enrique longingly, his fingers twitching to explore the room. But he dutifully followed the rest of them.

The southern hall broke off into the kitchens and a small infirmary. At the entrance to the eastern hall, goose bumps prickled along Laila's arm. In the distance, she thought she heard . . . growls? No, *snoring*. A pair of arched double doors etched with designs of wolves and snakes opened up into a dimly lit room where huge, jagged bumps covered the marble floor. Zofia broke off a phosphorous pendant, and the light revealed that she wasn't staring at bumps at all, but a menagerie of dozens of ice Forged animals. Lions with delicate ice whiskers, peacocks with a train of frosted feathers, wolves whose glassy fur bristled and gently rose and fell as if they lived and breathed.

Laila instantly recoiled, but none of the creatures moved. She studied them a moment longer, her fear giving way to awe.

"They're *asleep*," she said.

The animals slept with their paws bent, hooves tucked, and wings folded upon a creamy marble floor. Only one animal—an ice rhino—bothered to open its eyes at the sound of the doors. Its gaze flicked toward them, but it did not move.

"I hate everything about this," said Hypnos.

"Me too," said Enrique. "Shut the door before they wake up."

"The treasure wouldn't be in here anyway," said Séverin, frowning once more at the animals before shutting the door.

At each hallway, Séverin stopped to check the rooms for triggers that would activate any guard mechanisms. With the Fallen House, anything was possible. But none of the doors betrayed them, and none of the floors reacted. The spherical detection devices yielded nothing either. It was as if the Sleeping Palace were truly asleep. At every point, Zofia raised her phosphorous pendants, searching for signs of a Tezcat door in plain sight, but nothing revealed itself. As they walked down the final hall, the northern passage, Enrique pulled his coat tighter, glancing at the carvings where the wall met the ceiling.

"All the iconography shows women," he said.

Laila hadn't noticed that before, but he was right. All of the women in the frosted images covering the walls reminded Laila of priestesses. The detail of the ice didn't seem to have faded over the years, and there was a curious sharpness to their eyes.

"None of their hands are showing," said Enrique.

Small shivers crept down Laila's spine, and she quickly averted her eyes. Their posture was too familiar. How many times as a child had she shoved her hands behind her back so her father wouldn't be reminded of what she could do, or, as he later said, what she *was*.

So far, the northern hall was the longest. It grew colder the farther they ventured. At the front, Séverin looked over his shoulder and caught her eye. Laila discreetly made her way to him.

"Usual procedure," called out Séverin.

"Here, Hypnos, hold the detection device—" said Enrique, as the rest of them busied themselves.

Now it was just her and Séverin.

Séverin didn't look at her. "Anything?"

Laila took off her gloves. She reached for the icy carved door in front of them, letting her hands skim over the strange indentations at the threshold.

"I can't read it," she said. "It's all Forged."

"No trapping devices detected," called Enrique from the back. "Let's enter. Why's it so narrow?"

"It's like a corridor to a room of meditation," mused Séverin. "Designed to make someone feel as if the path they walk, they walk alone."

"Well, rather than standing here, let's get on with it and go inside," said Hypnos, crossing his arms.

"Can't," said Séverin.

"There's no handle," said Zofia, her blue eyes quickly scanning the door.

Séverin tried pushing it, but it made no difference. The door wouldn't budge. Séverin dropped his gaze to the floor indents. "This place was designed like a cathedral. It doesn't *want* brute force. It wants something else . . . something that's honoring whatever is sacred inside here."

Laila watched his face come alive with the puzzle of the room.

"Light," he said, holding out his hand.

Zofia passed forward one of the pendants from her necklace. Séverin snapped the phosphorescent chip. The sudden glow carved out the shadows of his face, throwing them into sharp relief.

"Move back," he said.

The four of them crowded into the small space of the hallway. Séverin dropped to his knees, flashing the light across the strange ripples and indentations covering the door.

"Found the opening," he said.

He held his hand perpendicular to the ice and slid it down where it disappeared as if into a slot. But still the door wouldn't budge.

"It's like a keyhole," said Enrique. "But why would someone put it where it's only eye level to a child?"

That thought disturbed Laila. No part of the palace made sense, from the menagerie full of ice animals to the empty corridors. Even now, she shuddered thinking of the ice rhino's slow gaze tracking them across the room. It hadn't moved. Yet.

"Eye level to a child . . . or to a supplicant," said Séverin.

Still crouched, he slid his knees into the dents of the floor. He dropped the phosphorous pendant on the ground, and the blue light silhouetted him. In the past, when they had gone on hunts for acquisitions, Laila had always been taken by how differently Séverin saw the world. He had a sense of wonder unlike anyone she'd ever met. It made her remember the first evening she realized she wanted to kiss him. At the time, he had commissioned a garden installation based on *cobwebs* of all things. She'd thought it was a disgusting idea until he'd reached out, tilted her chin back, and asked softly: "Do you see the wonder now?" That was all it took for the night sky to transform above them. One turn of her head, and the world seemed crisscrossed with the starry thread of soon-to-be constellations.

Séverin still had an uncanny sense for performance. But now, he had the look of someone too eager to be sacrificed, and Laila had to stop herself from the strange impulse to run to him and pull him to his feet.

"It's like an altar," Séverin said, so softly that Laila couldn't tell if he meant for them to hear. "And I kneel in worship."

Then, he pressed his palms together as if in prayer, pushing them into the depressions of the door. A silver light ran down the vines, as if it was stirring awake after a long slumber. The door's ice and metal hinges groaned as it swung back, revealing a room lit within by a silvery glow.

Beside her, Enrique crossed himself, and Hypnos drew in a sharp breath. Séverin rose to his feet, but he didn't enter.

"Why isn't he going in?" muttered Hypnos.

"Fear of dismemberment," said Zofia. "If I were designing thief-catching mechanisms, I would have a device rigged to attack the first three people who entered."

Hypnos stepped behind Zofia. "Ladies first."

Enrique threw the spherical detection device to Séverin who caught it one-handed.

"What do you see?" asked Enrique.

Usually, Séverin would have been narrating the whole scene— from the number of walls to the shape of the ceiling. But whatever he saw here was worth hoarding the whole sight to himself. Laila held her breath.

"Stars," said Séverin simply.

Laila and Enrique looked at each other, confused. What about the treasure? The *book*?

"No detection devices," said Séverin. "It's clear."

They filed in one by one—Hypnos clinging to Zofia's coat—into a room Laila could only describe as an ice grotto. Séverin was right about the stars. Above them stretched a rendering of the night sky, but it wasn't real, even though it looked fathomless. It was like an image suspended of a former night, and at the center hung a pendulous moon that changed before their eyes, growing slimmer with every passing second as if it were counting down to something.

The ice grotto resembled a sunken courtyard. Farther into the room, shallow steps descended to an empty floor bearing a single, jagged pool revealing Lake Baikal's sapphire water. Splayed against the far wall loomed three, huge shield-like structures. If there was writing or symbols on them, the cobwebs of ice concealed it from view. Above those three shields appeared more carvings of women. They seemed to lean out of recessed niches within the ice wall, their arms outstretched and their hands . . . *missing*. When the light flashed over them briefly, they looked terribly lifelike.

The pale light of the stars above them only gradually revealed the room's contents, but one thing was for sure . . .

There was no treasure here.

Laila's heart sank, but she refused to be discouraged. Treasure liked to hide. She knew that well enough after two years of working with Séverin. As they moved to inspect the eastern wall, Enrique jumped back with a squeal. Laila whirled around, her pulse racing as she beheld what made Enrique nearly scream. When the light hit the eastern ice wall, the wall turned translucent and revealed the entire menagerie of animals they'd glimpsed moments ago.

"Interesting," said Zofia. "A Tezcat wall connecting the menagerie that requires no key but light. That's clever."

"That's horrific," said Enrique. "Look at them . . . they're *awake*."

Laila turned slowly toward the creatures. Where they'd once slumbered, now they were awake. Each of their heads had turned to face them.

"I hereby volunteer to guard the door," said Hypnos. "From the hall. Actually, the end of the hall."

Séverin ignored him. "Let's keep documenting. I want to see what's down those stairs."

"How?" asked Enrique. "It's far too dark. We should come back with more light. I want lanterns trained just on that eastern wall."

Then, Laila heard the unmistakable *rrrip* of a lit match. In seconds, Zofia had created a makeshift torch.

"Much better—" said Enrique, but his words were cut off by a sharp scream from Hypnos.

"Séverin, *wait!*"

Too late, Laila realized Séverin had broken off from the group, venturing toward the stairs at the far end of the grotto that led to the north wall. He didn't wait. With his lantern aloft, Séverin took the first step—

Everything changed.

Time held still. As if in slow motion, Laila saw Séverin take a deep breath, his breath pluming in the air, the silver fog of it suspended for one perfect moment of silence . . . and then *sound* rushed in. From the eastern corner of the wall, the ice rhino crashed through the glass barrier. Shattered ice rained down, scattering across the floor. The rhino charged, a deep sound bellowing from its lungs. Out the corner of her eye, Laila watched as the other animals slowly came to life. A jaguar's crystal fur rippled. It swung its head and pawed the ground.

The staircase had triggered life.

"Get back!" she called.

Séverin turned his head, but a small ball of ice launched at him from opposite the wall, splattering on his face and covering his mouth and nose in a cobweb of ice. He stumbled back, falling onto the stairs. Laila moved to run toward him, but the rhino blocked her way.

"Someone get him!" she called.

Zofia tossed her torch to Enrique and quickly threw an explosive net across the rhino.

"*Ignite*," she willed.

Behind them, Hypnos dashed out into the hall, shouting for help.

The Forged net caught flame, and the rhino shrieked, exploding into a thousand shards of ice. Zofia and Laila ran to Séverin. They each grabbed one arm, hoisting him off the staircase. The moment he crossed the boundary, the ice animals once more fell still and silent. Laila pulled at the ice covering his mouth, but it was too slippery.

Laila grasped again, and *again*, but the ice only burned her hand and stuck fast to his skin. Her breath turned jagged inside her. She risked a glance at Séverin and wished she hadn't. His pupils were blown wide, the veins of his throat bulging as he threw off her hands and started to claw at his face. He was dying right before her eyes.

Zofia reached for a match, but Séverin clutched her wrist.

"You'll burn him!" cried Laila.

"Disfigurement and death are not comparable options," said Zofia fiercely.

Then, out the corner of Laila's eyes, she caught a whip of red as a figure rushed toward them. Eva dropped to the floor beside them, breathless. Séverin's head listed to one side. A blue sheen crept over his skin, and his eyelids started fluttering shut. A sob caught in Laila's throat.

"I can save him," said Eva, shoving Laila out of the way. "I've seen this kind of attack before."

Eva grabbed Séverin's face, then pressed her mouth over his. Her red hair fell over them both, and Séverin clung to her, his hands grabbing at her back. Immediately, the ice melted from Séverin's mouth. He gasped for breath as Eva pulled away, his face still cradled in her hands. The sight sent a strange twist of acid through her stomach. She watched as Séverin blinked rapidly. Ice rimmed his eyelashes. His gaze pinned Eva as if he were a cursed prince and she alone had freed him.

PART III

From the archival records of the Order of Babel
author unknown
1878, Amsterdam

Blood-Forging is a particularly vulgar art, fit only for the meanest of brothels. That it is not banned in every country is, I believe, an utter travesty.

16

LAILA

Laila crossed and uncrossed her ankles, fidgeting with the end of her dress. Nearly four hours had passed since Eva rescued Séverin. Since then, he had been holed up with her and a physician Ruslan had brought in from Irkutsk. No one was allowed to enter his chamber despite Laila's protests. On the one hand, she wasn't waiting alone . . . but she was the only one left awake.

After two hours, Hypnos had commandeered Enrique's left shoulder as a pillow. After three, Zofia started to doze off, though she kept jerking her head back until Enrique—terrified she'd snap her neck—maneuvered his right shoulder into her pillow.

"Don't worry, Laila," Enrique had said, yawning. "There's no way I'll fall asleep like this. We'll see him soon. I'm sure of it."

That was twenty minutes ago.

Now he was lightly snoring.

Laila sighed and removed her blanket. Gently, she tucked it across the three of them and started clearing the papers on the

table filled with Enrique's notes recounting what he'd seen, and
Zofia's diagrams of the hallway. Hypnos had also asked for paper, for what purpose Laila couldn't fathom until she looked
down and saw doodles of snowflakes and the animals from the
ice menagerie.

Outside the window, the frozen lake gleamed sleek with new
snow. Earlier, it had seemed so isolated. Now, activity buzzed
around the palace. Armored Sphinxes stood, unmoving, around
the perimeters. The familiar bloodred shimmer of Forged alarm
nets stretched across the ice. Necessary precautions, Ruslan had
explained, to keep them safe from the Fallen House members who
had attacked them in Moscow.

"What's left of them is a small knot of fanatics," Ruslan had
said. "They won't be able to make it past Irkutsk without our resources. Don't worry. You're under House Dazbog's protection."

A small knot of fanatics could still kill, though. Laila had remembered that truth each night before bed, when she whispered
a prayer for Tristan's restless soul. With one slice of that blade-
brimmed hat, Roux-Joubert had killed him. She'd never forget the
fevered light in his eyes, or the way he had pathetically crumpled
at the feet of the doctor, the masked leader of the Fallen House.
She hadn't been able to read anything of the man, but she hadn't
forgotten the *stillness* of him. It looked inhuman.

The sound of footfalls on the staircase made her sit up straight.

Ruslan appeared, carrying more blankets in his uninjured arm.
He smiled apologetically when he saw her, and a warmth of gratitude spread through her. It was Ruslan who had thought to bring
an extra couch, quilts, vodka, and several thimble-sized glasses,
and a spread of Lake Baikal cuisine—cold, smoked *omul* fish, taiga
meat wrapped in forest ferns and frozen berries, cloudberry jam

cakes, and golden *pirozhki* baked into the shapes of fish and wild fowl. Laila couldn't summon much of an appetite after what happened in the ice grotto, and so Enrique had eaten her share . . . as well as everyone else's.

"I know it's not much, but, no need to wait in the cold," said Ruslan. "Bad for the heart and the hair, and you have got the *loveliest* strands. Like a girl from a myth." Ruslan held his slinged arm close to his chest. "Are you familiar with the eleventh-century Persian poet Ferdowsi? He wrote a fabulous poem called the *Shahnameh*, otherwise known as *The Book of Kings*. No?" Ruslan swayed a little, closing his eyes as if that simple act would pull him into another world. "Just imagine it . . . elegant courts and citrus trees, jewels in the hair and poetry dissolving like sugar on the tongue." He sighed, opening his eyes. "With that hair, you remind me of the Princess Rudaba, and your Séverin is like King Zal! In the tales, she let down her mesmerizing tresses, and King Zal used them as a rope. I hope you do not use yours as a rope. Very unhygienic."

Laila laughed in spite of herself. "I assure you, I do not."

"Good, good," said Ruslan, rubbing his head.

Ruslan seemed lost in thought after that, murmuring to himself about braids and orange trees. House Dazbog—with its focus on the accumulation of knowledge rather than objects—was unlike the other Houses. And Ruslan seemed unlike most patriarchs. He didn't even look European. His high, broad cheekbones reminded her of the perfume ateliers who had arrived from China and set up shop in Paris. There was an upswept tilt to his eyes, like Enrique, and his face seemed to belong to two worlds: east and west.

Down the hall, the door to Séverin's suite opened, and the physician poked his head out.

"Patriarch Ruslan?"

Laila moved toward the door, but the physician held out his hand.

"I apologize, but the blood Forging artist said the mistress can't come in yet. It might alter his heart rate and blood pressure, which we've only just stabilized."

Laila's hand curled into a fist, but she stepped back as Ruslan made his way to the door.

"I'm sure it will only be a moment longer," he said kindly.

When the door closed behind him, Laila heard the faintest laugh. She whirled around to see Delphine standing once more at the stair landing. Every twenty minutes she had arrived, each time demanding entry.

"I am his patron, after all," she'd said to the physician.

To Laila, she sounded more like a worried parent.

"No admittance yet? I believe the girl who resuscitated him has not encountered the same problem," said Delphine, with a slanting smile. "She's very pretty."

Laila remembered the crimson fall of Eva's hair when she bent over Séverin.

"She is," said Laila stiffly. "And we are indebted to her."

Laila walked back to the others, taking a seat by the window and ignoring the other woman. Delphine sat beside her anyway, pushing aside the vodka bottle and reaching for the last remaining cake. Laila thought for sure Enrique would jolt awake, somehow sensing the last cake would be taken from him, but instead, he snored louder. Outside, dusk quickly descended into night, and the number in Laila's ring changed shape. She forced herself to take even breaths. She still had sixteen days left. There was still time to live.

"They said you were a nautch dancer when you broke into my home," said Delphine.

Laila smiled. She preferred this skirmish to the battle for her very life.

"They lied. I'm not a nautch dancer."

"A small lie," said the other woman, shrugging. "I understand that's not far off from your actual profession. A courtesan, am I correct?" Delphine snorted, not waiting for her answer. "A euphemism for a prostitute, if I ever heard one."

Laila wasn't offended, though perhaps the other woman wished her to be. Delphine's hands stilled, waiting. Testing.

"We have many things in common, Madame."

"And how do you suppose that?" asked Delphine drily.

"Me and my ancient profession, you and your ancient Order. Me and my wiles to part men from coin, and you and your Order's manner of forcing their hands," said Laila, ticking off the reasons on her fingers. "The only difference being of course that my wares never go out of style. Corruption, murder, and thievery are, I imagine, not as easily welcomed into people's beds."

Delphine stared at her, shocked. And then, impossibly, she laughed. She reached forward, pouring the vodka into two delicately etched quartz glasses.

"To our shared interests, then," she said.

Laila knocked her glass against Delphine's, and when she'd finished, she found the other woman staring at her. She seemed as if she wanted to say something more, but then the doors of Séverin's suite swung open.

Laila and Delphine sat up eagerly, and a House Dazbog servant poked his head out into the hall.

"Mr. Montagnet-Alarie will see you now," said the servant.

Instinctively, Laila looked over her shoulder, expecting Enrique, Zofia, and Hypnos right behind her—but they were fast asleep.

"Very well—" started Delphine, but the servant shook his head.

"He did not ask for you."

"It doesn't matter if—"

"He specifically asked *not* for you," the servant finally admitted, his gaze downcast.

Laila felt a pang of sympathy for the older woman. She'd been waiting so long to make sure he was well. Once, Séverin had confided that Delphine had treated him like her own child. When she abandoned Séverin, Laila thought her heartless. But looking at the matriarch now—her head bowed and lips pursed, hands clasped and ermine stole slipping off her shoulder like breaking armor—she wondered not at what she knew of her, but at what she didn't.

"Good to see his fond enmity remains intact," said Delphine lightly.

THE FIRST THING Laila's gaze went to was the giant four-poster bed, covered in silver damask silk and pale sapphire pillows. A Forged canopy of thinly hammered ice shot through with strands of silver draped over the bed and moved lightly to an invisible breeze. An irregularly shaped rug stitched together from the pelts of various white-furred animals stretched out beneath it, and at its four corners curled the yellowed talons of dead beasts. Polished ice formed the ceiling, and she caught her reflection wavering on its mirrored surface. In the blue light and dressed in furs, she hardly looked like herself, and her mind conjured up Enrique's tale of Snegurochka, the snow maiden. Perhaps that girl would have known what to do in this cold, beautiful room with a cold, beautiful boy waiting to see her.

As she took one step into the room, the diamond necklace on Laila's skin felt like a collar of winter at her throat.

You have just agreed to spend every night in my bed for the next three weeks. I will hold you to that.

Sitting in a carved ice throne was Séverin. He looked up at her, his dusky eyes burning. She could tell someone else had changed him out of his clothes because he wore a black silk night robe that opened at his throat. He used to hate dark sleepwear after Tristan once said it made him "look like a bat striving for glamour." The memory almost made her laugh when she noticed who else was with him.

Eva stood behind him, her hands raised, blood glistening on her fingertips. She didn't smile when Laila entered the room, instead shooting a glance of dismay at Ruslan.

"It may not be safe for her to be here," said Eva.

Ruslan made a *tsk* sound. "Oh hush, cousin."

The doctor put away the last of his tools and bid them a good day. "How attentive of you to wait on him. You're a lucky man, Monsieur Montagnet-Alarie, to have so many beautiful girls concerned for your health."

Ruslan scowled, and Laila thought she heard him mutter, "What about me?"

When the door shut, Eva glided to the basin at the end of the room, plunging her bloody hands into the water. Laila glanced at Séverin, but he was sitting too still . . . altogether too quiet.

"What did you do to him?" she asked.

"Aside from save him?" shot back Eva. "I regulated his blood pressure, but it has a slight sedative effect. He could've gone into shock from the hypothermia, so his limbs are momentarily paralyzed to allow a heating effect to work through his body and restore him back to perfect health."

Laila raised her chin higher. "You have our thanks," she said icily.

"And what about your trust?" demanded Eva. "If you'd just let me work with you from the beginning, he wouldn't even be in this state."

"Cousin—" Ruslan warned.

"As I pointed out to Monsieur Montagnet-Alarie earlier, I am proficient in Forging affinities with ice. I could help when you return to the chamber tomorrow. You *need* me," said Eva. She lightly touched her lips the way a lover recalls a caress. She looked to Séverin and then back to Laila. "But there were some benefits, at least."

Laila bit back a glower. Eva and Ruslan had to leave . . . and there was only one way to do that. She walked to Séverin, placing her hand at his cheek and looking over her shoulder.

"What *I* need is time alone with him." Laila smiled sweetly. "Thank you for taking care of him, but I can handle it from here."

"I don't think that's a good idea," said Eva, crossing her arms. "He needs rest and sleep. Maybe you can retire elsewhere tonight, and I can watch him."

"As it so happens, I know just how to put him to sleep."

Séverin looked up at her, and for the first time, the haze in his eyes had subsided somewhat. She sank into his lap, and his body stiffened beneath hers. In her mind, she ignored what she was doing. But her body noticed. Every part of her remembered and catalogued the hardness of his muscle, sinewy and lean from days spent working alongside L'Eden's workers for various installations; the heat that rose off his skin despite being in a palace of ice; and the faint scent of cloves that he could never get out of his garments.

"Put your hands on me," she whispered in his ear.

Séverin glanced at his limbs, his jaw clenching slightly.

"I cannot," he said, the words halting as if it took effort to fight the sedative. Séverin tilted his head forward, his lips at her ear. "If you want my hands on you, Laila, you'll have to do it yourself."

So she did.

The whole rhythm of their movements—of sinking against him, draping one arm around his neck—took up only a couple of seconds, and yet time felt slow as poured honey. Séverin's hand seemed heavy and burning, and when she placed it at her waist, his fingers dug into her skin. His brows knitted together, as if touching her physically hurt him. Laila almost forgot why she'd done this at all until she heard someone clearing their throat. At the entrance to the suite, Ruslan was practically shoving Eva out of the room.

"Until the morning, then," he said.

"Yes," said Eva, her eyes on Séverin. "The morning."

Laila waited until the door of their chamber closed. She held her breath, all too aware of how close they were, how the hair curled at the nape of his neck was damp . . . the pressure of his fingers at her waist. She immediately slid off his lap.

"Tell me what everyone saw in the ice grotto," demanded Séverin haltingly.

Laila quickly filled him in on all they had discussed. As she spoke, she watched as his fingers slowly curled and uncurled, movement returning to him. When she was finished, he said nothing except: "Tomorrow morning, we go back."

After a few minutes, he flexed his hands. "It's finally wearing off."

Soon after, he rose and disappeared into the adjacent bath suite. A rush of foolish nerves hit Laila as she walked to the bed. He would be here. With her. All because of an impulsive oath she'd wrung out of him.

You have just agreed to spend every night in my bed.

A low rustle of movement across from her made her head snap up. Séverin stood on the opposite side. He hadn't changed out of the supple, dark silk nightclothes, and she saw that the color shifted from indigo to black. It matched his eyes, though she wished she hadn't noticed. He looked at her and raised one eyebrow.

"You must want it very badly," he said.

Laila jolted. "What?"

"*The Divine Lyrics,*" said Séverin coolly. "You must want it very badly if this is what you'll put yourself through."

But the corner of his mouth twitched up. It was the ghost of his former self pushing up against this new, ice exterior. *Stop haunting me*, she pleaded silently.

"Of course I want the book," she said.

"Yes, I know," said Séverin flippantly. "For the purpose of dis-covering your origins, etcetera . . ."

Laila smiled grimly. He had no idea that her life hung in the balance. He didn't deserve to know.

". . . or perhaps it was all an excuse to get me here," added Séverin with a cruel smirk.

She could have wrung his neck. "I didn't need an excuse last time."

If he'd meant to taunt her, to push her farther away, he'd misstepped. And judging by the look on his face, he knew it. So she went in for the kill. She wanted him to flinch again. She wanted any ghost of his former self to retreat so far inside that fistful of snow he called a heart that she would never be reminded of how much he had changed. She crawled onto the bed, rising up on her knees, watching as his eyes narrowed.

"Remember that last evening in your study? You said yourself I was not real, Séverin," she taunted, enjoying how he flinched. "You could always rediscover that for yourself."

She reached for him, knowing she'd gone too far the second he caught her wrist. He stared at his fingers encircling her skin.

"I know you're real, Laila," he said. His voice was a poisonous silk. "I merely wish you weren't."

He let go of her hand then shut the gossamer curtains. Laila watched him retreat to the armchair. It took a few moments before she realized he wouldn't return. Good, she thought, easing herself into the large, empty bed. *Exactly what I want.*

As she closed her eyes, she imagined the cold, unlit spaces of the Sleeping Palace. Somewhere inside this place lay *The Divine Lyrics*, the secret to more life. But nothing was without sacrifice.

The week before she had left her father's home, he had given her a gift. Not her mother's wedding bangles as she had asked for, but a small knife inlaid with ivory and gold filigree that swept like a peacock's tail over the hilt.

"Better by your own hand, than the *jaadugar*'s," he'd said.

His meaning was clear. Laila thought of it now as she pulled the covers to her chin. She turned her back on Séverin, on the evenings they'd spent playing chess, the minutes she pretended she didn't see him waiting for her outside the kitchens of L'Eden, the way he didn't realize he smiled when he looked at her, and every single second when he never once made her feel like she was anything less than his equal.

She thought of her father's knife and words, of snow maidens with thawed hearts, and the collar of winter at her throat.

If surviving meant cutting out her heart, then at least she could do it by her own hand.

17

∞

SÉVERIN

Six days until Winter Conclave ...

Séverin had seven fathers, but only one brother.

There was a time, though, when he thought he might have two.

Wrath had dragged him to a meeting inside the Jardin du Luxembourg because now and then, Séverin's trust lawyers needed to see he was hale before they allowed Wrath more finances. They did not listen when Séverin told them about the Phobus Helmet that conjured forth nightmares, the thorny rosebush where he and Tristan hid every afternoon, the bruises on his wrist that always faded in time for a new meeting. Soon, he learned to say nothing at all.

On one of those meetings, he saw Hypnos, walking hand in hand with his father beneath the swaying linden trees.

"Hypnos!" he'd called out.

He'd flailed his hand, desperate to catch his attention. If Hypnos saw, maybe he could rescue them. Maybe he could tell Séverin what he had done *so wrong to make Tante FeeFee leave him behind. Maybe he could make her love him again.*

"Stop this, boy," Wrath had hissed.

Séverin would have called Hypnos's name until his throat turned raw had the other boy not caught his eye . . . only to look away. Séverin felt the turn of his head like a blade to his heart.

Some months later, Tristan saved them with a plant. Tristan confided that an angel had visited him and given him poisonous aconite flowers that—when steeped into a tea—freed them from Wrath.

Years later, the two of them would stand on the newly tilled earth that would become L'Eden Hotel. Tristan had hoarded his savings to buy a packet of rose seedlings that he promptly dropped into the ground and coaxed to live. As the slender tendrils spiked out of the earth, he'd thrown his arm around Séverin, grinned and pointed at the fast-growing roses.

"This is the start of our dreams," he'd said. "I promise to protect it."

Séverin had smiled back, knowing his line by heart: "And I protect you."

SÉVERIN COULDN'T SLEEP.

He sat in the armchair, his head turned from the unmistakable shape of Laila's silhouette behind the layers of gauzy curtains. Eventually, he drew out Tristan's penknife, tracing the silver vein near the blade full of Goliath's paralyzing serum.

Séverin reached for his greatcoat and shrugged it on. He didn't look at Laila as he opened the door to their suite and took to the stairs. Instead, he turned Tristan's knife over in his hand. He twirled it once, watching the spinning blade turn to molten silver. The roses Tristan had planted were long since dead, torn out of the dirt when he had ordered the hotel landscapers to raze the Seven Sins Garden. But a cutting remained in his office, waiting for new ground and a place to put down roots. He understood that. In *The Divine Lyrics*, he sensed richness. A future where the alchemy of those ancient words would gild his veins, cure him of human error, and its pages would become grounds rich enough to resurrect dead dreams.

THIS EARLY, THE SLEEPING Palace still slumbered.

The ice blossoms once open had closed. The gargoyles curled into tight crystals, horned heads tucked beneath their wings. From the windows, the blue light streaming into the glass atrium was the color of drowning and silence. Though the floor was mostly opaque, a handful of transparent squares revealed the lake's depths far beneath him, and as he walked, Séverin caught the pale underbelly of a hunting lamprey.

In the eaves stood bent and broken statues of women with their hands either sliced off or tied behind their backs. With every step, the small hairs on the back of Séverin's neck prickled. It was too cold, too bare, too still. Whoever made this place considered the Sleeping Palace holy . . . but it was holy in the way of saint's bones and bundles of martyr's teeth. An eerie rictus of a cathedral that called itself hallowed, and one needed to believe it just to bear the sight of it.

Séverin crossed the atrium, running through what he'd seen the day before in the ice grotto . . . the stairs leading to the sunken platform and the three iced-over shields, the pool of water and the ice menagerie turning their heads as one to watch them. Out of all the rooms and floors of the Sleeping Palace, *that* was the one that felt like its cold, beating heart.

He was on the verge of rounding the corner to the northern hall, when he heard footsteps chiming behind him. He frowned. The others couldn't possibly be awake already. But when he turned, he didn't see any members of his crew. Delphine approached him, carrying a mug of coffee in one hand. In the other, a plate with a piece of toast, the edges cut and sliced in diagonals. It was heavily slathered in butter, and she'd used raspberry-cherry jam. His favorite combination as a child.

"I guessed you would be up early," she said. "This is the time where only ghosts rouse us from sleep."

She glided forward, offering the food. Séverin didn't move. What game was she playing? First, there was the tea, then she'd requested access to him during his convalescing, and now she was bringing him toast?

"Then why are you awake?" he asked coldly.

"I have ghosts myself," she said. "Ghosts of decisions made. Ghosts of loves lost . . . of family departed."

She hesitated at the last part, and memories of Tristan knifed into his thoughts. She had no right to conjure him.

"He was a good boy," she said. "Kind, and, perhaps a little too fragile—"

"*Stop,*" said Séverin. Tristan wasn't hers. She didn't get to talk about him. "What do you think you're doing?"

Delphine stiffened under his gaze.

"It's a little late to try your hand at motherhood, Madame."

Pain flashed in her eyes. He hoped it hurt. After he'd built L'Eden, he'd researched what became of his favorite *Tante*

FeeFee. He knew her husband had died, and that she'd named her nephew—a boy who had wanted to go into the priesthood—her heir, once it became clear that she could have no children of her own. He felt no pity. She'd had her chance to take care of a child, and she'd forsaken him. Meanwhile, he'd spent days waiting for her at windows; hours praying to be someone else, someone she would want to keep.

"Séverin—" she tried, but he raised his hand.

He swiped the toast off the plate and grabbed the coffee.

"Thank you for your generosity," he said, turning on his heel.

"You should know they're growing curious," she called out after him.

He stopped and looked over his shoulder.

Delphine continued. "The Order," she said. "The Winter Conclave is in six days, and they want to know why House Kore, House Nyx, and House Dazbog have yet to arrive. They want to know if we've *found* something worthy of their notice. I am oath bound to inform them of my whereabouts should I not arrive on time to the Winter Conclave. I cannot keep them away from here forever."

Séverin clenched his jaw. The last thing he wanted was this place crawling with members of the Order . . . contaminating his hunting grounds.

"Then allow me to make haste, Madame."

HE UNDERSTOOD THE ICE grotto now.

Alone, he'd flooded most of the room with light from Forged floating lanterns. About fifteen feet away from the entrance appeared the stairs leading to the sunken platform. At the right stood the menagerie of ice animals. On the left, the wall of ice. Against the northern wall, three iced-over shields that looked roughly waist-high gleamed beneath a row of unsettling statues. The ice would need to be removed to figure out if there was any writing on the shields, but for now, Séverin turned his attention to the pool on the left of the statues. There, the waters of Lake Baikal silently churned. The pool was the size of a small dining table, its edges jagged and glittering dully.

He'd tested the other aspects as well. Yesterday when he'd taken a step onto the staircase, something had shot out of the walls. Now, he could make out the sign of three bullet-shaped protrusions situated at the angles of the room . . . right where an intruder might cross. He had an inkling of how he might have triggered the alarms, but it was worth testing just to be sure.

Séverin took one of the floating lanterns, removing the Forged device that allowed it to hover so that it dropped to the floor. He kicked it, and it rolled to the staircase. The moment it crossed the boundary, the protrusions on the wall swiveled, facing the lantern. At the other end, where the ice menagerie stood, a creature—this time a crystalline moose—swung its head, loping into the room. Séverin didn't move. Instead, he watched the lantern. From the wall, an ice bullet identical to the one that had caught him yesterday on his nose and mouth shot out, splintering the lantern and gutting the light.

Instantly, the moose stopped moving, It lowered its head for a beat, its hooves poised to paw the ground and charge. A few seconds later, it lifted its head, turned, and trotted back into the menagerie.

Séverin smiled.

He'd just confirmed what triggered the security system: *heat*.

Which meant he needed someone who could counteract it. Someone good with ice.

HOURS LATER, he was no longer alone. Laila stood wrapped in an extravagant coat just outside the entrance of the ice grotto. Hypnos, Zofia, and Enrique fanned out around her, as if she were their center. In the middle of the ice grotto stood Ruslan and Eva. Ruslan wore a hideous fur hat and kept stroking it as if it were a pet.

"Is it necessary that I am a trial rat in your inventions, cousin?" he asked Eva.

She nodded. "It is also entirely unnecessary for you to speak."

Ruslan scowled. They all watched as he took one step toward the sunken platform . . . then another . . . until his boot crossed the boundary. Everyone held still. Séverin looked at the ice menagerie, but the animals neither moved nor blinked. Ruslan turned slowly on the spot. Eva triumphantly tossed her red hair over her shoulder:

"See? I told you, you needed me."

Séverin nodded, not looking at her, but at the boots on Ruslan's feet, Forged to conceal a person's body temperature and allow them to walk down the staircase and access the sunken platform without triggering the creatures. He was dimly aware of the way her gaze fixed on him. She'd saved him, and he'd thanked her. If she mistook resuscitation for romance, it was hardly his problem, so long as she didn't get in his way.

"Well done, Eva!" said Ruslan. "And well done, *me*, for not dying."

Eva rolled her eyes, but she looked pleased with herself. Ruslan walked back up the stairs. When he reached them, he took off his boots and handed them to Séverin. His eyes shone with unnerving sincerity.

"I am so *deeply* eager to see what you will find," he said, clapping his hands excitedly. "I can still sense it, you know, that pulsing thrumming deliciousness of the universe waiting for her secrets to be unearthed."

"What, exactly, do you expect us to find?"

"*I* expect knowledge. That's all," said Ruslan, stroking the sling of his injured arm. "That is all I ever want. It is in knowledge, after all, that we find the tools to make history."

"A rather ambitious goal to make history," said Séverin.

Ruslan beamed. "Isn't it? I'm delighted. I never had the head—or perhaps the hair—for ambition, and I find that I like it." He smiled and patted Séverin on the head. "Goodbye, then."

Annoyed, Séverin smoothed his hair. When he turned around, the others had been fitted with their new boots. Zofia had first designed a pair of shoes for traction on ice and an ability to shift from shoe to ski at a moment's notice. But Eva had now Forged it to conceal temperature, which turned them glossy and iridescent, like an oil slick on a frozen pond.

"No thanks from you, Monsieur Montagnet-Alarie?" asked Eva, sidling up beside him.

"You have my thanks already," he said, distracted.

"So taciturn!" Eva laughed. "Is that how he thanks you, Laila?"

"Not at all," said Laila, her fingers grazing the diamond necklace at her throat.

Eva's gaze narrowed, and her smile sharpened. Her hand went to her own throat and to a slender silver pendant hanging from a chain. She tugged it sharply. "Diamonds for services rendered. You *must* be exceptional—"

Out the corner of his eye, Séverin saw Enrique's head snap up in fury, while Laila's fingers stilled on her necklace.

"Leave," said Séverin sharply.

Eva startled, her sentence left unfinished.

"Your help is much appreciated, but for this next part, I need to be with my team. Patriarch Hypnos will serve as Order witness. It's nearly noon, and we have no time to waste."

Eva's eyes flashed.

"Of course, Monsieur," she said tightly, before stalking down the hall.

Enrique coughed awkwardly, nudging Hypnos beside him. Laila stared at the floor, her arms crossed. Only Zofia serenely continued to lace her boots.

"You know, I really do *adore* this sheen," said Hypnos, pivoting on one heel. "*Très chic.* I wonder, though, what other garments might work as ice? Ice robe? Ice crown? Nothing too cold, though. One's tongue tends to stick to these things."

Zofia frowned. "Why is your tongue relevant to this discussion?"

"You mean: 'When is my tongue *not* relevant?'"

"That is not what I mean," said Zofia.

Laila straightened her coat, then looked down the hall. "Shall we?"

One by one, Laila, Enrique, and Zofia walked down the narrow aisle and into the ice grotto. Séverin was on the verge of following when he felt a touch at his arm. Hypnos.

The other boy stared at him with concern, his mouth pulled down.

"Are you well? After yesterday?" he asked. "I meant to ask, and I waited with the others but then . . . then I fell asleep."

Séverin frowned. "I'm here, aren't I?"

He started moving away when Hypnos lowered his voice. "Have I done something wrong?"

Séverin turned to look at him. "Have you?"

"No?"

But there was a flicker of hesitation behind his eyes. As if he knew something.

"Is it so impossible for me to express some concern about you?" demanded Hypnos. His blue eyes flashed, nostrils flaring just slightly. "Did you forget that we were practically raised together for some time? Because I *haven't*. For God's sake, Séverin, we were practically brothers—"

Séverin squeezed his eyes shut. That terrible memory in the Jardin du Luxembourg bit into his thoughts, and for a moment he was a small boy once more, calling out to Hypnos, with his hand outstretched. He remembered the moment when Hypnos saw him—their eyes meeting across the park—before the other boy turned.

"We were never brothers," said Séverin.

Hypnos's throat moved. He looked at the ground. "Well, you were the closest I had to one."

For a moment, Séverin could say nothing. He didn't want to remember how he and Hypnos had played next to each other, or how he had once cried as a child when Hypnos had to go back to his own home.

"Perhaps you felt I'd forgotten you after your parents died, but I never did, Séverin. I swear it," said Hypnos, his voice breaking. "There was nothing I could do."

Something in Hypnos's voice almost convinced him . . . but that thought held terror. He could not be trusted with another brother. He could barely survive Tristan dying in his arms. What if that happened to Hypnos next? All because he had let him get too close? The thought pinched sharply behind his ribs.

Séverin turned from him. "I only had one brother, Hypnos. I'm not looking for a replacement."

With that, he walked down the hall.

"TAKE A LOOK AT this!" called Enrique.

Enrique held up a lantern. Finally, the sunken platform was truly illuminated. Séverin staggered back in disgust as the light · caught hold of the female statues. From their recessed niches in the wall, they leaned out, extending their arms severed at the wrist. They looked grotesque. Their jaws had been ruined—or clawed— and designed to look unhinged.

"They're downright eerie to look at, don't you think?" asked Enrique, shuddering. "Almost lifelike. And, wait, I believe those markings on their mouth are *symbols* . . ."

Enrique held up his Mnemo bug, recording the statues and talking rapidly, but Séverin was no longer paying attention. He was watching Laila's face as she moved toward the statues, utterly transfixed. She'd slipped off one of her fur-lined gloves, stretching up on her toes as her bare hand reached toward the statues.

Above them, the giant moon changed shape with each passing minute, gradually growing full. He glanced at his watch and realized it would show a "full moon" right at noon. Séverin glanced over the room. He was missing something. If this place was supposed to be a sanctum, then why keep an eye on the time? What was the point?

His watch struck noon.

From the still pool of water came the sound of distant churning, like a submerged roll of thunder. The ground quivered. Hardly a moment ago, that great oval of water had lain smooth and flat as a mirror.

It wasn't smooth and flat anymore. It rippled, small waves sloshing out the side.

Something was coming.

"Move! Get *back*!" shouted Séverin.

Out the corner of his eye, he saw Laila's hand splayed against the statues, her eyes wide and shocked. He lurched forward, grabbing her and pulling her backward just as a creature made of metal shot out of the water. A biblical word rose to his mind: *leviathan*. A sea monster. It surged out of the oval, sinuous, snake-like, with a sharp snout like that of an eel shooting from the waves as steam plumed from the steel-fretted gills at its throat. When it cracked open its mechanical jaws, Séverin saw a hellscape of iron eel teeth. Its bulbous, glass eyes roved wildly as it dove back down—

Toward *them*.

Séverin ran to the door, yanking open the entrance and bracing himself for an attack that never came. The leviathan dove up, then curled down, its giant head resting on the ice and its jaws propped open.

The clock on the wall struck the third chime of noon.

Séverin felt his thoughts ram together, trying to arrange a puzzle that was missing a critical piece. But then he felt Hypnos pulling him through the door—

"What the hell were you waiting for?" he demanded.

The door closed, seaming the monster shut behind its walls. His heart raced. His mind tried to cling to every detail that he'd just seen: pale eyes and teeth, the chime of noon.

Hypnos clutched his heart. "Will it come after us?"

"I don't think it can fit through the door," said Zofia.

Enrique crossed himself. "Laila, did you—"

But he stopped. All of them stopped when they looked at Laila. Tears streamed down her face. The sight twisted inside Séverin.

"Laila, *ma chère*, what is it?" asked Hypnos.

"Those s-statues," she choked. "They're not statues."

She raised her gaze, her eyes finding Séverin's. "They're dead girls."

18

ENRIQUE

Enrique caught his breath.

He knew they had just gotten attacked by a mechanical leviathan, but it was the statues—no, the *girls*—who kept pushing to the forefront of his mind. There was something across their mouths, something that demanded noticing.

"Did anyone notice the symbols—" he started, only for Séverin to whirl on him, his eyes feral with anger.

"Not *now*," he said harshly.

Shame spread hot through his stomach. He was only trying to help. There was something about the arrangement of those girls that reeked of intention. Follow the intention, find the treasure. That was what Séverin used to say. Enrique was only trying to do that, and not for himself and whatever glory it might buy him, but for Laila. Out of the faith that what he did could have meaning to the people who mattered most.

What if what he'd seen could help them find *The Divine Lyrics*?

Then she would live. His research on the book had sometimes mentioned the lore of female guardians. Between that and the dead girls in the grotto, Enrique sensed the possibility of a connection. It called to him like a kernel of a secret, and he needed to root it out.

By now, Eva had rushed to meet them in the atrium of the Sleeping Palace. Séverin quickly told her what had happened in the ice grotto.

"A mechanical *leviathan*?" Eva repeated, staring back down the hallways.

"And all those girls," whispered Laila. "Strung up like . . ."

She couldn't finish her sentence. Enrique tried to reach for her hand, but she startled when the matriarch rushed into the atrium. Delphine Desrosiers never had a hair out of place. He didn't even think her shadow dared to stretch across a sidewalk without her permission. But when she ran in now, her eyes looked wild and her steel-colored hair frizzed around her face.

"They said there was an attack," she said breathlessly.

Her eyes went straight to Séverin, but he wasn't looking at her.

"Are you hurt?" asked Delphine.

"No," said Séverin.

Finally, she wrenched her gaze from Séverin and glanced over everyone else. When she caught sight of Laila, her face softened. She took off her own cloak and draped it around Laila's shoulders.

"I'll take her. She needs some hot broth and a blanket," said Delphine. She narrowed her eyes at Séverin when he moved to block her. "Not you."

Laila looked so frail, the great fur coat hanging off her shoulders. Beside him, Séverin watched her a beat too long . . . and then he turned his face and stared down the hallway.

"We need eyes on whatever is inside that room," he said darkly. "And we need to make sure it can't get *out*."

Zofia nodded. "I've got an incendiary net prepped and ready. There are Mnemo bugs already positioned to record its movements inside the grotto."

"I'll get the Sphinxes," said Eva. "They've got motion-sensitive thread and enough weapons to alert us if it makes it past the door."

"I'll come with you," said Hypnos, looking at Eva. "For all we know, that *thing* might already be planning to sneak into the atrium—"

"The leviathan didn't look as if it was designed to leave . . . ," said Enrique, thinking of how the creature had shot into the air only to rest its head, snake-like, on the ice.

"I agree," said Zofia. "Its dimensions are not compatible with the hallway space. It would destroy the beauty of its mechanism."

At least someone was listening to him, he thought glumly. While Séverin and Hypnos discussed new schematics, and Eva and Zofia examined a Forging net, Enrique stood there with the Mnemo bug clutched in his sweaty palm. Invisible.

"We need to discuss the girls."

Enrique didn't say statues. He wouldn't disrespect them that way, but he could feel his word choice shuddering through the group.

"Not *now*, Enrique, just go and—" Séverin stopped mid-sentence as another attendant ran forward with news about the leviathan in the grotto.

Enrique clutched his Mnemo bug tighter. He wished Séverin cared enough to at least finish his insult. Commotion whirled around him, and he decided, suddenly, that if he was useless here, then he might as well make himself useful elsewhere.

"I am going to find the library," he announced to no one.

Zofia looked up from her work. "The one that didn't have books?"

"The very same," said Enrique tightly.

Aside from Zofia, no one said anything. Enrique stood there a moment longer, then awkwardly cleared his throat. Hypnos looked up, his blue eyes slanted in confusion.

"Perhaps you could escort me to the library?" asked Enrique.

Hypnos blinked. For a second, his gaze slid to Séverin as if waiting for permission. The gesture rankled Enrique, who nearly turned on his heel when Hypnos finally nodded and smiled.

"Of course, *mon cher.*"

Away from the others, Hypnos seemed lost in thought, his brow creased as he fiddled with the crescent-shaped Babel Ring on his hand. Enrique waited for him to ask about the girls, to notice that Enrique had been trying to speak, but Hypnos said nothing. The wide double doors of the library loomed ahead. Hypnos would leave him there, and finally Enrique's impatience won out.

"Do you think those girls are the missing victims from twenty years ago?" asked Enrique.

Hypnos looked up from his ring. "Hmm?"

"The girls . . . ," prompted Enrique. "They might be the same ones from the stories in the area."

Hypnos grimaced. "I think you're right."

"And the way they were *arranged,*" said Enrique, emboldened. "It seemed purposeful. What if they're part of the key to finding *The Divine Lyrics*? I was thinking about how in the seventeenth century, there's a connection between—"

"My handsome historian," said Hypnos. He stopped walking

and turned to him, rubbing his thumb along the top of Enrique's cheekbone. "Your words are dazzling, but now isn't the time."

"But—"

"I have to go, *mon cher*," said Hypnos, backing away. "Right now, Séverin needs me. I need to consult with Ruslan, check with the Sphinxes, etcetera, etcetera." He flailed his hand. "Normally, responsibility gives me indigestion, but I find myself rather motivated."

He leaned forward, kissing Enrique.

"I have every faith you'll solve what needs solving and dazzle us all! Immerse yourself in your research, *mon cher*, it's—"

"What I do best," finished Enrique flatly.

Hypnos looked puzzled for a moment, then smiled and walked away. Enrique stared after him, trying not to let those words—*what you do best*—sink their teeth into his heart. Of course Hypnos was preoccupied. That's all. He would've listened otherwise, wouldn't he?

Numbly, Enrique reached for the door handle. Only once did he look over his shoulder to see if Hypnos noticed that he'd paused outside the doors. But the other boy never turned. As Enrique walked inside, he felt as if someone had taken the nightmare of waiting for the Ilustrados in the library auditorium and turned it inside out . . . the slow dread of waiting and hoping to be heard inverted to standing before an audience that could not hear him.

THE "LIBRARY" SEEMED to Enrique like the entrance to an abandoned temple. Past the double doors lay a marble aisle stippled with light from the panes of skylights above, so that it seemed to undulate. Marble pillars held up the ceiling. Four on each side of the aisle, and one at the end, each of them carved with the likeness of one of the nine muses.

On his right stood Clio, for history; Euterpe, for music; Erato, for love poetry; Melpomene, for tragedy. On his left stood Polymnia, for hymnals; Terpsichore for dance; Thalia, for comedy, and Ourania for astronomy. At the end of the long aisle stood one muse set apart from her sisters as the chief of them all . . . Calliope. The muse of epic poetry, revered in mythology for the ecstatic transcendence of her voice.

All of them held an object most associated with them: writing tablets and masks, lyres and scrolls. And yet, when Enrique looked closer, wandering over to examine the pillars, he saw that each of the objects were *broken*. Split down the middle or else lying in stony heaps at the goddesses' feet. It struck Enrique as a strange artistic choice.

Empty bookshelves covered nearly all the wall space, and yet, when Enrique breathed deeply, he caught the scent of books. Of binding and pages and tales eager to be known. Knowledge was coy. It liked to hide beneath the shroud of myth, place its heart in a fairy tale, as if it were a prize at the end of the quest. Perhaps whatever knowledge here was similar. Perhaps it wished to be wooed and coaxed forth.

Each of the nine muses leaning out of the pillars had one hand extended, as if in greeting or invitation. Enrique hoisted up the dossier of his research beneath his arm, then touched the icy marble hand of Erato, muse of love poetry.

At his touch, the marble muse shivered and split down the middle like a clever pair of double doors that unfurled into shelves. Enrique stepped back, awed. The shelves stretched higher than his head, the sound of the churning wooden gears chewing up the silence around him. When they fell silent, still at last, he reached for the books. At first glance, each tome seemed to be related to love poetry. Enrique studied the titles down the spines: *Pyramus and Thisbe, Troilus and Cressida . . . Laila and Majnun.* That stopped him. Laila and Majnun? Wasn't "Majnun" what Laila had once called Séverin? Enrique's skin crawled. He had an uncomfortable flashback to throwing open the door to his parents' bedroom after a harrowing nightmare only to be met with another one.

"Ugh," he muttered, putting the book hastily back on the shelf.

As he turned his head, a strange design leapt out at him, whittled onto the edge of Erato's hand. He hadn't noticed it until the statue, or bookcase as it were, had fully opened. It was like the number *3* flipped:

Enrique traced it delicately. Curious, he thought. Was it the signature of the artisan? He made a quick notation of the symbol and returned to the muse of history. He set up a stand and a projection display for his Mnemo bug.

In his hands, the Mnemo bug felt heavy.

Either he was a fool who had seen nothing on those dead girls' mouths or he had seen something, and, well, perhaps he was still a fool, but at least he was a fool with observational skills.

Moment of truth, he thought, fixing the Mnemo to the projection.

Just before he could press the display button, the doors of the library flew open, and in stepped a pair of unfamiliar guards. Judging by the snow-dusted fur collar at their throats, they were sentinels positioned outside the Sleeping Palace. The metallic sun that flared on the lapels of their fur coats marked them as delegates from House Dazbog.

"What business do you have here?"

"I am with Séverin Montagnet-Alarie, on business with the Order of Babel—" he started.

One of the guards interrupted, "Oh, now I remember you . . . What are you, his servant?"

"Valet?" said the other with a laugh. "What are you doing in a room full of books?"

Enrique's face burned. He was so tired. Of no one listening, or bothering to listen. But then, behind the guards came the fall of thunderous footsteps as Ruslan entered the room and scowled.

"This man is a scholar," he corrected.

The Dazbog guards looked chastened.

"Our apologies, Patriarch," said one, kneeling.

The other kneeled too, muttering his apologies.

"Remove your hats!" said Ruslan.

The guards did as told, their hair snow-damp and rumpled. Ruslan made a *tch!* sound at the back of his throat.

"You don't deserve your hair," he muttered. "Go away before I shave your heads."

From Ruslan, this seemed like a legitimate threat, and the guards immediately scuttled away. Ruslan watched them go, then whirled back to Enrique, his eyes bright with regret.

"I am sorry," said Ruslan.

Enrique desperately wanted to say something suave like Hypnos or enigmatic like Séverin . . . but all he had was the truth.

"It's fine. It's not the first time," he said. "And it probably will not be my last."

Ruslan regarded him for a moment, and then his shoulders fell a fraction. "I understand that."

That took Enrique by surprise. "How do you mean?"

With his uninjured hand, Ruslan gestured to his own face, turning from side to side.

"Not the most Russian profile in the world, is it?" said Ruslan.

"Well . . ."

Enrique knew the Russian Empire was huge, with citizens who looked as varied as hues in a rainbow, but there was something Enrique recognized in Ruslan's features. A gap, in a way, where *otherness* snuck in and blurred his features. He recognized it because he saw it in his own reflection every day.

"I know," he said, then patted the top of his head. "I don't know who my mother was. I imagine she was a Buryat native or a Kyrgyz woman or what have you. Then again, they have such *excellent* hair that one would think I would've inherited it! Rude. Ah well. It does not matter. What does matter is that the part of her that clings to me is the part no one seems to like. So I understand, Mr. Mercado-Lopez. And I see what you wish to hide."

Enrique felt a hard lump in his throat. It took him a while before he could muster the strength to talk again.

"I'm glad I'm not alone."

"You most certainly are not," said Ruslan kindly. He thrummed his fingers against the sling of his injured arm, then turned about the room. He let out a sigh. "Eva told me all about your rather disturbing discovery. Young women *dead* in these halls?" He shuddered. "I don't blame you for escaping into the quiet of this room."

Escaping? Was that what everyone thought he was doing? His cheeks warmed.

"I didn't come here to be alone with my thoughts," he said, fumbling with the Mnemo bug. "I came here to research and study what I saw in the grotto. I think there's a link between those girls and the Fallen House's treasures. And I'm quite certain those girls are the truth behind the ghost stories here."

Ruslan blinked at him. "Ghosts?"

"The . . . ghost stories about this area?" clarified Enrique, but Ruslan's face was still blank. "Hyp—I mean, Patriarch Hypnos— told me that this area terrified the locals so badly that House Dazbog even investigated. Nothing was ever found, though."

"Ah, yes," said Ruslan, shaking his head. "If those really are the same victims, I am glad they can be laid to rest. Though what does it have to do with the Fallen House's treasures?"

Enrique had his ideas, but maybe they were foolish. He was about to say so when he caught the way Ruslan looked at him. Wide-eyed and excited. Tristan used to be like this, eager to hear what he had to say, even if he hadn't the faintest clue what he was talking about. It was intoxicating, he thought, to be so clearly seen by someone else.

He slid the Mnemo into the projection. He did not want to go straight to the image of the girls. He needed to think through his process before jumping to a conclusion that could change the course of how they treated the ice grotto. Instead, he brought up a couple of images that had cropped up throughout his research in Paris. One was of the Matsue Castle of Japan. Another image followed, this time of a bridge, then another temple, then a design torn from the pages of a medieval book on Arthurian legends showing a tower balancing atop a red-and-white dragon fighting beneath the ground.

"All of these buildings have one aspect in common," said Enrique. "Foundation sacrifice. In Japan, they called this practice *hitobashira*, an act of human sacrifice specifically done around the construction of institutions like temples or bridges. In this area, in and around the Ural Mountains, the ancient Scythians and Mongolians had similar constructions with their *kurgan* burial sites, where warriors would be buried with all their riches and sometimes various servants and guards, so that the spirits of the sacrificed went on to act as guardians."

As he spoke, he saw the stories he referenced stretch out before him. He saw them linking back to the girls in the ice grotto and their ruined mouths. He wondered at their pain and their fear, all of it sliced through with the taste of snow and blood, metal and cold.

"In terms of the positioning of the girls . . . it feels similar to that ritualistic sacrifice, though we need more concrete proof before I can make that leap," said Enrique.

"But you think that the presence of the dead girls might be proof that there's treasure in that room? That there's something to be guarded?"

Enrique nodded hesitantly and then maneuvered the Mnemo bug to the last and final image, the one of the dead girls above the three shields. It was bad enough they had been murdered and strung up, but if their jaws held a symbol, then it might be a clue.

"Dear God," breathed Ruslan, his eyes widening in horror.

Enrique stared up at the image, his heart twisting. He made a quick sign of the cross down his body. He wasn't like Séverin or

Zofia, who could separate the human story from the treasure hunt. All he *saw* were stories . . . lives cut short, dreams withered from cold and forgotten, families torn apart. How many girls had gone missing for this? How many people had been left wondering where they'd gone? When all this time, they had been here, and no one could find them.

Across the mottled skin of the girls' mouths and cheeks lay precise and terrible slashes and puncture wounds, a grisly and unmistakable cipher that weighed down Enrique's next words:

"Those girls are the key to the treasure."

19

ZOFIA

Three days until Winter Conclave . . .

Zosia,

Do you remember the chicken soup Mama made with ey-erlekh? You used to call it "sun soup." I crave that so dearly right now.

I do not wish to worry you, but my cough has returned, and though I feel weak, I know I will get better. The boy delivering my medicine left me a flower today. He's handsome, Zofia. Handsome enough that perhaps I don't mind having to stay in bed all day if it means he comes to visit. His name is Isaac . . .

ALONE IN THE GROTTO, Zofia decided to test a theory.

"Seventy-one, seventy-two, seventy-three," she said aloud, counting the leviathan's teeth.

For the past three days, Zofia had tracked every movement within the ice grotto. Every day at noon the grotto moon turned full, and the mechanical creature surged out of the water, placed its head onto the ice, and opened its jaws. For sixty minutes, it would stay still before sliding back into the water.

Zofia considered the leviathan a calming presence. The machine never deviated from its schedule. It was not alive, but the quiet whirring of its metal gears reminded her of a cat's rumbling purr.

As of this morning, Zofia's recorded observations had convinced Séverin that the leviathan followed a pattern, and that the grotto was safe to explore. From there, Order members had removed the dead girls from the walls, leaving behind a Mnemo projection that outlined their original positioning and the symbols carved into their skin. Laila had not watched the removal process, but Zofia knew that she would be with the girls now.

The thought turned her stomach, reminding her once again that Laila could die. She couldn't let that happen, and yet she didn't know what to do. Lately, Zofia suspected she had more in common with the mechanical leviathan than anyone in the Sleeping Palace. She understood what it meant to be powerless, treading the same routine, the same path. She had felt it with Tristan. The night he died, she had sat in her laboratory for hours, counting all the objects that could not save him. She had felt it with Hela when she had gone back to Poland, unable to do anything but hold Hela's hand and watch as her sister fought to breathe.

She would not do that with Laila.

Zofia reached up and held onto one of the leviathan's fangs as she took one step into its mouth. The waters of Lake Baikal rushed around her ankles. Beneath her shoes, the surface was flat and grooved for traction.

Zofia snapped off a Forged button from her coat, and it lengthened into a small unlit torch. Ignite, she thought, and a flame rasped alive. For the first time, she could see *down* the metal creature's throat. The terrain changed, opening into a flat space, then a steep drop, followed by another flat space . . . like a staircase. Above her, splayed against the back of the creature's throat lay deep grooves, symbols clearly engraved in the metal—

It looked similar to the symbols Enrique had discovered on the dead girls' mouths. Zofia pressed the record function on her moth-shaped Mnemo bug. Enrique still hadn't cracked the code. Maybe this could help. In her other hand, Zofia drew out a pendant, Forged to detect the presence of a Tezcat door within a fifty feet radius. The pendant lit up slowly, and Zofia's pulse kicked up.

There was a Tezcat presence inside the grotto. Where did it lead? Outside? Or somewhere else entirely? Zofia eyed the leviathan's throat. It might even be farther inside the leviathan. She was about to take another step when someone shrieked: "What the hell are you doing?"

Enrique ran toward her, nearly skidding on the ice. Zofia paused. She'd thought Enrique was in the library. Instead, he ducked his head beneath the leviathan's jaws, grasping her by the shoulders and tugging her out until she stumbled and fell against his chest.

"Wait!" she cried out.

The Tezcat pendant in her hand went flying, skidding across

the ice and landing with a metallic chime against one of the three shields on the far wall.

Enrique's brown eyes looked hectic, and sweat sheened his face. He was—as Laila would say—"in a state."

"Are you all right?" asked Zofia.

Enrique stared at her. "Am *I* all right? Zofia, you nearly got swallowed up by that . . . that *thing*—" he said, flailing a hand at the leviathan. "Wh-what were you doing?"

Zofia crossed her arms. "Testing a theory."

"A theory of what?"

"A theory that there is a Tezcat portal presence within the grotto. The leviathan does not stay on the ice for more than an hour, thus it was the highest priority to explore. After that, I was going to test the three metal shield plates on the back wall," she said. "The leviathan deserves further examination. There appeared to be stairs inside it, and I plan to see where they lead."

"I think *not*," retorted Enrique. "If there were stairs to hell, would you venture down those?"

"It depends on what was inside hell, and if I needed it."

At that moment, Enrique's expression became unreadable. Zofia searched his features, feeling that same pulse of awareness that now followed when she looked at him too long.

"You're something else, Phoenix," said Enrique.

Her stomach fell. "Something bad."

Enrique's face warred between a scowl and a smile, and she could not decipher it.

"Something . . . brave," he said finally.

Brave?

"But that's not *always* a good thing," he rushed to say. His

206 ᘓ ROSHANI CHOKSHI

eyes darted to the leviathan, and he shuddered. "That thing is terrifying."

Zofia disagreed, but she understood. "Why are you here?"

Enrique sighed. "I can't crack those symbols. I'm sure it's a coded alphabet of some kind, but I thought perhaps leaving the library for a change might give me a burst of divine inspiration."

Zofia lifted the Mnemo bug: "I found more of those symbols inside the leviathan's mouth."

"You *did*?" asked Enrique. He glanced at the leviathan and back, then stood straighter. His brows pressed down and he pursed his lips. Zofia recognized it as the expression he assumed when he was about to do something he didn't want. "Can I see it—"

Just then, a huff of steam escaped through the leviathan's gills, and Enrique jumped back with a squeak.

"And my sense of self-preservation reasserts itself once more," he said, crossing himself. "Please tell me you recorded the symbols? And, hold on . . . wait." Enrique paused, staring at something just over her shoulder. "What's *that*?"

Zofia followed his gaze. On the ice lay the Tezcat pendant. Only now, instead of its dim glow, it had turned brighter, like a beacon. Which was something it only did in the direct presence of a Tezcat portal. She turned from Enrique, walking toward the pendant and the three shields still covered in ice.

"Zofia," hissed Enrique. "The leviathan is *right* there! Get away from it!"

She ignored him, walked past the leviathan—but not before patting its jaw and hearing a muted whimper from Enrique—and headed to the wall of ice. The three shields in the wall had a radius of at least ten feet each. Ropes of thick ice splattered across the front, but she could see a pattern under it: the metal beneath was not smooth. Zofia bent to pick up the Tezcat pendant, still glowing brightly before the first shield. Enrique's boots crunched on the ice as he joined her.

"Once you get that pendant, can we leave? We'll tell the others to join us after that creature disappears in the water," he said. He had his shoulders hunched up around his ears. A pattern of fear. When he looked once more at the metal shields, his shoulders dropped and he frowned. "There's something written under here. Or drawn? I . . . I can't tell."

"You can go because you are frightened," said Zofia. "I'll stay."

Enrique groaned, glancing at the shield and then the leviathan before letting out a sigh.

"I am frightened," he said quietly. "It's a constant state of being I have yet to make peace with." The corner of his mouth tipped up in a smile. "Perhaps constant exposure will help."

"You're not leaving?" asked Zofia.

Enrique squared his shoulders. "No."

She liked that Enrique could say he was scared and still be brave. It made her want to be brave too. When she considered this, an unfamiliar warmth curled through her belly.

Enrique tilted his head. "Hello? Phoenix?"

Zofia shook herself, then turned her attention back to the glowing phosphorous pendant in her hand.

"My inventions haven't been wrong before," she said. "If this is glowing before that shield, then it's a Tezcat. In fact—"

She crossed the length of the wall, passing each of the three shields as she held up the pendant. Not once did the glow fade.

"All three of these shields are separate Tezcats," said Enrique, his jaw falling open slightly.

"What do you think is behind it?" asked Zofia. "The treasure?"

Enrique made a face. "I don't know . . . why would it be behind a portal? That would mean it wasn't actually in the room but somewhere else, and after all the symbols and the girls . . . something about that doesn't seem . . . appropriate. Maybe the symbols on the metal will tell us more, but we need to melt the ice. Perhaps I can ask the matriarch for one of her heat fans or . . . oh. Well. I suppose that works too."

Zofia had pocketed the phosphorous pendant and reached for a heat-radiating locket from her necklace. She slapped it onto the shield. The ice glowed orange. With a sound like a faucet slammed to full blast, melted ice puddled to the floor. Zofia repeated this method with the two other shields, until they revealed a set of images engraved in the metal.

Enrique stared at her. "Don't take this the wrong way . . . but you strike me as dangerously flammable."

Zofia considered this. "Thank you."

"Why not," said Enrique, before turning his attention to the Tezcat door.

The circumference was entirely smooth, with no hint of a hinge or anything that might be twisted or pinched to open it and reveal what lay behind the shields. A grooved design stretched across the metal. When Zofia touched it, a familiar buzzing gathered at the edge of her thoughts, signaling the piece was Forged.

"The metal is designed to absorb something," she said, frowning. "A liquid. But not ice. Although, perhaps something that could also be present in ice, judging by the small pockmarks in the metal. It looks like it reacted to something."

Enrique pulled out a notebook and started to sketch the design.

"This symbol . . ." he said, holding it up to her. "It's weathered down quite a bit, but I recognize this."

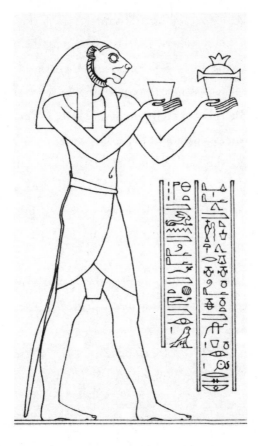

"Why does it look like a lion with a glass?" She squinted. "And . . . an urn?"

"Because it *is* a lion with a pot . . . and a *wine*glass," said Enrique. "It's showing an Egyptian god that I haven't seen depicted in ages."

Behind them came the sound of metal on ice. Zofia whirled around to see the leviathan close its jaws and slide back into the water. She glanced at the Forged moon in the grotto.

It was exactly on time.

The moment it slipped back into the water, a new sight came into view: Hypnos and Eva, standing in the entrance. The red-headed girl was holding a platter of food in her hands.

"I was looking for you both!" said Hypnos. He cast a glance at the oval of water where the creature had disappeared. "But then I was waiting for *that*"—he gestured in the direction of the leviathan—"to leave. What are you doing? Why didn't anyone invite me?" He tilted his head to one side. "Why is that lion holding a wineglass? Also, Eva brought food."

Eva gripped the platter so tightly that her knuckles looked white.

"Ruslan asked me to check on everyone's progress," she said, glowering. "I *won't* leave until that is done, so don't waste your time asking."

Zofia was still mentally sorting through Hypnos's questions and only nodded at Eva. Beside her, Enrique rubbed his temples.

"Yes," he said.

"Yes to what? To the food? The questions?" asked Hypnos. "Because 'yes' does not explain why that lion is holding a wineglass."

"Definitely yes to the food." Enrique gestured them over, and they crossed the grotto to stand before the ice wall.

Hypnos smiled at Enrique, and Zofia noticed that he did not return it. Instead, he turned toward the shield, his face blank.

"See how the symbols stretch across all three shields? They represent a god."

Hypnos frowned. "There's a god of lions and wineglasses? That seems incredibly specific."

"This god is Shezmu," said Enrique, rolling his eyes. "He's seldom depicted, perhaps because he's at such odds with himself. On the one hand, he's the lord of perfumes and precious oils, often considered something of a celebration deity."

"My kind of god," said Hypnos.

"He is also the god of slaughter, blood, and dismemberment."

"I amend my original statement," said Hypnos.

"Technically, the 'blood' translation might also stand in for 'wine.' I'm not quite sure," said Enrique. He eyed the platter of sandwiches and started to reach for one. "Either way, I'd bet he's critical to understanding how to open these Tezcats."

"Opening them?" repeated Eva.

The platter dropped from her hands and hit the floor.

"The sandwiches!" moaned Enrique.

"Why would you open it?"

"We're here to find the Fallen House's treasure," said Zofia. "That means opening things that are closed."

Eva narrowed her gaze, while Hypnos rubbed Enrique's back.

"Now about the treasure, *mon cher*," said Hypnos.

"You can't eat treasure," said Enrique, staring mournfully at the sandwiches.

"Yes, but we can still find it."

Zofia touched the metal shield once more. Through her metallurgy affinity, she knew the artist had fused together the properties of corkwood and metal . . . but there was a specific metal that affected the shield most. Something that was also present in ice, apparently, considering the minimal damage done to the original structure.

"The door wants something," said Zofia. "The metal had absorptive properties, so it seems as though it wants a liquid."

Hypnos sighed. "The longer I stare at this, the only liquid I want is wine."

Enrique snapped his fingers. "What if that's it?"

"Can't be," said Zofia. "There's no wine in ice."

"There *is* ice wine, though," said Hypnos. "Very sweet. In fact, they make an excellent vintage in Russia."

"You said he was a god of celebration—"

"And blood," said Enrique. "Or wine."

"Blood . . . or wine."

As far as she knew, there were no metallic properties in wine that someone could manipulate with an affinity.

"It's blood or *ice*," said Eva.

All of them turned to face her. Eva flexed her hand, and for the first time Zofia noticed a strange ring she wore on her pinky. It was curved like a talon.

"All blood Forging artisans are well versed in matter and mind, but we particularly excel at ice because of its metallic content."

"There's iron in both ice and blood," said Zofia slowly.

"*Naturally* occurring ice, at least," said Eva. "Boiled water left out in freezing temperatures isn't nearly as receptive to my affinity, but ice from lakes and oceans? Very rich in metal."

Enrique inched away from the shield. "So you think the door wants . . . blood?"

"Only experiment confirms hypothesis," said Zofia.

"It's *your* hypothesis. Might as well commit to it," said Eva. She uncurled her hand, her metal talon glinting. "I can make it painless."

Zofia swallowed, then held out her hand only for Hypnos to step between her and Eva. He gently pushed down her arm.

"I cannot see you hurt, *ma chère*," he said softly. "Allow me."

"Allow" was a strange word. Zofia had never considered that she might grant someone permission to protect her, and a feeling of warmth—like gulping down not-too-hot soup—settled into her chest. She stepped back wordlessly.

"You look like you have practice in such recreation, Patriarch," said Eva.

Hypnos merely held out his hand. Eva slashed her taloned ring across it, leaving his palm bloody. Grimacing, Hypnos pressed his hand to the metal. A moment passed, then two . . .

"I hope I did not ruin myself for nothing," muttered Hypnos. "That was my favorite palm, you know."

But a moment later, a change took place in the metal shield. The edges of the metal lit up, making a small puffing sound of release as it broke away from the ice wall. Enrique moved closer, and the three of them formed a tight knot as the metal door swung open like a lid covering a tunnel to reveal—

"A boarded-up brick wall?" demanded Hypnos. "I wasted my blood on *that*?"

Enrique got close to the wall, scratching at it with his nail.

"It smells awful," said Eva, recoiling.

"It's been boarded up for a long time," said Enrique, pointing to the fine trellis of moss that had broken up the brick.

"Let's try the other doors," said Zofia.

Clutching his hand, Hypnos walked to the second door. Again, he placed his palm against it. Again, the portal opened.

"Oh good, more brick," said Hypnos.

But this brick was different. A smell, like a stale pond in summer, hit her nose. The brick was damp, and when Zofia poked her head through the opening, she saw murky water far below. Above, but barely visible through the slats of boarded wood, she glimpsed cutouts of a blue sky. She could even hear the chittering of townspeople. Their language sounded close to her native Polish.

"It opens into a well," she said.

Enrique moved beside her.

"Do you see this writing?" he asked, pointing to marks on the dark bricks that made up the well. "These are signs of talismans and amulets, languages meant to ward away demons . . . There's even a name carved into the stone . . . Horowitz? Does it ring a bell?"

"It sounds Jewish," she said.

"Maybe it's the name of the well builder?"

Zofia didn't answer. She'd already moved on to the third Tezcat. After all, a door that opened into a bricked-up well would not save Laila.

"This one now," said Zofia.

"I think there's still some writing here," protested Enrique. "We've barely looked into the second door!"

Hypnos followed after her and placed his palm on the third shield. Again, they waited. Again, it opened with that same puffing sound of release.

A new scent flooded Zofia's nose. It smelled of *spices*, like the kind Laila put in her morning tea. Hot sunlight spilled out onto the ice grotto. The wide door had flung open to reveal a three-foot drop into a deserted courtyard below them. Nine broken pillars surrounded the walls of the stone courtyard. The wall on the opposite side wasn't made of stone like the others, though, but appeared to be slatted pieces of wood, through which Zofia glimpsed what looked like the green waters of a lake. Above the courtyard, open sky appeared between wooden slats draped in stained ribbons. There was writing along the wall in a language Zofia couldn't decipher. Beside her, Eva's hands had dropped to her side, her mouth slightly agape, and Enrique quickly crossed himself.

Hypnos sucked in his breath and then clapped his hands. "I'm going to get Séverin and Ruslan! No one move! Say 'promise'!"

"Promise," muttered Zofia, her eyes never leaving the statues.

The moment she knew Hypnos had gone, Zofia took a step forward. She had everything they needed already packed from her venture into the leviathan: rope, torches, sharp-edged knives, and the folded-up tools around her necklace. She needed to know whether this place held the answers they sought. Whether this place could save Laila. But no sooner had she taken a step, then Enrique caught her arm.

"What are you doing?"

"I'm only taking a look," she said, shaking him off.

"But," said Enrique in a smaller voice, "you said 'promise.'"

Zofia looked over her shoulder, one hand on the entrance to the courtyard. "I did say 'promise.'"

Out the corner of her eye, she saw Eva grin.

"I am only taking one step," said Zofia.

"Just the *one*," warned Enrique.

Small hairs on Zofia's arm bristled. *Just the one. Stay in sight. Don't move.* She could *do* this, she told herself. She could save Laila. Zofia brought out her Mnemo bug and toggled the switch to record as she hopped onto the ground. Eva landed gracefully beside her. Enrique craned his neck, but the rest of him stayed in the ice grotto.

"This place looks abandoned," he said.

Broken glasses and rusted knives littered the hard-packed dirt floor. Gouged-out holes, like the divots left behind from bullets, dotted what remained of the walls, and Zofia's stomach lurched. Her parents talked of riddled walls like this, witnesses to moments where their own people were driven out of villages. Whoever had been here had also been chased out.

And then there was the writing along the wall . . . the way the blasted pillars were not pillars after all, but statues of women. Women with their hands behind their backs. It looked familiar.

Hadn't Enrique pointed out something similar when they had first walked down the hall that led to the ice grotto? She took another step forward.

"Zofia, wait!" called out Enrique.

"Oh, don't be such a coward," said Eva. "This place is practically dead."

Zofia shrugged off her fur coat.

"I recognize the writing on the wall," said Eva. "I think . . . I think we're in Istanbul."

"In the *Ottoman Empire*?" asked Enrique from above her.

But Eva didn't have time to answer. Because from the wall on the right came the sounds of a chair scraping back. The next second, she saw a plume of smoke. Someone stepped into the shadows of a statue. Instantly, the pillars lurched to life, the broken faces of nine statues swiveling toward them.

An old, smoke-rasped voice declared:

"You shall not take another."

20

LAILA

When Laila was a child, her mother made her a doll.

It was the first—and last—toy she ever owned.

The doll was made from the husks of banana leaves, stitched together with the ends of the gold thread that had once fringed her mother's wedding *sari*. It had burnt eyes of charcoal, and long black hair fashioned from the mane of her father's favorite water buffalo.

Every night, Laila's mother rubbed sweet almond oil into the scar on her back, and every night Laila held still, terror gripping her heart. She feared that if her mother pressed too hard, she would split down the middle. And so she held her doll tight, but not too tight. After all, the doll was like her: a fragile thing.

"Do you know what you and this doll have in common, my love?" her mother had asked. "Both of you were made to be loved."

To Laila, the doll was a promise.

If she could love its stitched-together form, then she too could be loved.

When her mother died, she took the doll everywhere. She took it to dance practice, so it could learn the same movements she did and remember her mother with each sharp stamp of her heel and flick of her wrist. She took it to the kitchens, so it could learn the harmony of spice and salt, and the relief that this place was a sanctum. Every night, when Laila held the doll close, she felt her own emotion and her own memory replaying behind her eyes like a dream that would not end, and though she had grief, she did not have nightmares.

One morning, she awoke to find it gone. She rushed into the hall . . . but it was too late. Her father stood by the hearth, watching as scarlet flames fed upon the doll, charring out its eyes, gulping down the single braid of its hair that Laila had so carefully arranged to match her own. The room smelled of singed parts. All the while, her father did not look at her.

"It would've fallen apart sooner or later," he said, crossing his arms. "No use keeping it around. Besides, you're far too old for such childish things."

Afterwards, he left her to kneel before the flames. Laila watched until the doll was nothing more than soft ash and the muted glimmer of golden thread. Her mother was wrong. They were not made to be loved, but to be broken.

After the fire, Laila stopped playing with dolls. But despite her father's efforts, she had not stopped carrying around her own death. Even now, all she had to do was look down at her hand and the bright garnet ring waited to taunt her.

Laila stood in the icy makeshift morgue, the only living girl in the room. For today, she wore a funereal-black dress. On a small table beside her lay pen and parchment, and the diamond neck-lace Séverin forced her to wear. It hadn't felt right to lean over these girls with such extravagance on her skin, even if it was only a fancy means of summoning her.

Spread out on nine ice slabs were the dead girls taken down from the walls of the ice grotto. In the dim light of the Forged lanterns, the girls looked as if they were made of porcelain. As if they were simply playthings that had been loved too hard, and that was why their pearl-pale legs were mottled, why the thin shifts they wore clung to them in tatters, why the crowns placed on their heads had been knocked askew and tangled into the frigid clumps of their hair. At least, it seemed that way until one looked at their hands. Or, rather, the lack of them.

Laila fought back a wave of nausea.

It had taken all the attendants of House Dazbog, House Kore, and House Nyx combined to remove them from the walls. Forging artists brought in from Irkutsk had created a morgue, and House Kore's artist gardeners had crafted ice blossoms that gave off heat without melting. A physician, a priest, and a member of the Irkutsk police force had been summoned to administer final rites and identify the bodies, but they would not be here for a couple of hours, which left Laila some time alone with them. The others thought she was there to document what she saw, but the real reason lay in her veins. Her blood let her do what no one else could for these girls—know them.

"My name is not Laila," whispered Laila to the dead girls. "I gave that name to myself when I left home. I have not said my true name in years, but since I don't know if we'll ever discover who you were . . . I hope you find peace in this secret."

One by one, she walked among them and told them her real name . . . the name her mother had given her.

When she finished, she turned to the girl closest to her. Like the others, her hands been removed. There was a crown around her head, and in some places frosted petals still clung to the wire. Laila withdrew a piece of cloth from a basket at her feet. For what she had to do, she could not bear to look at the girl. What was left of the girl's face reminded her too much of a young Zofia . . . the suggestion of a pointed chin and a delicate nose, the slightest lift of her cheekbones and the fey-like sharpness of her ears. This was a girl who was too young to be beautiful, but might have become so had she lived long enough.

Laila covered the girl's face, her eyes stinging with tears.

And then, she read her.

Laila started with the crown of wire, the cold metal burning her hand. Her abilities had always been temperamental. The memories—sights, sounds, emotional impressions—of an object lingered close to its surface for a month before vanishing. After that, what remained was residue, an impression of the object's defining moment or emotion. Usually, they were textures to Laila— the spiked-rind of panic; the silk-melt of love; the thorns of envy; the cold solidity of grief. But sometimes . . . sometimes when it was strong, it was like living *through* the memory, and her whole body would feel strung out from the weight of it. That's how it had felt with Enrique's rosary, like witnessing a scene.

Hesitantly, Laila closed her eyes and touched the crown. In her head flowed a piercing tune. Haunting and vast, like what a sailor might grasp of a siren's song seconds before drowning. Laila drew back her hand, her eyes opening. The wire had been taken from an instrument, like a cello or harp.

Next, her fingers coasted over the cloth covering the girl's mauled face and the strange symbols cut into it. Laila's soul recoiled at the thought . . . whoever had done this to them hadn't even seen them as people, but something to be writ upon like so much parchment.

She didn't want to look, but she had to.

Laila touched the strap of the girl's dress. Immediately, the taste of blood filled her mouth. The force of the girl's last moments of life shrieked through her thoughts like a thunderstorm—

"Please! Please don't!" screamed the girl. "My father, Moshe Horowitz, is a moneylender. He can pay whatever ransom you name, I swear it, please—"

"Hush, my dear," said an older man.

Laila's skin prickled. The man's voice was kind, like someone soothing a child in a temper tantrum. But Laila felt the pressure of the knife as if it was pushed to her own throat. She tasted the ghost of blood in her mouth, the same iron-tang the girl must have felt when she realized what was happening and bit down too hard on her own tongue.

"It's not about money. It's about immortality . . . we are the made creatures that have surpassed our creator, why should we not become His equals? The sacrifice of your blood shall pave the way, and you shall be an instrument of the divine."

"Why me?" whimpered the girl. "Why—"

"There now, my flower," said the man. "I picked you because no one will look for you."

Laila clutched her throat, gasping for breath.

For a moment it had actually felt as if . . . she touched the skin of her neck and looked at her fingertips, wondering if they would come away red . . . but they didn't. It was just a memory from long ago, strong enough that it grabbed hold of her whole person. Laila forced herself not to cry. If she wept now, she wouldn't stop.

Though the ice blossoms kept her warm, Laila couldn't stop

shivering. When Enrique had shared his findings about the symbols on the girls, he had told them he believed they were meant to be sacrifices . . . and he was right. She couldn't get the sound of the man's voice out of her head. He had to be the patriarch of the Fallen House, and yet she hated how sickeningly *kind* he sounded. Nothing at all like the flat affect of the doctor when he'd descended upon them inside the catacombs.

Laila gripped the edge of the ice slab, her stomach heaving. Months ago, she remembered hearing Roux-Joubert's confession:

The doctor's papa is a bad man.

They had all assumed it meant the doctor's father had once been the patriarch the Fallen House. It had sounded so silly. "A bad man." Like something a child would say. But the girls, their mouths, the ice . . . they didn't fit in the scope of words like "bad." Laila had always thought that the Fallen House's exile was about power. They wanted to access the power of God by rebuilding the Tower of Babel, but all they achieved was exile. And yet, he had sacrificed these girls, cut off their hands, and for *what*? She needed to find out.

Heart pounding, Laila reached for the next girl. Then the next, and the next. She read them in a daze, the same words knifing into her thoughts over and over:

You shall be an instrument of the divine.

No one will look for you.

The patriarch had grabbed the girls too dark to be visible in the world's eyes; whose languages fell on deaf ears; whose very homes at the edge of society pushed them too far into the shadows for notice. A part of Laila hoped he was still alive, if only so she could show him what vengeance meant.

When she reached the last girl, her hands shook violently. She felt as though she had been stabbed and strangled, dragged through the snow by her hair and thrown into the dark and kept there for hours. In her head, she heard what sounded like the slosh of water. On the soles of her feet, she felt the slide of freezing metal. Always, she tasted blood and tears. And at the very back of her thoughts curled a terrible dissonance. What decided that they should die while she—born dead, as it were—would walk between their bodies? Laila wanted to believe in gods and inscrutable stars, destinies as subtle as spider silk caught in a shaft of sunlight and, beautiful above all, *reason*. But between these walls of ice, only randomness stared back at her.

Laila forced herself to turn to the last girl. Her hair, dark and threaded with ice, fanned out behind her neck. Though her skin had long since paled and turned mottled from the cold, Laila could tell she was dark-skinned. Like her. Laila steeled herself as she reached out and heard the girl's last moments:

"My family will curse you," spat the girl. "You will die in your filth. You will be slaughtered like a pig! I will be a ghost and rip you to shreds—"

The patriarch of the Fallen House gagged her mouth.

"Such a sharp tongue for a pretty face," he said, as if scolding her. "Now, my dear, if you please . . . hold still."

He raised the knife to her face and began to cut.

"You were to be my last attempt," he said, talking over the muffled sound of her screaming. "I thought the others would be instruments of the divine, but it would seem as though my greatest treasure wants a particular sort of blood . . . picky, picky." He sighed. "I thought you might be the one to see it, to read it, but you've disappointed me."

Laila winced, her eyes rolling back at the ghost of the girl's pain.

"I know one of you is out there, and I will find you . . . and you will be my instrument."

Laila pushed back from the last slab, a terrible numbing sensation creeping through her body. It happened when she read too much, as if there wasn't enough left of her to be in the present. Her mouth felt dry, and her hands wouldn't stop shaking. All those girls had been killed as a sacrifice that hadn't even worked. They were dead for nothing.

Laila slid to the ground, her face in her hands, her back pressed to the ice slab. She didn't feel the cold. She felt nothing but the aching thud of each heartbeat.

"I'm sorry," she choked out. "I'm so sorry."

Moments, or maybe hours later came the urgent footfall of someone outside the morgue. Her back was to the door, and she didn't turn right away. It was probably an attendant come to tell her the physician, priest, or police officer would take it from here. She would look like a fool to them, standing and weeping, her hands shaking. But instead, she heard:

"Laila?"

Séverin. His voice sounded choked, out of breath.

"Laila!" he called out again, just as she grabbed the slab and hauled herself up to see Séverin standing in the doorway.

In his sable coat with his snow-damp hair, Séverin looked like something summoned by a curse. And when he stepped forward, the ice-light of the morgue rendered his eyes the color of deep bruises.

For a moment, they merely regarded each other.

Mistress she might be in name, but not in any practice.

He might walk with her to the bedroom suite they shared at night, but he had never stayed there since that first night, much less ever got into the bed with her. The past few mornings, she had woken up alone. To see him now—standing hardly five feet from her—jolted her. So much reading rippled her own perspective, and she felt, for an instant, dragged back into a past that belonged to another life. A past where she was happily baking a cake in the kitchens of L'Eden, her hands dusted with sugar and flour. A past where his eyes were once lit up by wonder and curiosity. A past where he once jokingly demanded to know why she called him *Majnun*.

"What will you give me to know the answer?" she asked. "I demand offerings."

"How about a dress sewn of moonlight?" asked Séverin. "An apple of immortal youth . . . or perhaps glass slippers that would never cut your skin."

"None of those things are real," she'd said and laughed.

He stared at her when she laughed, his eyes never leaving her face. "For you, I'd make anything real."

The memory faded, dragging her back to the cold present.

"You're here," Séverin finally managed. "I tried to . . . I kept . . ."

Séverin raised his hand, not looking at her. The diamond jewel caught the light. Laila looked to the table beside him, the one holding her Forged necklace that he used to summon her.

"Why did you think I'd be gone?"

"The others," he said, raising his dusky eyes to hers. "They've gone missing."

21

ENRIQUE

As Enrique leaned out of the ice grotto and into the strange sun-steeped city, he wished he had a better sense of self-preservation. Part of him wanted to make Zofia and Eva return to the grotto, but the other part wanted to walk farther. His foot dangled off the precipice, and the sunlight held him in thrall. Only then did he realize the ruined courtyard had stolen something dangerous from him: his curiosity.

In the sanctuary, nine female statues served as pillars, propping up a ceiling of wooden slats. Time had eroded their details, but Enrique still caught the suggestion of gathered silk and slender diadems around their foreheads. Painted walls behind the statues caught his eye. The scenes showed nine hooded women prostrating themselves before the nine Greek goddesses of divine inspiration, the muses. Enrique recognized them by the emblems hovering over their heads—Erato and her cithara, Thalia and her comic mask—a bit of gold leaf still clung to the image of a lyre in the hands of

Calliope, the muse of epic poetry. The Forged paint allowed the images to shift, so that one moment, the objects the muses held were hale and shining. The next, they splintered apart in a cyclical pattern of made and unmade. When he looked at the women by the goddesses's feet, his whole body recoiled. Each of the nine women in the painting held out their arms, but none of them had hands. And there, piled behind the muses' feet: a collection of hands severed at the wrist. Like offerings.

Sacrifice.

Enrique flinched from the gruesome painting as bits of tales and research snapped together in his mind. His thoughts leapt to the dead girls in the ice grotto. Nine of them, all without hands. He suspected they'd served in some capacity as guardians, but now he saw the direct link to the Order's lore of the Lost Muses, the ancient line of women tasked with protecting *The Divine Lyrics*. What if it had never been a myth? What if—

A rasping sound choked off his thoughts.

"You shall not take another."

A wizened old man stepped into the light. He raised his hand in the air. The nine statues lifted their feet off their stone pedestals and brought them to the ground. Dust sifted through the air, and the ground trembled as nine blank faces turned toward them slowly.

"We're leaving!" shouted Enrique. "Right *now*—"

Zofia and Eva stumbled backward. Enrique leaned farther out of the Tezcat portal, clutching it one-handed, his other hand held out to hoist them back inside when something whizzed past him.

He jerked back, but not before something sharp flew past his ear. His grip slipped on the rough stones of the portal wall. Just as he tried to grab hold, Eva pulled on his hand and the icy floor skidded out from underneath him. Blood rushed through his ears. At the last second, he flung out his arms, breaking his fall against the hot, sandy floor of the courtyard.

"The portal!" shouted Eva.

Zofia hauled him to his feet. Enrique whirled around, ready to clamber back inside the portal . . . but it was gone.

"It just . . . it just *disappeared*," said Eva, blinking back tears. "We're trapped."

"More blood," he said breathlessly. "Maybe that's the only way to open it back up—"

Another arrow whizzed past his face. The feathers on the fletching slashed across his cheek, and a moment later, he heard the snap of rock as the arrow stuck fast in the broken rock wall. The hairs on the back of his neck raised and a shrill hum lingered in the air.

Zofia grabbed his hand. "Move!"

Enrique sprinted across the ground. Up ahead, Zofia fumbled at her necklace. Enrique dove forward, shoving her out of the way. Zofia fell to the ground, rolling onto her side just as an arrowhead stabbed into the dirt.

"Stop!" screamed Eva. "We just want to leave!"

In front of them, the old man moved out of the shadows and into the light. His eyes were milky with blindness. Deep gouges framed his sockets, and the raised scars looked purple and furious. This man had been made blind.

"We don't mean any harm," said Enrique, holding out his hands. "We were just following a lead from somewhere else—"

"Do not lie to me," said the old man. "I've been waiting for you since you took my sister. You are not welcome in this sacred place. You think to use us. You think to play at God, but the worthy choose not to wield their touch."

Zofia inhaled sharply, her hand frozen at her necklace.

"You speak Polish?"

"He's speaking Russian," said Eva, confused.

Enrique shook himself. To him, the man spoke his milk tongue of Tagalog, the language so familiar to him, he almost couldn't recognize that his language was out of place here. The man froze, and the statues of the muses paused midstep. He swiveled toward Zofia's direction, his eyes glassy.

"Girls," said the man, his voice breaking. "Have they taken you too?"

He raised his head, his unseeing eyes fixed somewhere above Enrique's head. "How many girls must you take before you realize that no matter how much blood you offer, you will never be able to see? If you cannot see, then you do not know where to use the instrument of the divine. And without that"—the old man laughed—"the will of God is safe." The man pointed at his gouged-out eyes. "You cannot use me either. I made sure of it."

Then he turned to Zofia and Eva. "I will save you, children. I will not let them take you."

He flicked his ancient wrists. The statue to the left of Enrique lurched forward, casting a cold shadow across them. Enrique flinched back, but the statue never struck. Instead, it loomed behind them, its arms spread wide to block their way back to the Sleeping Palace. Dread iced over his veins.

"There's been a misunderstanding—" he tried to say.

The old man flicked his wrist again. The eight remaining statues lifted their stone arms, and the three of them took off down the courtyard. Far ahead, cut off by the gauze of silken curtains, Enrique glimpsed the waters of a lake. He could make out the colorful tents and crowds flocking through a local bazaar.

"Help us!" he yelled.

No one glanced in their direction. It was as if they couldn't see them. Enrique looked right and left, but solid brick walls flanked them. That made no sense. Where did the old man come from, then?

"It's a dead end," said Enrique.

He looked over his shoulder, then immediately regretted that choice. The muse statues moved quickly, their stone tunics slicing through the dirt. "They're both Tezcats," said Zofia, holding up one of her pendants. She touched a spot on the brick wall, and her hand disappeared up to her elbow. "This way!"

Zofia barreled through the wall, Eva and Enrique following after her. Enrique braced himself, turning his face to the side, but all that met him was a rush of cool air as they fell through the portal and onto the rich, silk rugs of a carpet merchant. His chin banged onto the rug, and he winced as his teeth caught his tongue and hot, coppery warmth flooded his mouth.

Through the silk flap of the merchant's kiosk, Enrique glimpsed the curvature of the road he'd seen from the courtyard. The reflection of the bottle-green lake bounced off polished mirrors in the bazaar. That road must run through the whole of the bazaar, including the courtyard. All they had to do was follow the road, and they would arrive back at the portal to the Sleeping Palace.

Enrique turned his head. There, a merchant sat cross-legged amongst his wares, staring at them in shock. Above, delicate Turkish lanterns swayed gently, casting jewel-stained light all around them.

"This . . . this is a lovely rug?" said Enrique, patting the silk beneath him.

"*Ne yapiyorsun burada?!*" demanded the carpet merchant.

The merchant leapt to his feet, a sharp stick in his hand. Enrique clambered backwards, his arms flung out to block Eva and Zofia when the walls of the shop began to tremble and shake. A lantern broke loose, shattering glass across the silk, and the smell of wax and incense stamped the air.

"We need to—" started Eva, but a crashing sound drowned out her words as a stone hand the size of an armchair pummeled through the ceiling.

The man shrieked as the three of them darted out the entrance and into the mass of people. There, a different chaos enveloped them. In the bazaar, pyramids of cinnamon and nutmeg, golden saffron and matted heaps of hemp lined the outside of spice shops. Peddlers shook jars of star-shaped anise and dangled garlands of glossy red peppers. In the air, the sounds of the *muezzin* calling the faithful to prayer suffused the bazaar.

It was a moment of shining perfection—

Until the carpet merchant ran screaming out of his shop.

One of the muse statues tore straight through the tent. The crowd panicked, overturning piles of spices and salt as they ran.

"This way!" said Enrique. "It's a circle—we can run back to the Tezcat!"

"Or we could hide," said Eva, wincing as she gripped her leg.

Too late, Enrique remembered the slight limp in her gait. But then the muse statue's head swiveled to them.

"Afraid not!" said Enrique.

The three of them dove into the streets, nearly tripping over teaglass stands and knots of old men smoking their water pipes. The tops of tents flashed overhead. Behind them, Enrique could hear the groaning stone steps of the muse statues. He glanced back—there were only four. Their arms stretched out, blank eyes fixed on nothing. Around them, the bazaar had descended into chaos as storefronts started to break. Footfalls rang in his ears, but he kept his eyes on the patches he could see of the road. They just had to make it to the other side, he said to himself over and over.

A collapsed shop front loomed before them. Zofia threw one of her pendants at the pile of debris and wood, and it crackled, hissing into a wall of flames that would—hopefully—slow down the statues. The road curved once more, and Enrique's heart nearly sagged with relief. It couldn't be long now until they arrived back at the courtyard—

A soft cry pulled Enrique's attention. He turned to see Eva struggling. A fractured beam had caught her dress, yanking it to the thigh. Under normal circumstances, Enrique would've immediately looked away, but the sight of Eva's leg stopped him. Thick, raised scars mottled her skin. The muscles of her thigh looked shrunken.

"Don't *look at me*," she snarled. "Just *go*! Leave!"

Zofia turned back around, her gaze going once to Eva and then beyond her to where the tops of the muse statues loomed above the wall of fire. Without hesitating, Zofia ran back to the other girl, ripping her dress from the outpost. Eva let out a ragged breath.

"I can't keep up," said Eva. "I have trouble after . . . after a while."

Pain twisted her voice at the admission, and Enrique went to her, his hand outstretched.

"Then let us help you," he said, lowering his eyes.

Eva hesitated for only a moment and then nodded. The heroes in Enrique's imagination always ran off with maidens in their arms. So he rolled up his sleeves, put one arm around her legs and the other at her waist, hoisted her up—and then immediately put her down.

"I'm weak," he groaned. "Help. Zofia?"

Zofia shouldered past him. "Put your arm around me."

Enrique took Eva's other arm and vowed to mourn his pride later. The three of them hobbled across the curve of the road, staying close beneath the tent awnings that hadn't been pulled down in the attack. Close behind, the sound of crashing wood caught up to them. The earth quaked, trembling with every stomp of the approaching statues.

Enrique shoved down his panic, focusing instead on the lake as it came into full view. The damp earth fug of still water hit his nose. On the other side of the shore, he could just make out the wooden panels that hid the ancient courtyard and Tezcat entrance from the public. The three of them huddled beneath an abandoned shop tent as silence fell over the market.

"There were nine muses," said Zofia suddenly.

"What a brilliant observation," snapped Eva.

"Only four were following us."

"So—"

With a ripping sound, their tent gave way. Five of the muse statues stood there, holding the ragged tents in their arms as if they were nothing more than scraps of silk plucked off the ground. Instinctively, he moved backwards, but Eva stopped him.

"They're behind us . . ."

Cold shadows fell over him. The nine muse statues closed in while not twenty feet away stretched out the lake and, beyond it, the way back to the Sleeping Palace.

"We have to swim," said Enrique, his heart beating wildly in his chest. "Go now! I'll distract them."

"We can't leave you—" said Zofia.

But Eva didn't hesitate. She fixed Enrique with a hard stare.

"On the other side, then."

"Enrique—" said Zofia, her voice straining.

He let himself look at her, let himself drink in the candle-brightness of her hair, the blue of her eyes. And then he shrugged off Eva's arm from around his shoulder and darted in the opposite direction toward the merchant tents. *Look at me, look at me,* he willed. His breath scraped through his lungs, and he could hear nothing save for his own thunderous pulse.

"Over here!" he shouted. "Look! *Look!*"

Finally, he turned. But he couldn't make himself open his eyes until he heard it: the creaking groan of rock hinges. His eyes flew open to the sight of all nine muses circling him. Through the gaps between the statues, he watched Eva and Zofia wade into the lake.

But his relief was short-lived. Seconds later, one of the muses slammed her hand into the ground, throwing off his balance and sending him sprawling. Dust flew into his eyes, clearing only a second before he saw a stone fist heading toward him—

He gathered his energy, rolling out of the way just as another fist pummeled the earth. From behind the statues, the old man called out, "Can't you see that we are not meant to be gods? That it only brings ruin?"

Enrique dodged another blow, flinging himself behind a statue.

"No mortal can hide from the gods," laughed the old man.

When another blow came, Enrique crouched and then leapt—catching hold of the statue around its clenched fingers while his stomach muscles burned in protest. The statue tried to fling him off, but he held tight. At this height, he watched Eva and Zofia clamber onto the opposite banks and then, finally, disappear through the wooden slats . . .

The statue shook its wrist again, and Enrique dropped to the floor, crashing onto his side. Pain burned through his arm. This was it. Through the pain, pride flickered dimly inside him. He'd saved them.

He'd done something heroic after all.

"This is the end for you," said the old man.

Enrique raised his head. He knew it was useless to defend himself, but he couldn't help it.

"I'm no thief," he rasped.

The muse statues held still. Their stone bodies flanked him on all sides. Even if he could somehow get to the lake, he didn't know that he could find the strength to swim.

"Please," he heard himself say.

He was going to die. He knew it. Even the shadows cast by the statues were unnaturally cold and . . . icy? A thin layer of ice crept onto the ground in front of him, wrapping around his pant leg like an insistent vine. He raised his gaze and then, through the slim gap between two of the muse statues, he spied a delicate crystalline bridge knitting itself across the lake, layer by layer building until it could hold weight.

"I will not give you a merciful death," gloated the old man. "Just as you did not give one to her."

Enrique pushed himself to a stand.

Get to the lake, he told himself. *Just get to the lake.*

He held himself just so, little by little stepping toward the gap between the muses. In one smooth motion, the muses raised their arms. Enrique angled his body, timing himself, gathering one last burst of energy—

And then he dove forward.

He shoved himself through the gap between their bodies. The statues tried to turn, but he'd drawn them so close together that they tangled on themselves.

"Kill him!" screamed the old man.

Enrique sprinted for the lake, his legs pumping. The ice bridge was still ten feet out. He half ran, half swam toward it, even as the water chilled him and too-slick seaweeds brushed against his skin. The earth quivered beneath him, but he didn't stop. He threw himself onto the bridge as cold shocked through his body. Slowly, then quickly gaining speed, the bridge shifted. It yanked him toward the shore, contracting on itself. Enrique sank against the ice, letting the bridge pull him on and on while the old man's screams chased him into unconsciousness.

"WHAT THE *HELL* was he thinking?"

Enrique blinked a couple times . . . his room swimming into view.

"Don't yell at him," scolded Laila.

Enrique groaned. He knew he was still sore, but now a pleasant hum settled through his blood. Eva's work, perhaps. When he turned his head, he saw Zofia and Ruslan on the left side of his bed, while Laila and Séverin stood near the foot.

"Bravery is physically exhausting," he managed.

"You're awake!" cried Laila, hugging him.

"You're *alive*."

"And your hair remains exceptional," said Ruslan kindly.

"*C'est vrai*," said a warm voice.

Enrique turned to his right, and there was Hypnos, one warm hand at his shoulder. That cold knot of rejection that had coiled in his heart the moment Hypnos had left him at the library eased into warmth. He could've been at Séverin's side, but he'd chosen him.

"What did you find out?" asked Séverin brusquely.

"Can't this wait?" asked Laila.

"No," said Enrique, pushing himself up on his elbows.

The longer he looked at Laila, the more the world sharpened with urgency. In that second, he felt the weight of their eyes on him. The irony of it was almost funny. Finally, he thought, they were all listening to him. Except it happened to be at the exact moment when all he wanted was silence. And sleep. But he didn't want to imagine what nightmares would chase him through sleep. He'd given those dark dreams too much to feed upon—the dead girls in the grotto, the piled-up hands behind the stone-faced muses. A shudder ran down his spine, and he forced himself to sit upright.

"We were wrong about the Lost Muses," said Enrique.

Ruslan tilted his head. "The women who supposedly guard *The Divine Lyrics*?"

"Not just guard," said Enrique. "There was apparently something in their bloodline that allowed them to read the book itself. I don't think it's a myth. Not anymore."

"But that's impossible, *mon cher*," said Hypnos. "What woman has a bloodline like that? And what does that have to do with those poor girls?"

Enrique stared at his lap. He could think of only one woman with a bloodline that let her do the impossible: Laila. And her very existence depended on finding *The Divine Lyrics*. He avoided her eyes.

"Enrique?" prompted Séverin.

"I don't know who would have that bloodline," said Enrique, forcing his thoughts back to the conversation. "But it's clear the Fallen House believed in it. In the portal courtyard, I saw depictions of women without their hands, offering them to the muses. And none of those girls that we found—"

"—had their hands," finished Laila softly.

"I think once the Fallen House got *The Divine Lyrics*, they tried to find women of the bloodline necessary to read the book. And when they couldn't do that, they . . . they sacrificed them, arranging them like a shadow of the Lost Muses, like guardians for their treasures and *The Divine Lyrics* that they couldn't decipher. They might have kept finding more girls, but then they were exiled."

Laila's hand flew to her mouth. Beside her, Zofia and Eva looked sick.

"And it's not just blood," said Enrique, thinking of the old man's gouged-out eyes. "I think there's more to it, like sight."

"The old man," said Eva, her eyes narrowing. "He said something about how if you cannot see the divine, then you don't know where to *use* it? I didn't understand what that meant."

"I didn't either," admitted Enrique.

Séverin turned a small knife in his hand, and spoke slowly, as if to himself. "So to read *The Divine Lyrics*, someone would need a girl of the bloodline."

A frisson of cold traveled down Enrique's back. The way Séverin said it . . . as if. No. No, thought Enrique firmly. He would never do that. He wanted the book to avenge Tristan. Anything else was madness.

"But what about the other treasures of the Fallen House?" asked Ruslan. "Did the symbols lead to anything?"

Enrique shook his head. "I believe it's a coded alphabet, but without more symbols or a key, I can't crack it."

At this, Zofia cleared her throat. She held up a Mnemo bug, and he remembered that she'd seen something inside the leviathan.

"I found more symbols," said Zofia. "I think we can crack the code."

22

LAILA

Laila lingered at the entrance to the Sleeping Palace's kitchen quarters, caught between wanting to join the servants in their food preparations and avoiding the kitchens altogether. She used to love this—examining ingredients like scraps of a universe not yet made. She used to savor the safety of the kitchens where no memories could bite her, where all her touch conjured was something worth sharing amongst friends.

Once, she'd even baked edible wonders.

Now all that remained was wondering: How would she live? How would she die? She glanced down at her hands. They seemed alien to her. Long ago, when she'd asked the *jaadugar* how she might keep living, he'd only instructed her to find the book and open it, for therein lay the secrets to her making. He hadn't said that she would need to find someone else to read it for her, and yet that's what Enrique and Zofia's findings confirmed. To read *The Divine Lyrics*, one needed someone of the Lost Muses bloodline.

"Mademoiselle?" asked an attendant. "You came to give us certain instructions for the tea?"

Laila startled from her thoughts. The attendants must have noticed her standing at the entrance. Beyond them, she spotted tea carts already loaded with samovars and gilded *podstakannik* designed to hold the thin glasses, mounds of glistening caviar beside slender mother-of-pearl spoons, jam sandwiches the color of blood, and fragile sugar cookies that looked like layers of lace. All in preparation for the meeting to be held now that Enrique was conscious once more. Laila cleared her throat. *One step at a time.* First, she needed the book. From there, she would figure it out.

"No pork for platter number two," said Laila, pointing at Zofia's tray. "Please do not let anything on the plate touch."

She scrutinized Enrique's tray and frowned. "More cake on that one."

For Hypnos's plate, she pointed at the water goblet. "Could you put that in a lovelier glass? Something etched and in quartz? And put the wine in a plainer goblet."

Hypnos had a higher tendency to drink from a prettier glass, and they needed him sober. Laila hesitated at the last tray. Séverin's.

"What does Monsieur Montagnet-Alarie want?" asked the server.

Laila stared at the tray and felt a mirthless laugh rise in her chest.

"Who knows," she said.

The attendant nodded and promised to send the trays to the library within the next half hour.

"One more tray," said Laila. "A little bit of everything on it . . . I'm not sure what she likes. And you can give it to me directly."

The server frowned, but did as asked. With the platter in hand, Laila made her way through the intricate lower hallways to the room Ruslan had told her served as the infirmary. By now, the others would be gathering in the library, ready to break the code that Zofia had found in the leviathan's mouth, but Laila needed one more minute of silence. She hadn't had a chance to mourn the girls she'd read. She hadn't even had the chance to catch her breath after Eva, Enrique, and Zofia had gone missing, and all that she and Séverin had found was a blood-flecked arrow spinning across the floor of the ice grotto.

What she needed was to give thanks, and to the right person.

Laila knocked on the door of the infirmary.

"What do you want?" snapped a voice from within.

Laila took a deep breath and opened the door. Lying on a make-shift cot in the center of the room was Eva. Immediately, Eva pulled up the covers, hiding her leg beneath the blankets. In those unguarded seconds, Laila caught sight of the thick, mottled scars on Eva's skin and the shrunken muscle.

"Oh, it's *you*," said Eva, settling into her pillows.

"Who did you think I'd be?"

"Someone important." Eva lifted her chin. "I had put out an in-quiry to find out more about Moshe Horowitz. I thought you might be someone bringing me useful information."

Laila ignored the insult, caught off guard by the familiarity of that name, though she couldn't place it.

"It was a name we found in the well," added Eva.

Laila's hands twitched and turned cold, as if she'd touched a slab of ice and a crown of frosted petals. In her head, she heard the last memories of the dead girl: *My father, Moshe Horowitz, is a moneylender. He can pay for whatever ransom you name, I swear it, please—*

Laila gripped the platter harder, her heart aching. "I don't have any information, but I brought this. May I come in?"

Eva narrowed her eyes, but eventually nodded. As Laila drew

closer, Eva's hand went to her throat, nervously tugging at the pendant she always wore. This close, Laila could finally see that it was
a silver ballerina spinning on a thin chain. Eva caught her looking
and quickly tucked it away.

"If you think you can bribe my friendship—" she started, then
her stomach growled. Eva blushed furiously.

"I wouldn't dream of bribing you," said Laila. "Your stomach,
however, is a different creature."

She pushed the platter forward. Still, Eva did not take it. Laila
sighed.

"It doesn't have to be an overture of friendship," she said. "Call
it gratitude. Without the ice bridge you made, Enrique would be
dead, and my heart would be broken. So whether you want my
friendship or not, you have my thanks."

When Eva still said nothing, Laila stood and made her way to
the door.

"You don't like me," called out Eva. "And I don't like you."

Laila's hand paused at the door. When she looked at Eva, there
was such hardness on her face that something softened within Laila.

"Then perhaps we can just agree on mutual respect."

Without waiting for an answer, Laila left her. She only made it
a couple paces down the hallway before she felt a tightening sensation around her neck. It never tightened to a choke, but her breath
caught anyway. Séverin was summoning her.

Laila made her way through the winding crystalline halls. It
was almost entirely silent. The light cast off from the Forged lumi-
nescent threads set into the walls looked eerie, like glowing roots
for unearthly halls. Cracked-open doors revealed rooms empty of
furniture, but not of wonder. In one, intricate snowflakes sifted
down from the ceiling. In another, sharp carvings of impossible

plants and creatures opened their eyes and bared their crystal teeth as she passed. When Laila emerged into the atrium, she was greeted with another inhuman sight. Séverin stood wrapped in his long, sable coat, the lights catching in his dark curls, shadowing the cruel set of his mouth. If the frosted lights of the Sleeping Palace reminded her of stars crowding the night, then Séverin appeared amongst them like an eclipse. Everything about him was the opposite of radiance, and he drew her eye like a blight on the horizon. Unwanted, and yet, impossible to look away from.

Behind him shuffled artisans hired by House Dazbog, their hands raised as they led out the menagerie of ice animals. It was like something from a child's tale. Laila half expected Snegurochka to walk amongst them, cold hands pressed to her colder heart lest she fall in love and melt. Huge stags with glittering antlers stepped lightly onto the ice. Giant bears dragged their translucent bellies over the floor. Jaguars whose carved paws clinked like champagne flutes on the crystal floor padded after the ice artisans, who led them into the atrium. They looked like the ghosts of dead animals trapped in frost.

"Ruslan had the idea to reconfigure their Forging mechanisms," said Séverin, his voice low as he walked toward her. "Makes them safer to be around if they can't attack."

He closed the distance between them, his hand sliding around her waist. Laila wondered how cold she must be if a boy made of ice still shivered at her touch. She knew this was a show put on for the benefit of the attendants, but her pulse betrayed her anyway and Séverin knew it. A faint smirk touched his mouth, and Laila bit back her fury. She brushed her thumb over his lip and was rewarded with the faintest tremble in his fingers.

"You're overplaying your part," he said coldly. "Again."

"You summoned me, my love," she said, her voice a touch louder than it needed to be. "In full view of everyone. Are we to have an audience?"

Séverin's gaze snapped to hers. The ice in him hadn't reached his eyes. They were still that vespertine shade of violet. Still unsettling.

"I summoned you to know what you saw when you read those girls," he said, lowering his voice. "Does it corroborate with what Enrique, Zofia, and Eva saw in that courtyard?"

Laila nodded, even as her soul recoiled. "Those girls were failed sacrifices meant to act as 'instruments of the divine,' whatever that means. The patriarch was insane, Séverin. What he did to them—" Her voice broke for a moment and she struggled to continue. "What Enrique said was right. They didn't have the bloodline needed to read the book, and the patriarch of the Fallen House hoped his son would have more luck. That's why he left clues across their faces. And the way he chose them . . . he specifically said he went after them because he thought no one would look. Eva is tracking down the families now."

Séverin nodded, then regarded her curiously.

"You have been searching for that book a long time," he said lightly. "How will you read it?"

Laila raised her eyes to him. "Who said I needed to read it?"

"Could you?"

When he asked, his eyes looked molten. Desperate, even, and it threw off her thoughts. All this time, Laila thought he wanted the book to avenge Tristan. After all, robbing the Fallen House of their most precious treasure would be a killing blow. But she saw no hunger for vengeance in Séverin's face. It was something else . . . something she couldn't put a finger on, but it unnerved her all the same.

"I don't know," she said finally.

The *jaadugar* had merely told her to open the book. That was all. It was flimsy ground for faith, and yet her hope balanced upon it anyway.

Séverin touched her throat, fingertips resting on the diamond jewels there.

"Don't keep me waiting."

Laila grabbed his wrist, squeezing the oath bracelet.

"Don't make demands you haven't earned," she said.

"Earned?" asked Séverin, raising an eyebrow. "Oh, I've earned my demands. I've kept my promises. I promised to share all I knew with you and to take you with me. I promised to make you my mistress."

Behind him, an attendant strode across the atrium, leading a crystal tiger behind it.

Séverin leaned in. "I made no promise to treat you as one. Is that the issue?" he asked mockingly. "Do you want me in your bed, Laila?"

Laila dug her nails into his wrist until he winced.

"I just want you to remember your promises."

IN THE LIBRARY, the statues of the nine muses glimmered like nacre. A Mnemo projection hovering midair showed two sets of symbols. Laila recognized one of them as the images carved across the girls' jaws.

The other set must have come from what Zofia had seen inside the leviathan.

⌐⌐⌐⊡⟩⊓⊓⊐⊐⋀⌐⊡

Delphine greeted Laila with a huge scowl. As usual, the other woman was dressed impeccably—her steel-blond hair in a tight chignon, a dark sapphire cape trimmed in fox-fur cascading from around her shoulders. Laila considered her. Delphine was not . . . *nice*. But she was kind, and therein lay all the difference. When Delphine had led her away after they discovered the bodies, Laila managed to drag her fingers across the other woman's scarves and furs. What she felt was the crush of loneliness like a clamp to her heart, and what she glimpsed was the memory of Séverin as a child: violet-eyed and cherub-cheeked, his eyes aglow with wonder. Shame tended to warp memories, conjuring slick and grimy textures in Laila's readings. But the matriarch's memories of Séverin ran through her mind like a river of light . . . and she couldn't reconcile what Delphine had felt for him and what she had done to him. It made no sense.

"Are they *always* like this?" asked Delphine.

Laila looked beyond the other woman's shoulder to where Hypnos and Enrique argued over the positioning of pillows on a chaise; Zofia absentmindedly lit matches and watched them burn; Séverin—who had left the atrium before her—pretended as though he noticed nothing; and poor Ruslan could only rub his head in confusion.

"They're hungry," said Laila.

"They're *feral*," said Delphine.

"That too."

"Should I call for food—"

Behind Laila, the doors opened once more and the attendants came in pushing a cart of food. Laila heard a sigh of "cake" as the food was distributed. Séverin, she noticed, took nothing.

"Let's get started," said Séverin loudly.

Delphine lifted an eyebrow, and had made her way to the small arrangement of chairs when Séverin held up his hand.

"Not you."

Delphine stopped short. Hurt flashed across the other woman's face.

"I am the one sponsoring your acquisition, therefore I can stay."

"We already have the presence of two Order patriarchs."

Delphine let her gaze settle over Ruslan, who waved apologetically, and Hypnos who was frowning over the stemware on his tray. Even Laila felt a slight cringe in her heart.

"What an inspiring sight," said Delphine. "Two Order representatives strikes me as rather extraneous."

"Fine," said Séverin. "I will send one away."

Across from Laila, Hypnos went still.

"Patriarch Ruslan, would you give us the room please?"

Ruslan blinked owlishly. "Me?"

"Yes."

Laila caught the sudden sag of Hypnos's shoulders. Relief clear in every line of his body. When he looked up at Séverin, something like hope touched his eyes.

Ruslan grumbled and pouted, before finally joining Delphine at the front of the room and offering her his uninjured arm. She took it as gingerly as if it were a soiled cloth.

"I will leave you to your work, then," said Delphine. "But you should know that the Order continues to grow impatient."

"Do they know where we are?" asked Séverin.

"They will soon enough," said Delphine. "It's a secret that neither I, nor Patriarch Ruslan nor Patriarch Hypnos, have the right to keep from them when the Winter Conclave begins in three days."

"Then I suppose we'd best hurry," said Séverin.

Ruslan gestured toward the door, and with that, the two of them left the library. Laila made her way to Zofia, who nibbled on the edge of a sugar cookie.

"Not as good as yours," said Zofia.

"I'll make them again. When we go home."

Zofia looked up at her, confusion giving way to happiness. Beside them, Enrique had just finished swallowing half of a large piece of cake.

"Begin," said Séverin.

Enrique took a swig of tea. He still looked bruised and weary, but there was a new sheen to his eyes. A sheen he only got when curiosity grabbed hold of him. Before he looked at the symbols, he looked to her, and his expression was full of hope.

"The top set of symbols is what we found on the girls," said Enrique. "The bottom set is from the leviathan—"

Laila frowned. "Where exactly did you find those symbols on the leviathan, Zofia?"

"I walked inside its mouth."

Laila rubbed her temples. *"Alone?"*

"There was something inside. And it had stairs."

"Zofia, that's too dangerous to do alone," said Laila. "What if something happened to you?"

Zofia's gaze turned bleak. "What if something happens to *you?*"

That took Laila aback. Her palm pulsed with the memory of Zofia and Enrique tending to the wound on her hand just outside of St. Petersburg. They cared, and every time she remembered it, it felt like a beam of unexpected sunlight.

Hypnos shuddered. "That leviathan is a monstrosity—"

"It's not a monstrosity," said Zofia, a touch defensively. "Automaton pets are not so far out of the norm—"

"*Pet?*" repeated Hypnos. "Did she say pet?"

"A pet is a dog or a cat—" started Enrique, appalled.

"Or a tarantula," said Zofia.

"I beg your pardon—"

"There's no need to beg," said Zofia.

Enrique scowled.

"I can't imagine someone naming that thing and looking upon it fondly," said Laila.

Zofia seemed to consider this. ". . . I would name it David."

All of them went silent.

"David," repeated Enrique. "A tarantula named Goliath and a metal leviathan named *David.*"

Zofia nodded.

"Why—"

"The *symbols,*" said Séverin.

Zofia gestured at the last symbol on the pattern she'd identified. Enrique rubbed his thumb along his lower lip.

"There's other repeating ones as well," he mused. "Like letters. If I switched out a symbol with a vowel it might reveal a message. Let's try *A*?" Enrique stepped back, then shook his head. "Never mind. How about *E*?"

Zofia tilted her head, her blue eyes alight as she studied the pattern.

"Assuming *E* is the correct vowel for the stand-in, you can work backwards . . . It's all building on each other, like a grid . . ."

"Alphabet made from a grid?" wondered Enrique.

Laila watched Zofia stand, go to the board, bicker with Enrique, and then construct a loose grid . . .

Enrique let out a whoop of joy.

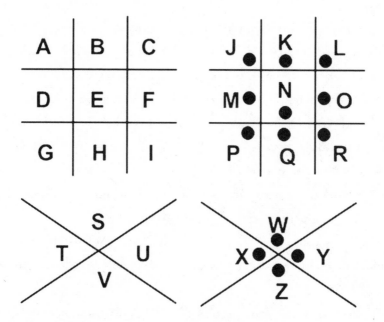

"Now we just have to line up the symbols with the letters. Zofia, you take the set from the leviathan. I'll take the original."

"What do we do?" asked Hypnos, leaning forward eagerly.

"Bask in their brilliance," said Laila, sighing.

Hypnos pouted in her direction, then moved to sit beside her. He reached for her hand, turning it this way and that.

"How do you do it, *ma chère?*"

Laila stilled. Had someone told him what she could do? Panic wound through her. Hypnos knew nothing of her secret. She didn't think Hypnos would view her any differently than the others, but she didn't entirely trust he could keep such knowledge to himself.

"Do?" she repeated.

"Yes, you know, in the sense that . . . and I mean no offense . . . but you contribute perhaps as much as I do in these meetings, do you not?" he asked. "There's the arrangement of food and such, but I tried to do that as well and was met with very pitiful success. How do you . . ."

He trailed off, and Laila knew the word he wouldn't utter: *belong*. Though Hypnos didn't realize it, as he turned her hand, a part of her couldn't help but to reach out with her own senses. She remembered what Hypnos had said in the music room of the Moscow teahouse. Of how music had filled his loneliness, and even in so small a thing as the cuffed edge of his shirtsleeve, Laila thought she could hear that loneliness clattering through her. It felt like icy rain sliding down her neck, like staring into a room full of warmth and missing the door to enter it each time.

"Give it time," said Laila, squeezing his hand. "I think most would place more value on knowing who you are . . . rather than who you're with."

Laila tensed, not knowing if he would find offense at her last comment. Everyone knew that he was involved with Enrique, but to what

THE SILVERED SERPENTS   253

degree? Hypnos's affection had always struck her as casual, despite its sincerity. What he had with Enrique hadn't seemed serious until Enrique had emerged unconscious from the Tezcat. At that instant, Hypnos had insisted upon tending to him. And yet, Laila noticed how his gaze went to Séverin far more than it did to Enrique; how his hand on Enrique's shoulder looked less affection and more like he was anchoring himself to a place in the room. Hypnos turned a couple of shades darker, and his gaze darted almost guiltily to Enrique.

"Knowing me," repeated Hypnos. "Are you calling me a cipher, Mademoiselle?"

"Don't flatter yourself."

"Someone has to," he said loftily. "How to crack a cipher, one wonders. Perhaps with names? Perhaps you might even tell me yours?"

Laila fixed him with an annoyed look. "Laila."

"And surely, I was born a *Hypnos*," he said, smirking. And then, after a moment, he let go of her hand. "Then again, the names we are born with can end up meaning so little. The names we give ourselves, well, perhaps that's the truth of us."

"And in truth, you wanted to be the god of sleep?"

Hypnos's smirk softened.

"I wanted to be a person I saw only in my dreams, and I named myself for that realm," he said quietly. "And you?"

Laila thought back to the day she'd plucked her name from one of her father's volumes of poetry.

Laila.

Night.

"I gave myself a name that hides all manner of flaws."

Hypnos nodded. For a moment, it seemed as if he would say something else, but then Enrique's voice rang through the air—

"Cracked it," said Enrique. "There was a message waiting for us this whole time."

Laila closed her eyes. Panic flared briefly inside her chest. She steeled herself, then opened her eyes to the translation of the first set of symbols:

The teeth of the devil call to me.

Then, her gaze shifted to the translation of the symbols Zofia found in the leviathan's mouth:

I am the devil.

23

ZOFIA

Zofia felt her pulse quicken as the words came into view . . . *I am the devil.*

The year before her parents had died, someone had vandalized the storefront of a well-known Jewish merchant, calling him a demon responsible for the death of Tsar Alexander II. All day, her father had helped scrub the paint off the bricks. When Zofia had visited him, he placed his hand on hers, and together they traced the stone still wet with painted slurs.

"You see that, my Zosia?" he had asked. "That is the devil. When a man cannot see a person as a person, then the devil has slipped into him and is peering out of his eyes."

A low, frantic buzz built up at the base of her skull. Zofia forced herself to take a deep breath. She started to count whatever she could see—the cookies on the plate before her, the number of tassels hanging from the carpet. She counted until she no longer had to remind herself to breathe. When she thought of evil, she did not think of mechanical monsters swimming in lake waters, but people. The people who had captured those girls and killed them; the people who hid cruelty behind politics. When the buzzing subsided, she tried to decipher the expression on everyone's faces. Laila's face was blank. Hypnos and Enrique wore matching expressions of what looked like horror. But Séverin's lip curled. The gesture unnerved Zofia. It reminded her of an animal's imitation of a human smile.

"We have to go inside the leviathan," said Enrique, breaking the silence.

"All of us?" asked Hypnos. "Can't we send, I don't know, an envoy into the terrifying beast?"

Enrique crossed his arms. "You're a paragon of bravery."

"Or perhaps I worry for you, *mon cher*," said Hypnos.

Zofia watched as color bloomed on Enrique's cheeks. The whole exchange—Hypnos's slow smile and the brightness of Enrique's eyes—disoriented her. Her pulse spiked, and her palms dampened . . . but to what purpose? Those small gestures felt significant for no reason. This was no equation that demanded solving. This was merely a scenario in which she had no place. And yet her center of balance felt tilted, and she didn't know why. Annoyed, she chomped on the end of a matchstick.

"When the leviathan returns at noon tomorrow, I will go," said Séverin.

"And *he* is a paragon of martyrdom," said Hypnos. "You're not going alone." He rolled his eyes. "I'll go."

"You're the one who just called the creature a terrifying beast," pointed out Enrique.

Zofia did not agree. A Forged invention was neither inherently good nor evil, but a vessel suited to a particular purpose.

"Perhaps it would be less terrifying if it had a name," she said. "I like 'David.'"

"*No*," said Hypnos, Laila, and Enrique at the same time.

Zofia scowled. Before she could defend herself, the doors of the library opened and Eva walked inside, carrying a slip of paper. As she approached, the limp in her gait seemed more noticeable. She stopped walking the moment she saw the translation of symbols.

"You shouldn't be here," said Séverin sternly.

At a snap of his fingers, the Mnemo projection disappeared. Enrique took a side step, blocking the translation from view.

"I brought news," said Eva.

Séverin frowned. "News of what?"

"One of the girls reported missing was the daughter of a man named Moshe Horowitz, the name we found in the well. House Dazbog's contacts were able to trace the name to a moneylender who lived in Odessa until 1881."

"And?" asked Laila.

At this, Eva's shoulders fell, and her gaze darted to Zofia. "Moshe Horowitz is dead. And so is his family. They were killed in a pogrom."

All of them fell silent. Zofia did not want to think about the dead girl's family in Odessa. They had lost their daughter, and then lost their lives. Before now, the dead girls had reminded her only of Laila. Now, she saw something of herself in them. That same powerlessness.

"The Fallen House patriarch targeted her because she was Jewish," said Laila angrily. "He thought no one would think to look for her. That no one would miss her. All those girls . . . he—" She swallowed hard, and Zofia knew that meant she was near tears. "He thought he could get away with it."

"How do you know that?" asked Hypnos.

Zofia noticed that Eva leaned forward curiously. Laila blinked back tears, then waved her hand.

"I found some writing near the bodies," she said.

Eva's eyes narrowed. "That's not possible—"

Séverin cut her off. "Why would they carve the Horowitz name inside a *well*?"

When no one answered, he said it again.

"Why a *well*?" he repeated. "That's not a normal place to memorialize the dead. There has to be a reason. Explore it again."

Enrique made a choked sound. "After we nearly got destroyed by automaton goddesses, you want us to open all those doors again?"

"Who said they *would* open?" asked Eva. "All but one of those Tezcats were completely boarded up."

It was true, thought Zofia. The old man in Istanbul could have blocked their way back inside entirely.

"I want you to look at them, study them. Don't go through them," said Séverin.

Zofia noticed he was only looking at her as he said this. She quickly looked somewhere else.

"Let me be clear, I am *not* volunteering my blood to open up those doors again," said Hypnos, crossing his arms.

"Am I alone in thinking this is a terrible idea?" said Enrique. "*Killer. Automaton. Goddesses.* We are *not* opening that door."

"The Istanbul Tezcat is closed," said Séverin. "I merely want to know if there's anything written on the other side, the way the bricked-up well has writing."

"How do you know it's closed?" asked Eva.

Séverin tapped a small Mnemo beetle on his lapel. "Because I'm watching it."

Enrique blinked. *"How?"*

"Before the door closed, I threw a bug at the opening to keep track. That old man in Istanbul has a giant statue positioned at the entrance. He doesn't want you to cross over, and neither do I. We have all the eyes we need on the place," he said. "Zofia, Enrique . . . go examine the doors—"

"And *me*," cut in Eva sharply. "I saved their lives. I have *just as much* to offer. And, besides, you have no representative from House Dazbog on this search."

Séverin looked from Enrique to Zofia. Eva was telling the truth, so Zofia did not correct her.

"She can come," said Enrique.

Eva smiled with all her teeth and lifted her chin in Laila's direction.

"We need to know what else might be there before Hypnos and I go into the leviathan tomorrow," said Séverin. "In the meantime, I'll be arranging what needs to be done with Ruslan and the matriarch."

Laila rose from her seat, making her way to Zofia.

"Please be safe," she said. "I can't have anything happen to you."

A sharp pain erupted behind Zofia's chest as she studied Laila's face. There was something about its arrangement that made her feel as if she were looking at Hela. It was not something physical. Their eyes were different shades. Hela's a smoky gray to Laila's dark chocolate. Their skin color was different too. Hela's the color of marble and Laila's the color of tree bark after a rainstorm. Maybe it was the effect they had on the world around them. The way they somehow made it safe.

"I'll be safe," said Zofia.

And then, she turned and followed Enrique and Eva out of the library. As she made her way to the ice grotto, Zofia watched the light play over the icy, vaulted ceiling and crystalline carvings of leaping rabbits and foxes beneath the balconies. Her parents had always told her to be a light, but the light she found brightest belonged in others. Some people were so bright that they shut out the dark of fear. After they lost their parents, Hela's presence drowned out the shadows. In Paris, Laila and Tristan, Séverin and Enrique—even Hypnos—had done the same. But losing Tristan let the shadows back in, and as the three of them passed beneath a darkened arch, Zofia feared that if she lost Laila and Hela, she might never find her way out of the dark.

IN THE ATRIUM, Zofia noticed how the ice menagerie had been emptied. Now, motionless crystal figurines of bears and swans, sleek leopards, and huge hawks covered the translucent floor of the Sleeping Palace, scattered throughout its rooms and halls. It was discomfiting merely to stare at the still statues, but Zofia had no choice. Enrique had forgotten his notebook in the library, and made them promise to wait.

"And don't just say 'promise,' Zofia."

Zofia crossed her arms.

"They're repurposing the ice animals," explained Eva. "They can't attack if their Forging mechanism changes."

Zofia watched as one of the artisans hauled out an ice stag with a snapped foreleg. One of them drew out an unlit torch, then raised a match toward it. She knew it was an ice stag, but for some reason, all she could see was the slain and forgotten girls on the slabs of ice, Hela's persistent coughing despite all the medicine procured, Laila's garnet ring and the ever-diminishing numbers within the jewel. All of it converged into some nameless fear that made her shout out, "Stop!"

The artisan looked up, first at her and then at Eva.

"Don't . . . don't destroy it."

"It's a broken machine, miss," said the artisan.

"I know, but—"

But it was hardly the machine's fault that it could not function in this world. That something about it was less desirable. That things had happened to it that it could not control. It did not have to be destroyed.

Eva stepped in front of her. "Have it put in the jail cell, then. Out of the way."

The artisan shot her a look of disbelief, but Eva narrowed her eyes.

"Do it."

The artisan nodded, hauling the stag elsewhere. Zofia's pulse slowly eased to its normal rate.

"Thank you," said Zofia.

Eva nodded brusquely, her hand going to the silver pendant around her neck. The other girl's face wore a pattern of hesitation— pressed brows, shifting pupils. Finally, she looked up at Zofia and smiled wide.

"We don't really know each other very well, do we?" asked Eva, shaking her head. She did not wait for Zofia to respond. "For in- stance, do you like the ballet?"

"I don't know," said Zofia. "I've never been."

"Probably for the best," said Eva. She tucked a strand of red hair behind her ear. "I stopped going years ago too. It's no good to be tempted by something one can't be."

"You wanted to be a ballerina?"

Eva's mouth tightened to a flat line. "Once."

To Zofia, Eva already looked like a ballerina. She was tall and slender, and though her gait dragged, she was no less graceful.

"I'm sorry," said Zofia.

She had no reason to be. It wasn't as though she had done something, but she figured it was the kind of response Laila would use.

"I am too," said Eva. Abruptly, she let go of the pendant she held. "Do you dance, Zofia?"

"No."

Eva tilted her head. "But Laila does?"

"Yes."

Although Zofia recalled that Laila did not always consider what she did at the Palais des Rêves to be dancing.

"I envy her that . . . among other things," said Eva. "Laila and you are close?"

When Zofia nodded, Eva made a *hmm* sound at the back of her throat.

"She's very astute, isn't she?" asked Eva lightly. "It's as if she knows the impossible sometimes."

Laila knew what other people did not because she could read what other people could not. But that was a secret, and so Zofia said nothing. Instead, she followed the commotion of the room, watching as an artisan opened one of the atrium walls and shoved in the broken stag.

"A prison cell," said Eva, following her gaze.

Zofia's throat tightened. She did not like cramped, lightless spaces. She had not even known there was a prison cell hidden within the Sleeping Palace's atrium.

"How did Laila and Monsieur Montagnet-Alarie become lovers?"

"They're not," said Zofia. A second later, Zofia realized she had said the wrong thing. Her pulse spiked. "They are. I mean—"

"Oh good, you waited!" called Enrique, jogging toward them from the library hall.

He shifted the mass of notebooks under his arm. When he got to them, he was out of breath. He looked to Zofia and grinned. Zofia felt the smile as if it were a tangible thing, and it made her feel uncomfortably warm. She did not smile back.

ONCE MORE, THE THREE OF them stood in front of the Tezcat doors.

Zofia could not shake the news that Eva had told them about the Horowitz girl and the pogroms. More than anything, Zofia wished she could hear from Hela . . . and then she paused. She hadn't heard from Hela.

Due to the Order's numerous inroads throughout Russia, Séverin had arranged to let her hear from her sister weekly. The last time had been exactly eight days ago when Hela had spoken of her cough returning and of meeting a boy named Isaac. Zofia told herself she should not be concerned. Statistically, there were a number of reasons why mail should go awry: human error, illegible handwriting, weather, etcetera. Any action must be accompanied with a standard deviation. If she had the figures to calculate the chances, she would not panic. And yet, without it, her panic often felt unquantifiable, defying the boundaries of a solid number, and instead, threatening to grow into a gaping hole that would swallow her thoughts whole.

"Ready?" asked Enrique.

Without answering, Eva drew her taloned pinky ring across her palm and pressed her hand onto the metal shield. The hinges of the Tezcat portal glowed a light blue, and then swung open. Behind the first door lay nothing but the damp moss that had grown over the brick which had become so tightly adhered to the Tezcat portal entrance that hardly an inch of space existed between the opening and the wall.

"As expected," said Enrique.

But Zofia could hear the slightest tremor in his voice.

"Now for the well in Odessa," said Eva.

Eva pressed her palm against the second door. Again, the hinges glowed fluorescent and then released. A bubble rose in Zofia's chest. She told herself to be calm . . . to count the things around her. When the door opened, she counted the bricks: eighteen; the bolts around the Tezcat Portal: forty-three; the beads of blood welling on Eva's palm: seven. But none of it prepared her for the sight of the bricked-up well once she knew why the name had been inscribed.

"I *knew* there was more writing here," said Enrique. He turned to Eva. "Knife, please."

Eva handed the blade to him, and Enrique began to scrape away the damp moss that grew around Moshe Horowitz's name. When he was finished, he read aloud the inscription:

"For the family of Moshe Horowitz, gone but not forgotten . . ." He scraped at the rest of the moss covering the brick. ". . . This being the site where Rebekah Horowitz went missing and, presumably, drowned . . ."

Rebekah.

An old hate scraped at the back of Zofia's mind.

When Zofia turned thirteen, she remembered her mother's belly swelling with child. Zofia had not wanted another sibling. She didn't like all the new changes—the sound of constant woodwork to build a crib, the stream of visitors, the unfamiliar dishes her mother now craved. But then her mother lost the baby. At first, Zofia could not understand how someone might misplace an unborn infant, but then she saw the midwife leaving her parents' bedroom with a basket of bloody rags, and she understood.

Was it her fault? She knew her will carried consequence. It was the age when her Forging affinity had started to manifest, the age when she realized that if she held a piece of metal and *wanted* it set aflame or bent . . . she could do it. What had she done . . . ? Jewish law held that the child had never lived, and so it never died. And yet, her mother whispered "Rebekah" at the grave, and when the rabbi at synagogue called members to stand for the Kaddish, she stood in the women's-only part of the synagogue and glowered at anyone who looked her in the eye. Zofia still thought of the name, Rebekah, though she never uttered it aloud. To her, it was the name of a change she did not know how to want. It was the name of a fear that never had a chance to become a joy, and it filled her with shame that she had not tried to love it, and would never have the chance.

Now, Zofia felt that same rush of urgency and powerlessness all at once.

The urgency to protect what she knew, and the dread of not knowing what to expect. She steeled herself, thinking of Laila's dark eyes and Hela's gray gaze, and she promised herself she would protect them.

Zofia broke off one of her Tezcat pendants, shining the fluorescent light against the bricks. Small, writhing insects burrowed back into the lining of the brick. Her light caught a molten, silver shape. Enrique held up his hand.

"I recognize that symbol," he said, frowning.

"Where?" asked Eva.

Zofia peered closer. There, buried right beneath Rebekah's name and no bigger than a thumbnail was a small, flipped number 3.

$$\mathsf{\varepsilon}$$

"I've never seen that symbol," said Eva. "Is it the letter *E*?"

Zofia tilted her head. The symbol reminded her of something she had seen in her father's study, a mathematic sign like the lowercase omega.

"I *know* I've seen it before," said Enrique, flipping through the pages of his notebook.

"It looks like a math symbol," said Zofia. "Like the transfinite ordinal number."

"Trans what?" asked Eva.

"Transfinite is a number treated as 'infinite' or far greater than finite numbers, but not quite infinite, and ordinal is a theory used to describe a number that describes the collection of other numbers."

Eva rubbed her temples. "What do those words even *mean*?"

"Knowing Zofia, I'm sure it will prove to be brilliant," said Enrique.

He shot her a warm smile. Zofia studded his face: brows pressed flat, mouth tipped up at the corners. A pattern of pity. He *pitied* her. And Eva was not even listening. Zofia's cheeks heated, and she walked away from the Tezcat portal to the third door. Enrique stayed behind, documenting the symbol.

"It still doesn't explain why her name would be carved in a well," said Eva. "Did the Fallen House climb into the well? Who saw her get in?"

"I have no idea," sighed Enrique.

"Maybe the third door will tell us," said Eva.

Enrique made a slight whimpering sound and stood behind Eva. A second later, he seemed to change his mind, and instead stood behind Zofia, muttering, *"Pleasedon'tlettherebeakillergoddess pleasedon'tlettherebeakillergoddess . . ."*

Rolling her eyes, Eva pressed her bloodied palm to the metal shield. It swung open with a creaking sound. Immediately, Eva leapt back. Enrique screamed.

"What?" asked Zofia.

Eva turned to her, her green eyes round. "There's . . . there's writing on the wall."

Enrique didn't move. "Metaphorically or—"

"You screamed because of writing?" demanded Zofia.

"Depending on the script, some writing can appear exquisitely intimidating," said Enrique. "And I didn't scream. I yell-breathed." He clutched his chest and scowled at her. "It's different."

Zofia peered into the third portal and saw the words written in a glowing ink:

TO PLAY AT GOD'S INSTRUMENT

WILL SUMMON THE UNMAKING

24

SÉVERIN

Séverin knew that the finding should make him happy, but he couldn't remember what happy was. His mind kept catching on a particular memory, like a silk scarf in sharp branches, from last year. The five of them had acquired a costly Fabergé egg, the sale of which supported an ancient Indonesian gold Forging community against the Dutch business interests. It was Zofia's birthday, though only Laila seemed to have known. As a surprise, she had hidden a cake shaped like a chicken's egg inside their escape hansom. Before Enrique could start talking about the mythological significance of eggs, Tristan had loudly asked: "What came first, the chicken or the egg?" Zofia was the first to answer: "Scientifically speaking, the rooster." The whole hansom went silent, and then they laughed so hard that Séverin accidentally put his elbow through the cake and all the bright yellow lemon curd that Laila designed like a yolk got onto Enrique's pants, which only made them laugh harder—

"Stop," Séverin hissed to his reflection.

He braced himself against the vanity of the bedroom, struggling to get ahold of his breathing. Ruslan and the matriarch had decided to host a formal dinner, which meant that he had a whole evening to get through before he would venture into the leviathan. He willed his pulse to calm.

Laila was, of course, accompanying him, but he hadn't seen her since the library when Enrique, Eva, and Zofia had rushed to show them the writing on the wall . . .

TO PLAY AT GOD'S INSTRUMENT
WILL SUMMON THE UNMAKING

It did not solve the mystery of the well, but he didn't need every mystery answered . . . that writing was as good as a warrant. *The unmaking* . . . vague words with vast consequences. He liked it. It meant *The Divine Lyrics* was every bit as powerful as he had hoped. Powerful enough to undo every mistake.

"Séverin," said a voice by the door.

He jolted upright.

The hairs on the back of his neck prickled. Out of all the things that jarred him, how strange that it was his own name. In the past, Laila would have called him *Majnun*. He never knew why she'd chosen that name and now it didn't matter.

When Laila entered the room, he first glimpsed her through the mirror, like a fairy tale where the hero crept upon the monster, risking only a glance at her reflection lest she turn his heart to stone. Only this was its inversion. Now the monster glanced upon the maiden, risking only a glimpse of her reflection lest she turn his stone to heart.

In the mirror, he saw that Laila wore a dress of smoke. Gray silk, Forged so the edges looked as if they dissolved into the air around her. The silk moved around her body, revealing a corner of her shoulder before sleeving it in gray plumes, then a plunging neckline for a moment before transforming into a high collar beaded with silver pearls. Her diamond necklace glinted just beneath it.

Every time she snuck up on him, it was like seeing her for the first time. Two years ago, she had arrived with a troupe of nautch dancers at L'Eden and thwarted an attack on his life. At the time, he'd hardly registered her revealing outfit. He had a vague impression of beauty, but something else had instantly transfixed him. It took him a few minutes before he could pin down what it was. Kindness. Laila's kindness was warmth freely given—like unasked for treasure—and it overwhelmed him as if he were a beggar gifted a king's ransom for as irrational a reason as the day of the week.

"There seems to be much more of you than meets the eye," he had said.

Laila had raised her eyebrow and gestured to her outfit. "But not much."

That was the first time she made him laugh.

Now, he looked at her in the mirror, at her beautiful gown and her burnished skin, her kindness drained to the dregs and nothing but a hard crust of wariness left behind.

"Tomorrow, you'll have what you want," he said, not looking at her directly.

And so will I.

The Fallen House couldn't read its own treasure, but the Fallen House didn't have Laila. Of course, Laila was not the type to consider how she might be the one carrying the bloodline of the Lost

Muses. But if anyone could read that book, he was sure it was her. How fitting, he thought, that he should need her as she needed him, though not nearly in the way he had once imagined. If he believed in such things, he might have called it fate.

"I hope you'll be satisfied," he said.

"And you?" she asked. "Will you be satisfied, Séverin?"

Again, that name that hardly felt his own.

"More than that," he said, smiling to himself. "One might even say reborn."

ON THEIR FIRST WALK-THROUGHS of the Sleeping Palace, the one place that had eluded them was the dining room. It had taken the work of House Kore and House Nyx's attendants to find it. The entrance was not through a door, but a balcony window on the second floor, fifty feet high, which looked out over the jagged, dusky belt of the Ural Mountains. An ice peacock perched before the huge window, translucent feathers fanned out to block the entrance. When it saw them, it swept its feathers aside and let out a mournful coo.

As if from midair, the matriarch stepped out into the vestibule and fixed them with a critical eye.

"Late," she said, by way of greeting. "Everyone else has arrived."

Laila sneezed, and her face softened. The matriarch—the same woman who had cast him aside without a second glance—once more shrugged off her fur coat and draped it around Laila's shoulders. The gesture summoned a cold lump in his throat.

"Thank you," said Laila.

"I hope your lover is impressively attentive in other respects considering he'd let you freeze at a moment's notice," she said, glaring at Séverin. She swept her hand toward the hall. "This way.

And do be warned that it looks as though a single step will send you plummeting to your death."

She stepped out of the window, and Séverin's stomach lurched, everything in him expecting that she really would fall. But she didn't. When he tilted his head *just so* he caught the glossy sheen of a clever, Forged glass floor. He and Laila followed after the matriarch, down a corridor that promised a drop of at least three hundred feet should they take any missteps. A molten golden door appeared as if in midair, and even though it was closed, Séverin caught the sounds of Hypnos playing the piano . . .

The door opened to reveal a great, domed dining room. A feast was spread out on a long, black table carved of onyx. Near the back of the room, Hypnos played at the piano, with Enrique, Zofia, and Eva beside him. As Ruslan made his way to greet them, Séverin eyed the room. Thinly hammered sheets of golden feathers served as the floor. Above, the Forged ceiling magnified the stars so that they seemed within plucking distance, and while the glass walls afforded a breathtaking view of Lake Baikal . . . they were ornamented with rotating lights that took on the shape of the Greek zodiac.

"It's beautiful," breathed Laila, tipping back her head. The light flared against the burnished line of her throat, and Séverin nearly caught himself staring.

"Yes, quite," said Ruslan, bending over Laila's extended hand. "And does the room please you too, Monsieur Montagnet-Alarie?"

"I find it morbid."

"*Morbid?*" repeated the matriarch.

But Ruslan's smile widened. "Tell me what you see."

Séverin tapped his foot on the floor. "The feathers of Icarus. And above, the too-close heavens. And around us"—he pointed at the zodiac—"inflexible fate. This room is a reminder of the great overestimation of men . . . a reminder of how far we might fall. I'm surprised the floor isn't bloodred."

Ruslan hummed in agreement, rubbing his bald head. "'Blood flow'd, but immortal; ichor pure, such as the blest inhabitants of heav'n, may bleed, nectareous.'"

"Who's reciting the *Iliad*?" called out Enrique from the back.

"Me!" said Ruslan gleefully. "Sometimes I surprise myself by remembering things . . . one imagines that without a ceiling of hair, all thoughts merely abandon the skull."

"What did you say?" asked Séverin.

"Skull?"

"No."

"Hair . . ."

"No."

There was something else. Something that had struck him in that moment.

Ruslan paused, and then said, "Ichor?"

"Yes, that's it. *Ichor pure.*"

Ruslan stroked his head. "The Fallen House loved any mention of the gods. It was even rumored they had found a way to *give* themselves ichor, of a kind. A way to manipulate their very human matter. A rumor, however."

"It's no rumor," said Laila. "We've seen it."

"Ah, yes . . . in the catacombs, correct?" asked Ruslan, looking from the matriarch to Séverin. "So it's true? You saw their ichor?"

As if he could forget. Sometimes he found himself touching his mouth, dreaming of sticky gold. Whatever alchemy rendered men to gods, he craved it.

"What let them do that?" asked Séverin.

"*Let?*" repeated Ruslan, his mouth twisting on the word. "They had objects the likes of which you and I cannot fathom."

Ruslan moved toward the dining table, pulling out a chair for Laila and Delphine as he spoke.

"House Dazbog specializes in the collection of Forging lore, and I believe the Fallen House had come across an ancient weapon . . . it had many names. In the Indian continent, it was known in the Tamilian language as an *aruval*, the medieval court of Baghdad called it a lost angel's *zulfiqar*, but when the Fallen House came upon it, they called it the Midas Knife, not only after the cursed king from Greek myth, but also for its alchemical properties: blood to gold, man to god."

"It sounds like magic," said the matriarch dismissively.

"Perhaps Monsieur Montagnet-Alarie can tell us better," said Ruslan. "Was it magic? What you saw?"

For a moment, Séverin was back in the catacombs. Once more, he kneeled on a stage, felt the sharp rip of wings searing through his shoulder blades, the pressure of horns at his head, and always the strange cadence in his blood that sang with divine invincibility.

"What is magic but a science we cannot fathom," said Séverin.

Ruslan smiled warmly.

"Well put," he said. "Though I would imagine such a weapon is wielded with great cost. It was said to be created from fragments of the top-most brick of the Tower of Babel, and thus closest in reach to God's power."

"Perhaps that's what made the Fallen House think they could become gods," said Séverin.

The matriarch scoffed, gesturing at the gold feathers of the floor, the intoxicating nearness of the stars. "One would think after all these reminders of fatality, they would've stopped themselves."

Ruslan rubbed his one injured arm, still limp in its sling. "But then we would not be human, would we?"

He grinned and signaled to a server, who rang a dinner gong. Hypnos continued to play the piano, lost in the music. It used to be impossible to pull Hypnos away from the instrument.

Eva called out over Hypnos's playing: "Do you take requests, Monsieur?"

Hypnos paused. "Yes!"

"Excellent," said Eva. "Then stop."

And she walked off. Hypnos's expression soured, but he rose from the piano and joined everyone at the table. When Séverin turned to his right, he found that he was seated next to the matriarch. A servant stopped beside her, handing her a small, bloody vial that he recognized as her immunity to any unwanted blood Forging.

"You always see so clearly into the darkness of men's hearts, Monsieur Montagnet-Alarie," she said, before adding in a softer voice, "But I remember when you used to see wonder."

Séverin reached for his water goblet. "And now I see truth."

For dinner, the spread appeared like burnt offerings, food presented to deities. All of it designed to look charred, though none of it was. In a silver bowl sat black figs, so velveteen and succulent, they looked as if someone had taken a silver spoon to midnight and scooped. Then a roasted haunch, served on a pillow of burnt sage; black pudding on ice terrines; soufflés the color of the night sky. Around them, the animals of the ice menagerie had been repurposed . . . a crystal jaguar prowled around the dining table, balancing carafes of delicate ice wine on its back. The onyx table reflected the sky above, and as the night stretched longer, the ceiling grew delicate stalactites that resembled thinly beaten strands of silver. Séverin moved through the motions of dinner, but he hardly felt present. As far as his mind was concerned, he was already inside the leviathan, already turning the pages of *The Divine Lyrics*, already watching as the blood in his veins turned to a god's rich ichor. He wouldn't need the Fallen House's Midas Knife for such a thing. He could have it on his own.

Séverin didn't realize dinner had concluded until the gong sounded once more. He pushed back from his chair, only to realize Zofia was standing beside him and glaring. He hadn't seen her leave her seat, much less walk toward him.

"What is it?"

"I haven't received word from Hela in eight days," she said.

Séverin frowned. There was no reason for a delay in messages. He had paid an exorbitant price so a courier would travel through the Order's inroads and fetch Hela's letters of health. Perhaps the man had gotten turned around in Irkutsk.

"I'll take care of it," he said.

Zofia hesitated for a moment, and then nodded. "I know."

Something flickered behind his heart, and the rime of ice he'd placed around it slipped for an instant. *How* did she know he'd take care of it? *How* could she trust his word after he'd made sure she couldn't go back to her family? After she'd seen what happened to the last person who trusted him so blindly?

Séverin clenched his jaw, and the cold in his heart reasserted itself. He had found the best physician in the area to treat her sister. By all accounts, the girl was responding to treatment better than expected. It was Zofia's trust that inexplicably annoyed him. This was a business transaction. It had no room for hope, and yet she'd shoved that burden on him.

Beside him, Laila touched his arm. As he readied to leave, he heard Ruslan call his name. He looked up and saw the patriarch of House Dazbog still seated at the table, dragging one finger across the dessert plate to collect what little powdered sugar remained.

"I can't decide if going into that leviathan's mouth makes you brave or mad," he said, with a small shake of his head. "But perhaps it's fitting." Ruslan looked to Laila, smiling. "With a name like 'Laila,' and a madman for a lover, I do hope you call your Séverin 'Majnun.'"

Laila's hand stiffened on his arm. "What did you say?"

Ruslan looked confused. "It's a reference to the sixth century poem 'Laila and Majnun' composed by Nizami Ganjavi—"

"I know what it is," said Laila quietly.

"Ah! Good, good," said Ruslan. "Do you, Séverin?"

Séverin almost didn't realize he was shaking his head. He felt numb all over.

"'Laila and Majnun' is one of my favorite tragedies," said Ruslan. "I've always considered it such a shame that they are overshadowed by their later counterparts, *Romeo and Juliet*."

Séverin fought to listen to their conversation, but his awareness felt pulled to every instance when Laila had called him *Majnun*. *Madman.* She'd told him what it meant, but he'd never known his nickname came from a poem. A tragic one, no less. Inexplicably, he felt like a fool. Once, that name had been a talisman to him. Now, it tasted bitter and prophetic.

"Ah, *Majnun*. The madman who lost himself to an impossible dream," said Ruslan. He laughed softly, then glanced at the clock. "I wish you both a good night, and am honored to have spent such an illuminating evening in your company. Good luck tomorrow, Monsieur Montagnet-Alarie."

He bowed once and turned back to his dessert plate.

SÉVERIN DIDN'T REMEMBER climbing to the top of the stairs, but he must have.

He didn't remember opening the door to their suite either, but he must have done that too, for here they were. The silence lay thickly around them, and perhaps that was why when he finally spoke, it seemed louder than he intended.

"Is it true?"

Laila startled. She had taken a seat at the ice-and-marble vanity in the corner of the room, her back to him as she drew off her gloves and removed her jewelry.

"Is what true?"

"My—" He stopped, gathered himself, started anew: "The name you called me. Did you take it from that poem?"

"Yes," she said.

It struck him then that even before she had kissed him and tangled up some roots inside him so deeply that he would—without thinking—*choose* her over his own brother . . . she had already marked him for someone who she would never belong to, an attachment that could only end in disappointment. How well she'd chosen his name.

He was mad, then, to think fate would let him be happy.

Perhaps he was mad, now, to try and change it.

Laila fumbled with the zipper at the back of her dress. Slowly, he went to her. He almost didn't realize what he was doing . . . all this time, he'd only ever tried to put distance between them. To get close to her now flew in the face of all of that, and yet he knew there was some transaction to be made if he wanted the truth. When he stood too close to her, he felt weak. No doubt she would feel weak by parting with her secrets, and so he must meet her on equal ground.

"Tell me what happens at the end of the poem, Laila," he said.

Laila closed her eyes, as if armoring herself. None of that, he thought. He reached out and swept her hair across one shoulder. Goose bumps prickled along her skin as she bowed her neck, graceful as a swan. His hands brushed against the caught zipper. Its teeth had gotten tangled up in the silk. At his touch, Laila flinched a little. She usually hated for anyone to see her scar, but this time she made no move to hide herself, as if just this once, she too was willing to be bare.

"Tell me, Laila," he said.

The zipper slid down an inch. In the reflection, Laila opened her eyes.

"Once, a boy and a girl fell in love, but they could not be together," she said. "The girl married another. The boy went mad, and—"

Her breath caught as he pushed the zipper farther.

"And?" he echoed.

"And he abandoned himself to the wilds of the desert," she said. She refused to look at him. "At the end, they had a chance to be together, but they chose not to."

Séverin slid the zipper farther. Now, he could count the delicate bones of her back. If he wanted, he could trace that glassy scar that some fiend had once led her to believe was a mark of her very unnaturalness. Once, he'd kissed his way down the line of it.

"In the end, they chose to preserve the thought of the other, uncorrupted, in their hearts."

Séverin's hand stilled. In the vanity's reflection, Laila finally met his eyes. "I don't think Laila could stand to see how much her Majnun had lost himself to the wilderness in his soul."

She made no move to cover herself or leave, even with her dress almost completely unzipped. He recognized the tension in the line of her shoulders, the lift of her chin . . . the taut stillness of *waiting*.

For him.

Unthinking, Séverin bent toward the hollow of her neck. He watched her eyes flutter shut, her head tilt back. Laila called to him like a long night's dreamless sleep after months of unrest. His lips were almost at her skin, when he stopped.

What was he doing?

Laila was a mirage glimpsed through smoke. A temptation in the desert that lulls the soul into thinking of false promises. Séverin had his promise, scrawled inside the jaws of the mechanical leviathan slumbering beneath the ice grotto. His promise lay behind the teeth of the devil. Tomorrow, he would have it, and he would be free.

Her words rang through his head.

I don't think Laila could stand to see how much her Majnun had lost himself to the wilderness in his soul.

Séverin drew back from the curve of her neck and met her eyes in the mirror. Whatever lay in her gaze instantly shuttered, all weakness replaced with wariness.

"I think he knew that she was never meant for him," said Séverin.

He grabbed his coat from where he'd dropped it to the floor. His hands felt as though they were burning. Then, he made his way to the library to wait out the long night.

PART IV

The Origins of Empire

Master Emanuele Orsatti, House Orcus of the Order's Italy Faction
1878, reign of King Umberto I

In debating the merits of pursuing hidden treasure, one must weigh the risk of whether it was never meant to be found and if so, why?

25

SÉVERIN

At noon, the devil waited for Séverin.

Séverin took his time leaving the library. He wanted to remember this . . . the indifferent faces of the nine muses. They were gargantuan, the tops of their marble crowns skimming the stained glass ceiling. They shadowed everything, and perhaps that was the architect's intent. To remind him of his own insignificance. His powerlessness. But Séverin needed no reminder. Every touch conjured the slip of Tristan's hot blood on his hands. Every breath carried the stench of the troika flames cornering them in St. Petersburg; the charnel sweetness of the fire that took his parents. Every sight promised unseeing eyes. To be powerless was the price of mortality. And he was done with mortality.

Along with Tristan's knife, he carried one last reminder of his past: the ouroboros carving that had once adorned his father's Ring. In another life, it would have been the Ring he'd worn as patriarch of House Vanth. Before, every time he touched the warm metal of the Ring and traced the jeweled eyes of the snake, he felt oddly light, as if someone had knocked loose his soul and it dangled outside him, always searching for a place to put down roots and always starved for light. Perhaps after all this time, his spirit had grown accustomed to the sensation. After all, what were roots when one could choose not be anchored, but instead be born aloft?

And yet, for all that he no longer cared about his inheritance, he couldn't forget that it had been stolen. He rubbed his thumb along the scar down his palm, remembering the blue light flashing across his eyes from the inheritance test. Proof that the Forging instrument had accepted his blood and still the matriarch had conspired against him. It no longer mattered why she'd lied or what she stood to gain, because in the end, all that mattered was what lay ahead. The alchemy of *The Divine Lyrics* might grant him the snowy plumes of seraphim or the lacquered horns of demons, but that golden blood would keep its promise:

Nothing would ever be taken from him again.

SÉVERIN HARDLY HEARD the conversation around him. He felt Eva's hands on his chest, the heat of a rushed, pressed kiss on his cheek. "For luck," she'd whispered in his ear. Laila stood unmoving by the entrance, her hand playing lazily at her diamond collar. Zofia had brought him and Hypnos an armband full of incendiary devices and spherical detectors, as well as several Mnemo bugs to capture all angles of what they found down there.

Enrique paced at the entrance of the leviathan's mouth, tugging the front of his hair.

"You're looking for a book," started Enrique.

"*Non!* A *book?*" repeated Hypnos, with a false gasp. "*Qu'est-ce que c'est?*"

Enrique swatted his arm, and Hypnos grinned.

"We know, *mon cher*," he said.

"It's not going to look like an ordinary tome. It'll be huge, probably. Bound with animal skin. According to my research, the last time it was seen, someone had tried to carve its name into the surface, but it was cut off at *D-I-V-I-N-E L-Y-R.*"

"Big, old fragments," said Hypnos. "Noted. Now kiss me. For luck."

Séverin watched the exchange. As someone who had been something of an expert in performance, he knew the difference between something genuine and something contrived. That kiss belonged to the latter. The question lay only in who was doing the performing—Hypnos or Enrique? Enrique smiled to himself, color blooming along the tops of his cheeks. Hypnos, however, turned to the leviathan without a second glance.

Séverin had his answer.

"Shall we?" asked Séverin.

Hypnos nodded. By order of the matriarch of House Kore, they only had one task: Go in, find *The Divine Lyrics*, and get out. It was the highest priority. After that, members from House Dazbog and House Nyx would follow and remove the objects to the library for further cataloguing. The moon in the ice grotto already began to shrink—moment by moment turning more slender, counting down the seconds before the metal leviathan would slip once more back into the waves.

Delphine waited for them near the leviathan, a plate in her hands.

As Séverin got closer, he recognized the familiar smell of raspberry-cherry jam smeared over buttered toast. The taste of his childhood before he'd abandoned all claim to one. When Delphine looked at him, something like hopefulness dared to touch the corners of her eyes. Séverin took the food without comment. He could feel Delphine's eyes at his back, but he didn't turn. Just as she hadn't turned when he'd stared after her, calling her name, even when she'd shaken his shoulders and told him they were no longer family, that she was no longer his *Tante FeeFee*.

"I'll call down the time," said Enrique. "Fifteen minute increments. The matriarch wants you out with ten minutes to spare."

The leviathan's mouth was too damp and narrow for them to fit in at the same time, so Séverin went first, his boots easily finding the grooves that led to the staircase. He broke a phosphorescent baton and the light climbed through the metal throat of the leviathan, catching on the tops of a spiraling staircase unwinding deep within its jaws. Séverin swallowed hard. He knew the creature was Forged, and yet it still seemed eerily alive to him. Steam plumed out from its metal joints like exhaled breath. He looked behind him, holding out his hand to Hypnos. The other boy stared into the tunnel, his blue eyes rounded with fear. Unbidden, he remembered Hypnos as he had been—the boy with the singing voice, the boy desperate for an invitation to join the game.

"You didn't have to come," said Séverin.

"Nonsense, *mon cher*," said Hypnos, even as his teeth chattered. "If I didn't come, who the hell would have protected you?"

The familiar barbs of those words dug into Séverin. He blinked once and saw Tristan wide-eyed, grinning. He blinked again and saw him dead. Séverin tightened his hand to a fist, feeling the raised edge of his scar, the sour taste of the promise he couldn't keep: *I protect you.*

"Come on, then," he said tonelessly.

The steps were slippery, and the metal joints groaned with the pressure of his weight. Arctic water sloshed over his ankles, soaking through his water-resistant trousers. Everywhere the light touched, Séverin saw ruin. There were still a number of steps to go, but at least he could see the slatted, silver floor of the leviathan's belly.

"Fifteen minutes down!" called Enrique, though his voice sounded faraway.

Right before they hit the bottom of the stairs, Séverin asked for the spherical detection device. Hypnos handed it to him, and they both watched as the detection light illuminated the gaping shadows, caverns and shelves of the Fallen House's treasure room.

In all that he had seen, the word "awe" rarely came to him.

But now . . . now he felt fresh wonder.

The light illuminated a world teeming with exquisite treasures. It felt like the inside of a holy place. Even now, Séverin could make out the tattered edges of a rich, scarlet rug. There was a water-damaged roll of cushion, a side table with a candle. Whoever built this had intended it as a place of meditation. Beyond the small area of meditation, the room opened to a cavern. Egyptian pillars of lapis lazuli propped up the walls. Huge, half figurines of roaring, golden tigers swiveled their heads in his and Hypnos's direction and narrowed their ruby eyes. Illuminated manuscripts Forged to the likeness of birds fluttered, shedding bits of gold leaf as they streamed overhead. There were statue busts and relics, necklaces of luminous stones, spinning orreries carved of jade . . .

"Dear God," said Hypnos. "The Order would *kill* for this."

Hypnos walked toward a pillar in the middle of the room. It was roughly four feet high and adorned with the international House symbols of the Order of Babel. Séverin followed after him. Each of the symbols bore a particular indentation. There, nestled among the thorns of House Kore and crescent moons of House Nyx, he recognized the ouroboros shape of the House that should have been his: House Vanth.

"Why have this here?" asked Hypnos.

Séverin followed the direction of the pillar to the low ceiling above which resembled a warped mirror. Or a Mnemo lens.

"I think it functions like a key," said Séverin, pointing at the indents within the House symbols. He took out his ouroboros carving and held it up against the sunken shape of it in the stone pillar. A perfect fit. In one smooth move, he pushed in the ouroboros and then looked up at the ceiling.

Nothing happened.

"Let me try," said Hypnos.

He pressed his House Nyx ring into the indent, and a ripple of light chased down the silver ceiling . . .

Séverin held his breath, wondering if it might reveal some proof that its final treasure lay here. Instead, the Mnemo screen showed the ice grotto above: Enrique pacing in a circle; Zofia burning a match; Laila stone-faced and unblinking.

"We can see them so clearly, but they can't see us, can they?" asked Hypnos. He waved his hands wildly beneath the screen, but no one's expression changed. "How is this possible?"

"The recording device must be on one of the leviathan's teeth," said Séverin, though that was not nearly as interesting to him as the Rings. He stared at the perfect fit of the ouroboros carving within the pillar. "My father's emblem didn't work."

Hypnos looked curiously blank as he withdrew his Ring. Instantly, the Mnemo screen went dark. Séverin noticed that the lines of his mouth had tightened, as if his mouth warred with his mind. It was the expression of a secret fighting to be known.

"Perhaps it only works on active Houses?" suggested Hypnos, not looking at him.

"The Fallen House was exiled long before House Vanth fell," said Séverin, pointing at the emblem of the six-pointed star in the pillar. "It works just fine."

"Yes, well," said Hypnos, shrugging. "Does it matter, *mon cher*? This is no treasure and holds no interest to us."

Séverin eyed the pillar a moment longer and then withdrew his ouroboros pendant. In the end, Hypnos was right. The pillar held neither hidden truths nor hidden treasure. They needed to keep looking.

While Hypnos turned to the wall of treasures, Séverin moved toward the northern section of the room. Built into the wall was a great steering wheel, the spokes encased in white.

The leviathan didn't just move, it could be *steered*. Controlled. Suddenly, the name of the Horowitz family in the well made sense. Each of those Tezcat portals had been routes for the leviathan to sneak through.

Hadn't Enrique mentioned there was a lake in Istanbul? And the well was just wide enough for the creature to fit through. Séverin scanned the area nearest the steering wheel, nausea creeping through his body. The Fallen House must have used the leviathan as a transportation vessel. To his right, a metal bubble protruded from the wall, an escape mechanism of sorts, equipped with its own small steering wheel and clouded orbs that he recognized as Shu Gusts, Forged breathing apparatuses full of oxygen

and named for the Egyptian god of the air. This part of the leviathan formed a partial narthex, which abutted the place of meditation. A table hunched half-hidden in the shadows. There, a stone
slab—like an altar—jutted up from the floor. On it lay something
dark and leathered.

Séverin took a step toward it. Something inside him hummed.
The scar on his hand tingled.

"Thirty minutes!" echoed Enrique's voice from far away.

This was it.

Séverin felt as though he were in a dream. That book called to
him. Strange paraphernalia littered the surface of the altar. The
book itself was as Enrique had described: huge and darkened, the
leather eaten away on the sides. Old blood spattered the stone.
A knife, now rusted, had fallen to the floor. There was a page of
hymns, litanies in different languages and a small, strange harp
pushed to the side; some of its strings glittered as if they had been
strung with starlight.

In that second, Séverin felt as if he'd caught the tempo of the
universe's pulse, as if he stood on the verge of an apotheosis. He
reached for the book. When he touched it, he thought he heard
Tristan's laugh echoing in his ears. He felt the pressure of horns,
Roux-Joubert's voice whispering to him: *We can be gods.*

He flipped open the book—

And then paused. It was impossible. And yet, the truth slammed
into him with all the force of a bludgeon.

26

LAILA

Laila watched as the afternoon light seamed through the cracks
of the ice, as if knitting the world back together in gold.

Or perhaps it wasn't gold at all, but rich ichor, that nectareous
blood of the gods that Séverin and Ruslan mentioned at dinner.
The thought unnerved her. If she looked at the world that way, it
turned the lake from something wondrous to something wounded.
She couldn't bear any more wounds, not from the dead girls and
their stolen hands nor from the raw ache behind her chest every
time she saw Séverin.

Near the entrance of the Sleeping Palace she found a slender
gazebo Forged of ice and marble, the pillars twisted round with
jasmine and bruise-colored violets to keep away the smell of fish
carcasses left out on the ice by the sleek seals that lived in the lake.
She breathed deep. Savoring all of it: the smell of life and death.
The fetid sweetness of life expired, the unripe bitterness of life cut
short. And always, that metal tang of ice.

In the distance, the jagged Ural Mountains appeared mirrored in the lake, as if an identical belt of them existed just beneath the surface of the water.

She hoped it was true.

She hoped there was another world pressed beside their own, a world where she had been born instead of made; a world where the girls bound to the Sleeping Palace had never died. Laila wondered who she might be in that other world. Perhaps she would be a married woman by now, like so many of the girls her age in Pondichéry. Perhaps a boy with skin as dark as hers and eyes that were not the color of sleep would hold her heart in thrall.

Laila twisted her garnet ring until the number blazed: *12.*

Twelve days left.

Or, depending on how soon Séverin and Hypnos could bring up *The Divine Lyrics* from the leviathan, hundreds of days to spare.

Laila's throat tightened, and she gripped the gazebo's railing, avoiding any sight of her reflection when a sudden crunch of snow made her look up. There, bundled against the cold, stood Enrique. He was dressed in a long trench coat, the chill wind mussing his hair.

"Can I join you?" he asked.

Laila smiled. "Of course."

She made room for him on the bench, and the two of them sat looking out at the endless stretch and prisms of ice and light. He fiddled with the edges of his coat. He opened his mouth, then clamped it shut.

"Spit it out, Enrique."

"You know how you can read objects with a touch?" asked Enrique in a breathless rush.

Laila feigned shock. *"I can?"*

"I'm being serious!"

"What of it?"

Enrique flipped over his notebook of ideas and research. He seemed agitated. In the past, he might have leaned against her, limp as a puppy angling for someone to scratch his head or, as Enrique used to say: *Annoy the ideas under my skull*. Something held him back now, and only then did Laila see part of the script written on the notebook:

TO PLAY AT GOD'S INSTRUMENT
WILL SUMMON THE UNMAKING

Strange words that cast shadows in her heart.

Enrique reached for her hand. "Have you ever considered that *why* you can do this has nothing to do with, um, the circumstances of your birth . . . ," he said delicately, and then, all in one breath, ". . . and more like, perhaps, a secret-lineage-in-which-you-are-descended-of-guardian-women-tasked-to-protect-a-powerful-book?"

"Enrique."

Enrique tugged at a piece of his black hair. "The more research I've conducted, the more this sacred order of the Lost Muses comes into play. Granted, they have different titles depending on which culture you look at, but they are prevalent! And then there's *you* with your goddess abilities, and need to find *The Divine Lyrics*, and the fact that all of those statues in the grotto and the dead girls didn't have hands. Their hands were a sacrifice, Laila, like giving up the power within them." He poked at her palm. "Just think about the power in your *own* hands."

Laila curled her fingers.

"Enrique," she said, this time more wearily.

He stopped, and the tops of his cheeks reddened. "We must be careful, is all, once they bring out the book. Especially you. There's far too much that's unknown and I . . . I worry."

He said this last part like a child, and Laila was reminded of the glimpses of boyhood she'd seen in the objects he handed her. The little boy who read by his mother's knee and wrote "books" from the scraps of merchant ledgers for his father. A boy who was brilliant and eager.

Overlooked.

She brought her hand to his cheek. "I hear you, Enrique."

He looked crestfallen. "But you don't believe me."

"I don't know what to believe," she said. "If I really were descended of the Lost Muses, I imagine my mother would have told me."

"Maybe she didn't have the time," said Enrique gently. "And it doesn't even have to be your mother. The man we saw in Istanbul had the bloodline and preemptively blinded himself because of it."

Laila bit her lip. Enrique had a point . . . but it felt too huge to wrap her mind around.

He squeezed her shoulder. "Will you come in and wait with us, at least?"

"In a minute."

"It's *freezing*. Why are you even out here, Laila?"

Laila smiled and exhaled, watching as her breath clouded.

"See that?" she said, nodding at the fading plume of air. "Sometimes I need to see that I can still do that."

Enrique looked stricken as he released her shoulder, tucking his arms around himself and huddling against the wind. He didn't meet her eyes. "Of course you can . . . and you will for a long, *long* time."

"I know, I know," she said, not wanting to worry him.

"No, but you really *must*," said Enrique, looking exceptionally wounded. "I can't feed myself, Laila. I'll perish left to my own devices. Life is cruel, and often without cake."

She swatted his arm. "There will always be cake."

He smiled, and then his expression changed to something pleading.

"Speaking of cake . . . or rather, the opposite of cake." He paused, frowning in thought. "What *is* the opposite of cake?"

"Despair," said Laila.

"Right, well, speaking of despair, I think you should tell him."

Enrique didn't have to define *him*. Laila already knew, and the thought twisted inside her. Séverin had no claim to her secrets, much less her death.

"I know he's been the opposite of cake, but he's still our Séverin," said Enrique. "I know these past months have been hard, and he's . . . different. But what if telling him changes how he's been acting? I *know* he's in there somewhere . . . I know he still cares . . ."

His face fell a little. Out of all of them, Enrique had always trusted Séverin the most. How could he not? Séverin had earned his loyalty through and through, but that was the past and now Laila felt as though someone had set fire to her veins.

"And what if it doesn't change him?" she said, her voice rising. "And even if it does, what does it mean that I have to be at death's door to bring him back to himself? My life, and whatever is left of it, will not be what his soul gnaws on to regain its strength. My *death* is not in service to his character, and I will not be a sacrifice simply for him to find peace of mind. He is *not* my responsibility to save."

It was only when she realized she was looking down at Enrique that she realized she'd shot to her feet.

Enrique's eyes went round, and he squeaked out, "Agreed."

"I know you mean well," said Laila, sighing as she plopped back down on the seat. "But I . . . I can't do it, Enrique. It would hurt too much."

Enrique's chin dropped a little, and his gaze went to the ice. "I can see that. I know how much it hurts when you realize you're not held in the same emotional regard as you thought. Or, perhaps, imagined."

"Promise me you won't tell him, Enrique," she said, gripping his hand. "I have had things taken from me my whole life. My death will not be one of them."

Enrique looked at her, his eyes bleak. And then he nodded. A moment later, he squeezed her hand and left. Laila watched him go as a light snow began to dust their clothes. Now, the Sleeping Palace looked as if it had been chiseled out of the pages of a cold fairy tale. The spires of frosted quartz looked like glass bones, and Laila wanted to imagine the palace belonged to Snegurochka. Maybe the snow maiden had chosen not to melt for love, but rather freeze for life. But her reverie was cut short at the sight of Delphine greeting Enrique at the threshold. Laila was too far away to catch the words exchanged, but she saw how Enrique went stiff. He looked back to her, but Delphine caught his arm, pointing him inside. Laila knew what it meant.

Séverin was back.

The book was here.

In the cold, Laila's ring felt wondrously loose, as if it wished to be discarded now that there was no point in wearing it.

The other woman approached her, black furs draped around her body. She cut a striking pose on the ice, and if Laila didn't know better, she'd guess that Delphine was the kind of woman who breathed as if it were an exercise in leisure rather than necessity.

"They're back?" asked Laila.

Delphine nodded.

Laila felt as if her life was waiting for her to run and catch up to it, but she couldn't make herself move. Something kept her back. Laila pushed through her misgivings, and rose to meet her fate.

They walked back in silence for a few moments before Delphine spoke. "It's hard to look at him, is it not?"

Laila knew she meant Séverin, and a long-dead piece of loyalty flared within her.

"I imagine it is just as hard for him to look at you."

"I owe you no defense of my choices," said Delphine haughtily. But then she smiled sadly, lost for a moment. "I only meant that I cannot see him as he is now. In my eyes, he will always be a child turned around in his seat at the theatre. A little boy staring at people, watching as wonder bloomed across the audience's faces."

Laila could almost picture him as a child. Slight and dark-haired, his dusky eyes huge in his face. A little boy who had to grow up too soon.

"Why are you telling me this?"

Delphine smiled, though it was fragile and did not reach her eyes.

"Because I need to tell someone what I remember," she said. "I envy you, child."

Laila bit back a snort. The matriarch had nothing to be envious of. Delphine could move through the world without expectation of a door slammed in her face. Delphine had *lived*. Laila had only dreamed of life.

"I assure you that any envy I inspire is ill-deserved."

Delphine looked down at the ice, considering the echo of her face in the lake water. "I envy you because you can look at yourself. You can bear your own reflection, knowing you can shoulder the weight of every choice you made and regret you carry. That is a rare thing as one gets older."

What feels rarer is the chance to get older, thought Laila.

INSIDE, THE SLEEPING PALACE was a rush of commotion. One of the House Kore artisans popped a bottle of champagne. A cautious wave of excitement wound through Laila.

"Treasure!" shouted one of them. *"Mounds* of treasure!"

Delphine accepted a glass of champagne. Laila stood in the shadows, her eyes tracking the room, catching on the glint of light bouncing off the slow-moving ice animals and the grand chandelier swaying overhead.

"The patriarch of House Dazbog had no choice but to send word to the Order of Babel according to Order protocol," said another. "They're coming, matriarch. *All* of them."

The glass dropped from her hand, shattering onto the floor.

"Here?" Delphine spluttered. "What about the Winter Conclave?"

"It would seem, matriarch, that they are bringing the Winter Conclave . . . to us."

Laila looked around the vast, empty atrium. Resentment coiled inside her gut. She didn't want hundreds of Order members running through here with their sticky hands grabbing for treasure. She might have felt differently if the Conclave admitted its non-Western members—those from the colonial guilds that had been absorbed into the Houses of the country that conquered their land—but they had no place here. It reminded Laila of the dead girls, hunted for their very invisibility in the grand scheme of the world.

"When are they coming?" snarled Delphine.

"Within minutes, matriarch," said the servant. "They plan to utilize their own Tezcat inroads, both above ground and under water. They will bring their own artisans to decorate before the annual Midnight Auction."

Delphine swore under her breath. Just then, Laila watched as the servants carried up baskets of treasure—books and statues, jewels dripping off platters and gleaming instruments. Her thoughts felt pulled in a thousand directions. She felt someone shoving a champagne flute into her hand. When she looked up, silver petals rained down from the ice ceiling, clinging to the blue floor. She'd always dreamed that when she got close to the book, her body would know. Maybe her veins would gleam with light, or her hair would raise up off her shoulders. Instead, her pulse turned sluggish. Time seemed to have forgotten to gather her in its momentum, slowing the room and its inhabitants around her. Doubt caught up to her. Her heart hurt for no reason she could name. And then, at last, she felt Enrique and Zofia at her side. Zofia—sweet, stoic Zofia—had tears streaming down her face. Enrique was talking too fast, and she couldn't catch anything but one phrase, so sharp she felt like she'd broken her life on it:

"There was no book."

27

ENRIQUE

Six hours before the Midnight Auction . . .

Enrique once loved the feeling of incredulity. It was the sense that the world conspired to dazzle him. It was how he had felt when he'd first visited L'Eden, on the hotel's anniversary when Séverin had designed the space to resemble the Garden of Paradise. A basilisk made of apples and twice the size of a dining table writhed between the pillars, twisting and snapping its jaws, perfuming the air with fruit. Topiary creatures gently grazed by silk couches. And Séverin moved among them like a well-tailored god still curating his universe. That was incredulity. That someone like Séverin could summon forth his imagination, and the world would not bowl him over but bow before him. Enrique didn't remember consciously deciding that he wanted to work for the strange hotelier with a taste for stranger artifacts . . . all he knew was that he wanted to know what the world looked like from his angle.

What he felt now was a different kind of incredulity. The kind where one has released a dream into the world, only to rediscover it on the ground, trampled and stained.

There was no book.

How . . .

How could they have been *so* wrong?

And at such cost?

Beside him, Laila hadn't moved. Her face was bloodless, her garnet ring sliding down her finger. Zofia stood on Laila's other side, their shoulders barely touching.

All around them pressed the members of House Dazbog and House Kore. The air seemed to quiver and shake with the promise of guests soon to arrive. At the entrance to the Sleeping Palace, the matriarch of House Kore fixed the lake with a haughty expression.

"How *dare* they," she said, under her breath. "They could not stand the thought of someone unearthing treasure without them. Well, that's fine. Let them bring the Conclave here. Let them see exactly what *my* patronage still yields."

She cast a scathing glance at Enrique.

"And you *still* need a haircut."

Enrique wanted to grumble at her like he normally did, but he couldn't find the right words. All he felt was Laila's hand in his . . . cold and still as a corpse. A warm hand gripped his shoulder, and Enrique turned to see Hypnos smiling down at him.

"Aren't you going to congratulate me?" asked Hypnos. His face shone with pride. "We've got the treasures of the Fallen House! The Order will have their infamous Midnight Auction. Séverin has his vengeance. Whatever is left of the Fallen House will never recover from this blow."

Enrique was in no mood to congratulate, and so he said nothing.

Hypnos didn't seem to notice. His hand slipped from Enrique's shoulder as he pointed to the ice. Beside Hypnos, Eva appeared, crossing her arms. A challenging smile curved her lips.

"They're here," she said slowly.

Enrique's pulse kicked up at the sound of paws scraping over ice. Hundreds of dogsleds poured across Lake Baikal's frozen waters. As they got closer, Enrique recognized different factions of the Order and the living treasure chests that kept pace beside them. A beryl wolf let loose a mechanical howl. Eva nodded in the wolf's direction.

"House Orcus," she said. "They specialize in collecting objects of torture, particularly ones used to punish oathbreakers."

Overhead, an obsidian eagle swooped low, its shadow stretched across the water.

"House Frigg of the Prussian Empire," explained Eva once more, pointing at the pale bird. "They have more of an agricultural taste when it comes to their acquisitions, particularly in tapping rubber trees—"

"A *taste* for agriculture?" repeated Hypnos, his lip curling. "I'm sure that's how those souls in Africa see it too."

A marble dolphin broke the surface of the ice before disappearing under the waves while an agate chamois goat and a stately onyx horse trotted beside two ornate carriages.

"House Njord, House Hadúr, and House Atya of the Austro-Hungarian factions," said Eva.

Hypnos crossed his arms and let out a low whistle. "And what do we have here? Ah, even the British decided to take a peek at our wares." He waved at a shimmering golden lion making its way slowly across the ice. Beside it, a smaller and less ornate carriage. Like an afterthought.

"They tend to keep their findings to themselves and their museums," said Hypnos, rolling his eyes. "But the Fallen House's long-lost wares tempt them all."

Enrique felt his stomach turn as he watched the procession of the Winter Conclave. The Order thought of themselves as guardians of Western civilization, but their might was far more powerful and terrible; they were custodians of history. What they took, the world forgot. And he had helped them.

Eva tugged at her silver ballerina pendant. "They're going to want to see all of you tonight . . . the great treasure hunters who found the hidden nest of the Fallen House."

"I don't want to see them," said Enrique automatically.

"Oh, come now," said Hypnos. "Even *I* don't like them, but that doesn't mean they can't be useful to us."

"I'm afraid none of us have any choice in the matter," said Eva, before pausing to look around the hall. "Where's Mademoiselle Laila?"

It was only then that Enrique noticed a weightlessness in his palms.

He looked down and realized he was no longer holding her hand. When he turned around, he only saw the icy archway of the Sleeping Palace. Laila had disappeared.

"Where did she go?" asked Enrique, turning to Zofia.

But Zofia's gaze was fixed on the arriving Houses of the Order of Babel. Enrique looked to Ruslan and Delphine, but they had broken away to greet the other Houses.

"And where's Séverin?" asked Enrique.

Eva shrugged. "The last I saw of him was an hour ago. He was supervising the transportation of treasures from out of the leviathan.

They still have to be catalogued and prepared for the Winter Conclave's Midnight Auction."

"Where are they keeping the objects?" asked Enrique.

"The library, I believe."

"It's nearly three in the afternoon," said Zofia.

Eva fixed her with a stare. "So?"

"The leviathan only stays for an hour. It mechanically cannot
stay longer."

"I'm not sure it has much of a choice when there's Forged metal
ropes involved," said Eva.

"David has been leashed to the ice?" asked Zofia, her voice
rising.

"*David?*" said Eva with a laugh. "We would've pinned that thing
to the ground earlier if those ropes hadn't taken so long to Forge."

Zofia glowered.

"Excuse us," said Enrique brusquely.

He nudged Zofia out of the crowd, then steered them far away
from Eva and the Order's procession.

"See, this is why you don't name mechanical monsters," muttered Enrique as he marched them deeper into the atrium.

"Why are we leaving?" demanded Zofia.

"One, we have to find Séverin in the library. And two, I didn't
want you to set Eva on fire."

"I would not waste an incendiary pendant," said Zofia grimly.

As they made their way to the library, Enrique dodged planners
and artisans, napping ice bears and a trio of crystal swans whose
translucent feathers had been edged in silver. In the atrium, a huge
podium had been erected for the Midnight Auction. Servants who
had arrived early from the various Houses bustled about, carrying
platters of quartz flutes filled with chilled ice wine. Once, the sight

would have dazzled Enrique, but now he hardly cared. He refused to believe that everything they had seen—the handless women, the muses with their blank stares and broken objects—had been for nothing. He refused to believe that Laila had only a handful of days left to live. And he refused to believe that Séverin didn't have another plan hiding up his sleeve.

Inside the library, the statues of the muses gleamed. Slabs of ice tables lined the floor where there had once been nothing but empty corridor space. Treasures lay piled atop the surfaces, each of them affixed with neat, white labels for the auctioneer to read. Another time, Enrique would have stopped and marveled at the objects he glimpsed—objects which had been deemed lost by the whole of the historical society—but that was before he saw Séverin.

In the midst of all that treasure, he looked like something out of myth, and Enrique was reminded of how deceptive myths could be. When Enrique was seven years old, he thought he'd seen a *si-yokoy*, a merman. This man clambered to the top of a cliff, looking out onto the ocean. He wore no shirt and around his neck lay strings of pearls. On his fingers, countless rings. His pants sagged with sea rocks, and a hundred silk scarves hung through his belt loops. At the time, Enrique stood with his family on a listing *paraw* boat, celebrating his mother's birthday. He'd called out excitedly, "The sea king!"

In his mind, only a man laden with treasure could be a sea king.

But that was not what his family saw. His father had panicked, screaming to the man to stop, to *wait* . . . His mother crossed herself, folding Enrique against her so he wouldn't see. He pushed against her hold, desperate to see the sea king, but all he heard was the splash of water and his father's anguished yell. It was weeks later that Enrique understood the man had drowned himself. He heard the whispers—the man's whole family had perished in a recent typhoon. At the time, Enrique didn't understand how a man laden with treasure could be so poor in life as to choose death. He was reminded of it now when he looked at Séverin, sitting in a room full of treasure with his eyes full of nothing.

All this time, Enrique had suspected that Séverin wanted *The Divine Lyrics* as the last, crushing blow to the Fallen House . . . but he looked as stricken as Laila, as if he'd lost his whole life. Something about it didn't fit right in his mind.

Wordlessly, Séverin pointed to a heavy tome situated on the table nearest him.

"Go ahead and look," rasped Séverin.

Enrique approached cautiously while Zofia trailed behind him.

As Enrique had suspected, there was some tracing of gold on the cover, and it was certainly made of animal skin. The dimensions were quite large for a book, and there was the suggestion of buckles along the binding, almost as if it was intended to be a book that held something within. Pressed into the surface was a burned marking . . . like a small, slanted *W*. The image bothered him, but he didn't know why he recognized it. Within the book lay nothing but empty space, with the vaguest depressions of something having been inside of it that was no longer there.

Enrique swallowed hard, letting his fingers coast down the spine.

"What if we've missed something?" he asked. "Maybe if we—"

"There's no point," said Séverin. "There's nothing left."

He didn't raise his voice. He didn't even make eye contact. But the air bent around him, and it was like skittering away from a sudden opening in the world. Enrique felt his face flush red. He wanted to scream at him. He wanted to tell him that Laila would die without their help. But in the end, his promise to her kept him silent.

Séverin rose from his seat. From the pocket of his jacket, he withdrew an envelope and handed it to Zofia.

"This came for you," he said tonelessly. "You can return to your sister as early as tomorrow. It doesn't matter."

Zofia took it, the line between her brows furrowing.

"Congratulations to us all," said Séverin tonelessly. "We found one of the greatest collections of treasures man has ever known."

Just as Séverin made his way to the door, Hypnos appeared at the threshold looking out of breath and confused.

"I was wondering where everyone went," he said, turning an accusing eye to Enrique. "I thought you and Zofia would come back, but you never did. If I'd known you were going to see Séverin, I would have joined you immediately."

Enrique felt Hypnos's words settle heavily inside him. Was Séverin the only reason he would have joined them?

Séverin pushed past him.

"Where are you going?" asked Hypnos. "We have to get ready for the celebrations later!"

Séverin walked out the door, leaving Hypnos to groan and throw up his hands. He adjusted his suit, took a deep breath, and made to go after Séverin when something in Enrique forced him to call out, "Wait!"

Hypnos looked at him, irritation flashing across his face.

"What is it, *mon cher*? Can it wait?"

Enrique felt a lump in his throat as he made his way to Hypnos. He felt, suddenly, foolish. The shadows of today curled darkly in his heart, and he craved the light and warmth of another person before he threw himself into examining the treasures. He thought

Hypnos would have recognized that plea in his face, but the other boy hadn't noticed. In fact, Hypnos looked ready to bolt.

"I could use your help?"

Even as he asked, he knew the answer.

"I cannot," said Hypnos quickly, his eyes going to the door. "Séverin needs me—"

"What if *I* needed you?" asked Enrique. And then, softly, "Would it even matter?"

"Séverin is the closest I have to family," said Hypnos. "I have to go to him."

Pity flashed through his heart.

"I don't think Séverin sees it that way," said Enrique gently. "Trust me, Hypnos . . . I recognize what one-sided affection looks like." His hand fell to his side. "At least, I recognize it now."

Hypnos went still. In his stillness lay all the answer Enrique needed. He saw, with a weary clarity, everything he hadn't wanted to notice. How he had reached for something Hypnos wasn't willing to offer. How the other boy seemed happiest when he was with the group, instead of just him. Hypnos had told him from the start that this was casual, and yet Enrique had kept trying to make it . . . *more*. An ache settled behind his rib cage. The room felt larger, and he felt all the more diminished.

Hypnos's mouth twisted with guilt.

"Oh *mon cher*, it is not one-sided, it is merely—"

"—Not enough," finished Enrique, looking down at his shoes.

Hypnos moved closer. Dimly, Enrique felt the other boy's warm fingers tipping up his chin.

"I am quite charmed by you, my historian," said Hypnos. "You and I . . . we understand each other's pasts."

But a shared past didn't make a future. And Hypnos seemed to know this too.

"I think, with enough time, I could learn to love you," said Hypnos.

Enrique reached up, slowly removing Hypnos's hand from his face. He held the other boy's hand, then curled it into a fist, brushing his lips once against Hypnos's knuckles.

"Perhaps we both deserve someone who is not so hard to love," said Enrique.

"Enrique—"

"I'll be fine," said Enrique. "You broke no promises to me. Just go."

Hypnos opened his mouth as if he'd say more, but in the end, chose silence. He met Enrique's eyes, nodded stiffly, and left the room.

Enrique stared out the empty door. He felt hollow, as if a stray winter wind would blow right through him. Haltingly, he took a deep breath. The library smelled of paper and ink . . . and possibility. And that, in the end, was where he turned his attention. He needed the sanctuary of work, and judging from what he'd glimpsed of the treasures, there was much work to be done. It was only when he turned fully from the door that he realized he wasn't alone. Zofia stood there, twirling a lit match between her fingers and eyeing a table full of treasures. She'd stayed, and he didn't know what to make of that. She looked him in the eye, her blue eyes fierce.

"Do you need help?" she asked.

AROUND THEM, THE LIBRARY seemed to take on new meaning. The caryatids of the muses had folded their hands against their breastbones, the iconography of their particular fields gleaming on their person and wrought in stone. Enrique saw the lyre of Calliope, the chief of the muses and the muse of epic poetry; the cornet of Clio, muse of history; the aulos of Euterpe, muse of music; the kithara of Erato, muse of love poetry; the tragic mask of Melpomene, muse of tragedy; the veil of Polymynia, muse of hymns; the lyre of Terpsichore, muse of dance; the shepherd's crook of Thalia, muse of comedy; and the compass of Ourania, muse of astronomy. A shiver ran down his spine as he regarded them. Once, they had been revered as the goddesses of inspiration, but what had they inspired in this place except murder? And why were all their objects broken?

"What are we looking for?" asked Zofia, walking to one of the tables laden with treasure. "Where else could the book be?"

Zofia reached out, touching a delicate Medusa crown, a Forged object from ancient Greece capable of rendering small objects to stone. One of the little stone serpents recoiled at her touch, and its body tightened to a sharp crimp . . . the shape struck Enrique as deeply familiar. Like a figure eight. It looked like something he'd seen only moments ago. He walked to the nearest muse, studying the sign he'd found etched on each of their palms days ago:

He held his notebook up to the symbol, and then . . . turned it to the side, the way he'd seen the Forged snake only moments ago.

His pulse fluttered. When the symbol was turned, it wasn't a backwards three at all, but the lowercase form of the last letter of the Greek alphabet, omega. *Alpha and omega.* All he had to do was extend and curve the lines *just so*, and it was nearly identical to the lemniscate symbol, which was the mathematical representation of infinity. Supposedly, the lemniscate's figure eight shape was derived from the lowercase form of omega, which in Greek translated to only one thing:

"The first and the last, the beginning and the end," whispered Enrique.

The literal power of God, the power that *The Divine Lyrics* was supposed to access. And he knew he'd seen it before somewhere.

"Zofia, can you get the tome?" he asked.

Zofia reached for it on the table and brought it over. There, embossed on the surface was that identical *W* shape . . . a buried lemniscate.

"See that?" he asked.

"The symbol for the first transfinite ordinal number," said Zofia.

Enrique had no idea what that meant. "Perhaps, but also—"

"A lowercase omega."

"Yes, precisely!" said Enrique, excitedly. "It also represents—"

"The first and the last, the beginning and the end," recited Zofia.

"That's what you said last year the first time you noticed the symbol. You said 'in other words, the power of God.' Yes?"

Enrique blinked at her, and she shrugged.

"What? I was listening to you," she said.

Enrique merely stared at her. She'd listened. That small sentence held a strange and unfamiliar warmth. Zofia opened the tome, pressing her pale hand to the hollow where the pages of *The Divine Lyrics* would have been.

"It looks more like a box than a book," she said.

Enrique studied the cavity, tracing the inside of the spine. As a book, it should have held thread or some other sign that the pages had once been bound together, but it was smooth.

"If it was always hollow and *held* something . . . then what if this symbol is what links it all together?" he asked, pointing to the lemniscate on the surface.

"Like a book inside of a book?" asked Zofia.

"It's the only thing that makes sense," said Enrique.

Whatever they were looking for had to bear the same symbol. Together, they turned and faced the piles of treasure heaped onto the tables.

Now, they just had to start searching.

28

ZOFIA

Two hours before midnight . . .

Zofia did not count the passage of hours as she and Enrique worked. But she did not have to count to hear how the sounds outside the library grew louder in anticipation of the Midnight Auction. All those *people*. It made her shudder. Zofia had hated being outside to welcome the Order of Babel. She didn't like everyone pressed close together, and she did not like that her height forced her to be eye level with the back of people's heads.

What she liked now was the stillness and the set tasks before them: pick up an object; look for the lemniscate symbol; move on when it wasn't there. At least she was doing something. Before, when she found out that there was no *Divine Lyrics*, she could not speak. Tears ran down her face. But it was not sorrow. She had felt this way once before, when her family had taken a trip to one of the lakes in summertime. She had swum too far, happy that under water, she couldn't hear the loudness of the other children. But somewhere in the lake, her foot caught on a net, and she could not keep her head above the surface for longer than a few seconds at a time. By chance, Hela had seen her struggling and called out to their father who had rushed into the lake and saved her.

Zofia never forgot how it felt—kicking out her legs, hitting the water with her hands, spitting out lake water, and gulping down air. She never forgot the frustration of powerlessness, the awareness that her movements made no difference, and that the water—vast and dark—did not care.

That was how she felt realizing Laila would die.

Nothing she did had made a difference, thought Zofia as she put down one object. But maybe this time, she hoped, reaching for a different artifact. There were 212 objects left to examine, and in each unexamined object, Zofia reached for the comfort of numbers, for the knowledge that no matter how small the chance, discovering a lemniscate symbol was not out of the statistical realm of probability.

Beside her, Enrique worked in semi-silence. He hummed to himself, and though Zofia normally preferred silence, she found the background hum an agreeable constant. Enrique talked to himself too, and Zofia realized that just as she found comfort in numbers, he found solace in conversation.

By now, they had tackled two of the seven tables with no results. When Zofia moved to a different table, Enrique shook his head.

"Save that one for later."

"Why?"

Enrique gestured to a different table. Zofia scanned the contents. Among them were a small notebook with a golden varnish;

a collection of gleaming feathers in a jar; a harp; a string of jade beads carved with the faces of beasts; and a pair of scales. It was no different from the other tables littered with similar objects. It possessed no greater likelihood of hiding a lemniscate symbol.

"Do you smell that, phoenix?"

Zofia sniffed the air. She smelled metal and smoke. She moved closer to where he was standing and caught a whiff of something else . . . something sweet, like apple peels thrown into a fire.

"The scent of perfume," said Enrique.

"Scent is irrelevant to this," said Zofia, turning back toward the other table.

"But the *context* . . . the context makes the difference," said Enrique. "The word 'perfume' comes from the Latin *perfumare . . . to smoke through*. Scent was a medium through which the ancients communicated to the gods."

Enrique pointed at the objects strewn on the table.

"Séverin was the one who explained how the whole place was designed like a temple, even their . . . their sacrifice altar," he said, shuddering. "My guess is they would have only used incense for their most precious objects, especially whatever was inside *The Divine Lyrics*, which makes me think we should look through whatever is here before we try elsewhere."

Zofia stared at the table, then stared at him. "How did you come to that conclusion?"

Enrique grinned at her. "Oh, you know . . . superstitions, stories." He paused. "A gut instinct."

He'd said something like that to her before, and it annoyed her no less than it did now.

Zofia reached for a new object. They had only just examined

the first two objects—a goblet and a cornucopia—when a gong sounded from outside. Enrique looked up, his eyes narrowing.

"This isn't good," he said. "We don't have much time before the auctioneer starts coming in and taking away the objects for sale, and I want to take a look inside the grotto and the leviathan once more."

"Why?"

"It's this symbol . . ."

Enrique picked up his notebook, tracing the sign once more.

"Now that we know what we're looking for, I just want to make sure we haven't missed any hints."

Zofia frowned. They wouldn't have enough time to go to the leviathan, search the premises, and return. One of them needed to go alone. One of them needed to try and buy more time.

The thought of venturing into that crowd turned Zofia's stomach.

But it was nothing compared to the thought of losing Laila.

Zofia stood straighter and felt the heavy, unopened envelope pressing against her chest. She had not recognized the envelope seal, and the penmanship did not look like Hela's. The unfamiliarity of it filled her with a strange unease that she couldn't name, stopping her hand each time she gathered the courage to read it.

Beside her, Enrique was talking to himself.

"If we could get Hypnos to come back, we could go, but he hates being left alone, and we can't ask Laila . . . she's been lying down and the sight of this will only upset her . . . and I have no idea where Séverin is . . . Ruslan could do it, but Séverin usually approves who knows what and how much time would we lose if—"

"I can go alone."

Enrique's gaze snapped to hers. For a second, Zofia barely registered that she had uttered such a thing. But the moment it was said, it calmed her.

"No, I couldn't ask you to do that," said Enrique. "I know how hard new situations can be for you. I'll go."

The words struck Zofia. She remembered Hela's earlier letters: *Oh, don't make them worry, Zosia. They might start fretting over who would have to take care of you when I'm gone.*

She was not a child who needed constant minding.

"I will go alone. You are better suited here."

Enrique held her gaze only a moment longer, and then nodded. "I'm certain the grotto will be empty. All you have to do is a quick search for the lemniscate symbol. If you can, on the way, try and buy us time? I'll work as fast as I can and join you as soon as I have something."

Zofia nodded and headed for the door. But just as she reached for the handle, Enrique called out to her:

"Phoenix?"

She turned and saw Enrique leaning against one of the tables, an object in one hand, a notebook tucked under his other arm. When he smiled, Zofia noticed the left corner of his lips quirked higher than the right. She liked that detail despite its asymmetry. Hypnos must like that detail too, she thought, remembering how he had kissed him right before they searched the leviathan. An uncomfortable pang hit her stomach.

"What?" she asked.

"You're a lot braver than most of the people outside," said Enrique. "None of them could build a bomb with their eyes closed and wander into a metal monster and still want to name it 'David.' Trust in yourself, Phoenix."

Zofia nodded and had the irrational desire to wish that some words could be solid and picked up off the ground and held close, so that she could reach for them whenever she needed.

"I will."

WHEN ZOFIA STEPPED OUTSIDE, the Sleeping Palace had changed.

Once calm, the gigantic atrium had transformed. Zofia lost count of the silver orbs covering the ceiling. She counted no less than eleven of the Sphinx patrolling the perimeter. The translucent floor had become another stage. Thirteen Forged illusions of *rusalka*, maidens from Polish folklore, dragged themselves out of the floor and appeared to wrap their arms around the dozens of laughing men and women gliding through the ballroom.

Beside the hallway that led to the library loomed a white tent. Zofia had no choice but to cross through it to reach the hall that housed her laboratory. She stepped over the sprawled out guests reclinining against pale cushions and swirling goblets in their hands. Chased-silver contraptions sheathed their pinky fingers, each ending in a sharp talon. They looked just like Eva's ring, and Zofia realized they were instruments of blood Forging. In one corner, two women laughed and then—at the same time—dug the talon into the other person's wrist. Blood beaded to the surface and the women crossed their hands, letting their blood drop into the other's goblet. Zofia moved quickly to the exit when another group blocked her path. Two men and a girl no older than Laila. The girl had her back turned to them, and the two men wore matching grins. One man threw back his drink. Instantly, his visage shuddered and twisted, until he looked identical to the other man.

"Tell us apart, love," said the one beside him, spinning the girl around. "Or perhaps you need the assistance of touch?"

One of the men looked up at Zofia and held out his goblet.

"You are more than welcome to join, lovely little fae."

Zofia shook her head and stumbled out of the tent as fast as she could to get to her laboratory. Once inside, it took a moment to catch her breath. Blood Forging confused her. She knew it was the science of pleasure and pain, and she knew that lovers enjoyed its artistry. Was she supposed to want . . . *that*? Bodies operated like machines, and she wondered at her own machinations that nothing in that tent interested her. At least, not with those people.

Zofia shoved aside the small twinge of pain, and hurriedly gathered heat lamps, more phosphorous pendants, a Mnemo bug, several pieces of rope, and a new matchbox. When she stepped back into the hall, she realized she was not alone.

Hypnos was slumped on the ground, his back against the wall, a bottle of wine tucked under his arm, and an emptied glass in his hand. When he saw her, he looked up and flashed a lopsided smile. It matched Enrique's own quirked smile in its asymmetry.

The pattern jolted through Zofia, opening up a chasm of heat within her. She remembered the day she had accidentally glimpsed them in the hallway of L'Eden. She was wearing a silk dress Laila had bought for her. After that, she could not bear the touch of silk. She remembered, also, Hypnos and Enrique's kiss in the ice grotto: brief and uncomplicated. Hypnos had often said it was not his fault most people wanted to kiss him just as it was not her fault she felt no compulsion to kiss most people. However, the one person who made her entertain such thoughts looked not to her, but Hypnos. Statistically, it made sense. Hypnos attracted far more people than Zofia did. Such a realization should cause no pain, and yet she felt a sharp twist behind the bones of her chest, and she did not know how to make it stop.

"Am I a terrible person?" asked Hypnos. He hiccuped loudly. "I didn't mean to *use* anyone. I thought it was fine?" He shook his head. "No, it was never fine."

There was a vague blurriness to his words that Zofia recognized as intoxication. Hypnos did not wait for her to answer his queries. Instead, he took another swig from his glass.

"I'm going back to the ice grotto—" started Zofia.

Hypnos shuddered. "It's eerie, cold, damp, and without food and drink. Why in the *hell*—"

"I have to," said Zofia. "I have to protect someone."

"Keeping secrets, are we?" asked Hypnos.

Zofia nodded. Hypnos let out a laugh, clutching his glass. His eyes looked glossy, and the corners of his mouth tugged down. He was sad.

"Secrets within the group which, I suppose, I will never be privy to," he said. "I envy whoever they are, to be worthy of such secrecy. And I envy you, too, for enjoying such trust. For being so"—he circled his glass, frowning—"*wanted.*"

Wanted.

It struck Zofia that they could be envious of the same quality. She remembered every time Hypnos had tried to help: when he brought them mismatched snacks, when he proposed a toast in the St. Petersburg warehouse, when he had hovered at her side and all she had thought to say was that he was throwing a shadow over her work. Tristan had done the same when he was alive. He had tried to be there, and she had not told him enough that while his presence did not improve the efficiency of her work, it was not unwanted.

"I thought we were friends," said Hypnos, hiccuping. "Notwithstanding cat sacrifice on Wednesdays, etcetera."

"We are friends," said Zofia.

She meant it. Zofia wished Laila were here. She would know what to say. Zofia gave her best effort and brought out her matchbox.

"Want to set something on fire?" she asked.

Hypnos snorted. "A rather dangerous suggestion given my current inebriation."

"You're always inebriated."

He pondered this. "True. Give me a match."

Zofia struck one and handed it to him. He squinted as he watched the flame eat its way down the wood until the spark extinguished and smoke unspooled from the burnt end.

"That *is* rather calming," he said, shrugging. "But I'd rather help than scavenge around for flammable things."

Enrique's words drifted back to Zofia: *If you can, on the way, try and buy us time.*

"I know how you can help," said Zofia.

Hypnos clapped his hands. "Do tell!"

"Make *others* drunk," said Zofia. "Delay the Midnight Auction. That will be the greatest help."

"Help!" Hypnos hiccuped and grinned. "Cause a drunken distraction? Bawdy songs? *Impromptu waltzes*? I love waltzes."

"Would you?"

A wide smile tugged at Hypnos's mouth. "Would I prove that I'd do anything to help my friends? *Oui, ma chère,* I would." He waved his hand. "Besides, you know I live for antics."

ZOFIA USED THE SERVANT ENTRYWAYS to avoid the main atrium. She did not want to see that white tent again. Two uniformed guards protected the hall leading to the ice grotto. An unfamiliar Order of Babel insignia was emblazoned on the front of their jackets.

Zofia considered the various scripts she had memorized over the past two years of working on acquisitions with Séverin. She set her teeth and touched her heart, not out of sentimentality but for the reminder of the letter from Hela pressed against her chest. Sometimes she needed help, but that did not make her helpless.

Zofia marched up to the guards.

"And who are you?" asked one of them.

"I am one of the Forging engineers who supervised the removal of treasure," said Zofia, in her best approximation of a haughty voice. "I was asked by the auctioneer to sweep the ice grotto for any remaining treasure."

The other one shook his head. "They already have someone doing that right now."

Zofia had not anticipated this. Enrique had figured it would be empty. Who was inside?

"I was told to consult with them," said Zofia.

The guard stared her down for one moment before sighing and stepping aside. Zofia moved past them, down the long, narrow, dark hallway. Inside the grotto, silence met Zofia. Many of the lanterns had been removed, throwing the grotto into darkness. The leviathan lay chained to the ice, Forged metal straps crisscrossing its neck and propping its jaws open.

"Hello, David," said Zofia.

The leviathan thrashed, and small fissures of ice spidered out around it. The sight of the chained machine angered Zofia, but it was the silence of the grotto that confused her. The guard had said someone else was here, and yet it was empty. Perhaps they had made a mistake.

Zofia placed one of her lanterns at the entrance to the leviathan. When she touched its metal lip, she felt it thrash, frothing the lake water around it. A pang of pity struck her as she stepped inside, holding out one of her phosphorous pendants for guidance. She thought the leviathan would be cold, but inside its mouth, the air turned humid and damp.

When she peered over the edge of the staircase, she glimpsed a red, wavering glow. The light unnerved her, nearly causing her to stumble backwards when a new image flashed through her mind: the faces of her friends and family. She thought of Séverin, how he walked as if he carried so much more than his own weight. She thought of Laila's liveliness. Of Enrique's asymmetrical grin and Hypnos's glossy eyes. All of it was light. From her father's tutelage, she knew that light belonged to an electromagnetic spectrum. The light the world perceived belonged to the visible spectrum, which meant there was light humans could not see. But Zofia wondered if they could feel it all the same, the way she could sense sunshine against her closed eyelids. Because that was how friendship felt to her, an illumination too vast for her senses to capture. Yet she did not doubt its presence. And she held that light close to her as step by step, she ventured down the stairs.

Five . . .

Fourteen . . .

Twenty-seven . . .

At the end of the staircase, she saw the room in full glow. Fifty-seven bare shelves stretched down from the ceiling. One water-damaged rug spread across the main space. In the corner on her right, Zofia recognized a podlike capsule containing one steering wheel and two seats. A built-in escape mechanism. Across the ceiling, she recognized a Mnemo bug projection, which showed the ice grotto she had just left. She could not recall such an apparatus in Hypnos and Séverin's recorded notes.

All of those observations paled before the source of the heat she had felt the farther she walked down the stairs. On a raised, stone altar, hundreds of waxen red candles burned brightly. The red light spread across the sculpted stone faces of the nine muses leaning over the altar. It did not make sense to leave the candles burning. She had seen a similar situation in the past. It could be a gesture of sentimentality, one that she recognized from the time her neighbors left candles beside the family elm tree when her parents died. Perhaps this was meant for the girls who had died. But then she noticed the writing on the wall . . .

Zofia lifted her pendant, scouring for signs of the symbol along the altar. But the lemniscate was not here. The closer she moved, the more the writing on the wall became legible:

WE ARE READY FOR THE UNMAKING

"Unmaking?" repeated Zofia aloud.

The word reminded her of the last time they had seen writing on the wall.

TO PLAY AT GOD'S INSTRUMENT
WILL SUMMON THE UNMAKING

What did it mean?

A glint in her peripheral vision caught her attention. A small object had fallen near the base of the altar. She bent down, picking it up off the floor—

It was a golden honeybee.

Zofia had not seen a honeybee pendant quite like that since the catacombs where the doctor opened his arms and let the Fallen House members flood the Paris catacombs. Panic zipped through her veins. She needed to warn the others. Zofia stepped backwards, but her foot slipped on the step, and she slammed into . . . *someone.* For a moment, all she felt was the rise and fall of their breathing.

Instinct took over.

Zofia dropped to a crouch. The ground beneath her turned damp and slippery. Her foot skidded as she leapt to one side, sending her crashing to the floor. Zofia clawed at her necklace, desperate to grab her incendiary device when a cloth-covered hand clamped over her mouth and nose. An ether-like odor tinged with sweetness filled her nostrils, and her eyes began to close.

"I hate that you've made me do this," said a familiar voice. "But I know you'll understand, my dear."

29

ENRIQUE

When it came to silence, Enrique always thought to fill it.

He'd thought that for something to be powerful, it needed sound to match in the same way a background growl of thunder turned the lightning ominous. Or the way words peeled off a page and *spoken*, gave them a new heft and weight.

The first time he had been chosen as a speaker for his debate team, he had been flattered. People trusted the weight of his words even when his topic of interest—*Universal Stories: A Defense of Filipino Folklore*—hadn't first seemed to grab any of his *escuela secundaria* classmates. All night, he prepared for his speech, his nerves practically fizzing. He'd even attended morning mass and prayed that he didn't get tongue-tied. But moments before he stepped onto the podium, a classmate handed him his lecture.

"What's this?" Enrique had asked, confused.

None of the writing looked familiar.

The classmate laughed. "Don't worry, *Kuya*, we did all the work for you."

"But . . ." said Enrique, limply holding up his own speech.

The classmate waved it away. "Oh, don't worry about that." His classmate lightly patted his cheek. "Your face will do all the convincing. Now get up there!"

Enrique remembered the cloying warmth of the theatre, his fingers leaving damp presses in the paper, and the audience exchanging smirks or looks of pity. Did he want to be heard for his face or philosophy? Or did he merely want to be *heard*? Cowardice chose for him. He spoke, reading off the page. Later, when they handed him the award of first place, Enrique went home shamefaced, shoved the trophy under the patio, and never whispered a word of it to his parents. Years later, he could not remember what it was that he'd said.

But it didn't really matter.

Enrique thought of that moment now as he analyzed the treasure before him. Maybe for the first time, he was doing something that mattered. The key to saving Laila's life could be —*had to be*— here. And none of it required speech. Only the silence of keeping his head down, his face away from the light.

Enrique looked at the door, then back at the table. That was the second time he'd done that since Zofia had left for the ice grotto twenty minutes ago. He told himself that was just because he didn't like being alone and the work went slower without her. And yet, he had to admit that he liked glimpsing the world through her eyes. It was like a curtain drawn back to reveal the slender, mechanical mechanisms holding up the stage, a world he didn't know how to see.

Enrique reached for another artifact. There were only three more treasures left on the table. A jar of feathers, a small and rusted harp with dull metal strings, and a handful of long, oval masks covered with cold, Forged flames. Enrique was about to reach for the harp when he heard a sharp knock at the door. He frowned. It was too soon to be Zofia. And though he needed the help, he wasn't ready to see Hypnos. Thinking of him—or rather, the disconnect between what he wanted and what they had—was like touching a fresh bruise.

"Hello?" he called out.

"It's me!" said a familiar voice. "Ruslan!"

Enrique wiped his hands on his smock, then went to open the door. Ruslan stood in the doorway, holding a plate of food in his one hand, while the other, as always, lay in a tight sling across his chest.

"Your hair looks very rumpled," said Ruslan, casting a critical eye over him. "Troubling thoughts, perhaps? Or a lack of a comb?"

"Both."

Ruslan raised the platter. "It looks like the Midnight Auction got delayed, and I thought you might want some food and company?"

Enrique flashed a tight smile. Truthfully, he didn't want to waste a second that could spare Laila pain. And if he was going to work with anyone, it was Zofia.

"That's kind of you," he said.

". . . but not particularly wanted?" prompted Ruslan, his smile tugging down. "It's quite all right, I understand. I figured once I saw the state of your hair, which, forgive me, is exquisitely dismal—"

"No, please," said Enrique, remembering himself. "Come in.

You have every right to be here. You're the patriarch who commissioned the expedition, after all."

Still, Ruslan didn't move, and Enrique had a sudden feeling that he had said precisely the wrong thing.

"I would rather rely on the strength of my personality than my privilege," said Ruslan quietly.

Enrique softened. He looked back at the table full of artifacts and sighed. Perhaps Ruslan could be of help. Séverin used to be strict about who was allowed to assist them, but these days Séverin was a ghost who couldn't even muster the interest to haunt them.

"I could use the help," said Enrique.

Ruslan gave a little hop of joy and then followed Enrique inside.

"What are you examining?" asked Ruslan, eyeing the table.

Enrique pointed at the symbol he'd found on the muses' palms and the outside of the box they had mistaken for *The Divine Lyrics*:

ε

"That's what we're looking for, but on one of the other objects," explained Enrique. "I think it might be the actual symbol of *The Divine Lyrics*. The book that Séverin and Hypnos found was hollow, so perhaps it's not a book at all? Or a book inside of a book? I'm not sure."

Ruslan seemed to absorb this carefully. "You think it may not be a book? Why?"

"Well, the word itself was an incomplete translation," said Enrique. "As far as we know, we only have the letters: THE DIVINE LYR to explain what it is . . . which may not be a full picture. There's certain iconographical missteps that keep leaping out to me, but I don't know what it means. For example, all the muses in this room are carrying broken objects, which was identical to what we saw when we followed the Tezcat portal to Istanbul. We know the Lost Muses guarded *The Divine Lyrics*, and we know their bloodline allowed them to read the book. Perhaps that's what connects the paintings in Istanbul and"—Enrique crossed himself—"the dead girls in the grotto. Their hands had been removed, perhaps as a nod to restraining their power from, I don't know, holding the book? Turning its pages? It's still unclear to me, but it demonstrates restraint of power—"

Abruptly, Enrique stopped. He felt a twinge of self-consciousness when he spoke. He didn't normally talk that long before most people told him to stop. Laila never did, of course, but he could always tell when she grew bored because her gaze went unfocused . . . and then Zofia. Well, actually, Zofia always leaned forward. Zofia always listened.

"I apologize," he said quickly. "I sometimes get carried away with my thoughts."

He looked at Ruslan, and saw that he was *rapt*. The sight was deeply humbling.

And deeply awkward.

"Er, if you want to help, could you start by picking up the objects on the far right side of the table to look for the symbol?" asked Enrique. "Some of them are a little dirty and need to be cleaned beforehand."

"Oh, of course!" said Ruslan, hopping to the table once more. He reached for the jar of feathers.

"I must say, I'm always a little shocked to hear you speak . . . You're so eloquent that it's, um—"

Dazzling? Awe-inspiring? wondered Enrique. He puffed out his chest a bit.

"Confusing," said Ruslan.

Well, never mind.

"Confusing?" repeated Enrique.

"A bit, yes. I heard about your meeting with the Ilustrados in Paris—"

Enrique froze at the mention. All over again, he remembered standing in the auditorium, the empty table and the cooling food. The way every sound outside the hallway brought a shock of hopeful nerves.

"—something about not feeling up to the task of lecturing; although, it was very kind of you to send each of them a check," said Ruslan, shrugging. "I thought perhaps you'd just been nervous, or perhaps not as eloquent as you'd hoped, and that's why you cancelled the meeting."

Enrique felt rooted to the spot. "I never cancelled that meeting."

All this time, he thought no one had cared. But that wasn't the case. Someone else had cancelled for him. Someone who had enough money to pay off the Ilustrados; who could speak on his behalf; who knew him well enough to know exactly what he wanted.

Séverin.

Enrique wished he didn't remember how Séverin had flung himself between the *troika* fire and Enrique. He wished he didn't remember the day that Séverin introduced him as the new historian of L'Eden and promptly dismissed anyone who spoke out against him.

Without meaning to, Enrique's hand moved to his heart. Whatever bruise Hypnos had left on it was nothing compared to the break he felt now. The secret snap of the heart where certainty crumbles. He'd always known a part of Séverin had died when Tristan was murdered, and Enrique had mourned them both. But at least Séverin was here, and though he was a shadow of himself, there was always the chance he would find himself once more. Now Enrique knew that he'd been holding out hope for a ghost.

The Séverin he knew was gone.

"Enrique?" asked Ruslan. "I'm sorry . . . should I leave? Did I say something wrong?"

Enrique pushed aside his thoughts.

"No, not at all," he said, returning his focus to the objects. "It's merely been a while since I've thought of the Paris talk. No matter." He met the other man's eyes. "Please stay."

He would let himself think of Séverin's betrayal when all of this was over. Too long, he had forgiven Séverin his temper and his coldness . . . but *this*. This, he could never forgive. Enrique set his jaw and reached for a new object.

"Is that a harp?" asked Ruslan, lifting an eyebrow.

"No," said Enrique, studying the shape. He looked behind him to Calliope, the muse of epic poetry. In her hands, a broken golden instrument.

"It's a lyre," he said.

The lyre didn't look like other treasures. For one, it was of a metal he didn't recognize, with etchings along the side. The strings, which normally would have been cat gut and thus disintegrated by now, looked metallic. He tried to pluck one of the strings, but it was stiff and intractable, hard as concrete. A hum gathered at the back of his thoughts as he slowly rubbed the surface of the lyre with a clean towel until the metal shone. There . . . etched into the left side appeared a symbol:

ε

Enrique hardly breathed as he lifted the lyre, gently taking it to the box shaped deceptively like a book. The lyre fit perfectly within the hollowed space. And just like that, the images fell neatly into his head. The reason all the women's hands were cut off. It wasn't for turning pages . . . it was for *playing* an instrument.

"It was never *The Divine Lyrics*," breathed Enrique. "It was always the *divine lyre* . . . a mistranslation. The words had gotten cut off and everyone thought it was a book, but we were wrong. That's why everything we've found keeps referring to it as an *instrument* of God."

No sooner had he spoken than he remembered the words painted on the Istanbul portal . . .

TO PLAY AT GOD'S INSTRUMENT
WILL SUMMON THE UNMAKING

Unmaking . . .

Enrique looked once more at the statues of the muses. The broken objects in their hands. He thought back to the paintings in

Istanbul . . . the way every painting showed a Forged object crumbling apart in the hands of the goddesses of divine inspiration. All this time, they'd known what they were searching for held the secret to the art of Forging . . . but what if that secret was not how it could create . . . but how it could *destroy*. And that meant that Laila, endlessly chasing what she thought would save her, was running straight to her death.

"Oh no," said Enrique, snatching back his hands as if merely touching the object would summon destruction.

He needed to find the others. He looked to the door. Where was Zofia? Surely she should have been back by now. And then he felt a shadow cross over him. Before he could turn, before he could even *speak* . . . the world turned black.

30

LAILA

One hour before the Midnight Auction . . .

In eleven days, Laila would die.

Maybe tomorrow, she would feel fear, but right now fear felt out of focus and far off, like something glimpsed beneath layers of ice. Maybe deep in her heart, she had always known it would end like this. Or maybe she had lost the ability to feel anything other than regret. Not that she wouldn't live longer, but that she hadn't lived *enough*. She should have stayed at L'Eden even if it hurt, because then at least she would have had more time with those she loved. She should have baked cakes and shared them with friends. She should have stayed even if it meant seeing Séverin . . . perhaps especially so.

She should have, she should have, she should have.

That mantra sped through her veins, bloomed into her pulse until her heart sang with it. Laila curled her hands into fists. Eleven days of life. That's all she had. These precious coins to spend as she wished, and she did not want to do it alone. She wanted to be with the people she loved. She wanted to hear music, to feel light across her skin. To step out on the ice and watch her breath plume.

Laila would meet death standing.

Earlier, she had made herself dress for evening, but she had skipped dinner entirely. Only now did she realize that not once had her Forged necklace of white diamonds tightened with a summons. Séverin was lost to himself. Perhaps he thought finding *The Divine Lyrics* would be the truest vengeance for Tristan, and now his guilt only thickened in his blood and forced him away from the world. Or perhaps . . . perhaps he thought nothing of her absence. He would never know that death raced toward her.

Each time she'd thought to tell him, fury stilled her tongue. She couldn't live with his pity, and she would die at his apathy. All that remained was his silence. Laila wondered if that was the truest death—being slowly rendered invisible so that all she inspired was indifference.

Laila glanced at the invitation on her vanity. The theme of the Winter Conclave was dusk and dawn . . . to herald the transition of a new year.

For tonight, she selected a gown steeped in midnight. The Forged silk clung to every contour. Its only nod to opulence was the ends of the gown, the tendrils of which appeared like ribbons of ink suspended in water. If she leaned forward, the top of the long scar down her spine peeked out. It used to make her feel like a doll hastily put together; now, she merely felt like she wasn't hiding her truth. Laila fastened the cold diamonds to her throat.

Now what?

"Now," said Laila, more to herself than to anyone else. "Now, I dance."

At the top of the staircase, the loud sounds of revelry reached her, thrumming with urgency and desperation. Candles lined the stair banister, Forged to appear like gleaming suns. Lustrous moons crowded the ceiling, and silver confetti spiraled slowly through the air so that it was like watching a constellation explode in slow motion. The members of the Order of Babel had dressed as gods and goddesses, demons and seraphs . . . all of whom embodied dusk or dawn.

Laila scanned the crowd, looking for the others. From the Midnight Auction's podium, Hypnos led the crowd in chanting the lyrics to a bawdy song while the auctioneer looked increasingly distressed and kept gesturing to the time. When Hypnos saw her, he winked. Not an uncommon gesture coming from him, but it made her pause. It felt intentional, like he was deliberately distracting the crowd. But to what purpose?

"Mademoiselle L'Énigme," said a familiar voice at her side.

Laila turned to see Eva, dressed in a ball gown of brightest green. Her red hair was arranged in a cascading coiffure, with a gold headpiece unfurling behind her ears like slender wings. Eva crossed her arms, and Laila caught the glint of her silver ring sheathing her pinky like a claw. Eva caught her looking and smiled. It was a cat's smile with all her small, sharp teeth. Eva opened her mouth, but Laila spoke before her.

"You look beautiful, Eva."

Eva paused, almost flinching at the compliment. Abruptly, her hand went to the ballerina pendant at her neck before she dropped it.

"We could still be friends," said Laila.

Death's shadow robbed her of subtlety, and she watched as Eva's eyes widened almost guiltily before she snapped back to herself.

"You have too many things I want, Mademoiselle," she said coldly, and then tilted her head. "Sometimes I wonder what it would be like to be you."

Laila smiled. "A short-lived wonder, I imagine."

Eva frowned.

"Who are you supposed to be?" she asked. "A goddess of night?"

Laila hadn't really considered herself dressed as a goddess, but now she thought of the stories her mother had told her, tales of star-touched queens who trailed nighttime in their shadows.

"Why not," she said. "And you?"

Eva gestured at the green of her gown, and only then did Laila notice the delicate pattern of insect wings.

"Tithonus," said Eva. "The ill-fated lover of Eos, goddess of the dawn."

When she saw the confusion on Laila's face, she said, "Tithonus was so beloved of the goddess of dawn that she begged Zeus for his immortality, so that he might stay with her forever . . . but she forgot to ask for eternal youth. He grew old and hideous, and pleaded for death that no god could grant until Eos took pity on him and turned him into a cricket."

The story raised goose bumps on Laila's skin.

"You're dressed as a warning, then?"

"Why not," said Eva, lifting one shoulder. "A warning to be careful of what we demand from the gods."

From the podium, Hypnos struck a gong and pointed at the musicians. "A dance before we divide our treasures!"

The crowd clapped. The auctioneer threw up his hands in surrender just as the musicians struck up a lively tune. When Laila turned back to Eva, she realized the other girl had moved closer, until she was hardly a handspan away from her.

"That necklace is beautiful," said Eva, tilting her head. "But it's gotten turned, and the clasp is at the front. Allow me to adjust it."

Without waiting for her answer, Eva reached out to her throat, freezing fingers slipping under Laila's necklace. Laila gasped from the cold, but it turned to a wince in her mouth as something sharp grazed her skin.

"There, all better now," said Eva. "Enjoy the party."

Eva turned, disappearing into the crowd of wings and haloes. Only then did Laila feel a slight trickle of blood at her neck.

Eva's ring had left a tiny cut. Laila touched it, confusion giving way to scorn. She had no time for Eva's small acts of spite.

Around her, the members of the Order of Babel had begun to dance. Dozens of participants wore Forged masks of ice— elaborate, glittering feathers, or cruel things with hooked beaks. Some of them had smeared gold paint across their mouths, as if they were gods recklessly bleeding out their own rich blood.

Laila stumbled back, only for a man wearing a crown of the sun's rays to catch her up in his arms. She hesitated an instant before surrendering to the dance. Her very pulse became an intoxicating cadence. *More*, she begged of her heartbeats. Laila danced for nearly an hour, switching from partner to partner, pausing only to sip the sweet ice wine in crystal glasses. She danced until her feet slipped out from beneath her, and she lurched forward, flinging out her arms before someone yanked her back at the last second.

"Are you all right, my dear?" asked a familiar voice.

Laila turned to see Ruslan, his uninjured hand still outstretched from breaking her fall.

Her heartbeat thundered loudly in her ears. "Yes, thanks to you."

"I was rather hoping I would see you," he said shyly. "May I convince you to take one more turn around the room?"

"I never need much convincing to dance," said Laila, smiling.

Ruslan beamed. As they danced, he held his injured arm close to his chest, though he was no less graceful because of it. His Babel Ring caught the light, and for the first time, Laila noticed a bluish tinge to the skin. His hand looked far too stiff.

"Does it hurt?"

His eyes softened. "Do you know . . . you're the only person who has asked me that. I wish there could be more people like you, Mademoiselle."

He spun her in a small circle, only to be interrupted by a server wearing a white rabbit mask and holding a bloodred platter piled with onyx glasses.

"May I interest you in some refreshment?" asked the server, holding out a bitter-smelling drink. "Specially made blood Forged drinks in honor of the Winter Conclave." The server grinned, and Laila noticed his teeth had a scarlet tinge to them. "To consume a drop of one's own blood allows you to submit to your innermost desires . . . a drop of another's blood and you could even wear their face for an hour."

Laila recoiled. "No, thank you."

Ruslan also declined, but he stared almost longingly after the drinks. "Too eerie for my taste, although it would be nice to look different for a change . . ."

He sighed, patting the top of his head.

"I quite like my own face," said Laila wryly.

"I am sure Monsieur Montagnet-Alarie would agree," said Ruslan, winking. "Might I ask where Mademoiselle Boguska and Monsieur Mercado-Lopez are for the evening?"

"Preoccupied, I believe," said Laila, staring after the platter of blood Forged drinks. "Poring over the recent treasures excavated from the metal leviathan before the Midnight Auction."

"*Midnight* is a flexible hour it seems," said Ruslan. "But it gives time for others to follow your lead, perhaps even change their attire."

Laila frowned. "How do you mean?"

"Well, not thirty minutes ago, I saw you dressed in a lovely green gown," said Ruslan. "You and Monsieur Montagnet-Alarie were heading to your suite—to change, I imagine, and, ah, well . . ."

Ruslan turned red, fumbling to finish his sentence, but Laila had stopped listening.

A green dress. An image of Eva's kitten-teeth smile flashed through her mind. She remembered the sensation of cold fingers on her neck, and the hot slick of her own blood on her fingers. *Sometimes I wonder what it would be like to be you.*

"I have to go," said Laila abruptly, turning on her heel.

Ruslan called out after her, but Laila ignored him. She ran back through the crowd, up the stairs. Her skin felt tight and burning, and as she raced up the stairs, she wondered whether they might just melt out from beneath her.

At the top of the stairs and down the hall leading to their suite, she saw their door had been left ajar. Laila pushed it open. The smell of spiced wine hit her nose, and the first thing she saw were two black goblets. Two pairs of shoes. Neither of them her own. Acid rushed through Laila's gut as she lifted her gaze from the floor and heard a soft groan coming from the bed. The curtains of the ice canopy shifted, and the sight froze her to the spot. Séverin's head was bent into the crook of a girl's neck, his hands digging into her waist . . . the girl looked up at the sound of the door scraping against the floor.

She was wearing Laila's face.

When their eyes met, she smiled one of Laila's smiles, but it looked all wrong on her. It was too sly.

"I had to sate my curiosity somehow," she said.

The girl was wearing Eva's dress . . . but spoke with Laila's voice. And around her pinky finger, Laila spied the sharp-taloned silver ring. The same ring that had punctured her skin and drawn blood. Laila advanced toward her. Eva's fright flickered across her own face as she scrambled backward on the bed. Séverin lifted his head, looking between the false Laila on the bed and the true Laila. Shock widened his eyes. He touched his mouth, disbelief slowly giving way to a look of blank horror.

Eva leapt to the floor, clutching her ring and circling Laila.

"*Leave*," said Laila.

"You should feel flattered," said Eva quickly.

"And you should feel my heel in your ribs," said Laila.

Eva stumbled back. She tried to grab her shoes, but Laila grabbed a candelabra from the top of a nearby dresser. Eva's eyes widened.

"You wouldn't."

"Just because you wear my face doesn't mean you know me," she growled.

Eva looked at her shoes and necklace, then back at Laila.

"*Go*," said Laila one last time.

Eva skittered around her, pressed against the wall before she raced out of the room. Laila slammed the door shut behind her. Fury vibrated through her. Fury and—though it felt like a cruel twist—*want*. That was supposed to be her on that bed, braced between his arms.

"How could you think that was me?" she demanded.

Or worse . . . had he known all along it was never her? Séverin looked at her, and the expression there, as if he'd been laid bare, banished her doubt. His shirt was undone, pulled from his trousers, and the topmost buttons exposed the bronze of his throat. He had the look of someone gloriously defiant even in his defeat, like a seraph freshly flung out of heaven.

"I saw what I wanted to see," he said, hoarse. "Only a desperate man trusts a mirage in the desert and I am desperate, Laila. Everything I came here for . . . it was nothing. And because it was nothing, I had no excuses left."

"Excuses?" repeated Laila. "Excuses for what?"

She moved closer, noticing the smudged line of blood on his neck and the blush tinge at his mouth. Dimly, she remembered the two goblets on the floor, and the server's words: *To consume one's own blood allows one to submit to their innermost desires.*

"Excuses to stay away from you," he said, the words rushing out of him. "Excuses to tell you that you're a poison I've come to crave. Excuses to tell you that you terrify me out of my senses, and how I'm fairly certain you'll be the death of me, Laila, and yet I can't bring myself to mind."

The words shuddered through her, and Laila felt a flicker of power in her veins. It was that same thrum of energy that she had once felt in the dance theatre of House Kore when he had watched her . . . his posture like that of a bored emperor, his stare like that of someone starved. She stared at Séverin now, propped against the pillows, his expression desperate and raw. The more she looked at him, the more a dangerous molten heat spread through her.

Laila turned her ring—and all its dwindling days—toward her palm, hiding it from herself. She hardly knew what she was doing, only that she couldn't stop herself. She climbed onto the bed, her pulse going jagged the second his eyes widened.

"How do you know I'm not a mirage . . . how do you know

I'm real this time, Séverin?" asked Laila. "You said so yourself I wasn't."

As she spoke, she straddled him, her hips above his. Séverin's mouth twisted up, dark and lupine.

"Perhaps," he said, his voice low. He trailed his hand up her thigh. "All goddesses are just beliefs draped on the scaffolding of ideas. I can't touch what's not real." Séverin looked up at her. His pupils were blown out. "But I can worship it all the same."

Laila's hands went to his shoulders . . . his neck.

"Can I, Laila?" he asked. His eyes burned. "Will you let me?"

Laila dug her fingers in his hair, tugging backwards so he couldn't look away from her. He winced slightly, the corner of his mouth twisting into a smile when she finally let herself say, "Yes."

Barely a second after she'd spoken, his hands went to her waist, dragging her swiftly off his lap so she fell to the bed. There was a moment when the perpetual twilight outside snuck across her vision . . . but it disappeared when Séverin moved over her and became her night.

LAILA WOKE UP WITH an unfamiliar ache in her chest. She brought her fingers to her throat, checking her pulse: *one, two . . . one, two . . . one, two . . .*

Her heartbeat was normal. So then what was this ache? Beside her, Séverin stirred. His arm slung across her waist curved, drawing her against him. Against his heartbeat. In sleep, he pressed a kiss to her scar, and finally Laila recognized the shape and flutter of this ache.

Hope.

It felt like the flicker of newly made wings, thin and chrysalis-slick, dangerous in its new power. Hope *hurt*. She'd forgotten the pain of it. Laila stared at her hand on Séverin's. Slowly, she twined her fingers in his, and that ache roared sharply the tighter he held their clasped hands.

They had seen the other bared before, but not like this. Séverin had revealed a corner of his soul, and Laila wanted to answer that strength. She wanted to wake him, to tell him of the handful of days she had left. She didn't want to give up in their search, but renew it. *Together.*

Giddy, she slipped out of bed. She refused to say anything to him with her hair in this state; her mother would've rioted. She reached for her robe on the floor when her fingers brushed against something cold . . . something simmering with pain and fury right beneath the metal. Laila yelped, then looked down; it was Eva's ballerina necklace and pendant.

She stared at it, then looked back at Séverin sleeping in the bed.

It felt wrong to spy into this part of Eva with Séverin so close to her. Gingerly, Laila pulled on her robe, then stepped out into the hallway and down the passage to the stair's landing. Eva's necklace vibrated with emotion, and the moment she touched it, the sensation of being *hunted* overwhelmed her, turning her pulse rabbit-quick with panic. Its most recent action had been last night, when Eva had removed it from her neck and concealed it in the palm of her hand after Séverin consumed the blood Forged drink. But there was a deeper memory within it. Laila closed her eyes, searching out the object's truths—

A small, red-haired Eva twirling before a painting of a beautiful ballerina with identical hair. She was in a room full of paintings and statues.

"I want to dance like Mama!" she said.

"You will never *end up like your mama. Do you understand, Eva?"*

Even in the memory, Laila recognized the voice . . . Mikhail

346 ~ ROSHANI CHOKSHI

Vasiliev. The art dealer from St. Petersburg. An image of a portrait flashed through her head of a beautiful ballerina, Vasiliev's lover who had killed herself after the birth of their illegitimate child. All this time they had thought the child was dead. They were wrong.

Laila remembered Vasiliev's last words in the salon:

She will find you.

It was never the matriarch. It was Eva, Vasiliev's own daughter.

Laila pressed the pendant harder, and the memories rushed forth—

A long, hot knife taken to Eva's leg. Her shrill screams as she pleaded for them to stop.

"I can't let you be like your mother. I'm doing this to protect you, child, you understand? I do this because I love you."

Tears prickled Laila's eyes . . . but it was nothing compared to the panic she suddenly felt when the memory changed. The memories before had been deep-seated . . . but this . . . this was within the past year.

"I know you want freedom, Eva Yefremovna. Do as I say, and I will give it to you. No more curfews, no more hiding, no more darkness. The Fallen House is depending on you."

The pendant fell from Laila's hand with a small, metallic chime. Too many thoughts raced through her head, but it was the *sound* that caught her attention. The Winter Conclave revels were said to go on for hours. It shouldn't be this silent.

"You should have stayed in bed," said Eva from the bottom of the staircase.

The other girl had changed out of her green ballroom gown to an outfit of a soldier. Slim, black trousers and a close-fitting jacket.

"How did you enjoy the doctor's gift?" said Eva, advancing toward her. "In his mercy, he wanted to give you both one last

night of pleasure. He figured that either you'd be too stubborn to
go to Séverin, and I would have to do the honors of giving him one
last night with you. Alternatively, I would have incited you to the
point you would go to him on your own."

Eva eyed her up and down.

"It seems I was successful. Well done, *me*."

Eva pulled out a dagger. Laila glanced over her shoulder. She
was too far from the door. She put up her hands, her thoughts
clamoring together. *The doctor*? He was here?

"Listen, Eva. I understand the Fallen House may have promised
you freedom, but we can *help* you—"

Eva's eyes widened. "How did you . . ."

She trailed off, her gaze snapping to her dropped necklace. At
that, Eva looked beyond Laila's shoulder.

"You were right," she said.

But she was not speaking to Laila.

Behind her, someone started to clap. Before Laila could turn,
the person grabbed hold of her, pulling her against their chest. Eva
lunged forward, grabbing her by the throat. Her ring talon dug
into her neck.

"*Be still.*"

Laila's limbs went numb. She couldn't even speak. All she felt
was a roiling sense of nausea.

"You must be wondering what the Fallen House wants with
you," said Eva.

"It's the same thing your darling Séverin craves, my sweet muse,
my divine instrument," said a familiar voice.

Laila felt her arms yanked forward, her hands brought up to
her face.

"Nothing but your *touch*."

31

SÉVERIN

Séverin awoke to a cold bed and a panic that felt like a thunderstorm had taken root in his skull. Laila was gone. Of course she was gone. If he could, he would've cursed that blood Forging drink for unlocking him so thoroughly. He must have terrified her. He touched the empty space beside him. Every exquisite detail of last night burned through him. Including everything he'd said. Shame burned his cheeks . . . but then why did he remember Laila smiling at him, her laughter against his skin? Laila was many things, but not cruel. Pity wouldn't have driven her to his bed. So then why had she left it so soon?

Séverin threw back the sheets, groping on the table beside him for Tristan's knife hidden under one of his notebooks. The heft of the wooden hilt in his hand calmed him. He unsheathed it, staring at the blade and the thin, translucent vein in the metal where Goliath's paralyzing venom ran thick. Perhaps more than the failure to protect Tristan was how he'd failed to know him fully. How could

Tristan inflict hurt and give love in the same breath? How was he supposed to live knowing that all of this had been for nothing? *The Divine Lyrics* had never been there. He'd failed Tristan. He'd failed all of them, left them unprotected . . . and left himself unprotected too. What he'd done with Laila . . . he felt like a creature yanked from its shell, all exposed flesh and raw nerves.

Silence pressed all around, and . . . wait. Silence?

Dread grabbed hold of his thoughts. Séverin threw on his clothes, pocketed a couple of Zofia's concealed weapons and Tristan's knife, and then opened the door. A sickly sweet smell immediately hit his nose. Like blood and spiced wine. He crossed the stair landing. On one of the steps, he spotted a familiar necklace . . . Eva's ballerina pendant.

Thinking of her brought a bitter taste to the back of his throat. She'd tricked him, and that mind Forging draught had turned him reckless, blurring the differences to show him who he wanted in his arms. Not who he had.

Far below came a strange scraping sound, like dry leaves on a road. Goose bumps pebbled his skin. The silence was all wrong. It wasn't the intoxicated, full-bodied silence of a crowd passed out, but something more sinister. More absent.

Séverin kept to the side of the stairs. Immediately, a rounded shape met his eye. He stepped closer and his stomach dropped.

A person was sprawled out on the steps.

With a normal Order function, he would have assumed they were just passed out from drink . . . but this person's eyes kept moving, roving back and forth wildly, his mouth frozen in an oval of panic. Paralyzed.

Séverin bent down, turning the man's chin ever so slightly. A slight puncture wound marked his skin. This had to be an act of blood Forging. The paralyzed person—a white man in his late fifties—stared hard into Séverin's eyes, silently pleading for help, but Séverin had no skill in blood Forging. And frankly, this man was not his concern. He cared about where Laila had gone; whether Zofia and Enrique were safe . . . and Hypnos.

As Séverin moved down the staircase and entered the atrium, he saw dozens of Order members slumped over, lining the frozen walls in neat rows. Scattered around them, the living animal-like treasure chests of the Order appeared as inanimate as rock, frozen just like their respective matriarchs and patriarchs. Hypnos was not among them.

The more Séverin looked at the paralyzed members of the Order, the more the details struck him. For one, they were too organized. Every single person had been arranged so that not one had their face toward the ground. It could have appeared merciful, a pose that allowed them to breathe . . . but Séverin had long practiced reading rooms full of treasure. This was personal. Whoever had done this to them had arranged them so they could see one another, so their own horror would be reflected back infinitely.

Someone wanted to make sure that everyone knew who had put them in their place. He needed to find out exactly who that person was, what they'd done with the others . . . and why they had chosen to spare him. The location of his suite was no secret. Clearly, he was meant to see this. He just didn't know why.

The atrium now held a gruesome beauty to it. Silver confetti still spangled the air. The champagne chandeliers drifted aimlessly, frost creeping over their stems. Down the hall leading to the ice grotto, Séverin spied a heat net composed of slender, crisscrossing patterns in glowing red that stretched from the floor to the ceiling. It blocked Forged objects, but not humans. If the others were taken, they could've been dragged through the net easily.

To his right, he heard the creaking sound of a door. Séverin took quick stock of his position in the wide atrium. The sound was coming from the library, the place where he had last seen Enrique.

A low growl emanated from the podium. Séverin snapped his head to the stage where the Midnight Auction was supposed to have taken place, but judging from the confetti and untouched champagne, they had never made it that far before the attack.

From between the rows of paralyzed Order members slithered out crystalline snakes. A transparent jaguar prowled out from behind a grand piano. Several birds of prey broke off from the moonstone chandelier, their crystal wings chiming loudly. All around him, the crouched silhouettes of animals started to stir. *Ice* animals, the same ones that had been hauled out of the menagerie, their internal mechanisms changed to turn them into docile, sentient tables.

The ice jaguar's tail switched, its jaws lengthening.

They weren't docile anymore.

Another banging sound came from the library door. As if someone was trying to get out. Séverin weighed the chances of death by the ice animals or death by whoever hid in the library . . . and then he took off down the hall.

Behind him, the heavy paws of the ice animals crunched against the glass floor. Séverin skidded to a stop near the front of the library entrance. Chairs barricaded the doors, and a table bearing vases of frozen lilies blocked him. Séverin pushed them aside, then lifted the chain holding the doors in place. When he jammed the handle, it was stuck fast . . . but from the other side.

"Who's there?" came a voice from within.

Enrique. Séverin could have fallen to the floor in relief.

"It's me, Séverin," he said. "You need to open up, there's—"

"*Séverin,*" spat Enrique. "Where are the others? What did you do with them?"

"Why would *I* do anything with them?"

"You're clearly intent on destroying anything around you, so where are they?"

Behind Séverin came a low growl and the sharp *scritch* of ice on ice. He risked a glance over this shoulder and saw an ice bear snuffling the ground. Séverin held still. The animals were drawn to heat and movement . . . it wouldn't move unless *he* did.

"Enrique—" said Séverin.

"You didn't think I'd find out about the letters you sent to the Ilustrados?" demanded Enrique. "How you cancelled the meeting and destroyed my dreams?"

Séverin froze, but only for an instant. Yes, he sent out a letter to every member of the Ilustrados. Yes, he had enclosed a check with each letter, so they would not attend. He didn't care if it looked like sabotage. He didn't even care if Enrique hated him for it. All he had done was try to protect him.

Enrique cracked open the door and stepped outside. "So unless you can explain why I should trust—"

The door swinging open caught the bear's attention. It roared, pounding the floor as it charged toward them. Séverin snatched the vase of frozen lilies, smashing it over the bear's head. A quarter of its face cracked off, splintering to the ground. Enrique screamed, and Séverin pulled him away from the wall right when the animal charged again.

"I'll distract, you run inside, and then we slam the door," said Séverin. "Understand?"

Before Enrique had a chance to answer, Séverin grabbed the white lilies from the ground, waving them off to the side. The creature looked between Enrique and the flowers. Séverin's hand lent the bouquet an illusion of heat. The bear leapt, springing for the flowers—

Séverin tossed them in its face, then grabbed Enrique, pushing them both into the library. Too late, the creature registered the falsehood. It charged at the library, but Séverin got to the door first, slamming it hard enough that delicate shingles of ice crashed onto the marble. The bear snarled and snorted, scrabbling at the door of the library.

"What the hell just happened?" gasped Enrique. "They're not supposed to act like that."

"Someone must have returned them to their original settings," said Séverin.

He glanced behind Enrique. The tables full of treasure looked just as they had left them.

"I still hate you," said Enrique raggedly.

"Not an uncommon sentiment today."

"You *sent out notes* to every member of the Ilustrados making sure they wouldn't come to my meeting? Do you deny it?"

"No," said Séverin. "We need to find the others. You can berate me later."

"I might *kill* you later, forget berating—"

"Shhh," said Séverin. He pressed his ear to the door and peered through the keyhole.

"Good. The ice creature left," said Séverin. "Tell me what happened. Where are the others?"

Enrique stared at him, still breathing hard, his face contorted in something between fury and worry. Finally, Enrique let out a sigh, and Séverin sensed that for now . . . he would put aside his hurt.

"I was knocked out," he said, rubbing his temples. "The last thing I remember is Ruslan saying he would deliver the lyre to the matriarch. There must have been something in our drink that was meant to knock us out, but Ruslan didn't take his goblet. He could be *dead*. And Zofia . . ." Enrique swallowed hard. "Zofia had left to examine a part of the ice grotto, but she never came back. I have no clue where Laila was last night."

Séverin opened his mouth, closed it, then rethought his words. "She was accounted for up until a few hours ago."

"Where was she?"

"In bed," said Séverin curtly.

"How do you know?" demanded Enrique.

"Because I was there," said Séverin, adding quickly, "What about Hypnos?"

"I haven't seen Hypnos since last evening and—wait a minute, what did you just say?"

"I didn't see him out there with the others," said Séverin.

"You were with Laila 'in bed'?" asked Enrique. "Like . . . beside her or—hold on, what do you mean out there with the others? What others?"

"The paralyzed members of the Order are lined up all around the atrium. Must have been a blood Forging artist," said Séverin. Then he frowned, running through what Enrique had said. "Why would Ruslan need to deliver a lyre to the matriarch?"

Enrique eyed him warily.

It hit Séverin then: Enrique didn't trust him. Enrique, who had once willingly walked into a volcano beside him and emerged on the other side craving marshmallow and bars of chocolate. This was the cost of what he had done, and to stare at it full in the face and have nothing to offer in return: no godhood, no protection, no recompense . . .

It was its own kind of death.

"Later," said Enrique curtly.

Séverin forced himself to nod and then turned to the door of the library.

"The ice creatures are drawn to heat and movement. There's a heat net blocking the grotto entrance, and they can't cross it. We just have to get there before them."

"And how, exactly, do we avoid getting mauled?"

He couldn't care less what happened to him so long as the others were safe, but he'd be useless to them if he was too wounded to help. Séverin looked around the library, then walked to one of the tables laden with treasure. There were statue busts, woven tapestries that shimmered and sang at his touch . . . but that wasn't what he was looking for. His gaze zeroed in on a handheld mirror the size of his palm.

Enrique moved behind him.

"That's a fourth-century replica of Amaterasu's mirror. It's a relic all the way from Japan, so be *very—*"

Séverin smashed it, eliciting a strangled choking sound from Enrique.

". . . *careful*," finished Enrique weakly.

Séverin picked through the shards, gathering a couple for himself, and then a couple for Enrique.

"Follow me."

Séverin opened the library door slowly, and they walked down the hall to the atrium. Beside him, Enrique muttered something about the "tyranny of indifference." Morning light changed in the

room, silvering the interior of the Sleeping Palace. The ice creatures weren't true animals; they couldn't see. Yet their Forging
function was identical to that of a Mnemo bug. It could track and
record movement like any ordinary pair of eyes . . . and respond in
kind.

Séverin weighed the mirror shards in his hand.

"Do you remember Nisyros Island?"

Enrique groaned. Séverin knew that Enrique, in particular,
held a special grudge against the island.

"Remember the mechanical sharks?"

"The ones you said wouldn't attack?" shot back Enrique.

In the past, Enrique had always mentioned this jokingly, but
there was no humor left. Now, Enrique's eyes dulled, as if whatever joy he'd found in the past had snapped beneath the weight
of the present. Séverin wanted to shake his shoulders, to tell him
that everything he'd done was *for* and not against him. But disuse
had turned his tongue clumsy for truth telling, and the window for
truths slammed shut at the distant growl of an ice animal.

"Those sharks followed patterns of light," explained Séverin.

"Which would carry a very faint heat signature to the ice animals," finished Enrique, nodding.

"Exactly," said Séverin. "Now. On the count of three, I'm going
to shine the mirror shards onto the wall behind us. At that point
you have to run."

Even without turning around, Séverin could feel Enrique chafe
at the thought.

"One . . ."

Séverin moved forward. The silhouettes of animals crowded the
stage, tensed for any sign of an intruder.

"Two . . ."

Enrique moved beside him, and Séverin remembered every other time they had stood like this. Like friends.

"*Three.*"

Séverin threw out the mirror shards. Patterns of light hit the floor.

"Go!" he shouted.

Enrique ran forward. Light splayed like diamonds across the translucent floor. The creatures leapt and snarled at the patches of light. But not all the creatures were so distracted. To them, any combination of heat and movement was worth chasing. Out the corner of his eye, Séverin saw a huge crystal wolverine break off from the rest of the group. Its head jerked sharply in their direction before it growled, leaping after them, the ground falling away beneath its loping pace.

Up ahead, the red Forged heat net grew closer. Enrique tried to match Séverin stride for stride, but he wasn't fast enough. The wolverine gained on him, one sharp claw was all it would take—

Séverin turned swiftly and barreled into the ice wolverine. It skidded to the right, scrabbling at the ice to get back on course.

"Don't stop running!" yelled Séverin.

Séverin tore an incendiary device from his belt, throwing it into the wolverine's gaping jaws. Seconds later, orange light burst across his vision. He threw up his arm as glass exploded in every direction. Growling and hissing filled his ears. All that the other creatures detected was heat and light, and they stalked it like a trail of blood left behind by wounded prey. Séverin couldn't run. The creatures closed on him from every side. He willed himself still, arms frozen. In front of him, a vulture hopped forward, snapping its beak.

Séverin slowly maneuvered the mirror shards down his sleeve

and into his palms. If he could distract them, he could make a run for it. He nearly had the shard in his hand when he heard the scrape of glass on ice. Out the corner of his eye, he saw a leopard sink back on its haunches. His heart pounded. He spun around in the same instant the creature leapt into the air. Light flashed in his eyes, his feet skidding beneath him. Séverin threw up his hands, only for cold air to burst onto his face. The animals had scattered. Sharp patterns of light knifed across the floor, blinding him.

"Run!" called Enrique.

Séverin twisted around. Enrique stood at the entrance to the Forged heating net, and for a moment, time froze with his shock: Enrique hadn't left him. Scrambling to his feet, Séverin took off at a run. Behind him, he could hear the ice animals giving way to chase. A claw caught the edge of his jacket, tearing it off him. The Forged net loomed closer, its warm red light searing into his vision. One step, then three—

At the same time, Séverin and Enrique dove through the Forged heat net. Séverin slammed into the ground. Sharp pain shot up his wrist, but he pushed past it.

"Behind you!" shouted Enrique.

A huge ice lion sprang toward them. Séverin clambered backwards on his elbows, turning his face sharply. Seconds later, a rush of water hit the floor. He looked up to see water soaking his pant leg.

The heat net had turned the creature to a puddle of water.

Beside him, Enrique fought to catch his breath, his arms around his knees.

"Thank you," said Séverin.

Enrique's eyes turned glossy. When he fixed him with a stare, it was dead-eyed. For a long moment, he could say nothing. He looked away from Séverin to the floor.

"How could you do that to me?" he asked quietly.

At the sound of his voice, something inside Séverin threatened to break. He had nothing left to offer but the truth. He closed his eyes, thinking that once more his head would be full of remembering the slick golden ichor on Roux-Joubert's mouth and the fleeting weight of wings.

But instead, he thought of Hypnos's last toast. *May our ends justify our means.* That was all he had wanted. And he'd failed.

"I needed you for this one last job," said Séverin, hauling himself upright. "I needed everyone's complete focus and attention, but it wasn't just for me. It was for all of us. *The Divine Lyrics* can grant godhood. That's what I wanted for us . . . Do you understand? If I had that, no one would ever hurt us. You could have anything you want. You could go back to the Ilustrados, and they'd fall to their knees to have you. Tristan could even—"

"Have you gone mad?" cut in Enrique. "Turning into a *god*? *That* was your solution to your problems?"

"You have no idea what I saw or what I felt when I was in those catacombs. I had *wings*, Enrique. I had golden blood in my veins, and what I felt . . . it was like knowing the fucking pulse of the universe," said Séverin. "You heard Ruslan in the dining room. The Fallen House had the means to do that, with their Midas Knife or whatever it was called. Imagine if there was more. Imagine what I could have given us if we had that book—"

He broke off when Enrique started laughing. Not a laugh of joy, but a laugh of hysteria.

"It's not even a book," said Enrique.

Séverin paused. Everything in his mind went still. "What?"

"It's a lyre."

"A lyre," Séverin repeated.

Once more, something stirred to life inside him. Something that felt dangerously like hope.

"But I don't think it will give you what you want, Séverin," said Enrique sadly. "The writing on the wall talked about the instrument summoning the unmaking. It could mean that every *Forged* thing in existence would collapse."

"It's supposed to grant the power of God—"

"And God creates and destroys in equal measure."

"So we make sure that only *we* play it—"

Enrique flung out his hand. "You're not *listening* to me! What about Laila? The Fallen House has been searching for someone of the Lost Muses bloodline—a *girl* with an ability to read what others cannot. That's Laila. If the Fallen House has taken her, what if it's because they know what she can do? They might have even connected her to the lineage of the Lost Muses."

Séverin's head was spinning. Blood rushed through his ears. He had to get to her. He had to make sure she was safe.

"Then only we play it, guided by Laila—who might be the only person left who can use it—"

"*No,*" insisted Enrique. "Don't you see how this could affect her if this instrument is played? She's *Forged*, Séverin. That could mean that she—"

Séverin's gaze snapped to him. "How do you know that?"

Two things hit Séverin at once. One, that he'd never even stopped to consider the nature of Laila's . . . making. To him, something Forged was inanimate. An object. Laila was life incarnate. The second realization was that Laila had told someone else about her origins. Before, he was the only one who'd known. The only one she had trusted with that secret.

Enrique's eyes flickered with guilt. He was hiding something. Séverin was sure of it.

"What aren't you telling me?"

Enrique crossed himself, looked upward and murmured, "I'm sorry, Laila. But he has to know."

"Know *what*?" demanded Séverin.

Enrique looked away from him. "Laila is dying."

A beat passed. Then two. Those words poisoned the air, and Séverin didn't let himself breathe as if one inhale might make those words true. And then, before he could speak, a hissing sound pulled his attention to the Forged net. The light quivered, flashing bright and dull. Just beyond it, the animals had lined up . . . tails whipping, hooves raking the frost-thick floor . . .

The net had begun to break.

32

ZOFIA

Zofia blinked a couple of times, her mind registering the unfamiliar surrounding in spurts: translucent floor, Lake Baikal's gem-colored water rushing beneath the surface. Cold, slippery ice burned the skin of her palms. When she glanced up, light bounced off a sharp curve she didn't recognize. Out the corner of her eye, she spied the tops of people's heads, their scalps pressed up against the wall and eye level to her. Zofia turned away sharply and flung out her arms, only for them to slam into the walls encasing her. She was trapped. The word zipped through her skull, and she doubled over, nausea building in her throat.

Not again.

When she blinked, she saw the laboratory fires . . . the students screaming . . . the way her mind and body failed her when she reached to open the door.

No. No. No.

Zofia curled in on herself only for the sharp edge of Hela's envelope to press against her skin, a stinging reminder of the people depending on her. Zofia forced herself to sit up straight, and remind herself of all that had happened. Her memories felt thready. She remembered the leviathan and the red candles, the writing on the wall . . . WE ARE READY FOR THE UNMAKING. After that, nothing. Zofia set her teeth and lay her palms flat on the ice floor, letting the cold shock her. She counted her breaths. *One. Two. Three.* She focused on the floor, counting the marbled trails left behind in the ice . . . *fifteen, nineteen, forty-seven.*

Only then did she finally lift her head.

Where was she? The room was long and rectangular, the width of it not sufficient to stretch out her arms. She could stand and turn easily in the space, and so she did, though she could not walk far, for she was not alone. Shoved against the western wall and propped at a sharp angle was the broken body of an ice stag. She remembered seeing it with Eva not two days ago. Eva had seen her discomfort and asked House Dazbog not to destroy the machine. The stag's chest was torn out, and the ventricles of ice that had once pulsed through it were dead, leaving nothing but hollow wire. Finally, Zofia knew where she was.

The prison of the Sleeping Palace.

Except for the north-facing wall, her surroundings showed nothing but an expanse of packed snow. When she faced north, the glass walls revealed the atrium of the Sleeping Palace. Members of the Order of Babel lay propped against the atrium's perimeter like strange dolls. A couple even leaned against one wall of her prison cell.

"Let me out!" shouted Zofia.

But they did not move when she tapped the glass behind their heads. They did not respond when she looked at the ones opposite the room, shouting once more.

No response.

Not even a blink.

She caught sight of something else. Two people dashing into the atrium from the western side of her cell: Enrique and Séverin. A pattern of shifting light sprawled out before them. From behind the pianos and tables, the empty stage and rows of people, ice creatures stalked to attack. A flash of silver caught her eye. Too late, she saw an ice cheetah dash toward Séverin's unprotected right side:

"Séverin!" she called out.

But he didn't hear her.

Zofia pounded at the glass with her fist. Nothing happened. Frantically, she reached for her throat, only for her hand to meet skin.

Her necklace of pendants and folded weapons was *gone*. Bile stung the back of her throat. She patted down the front of her jackets and pockets. She had nothing on her person except Hela's letter and—

Zofia stopped just as her fingers closed around familiar edges. Her matchbox. She drew it out, flipping back the silver cover: three matches. That was all she had. She looked at Séverin and Enrique, now trying to run to the ice grotto entrance, which was netted over with a Forged heat protectant. Her breath came quick. In Forging, her affinity had always been metallurgy. She had not been trained in the art of detecting and manipulating the presence of minerals in ice. The probability of success was low. But the probability of dying was higher.

Zofia lit one of the three matches against her tooth, then held it to the ice wall. If she could detect the minerals and ignite it with the presence of fire, she could create a hole within the wall. She pressed her hand to the ice, straining to feel the pulse of her Forging affinity . . . the thrum of ore within an object that responded to her touch. She pushed with everything inside her, but then the flame guttered out. Zofia scrambled to catch it only for her feet to slip out beneath her, throwing her to the ground. Her chin smacked into the ice floor, and she tasted blood. Wearily, Zofia forced herself to a stand.

Only two matches left.

Fingers trembling, she wiped the blood off her lips, then reached for another match. The sound of fire ripped through the air only for the match to slip out from between her wet, bloody fingers. A sob caught in her throat as the flame spluttered and died on the ice.

Zofia felt the rush of a thousand failures. She saw the blank expression on Laila's face; the pity in Enrique's eyes; Hela's worry tugging down the corners of her mouth. A thousand expressions she had easily deciphered. All of it dragged out something deep within her. Her skin felt like it was burning. A low buzz gathered at the base of her skull. It wasn't irritation. It wasn't annoyance.

It was fury.

Zofia remembered one of the last evenings in the kitchens of L'Eden, when Tristan had still lived. He had been making a chain of daisies, letting them grow into bizarre vines that snatched Enrique's book straight out of his hands. Laila had scolded them for making a mess, and threatened: "If you make a mess of my kitchen, I'll unleash the fury of a Zofia who has not had her daily sugar cookie." Zofia had frowned at that because she didn't know that she was capable of fury. Fury belonged to those with fiery temperaments, but the longer she sat there, the more she felt as if she was seeing a new part of herself.

When she looked through the northern glass, she saw Enrique stumbling . . . an ice wolverine gaining on him, and she remembered the last thing he had said to her:

You're a lot braver than most of the people outside. None of them could build a bomb with their eyes closed and wander into a metal monster and still want to name it "David." Trust in yourself, Phoenix.

She would not make him a liar.

Zofia turned to the crystal stag, inert and glittering. Beneath its hooves, she noticed a spider-like fracture spreading out from the ice. She could not burn through the ice. But the stag was a Forged instrument, powerful enough that its hooves, if moving, could shatter through the barrier.

Her last match in hand, Zofia knelt beside the stag. Days ago, House Dazbog had dismissed the machine for its broken internal metal mechanisms, its failure to respond. She could not manipulate ice. But she could work with metal. And she could work with fire.

Zofia let her hands run over its smooth artistry. In the gaping mess of its chest, she felt the slim, hollow wires . . . their tangled shape. She felt where the machine had gone silent. She struck her last match. At her touch, the once dormant metal *sang*. It was a low, thready song. Slowly, the gears began to grind together, the fire working its way through the flammable metal oxides.

The ice stag shuddered to life, its hooves pawing at the air. Zofia bent her will to the creature, just as she would with any of her other inventions. The stag kicked out, shattering the glass wall. It scrabbled to a stand, righting itself and arching the frosted line of its throat. When it shook its antlers, small icicles shattered on the ground. It lowered its head to Zofia, its huge antlers sharp as weapons. At the center of its chest now bubbled a small inferno. A heart of fire.

For a moment, Zofia was awed. All the tools and objects she had Forged were not like this. *This* was the art of Forging that felt like she had granted life. This was the part of the art form that others called a sliver of God's power.

It filled her with a sense of capability . . . as if she might go any-where and not count the trees; as if she might talk to anyone and never know panic. It was power, she realized, and she quite liked it.

Zofia reached for one of its antlers and then hauled herself onto its freezing back.

"*Go*," she commanded.

The stag reared up onto its front legs and then shattered the glass wall. In one smooth leap, it jumped over the heads of the frozen members of the Order of Babel. Ahead of her, Zofia could see the line of animals had converged into a knot at the entrance to the hall that housed the ice grotto. The Forged heat net flickered dimly. Soon, it would die. At the mouth of the hall, she watched as Séverin flung out his hand, his other hand pushing Enrique behind him.

The animals poised to strike.

Zofia urged the stag faster, her hand moving once more to her neck. Frustration gathered inside her. She needed a weapon, some-thing that would push back the creatures. She cast about and saw an ornamental sword lying across the lap of a frozen member of the Italian faction. The stag halted to a stop in front of him, and she reached down, plucking the sword.

"Thank you," she said.

She gripped the blade, finding the pulse of its metal that sang to her Forging affinity and then pressed it against the ice stag's flam-ing heart. Fire erupted across the sword.

"*Faster*," she whispered.

The stag galloped down the line of ice creatures, then skidded to a halt at the front of the Forging net. The net itself was made of metal, and when she reached out . . . letting her fingers skim across it, the thread felt cold to the touch. It needed fire. She looked behind her to make sure that Séverin and Enrique were safe. Séverin held a mirror shard in his hand and stared at her. Enrique yelped, hiding his face behind his arm. He poked his head up, his arm falling to his side. His jaw dropped, and he looked from her face to the flaming sword.

"*Zofia?*"

Indignation. Amazement. Confusion. It could be any of those emotions, thought Zofia, so she settled on the only reply that made sense to her: "Hello."

Then she turned back to the line of ice creatures. She brandished the fire sword. A handful of the creatures skittered back.

"Séverin and Enrique, get behind the net," she said.

She heard them step backward, and then she brought the tip of her sword to the net. Heat bloomed across it once more, and the ice creatures stepped backwards, hissing and growling. Zofia dropped the sword, then dismounted from her stag. It swung its head to her. Zofia patted its hindquarters once, and it took off down the atrium, far away from the fire net.

When she turned around, Séverin and Enrique were still staring at her.

"You rescued us," said Enrique, heaving. He smiled weakly. "This almost feels like a fairy tale, and I'm the damsel in distress."

"You're not a damsel."

"I am in distress, though."

"But—"

"Let me have this, Zofia," said Enrique wearily.

"Zofia . . ." started Séverin, and then he stopped.

If anyone appeared distressed, it was Séverin. He fell silent, his brows pressing together as he pointed to the ice grotto.

"I'm glad you're safe, but we're still missing Laila and Hypnos," he said, looking up at her. "Enrique said you'd gone to the leviathan. What happened?"

Zofia stared down the hall, unease creeping through her.

"I was attacked inside it."

"Did you see your attacker's face?"

She shook her head.

"What weapons do we have?"

Zofia touched her bare throat. *Nothing.* Séverin saw the movement and nodded. He looked to Enrique and then glanced down at the emptied arsenal of his belt.

"Stay behind me, and we'll go together," he said.

Zofia had hardly taken a step when she heard a low sigh from the end of the ice grotto. It was a sigh of reluctance, the sound she used to make when Laila would tell her to wash her hands before eating dinner or help tidy up the kitchens. But that sigh did not match the figure who stepped out of the shadows. A man wearing a golden bee mask . . . his hands steepled in thought, one hand pale and the other . . . the other *gold.*

She recognized the insect mask immediately. It belonged to the man in the catacombs, the man who the Fallen House had called "the doctor."

"I know you'll understand," said the doctor. "It may not be easy at first . . . but you will understand. I will show you before the day is gone."

"What—" started Zofia, just as three masked people stepped out from behind the doctor.

Séverin lunged at them, a mirror shard in his hand, but the man was too quick. He subdued him, forcing him to the ground. Séverin fought to turn his face toward them.

"Zofia, Enrique, *run—*"

The person kicked Séverin in the head, and he went still. A second masked man grabbed Enrique by the throat, holding a knife to his neck. Zofia raised her fists, fury gathering at the back of her skull when the doctor raised his hand.

"Fight back," said the doctor, turning his masked face to her. "And I will cut his throat. I *really* do not wish to do that. First, it's deeply unhygienic. Second, it's such a waste of a person."

Zofia looked down at her hands. Her veins still vibrated with the memory of power, and she hated that she could not use any of it now. Slowly, she lowered her fists.

"Very good," said the doctor. "Thank you for doing that, Zofia. I've never found violence to be the answer."

His voice . . .

There was something about it she recognized. And how did he know her name?

"Now," said the doctor, as the third man stepped toward her. "I need your help, my dear. You see, my muse needs some inspiration before she can work. I think you, Enrique, and Séverin will help us accomplish that. I hope you will agree."

When he stepped forward, Zofia noticed something tucked beneath his arm . . . something pale and white, bent at a strange angle. It was a hand. Attached to the finger gleamed a huge Ring. And then the doctor lifted up his mask, revealing a pair of kind eyes that she had grown used to, a curving smile that she had often answered with one of her own. For Zofia, it felt like two images that did not fit, and yet her observations could not lie.

The doctor of the Fallen House was Ruslan.

He grinned and then waved the hand that had never been his.

"Rather gruesome, isn't it?" Ruslan said. "Anyway, I do hope you can all help. After all, friends make incredible sacrifices for one another. And I've come to consider you just that." He smiled wide. *"Friends."*

33

SÉVERIN

Séverin woke up with his head pounding and his hands bound. He was propped up against a metal chair in a dark silver room that *pulsed*. The smell was familiar, the salt rust scent of blood. Light wavered across the ribbed metallic walls. A familiar raised podium cut the center of the room. Séverin blinked. He was inside the metal leviathan. Only it looked different now that it had been stripped of its treasures.

Séverin tried to inch forward silently, but the slight movement sent a burst of pain through his skull. His head pounded. The last thing he remembered was lunging at a guard, only to be thrown to the floor and knocked unconscious by a sharp kick. The hilt of Tristan's knife pressed against his ribs, and the sharp tip of the Mnemo moth pinned to his lapel pricked his skin.

Near-silence filled the room, broken only by the eerie, watery pulse of Lake Baikal sloshing against the metal leviathan. A slight stir to his left caught his attention. *Hypnos.* Séverin scooted forward. The other boy lay utterly still, and for a wild moment Séverin prayed that time itself had stopped because Hypnos lay far too still. He wanted to be like ice, but there were too many cracks in his armor. The closer he got to Hypnos, the more old memories slithered out from the fissures, scalding him. Séverin remembered the brothers they had been—cut from the shadows and resigned to them; Hypnos's singing voice; sunlight flooding the false theatre in which they had played at being the wanted sons of pale patriarchs. With his bound hands, he nudged at Hypnos's body, managing to flip him over. The other boy let out a low growl, curling his hand under his chin as he . . . sucked his thumb?

Hypnos was asleep.

"Wake *up*," hissed Séverin.

The sleeping Hypnos merely scowled harder, but didn't wake.

"He'll be fine," said another voice emerging from the darkened end of the leviathan. "I got to him before the second round of the blood Forging attack. The ice wine put the Order to sleep, and the blood Forging woke them up . . . though it won't let them move for another twelve hours."

The matriarch approached them. Her fur coat was clasped at her throat like a cape. But the rest of her attire was trousers and boots. *She* was the one who had knocked him unconscious. She gestured at her outfit and kicked lightly at a discarded mask on the floor. "Camouflage. I have you and your cohort to thank for the idea."

"You're—you're not—"

"Affected by the blood Forged drinks?" she asked. "I've thoroughly immunized myself to them."

Of course, thought Séverin, her little vials served with her suppers. The matriarch held out a tin of biscuits and a jar of the raspberry-cherry jam he had once loved.

"You took a bad fall . . . my apologies. Food will help. Besides, you need to eat before the journey."

Journey?

"Wh-what are you—"

"Rescuing you," said the matriarch abruptly. "You have no idea what's going on up there, do you? Allow me to illuminate the situation."

"Free me," demanded Séverin, raising his chained hands.

"After you see this," said the matriarch.

She gestured to the Mnemo-like screen above the podium and pressed her Babel Ring into the thicket and twist of stone thorns. The silver ceiling above flickered to life.

Séverin shot to his feet, only for the metal leviathan to lurch, listing heavily to the right and throwing off his balance. He staggered toward the Mnemo screen, which showed the ice grotto above. Enrique and Zofia were bound tightly, cloth stuffed into their mouths to keep them from screaming. Two pairs of Fallen House Sphinx stood on either side of them. But every sight was eclipsed by Laila. When he looked at her, he felt as if someone had grabbed his heart in a tight fist.

Ruslan gripped her arm, forcing an instrument into her hands.

Ruslan looked unaltered and unrecognizable in the same instant. An eccentric tilt to his mouth. Laugh lines around his eyes. And yet, his hand was pure *gold*. Gold as ichor. Gold as godhood.

Beside him, Eva looked stone-faced. She kept raising her eyes from the floor and staring at the others, her face inscrutable.

"*Read it*, my dear," demanded Ruslan. His smile cracked a little.

"Find the right strings that are to be played, and we might all pretend at being gods."

Laila's eyes darted back and forth between Enrique and Zofia.

"I—don't—know—how," she bit out.

Ruslan's smile hovered on his lips for an instant . . . and then he threw her against the ice. Séverin heard her skull thud against the wall. He wanted to rush to his feet, but he couldn't stand with his hands bound.

"Don't *lie* to me!" roared Ruslan. "I hate that. Do I look like a fool to you?" He paused, taking a deep breath and stretching his neck from side to side. "My father thought so . . . I'm sure the real patriarch of House Dazbog thought so too, but I killed him, so I can't ask. *I* think I'm clever, though. Look what I did! I became the patriarch. I released all his staff and brought in my own. I made sure your *troika* exploded in Moscow and almost finished the job before I realized that perhaps you could be of more use than I imagined . . . and, oh, how I imagined." Ruslan turned to Laila, smiling slowly. "Roux-Joubert whispered of you, my girl. He spoke of a girl who seemed to *know* things with just a touch. And he was right."

Ruslan rubbed his head with his gold hand, then he lowered it, turning it this way and that.

"So you see, I'm not a fool. Not yet, at least," he said quietly. "That is the cost of godhood, yes? Your Séverin was quick to recognize the ichor on the floor of the dining room . . . what I did not tell him was that there is a price to it all. I did not know, then, what it would cost to wield such a thing as the Midas Knife, to change the matter of humans entirely . . . to make us *different*."

He laughed.

"The hair goes first!" he said. "An annoying side effect. But the sanity quickly follows, and that's rather less easy to endure. Unless, of course, one has a permanent solution."

Ruslan spun the lyre in his hand, and in the space of a second, he was once more the mild-tempered patriarch of House Dazbog that he had pretended to be.

"Listen—hush, hush, I apologize for that outburst," he said, raising Laila to a stand. He stroked her cheek with the back of his golden hand. "It's important, you understand? I just want the world to be a better place. And I can do that if I had just a *touch* of God's power. Remake the world by remaking *us*. Don't you wish the world would be different? Don't you yearn for a day when you might walk freely through the world? Don't you, Zofia, wish to live without persecution? And you, Enrique, my sweet revolutionary historian . . . I know you dream what I dream . . . a world where people like us are not kept under foot, but restored to a place of equality." He turned Laila's chin toward Enrique and Zofia. "So, please. Don't make me hurt them. I hate doing that. For one, blood gets everywhere, which is so gruesome, positively uncouth"—he flashed a charming smile—"and for a second reason, I like them. I like *you*."

Tears streamed down Laila's face as she turned her face up to him.

"Don't you think I want to read it?" she demanded. Her eyes went to the glowing harp on the floor. "Don't you think that if I knew what strings to play, I would?" She flailed a hand at the instrument. "That is the only thing that could keep me *alive*, and it's useless to me. I can't move even a single string."

Ruslan let go of her face with a sound of disgust. "Again with this story of being"—he fluttered his hands, like waving away a swarm of flies—"*made*. You're lying. You're lying to protect your lineage, and I hate liars."

376 ☙ ROSHANI CHOKSHI

Séverin felt sick as Ruslan paced the floor, gently tapping a knife against the flat of his palm.

"The instruments of the divine . . . they have personalities. Like any of us!" said Ruslan. "And the personality of this one enjoys the company of ancient bloodlines rather exclusively. Now. This can be very simple. Play the instrument, and tell me the *place* that you see."

"Place?" repeated Laila wearily.

Ruslan itched his nose with his golden hand. "Of course there's a place, my dear! One doesn't merely strum a harp and become a god. No, no. *This* must be played somewhere special . . . in a temple. Played in the right temple—or theatre, if you will—and that lyre unlocks the power of God. Played anywhere else, and the lyre is very vindictive and destructive. Rude little object."

Laila's shoulders sank, and she looked up, not at Ruslan, but Eva.

"I don't know what's happening," she said. "I don't *know* what you're talking about, and I don't *see* anything—"

Eva's lower lip trembled, but she turned her head.

Séverin's gaze went to the lyre. Time seemed to move slower, and he wondered how hard he might have hit his head. He could see the strings glowing. Their delicate filament seemed softly hued, a rainbow glimpsed through an oiled pane of glass.

Ruslan sighed. "You don't give me much of a choice."

The Sphinx advanced on Enrique and Zofia.

"No!" Séverin tried to scream, but the matriarch clapped her hand over his mouth.

"Speak and you'll kill us all," she whispered harshly.

"What will motivate you to use your powers?" asked Ruslan. "I know you have them. I know just what your *touch* can do, Mademoiselle Laila."

Laila began to plead, and Ruslan sighed.

"Fine, I'll start with your lover, then," he said. He turned to one of the Sphinx. "Would you be so kind as to deliver me Monsieur Montagnet-Alarie?"

The Sphinx left.

"I imagine that will be an unfortunate surprise," said Delphine, glancing up at the Mnemo screen. "I was told to throw you in a jail cell and wait with you, but as you can see, we took quite a different route."

"Eva, please," whispered Laila.

But the other girl did not turn.

When the other Sphinx returned to the room empty-handed, Ruslan's smile fell.

"Gone?"

The Sphinx nodded.

"Well then, go find him! And make sure everyone is accounted for! Every matriarch and patriarch, every bloody fool with a ring on their hand. Go find them and make sure they know," he said. "Make sure they know who did this to them. Oh, and, wait—"

He paused, turning around to grab something lying on the ice. Séverin's stomach turned. It was Ruslan's hand. Or, rather, the hand of the real patriarch of House Dazbog.

"Slap them in the face with this," said Ruslan. He started laughing and then turned to Laila and Eva. "Truly? *No* laughs?"

Eva looked stricken.

"Perhaps I'm no dab *hand* at humor," said Ruslan, punctuating the word with a shake of the severed hand. "But hear me well, for I mean it, my dear. I'll even demonstrate on our good friend who wants to be listened to so dearly. I'm sure he'll appreciate the sentiment more than most."

He stalked toward Enrique. Too late, Séverin saw a flash of metal slice through the air. Enrique cried out, blood running down his neck . . .

Ruslan had sliced off his ear.

Laila shrieked, straining against her bonds, but Ruslan ignored her. Enrique fell to the floor, writhing painfully.

"An ear for an ear? Is that not a phrase?" mused Ruslan, kicking Enrique's severed ear across the ice. "Pity. Anyway." He turned to Laila. "You have ten minutes to make your decision. Time starting . . . *now*!"

Séverin jerked back from the matriarch's hold, catching his breath.

"We have to go," said Séverin. "We have to save them."

The matriarch watched him sadly. "There's nothing you can do for them. You cannot rush up the leviathan and free them. The leviathan can barely be held in one place with those broken tethers. Can't you see I'm saving your lives? We're leaving right now, through that pod—" she said, gesturing to the podlike device at the narthex. "From there, we can get to Irkutsk, and I can call for help. It leaves just enough time while he fools around thinking that girl has the Lost Muses bloodline."

But they could not do that in ten minutes. Which meant that Enrique, Zofia, Laila . . . all would die.

"You want me to let her die?" asked Séverin. "But you . . . you like her."

The expression on the matriarch's face was full of age and sorrow.

"And I *love* you," said Delphine. "I have always loved you, and look at what I still had to do."

Love? Séverin hadn't heard her say that to him in . . . in years.

He couldn't even mouth the word, it seemed to stick his lips together.

The matriarch removed her Babel Ring from the pillar, and the
Mnemo screen showing Laila, Enrique, and Zofia went blank.
And yet Séverin couldn't unsee the sharp light of those lyre strings,
or stop hearing the echo of the way Delphine had said the doctor
thinks *the girl has the Lost Muses' bloodlines.*

As if she didn't just know that Laila didn't have that bloodline,
but as if she already knew who did.

"Long ago, I made a promise to protect you," she said. "To take
care of you."

Séverin wanted to spit in her face. "To take care of me?"

"Sometimes protection . . . sometimes love . . . it demands hard
choices. Like the one I am asking of you now. I showed you this so
that you would know, and that you might make your own choice . . .
a luxury I myself did not have," said Delphine. "The Lost Muses
bloodline runs in *your* veins, Séverin."

Séverin opened his mouth, closed it. No words came to him,
and all he could do was stare numbly at her.

"All these years, I have kept you safe from the people who would
use it against you. Who would use you for their own gain. That's
why I had to keep you from the Order as much as I could. When
we performed the inheritance test, your blood could have made
those Forged objects snap in half. I had to hide you from yourself."
Delphine swallowed hard, fidgeting with her Babel Ring. When
she spoke, her voice was ragged with grief. "But I tried to help as
much as I could. When I saw how your first caretaker treated you,
I was the one who gave Tristan aconite flowers. I thought Clothilde
would mother you, but she was greedy, and the moment I found
out, I had you removed from their care. I was your first investor

in L'Eden. I fought for you from the sidelines. I mourned living without you every day."

Small things clicked in Séverin's head, but it was like a reed caught up in a river—there was simply not enough traction to let it stand and to wonder. *He* had the bloodline. He didn't have the space in his mind to process what that meant, or rather, what it failed to mean. Inheriting his House was a dream that had dried up in his soul, replaced with a desire that spanned eternity: a dream of godhood, the memory of invincibility that he had only felt through the Fallen House. All this time, he thought he had failed everyone by failing to find *The Divine Lyrics*, but the secret to its power lay in his very veins. It made him feel . . . absolved.

Around them, the leviathan began to list from side to side again. The sound of metal breaking and churning screeched through the silence. The leviathan was untethering. Soon, it would be fully beneath the lake, its belly full of water.

"You need to make a choice, Séverin," said Delphine quickly. "Escape or death." For a moment, he could say nothing, but then Delphine spoke again, and it was as if she'd peered inside his head. "You make the choice that you can live with. You do not have to like it."

She raised a knife and cut through his bindings. His hands were free, and the choice was his.

Séverin clung to Delphine's words in a way he had not done since he was a child. He glanced beside him to the sleeping Hypnos, and then to the silver ceiling where Laila stood with her head bowed, Enrique lay limply on his side, and Zofia stared numbly at the ice, tears streaking her cheeks. He wanted to protect them. He wanted to make impossible amends. He wanted to be a god.

What he had not considered was how a god acted, and this was his first taste—the bitter calculus of decision. Gods made choices. Gods burned cities and spared a child. Gods put gold in the palms of the wicked and left that miserable currency of hope in the hearts of the good. He could spare three and sacrifice one, and perhaps— by number alone—it held its own bloody logic. Laila would die if the lyre was played. Laila would die if the lyre was not played.

He closed his eyes.

When he breathed, he did not catch that scent of the leviathan's metal bones or the tang of raspberry-cherry jam. His lungs filled with *her*. Roses and sugar, the burnished silk of her skin, the force of her smile . . . powerful enough to alter the course of deep-rooted dreams.

He opened his eyes, reached into his pocket, and drew out Tristan's knife. The blade shimmering with the muted glitter of Goliath's venom. As he turned it, the scar on his palm gleamed. Even in the dark, he could make out the faint network of his veins, and the outline of the blood running within it.

You're only human, Séverin.

Therein lay the irony.

He didn't have to be.

To be a god, Séverin had to divorce himself from all that made him human. All his regret and, even, all his love. Sometimes to love meant to hurt. And he would be a loving god. Séverin looked up to the matriarch and felt as if that numbing ice had once more wrapped around his heart.

"I've made my choice."

34

ENRIQUE

Enrique's ear—or what had been his ear—throbbed with pain. He breathed slowly through his nose, trying to ignore the wet slick of blood dripping down his neck and focusing, instead, on the slender moon of the ice grotto. With every passing second, it thinned. Ten minutes had nearly passed, and still Ruslan kept turning the knife. Beneath them, the packed ice floor of the grotto began to splinter. Threads of water wept from the cracks. Enrique tried to speak, but the rough gag in his mouth held fast. Every part of him screamed that this was the end. He would die here, in this cold place that smelled of salt and metal, not at all like the sunshine-steeped earth of the Philippines.

And it was all his fault.

How fitting, he thought through the fog of pain, that Ruslan would take his ear. It was his own craving to be listened to that made him share the very information that damned them all. Ruslan had seen the weakness inside him and sharpened it to a weapon. Over and over, he replayed what Ruslan had said when he dragged them to the grotto. He'd secured the gag, humming to himself. And then he'd gripped Enrique's face, pressing their foreheads together.

"Thank you, my friend, for trusting me," Ruslan had said. "You know, I've always thought that I was meant to find *The Divine Lyrics* . . . but I now believe I needed you. And I understand with my whole heart that what I'm doing seems cruel . . . but I think you understand. It's all in service to the knowledge, is it not?"

True regret shone in his eyes.

"I wish, in war, there were no need for casualties," he said. "And yet, no one is truly safe. When the devil waged war in the heavens, even angels had to fall."

Now, the floor of the ice grotto trembled once more. The leviathan was slowly becoming unmoored. One of the tethers had broken loose, and the other—hooked around a mechanical gill—trembled. Its tail whipped against the underside of the floor, throwing Enrique to his side. His vision blurred for a moment, but he heard everything.

"Cousin," said Eva. "We should take this conversation to a different room."

Ruslan tapped the flat of his knife against his mouth, then closed his eyes.

"No," he said. "I'm waiting. Two minutes left, Laila."

"We could all *die*," said Eva.

"If we die here in pursuit of godhood, then I'll take the divine lyre to the bottom of the lake. I can live with that." Ruslan called out, "*Where* is Séverin? Why is it taking so long to find him?"

Enrique craned his neck. He could sense Zofia beside him, silent and unwavering. She stood straight-backed, her candlelight hair shining bright as a corona. Her eyes looked unfocused, hollow. The sight of her—so *defeated*—jolted him from grief.

Even though the minutes were sliding to nothing, even though he felt horror climbing up his throat . . . all he wanted was one moment to talk to her. They couldn't save the world. They couldn't save their friends. They couldn't save themselves. But he could tell her he was proud to know her, proud that he'd seen her wield a flaming sword and jump off the back of an ice stag. And if he could just tell her all the ways he knew they'd tried . . . it would have been enough.

"The last minute is up," sighed Ruslan.

Enrique tensed, expecting Ruslan to take his other ear or, worse, his very life. Beside him, Zofia closed her eyes. Enrique wanted to tell her not to worry, that everything would be fine, to keep her eyes closed. Ruslan took another step. Enrique braced himself. The pain in his ear was nothing more than a dull pressure. He could take it.

But then Ruslan stepped toward Zofia. The world slowed. *No. No. Not her.* Enrique thrashed, trying to get out of his bindings. His bound hands robbed his balance. Every time he tried to right himself, he failed and fell against the ice. He looked to Zofia, praying that her eyes had stayed shut . . . but they were open. Open and fixed on him, that blue-as-candle-hearts gaze scalding him like a flame.

"Please, you have to believe me!" shouted Laila.

"Believe? I have so *much* belief, my dear," said Ruslan. "That's why I do not hesitate in what I do."

He stroked the sides of the ancient lyre, attempting to pluck its dull strings for the thousandth time.

Enrique wanted to scream. He wanted to scream so badly that

when he heard a loud, shattering sound, he thought, for a moment, that it had come from deep within his soul. He looked up and saw that something inside the leviathan moved. A figure appeared. Séverin.

In spite of himself . . . in spite of how it broke something inside him to know that Séverin had destroyed his chances with the Ilustrados . . . he felt relief. When things fell apart, Séverin put them together. When they didn't know how to see what was in front of them, Séverin adjusted their focus. He would fix this. He *had* to fix this because no matter how much he'd changed . . . he was their Séverin.

Séverin stepped out of the leviathan's mouth, his face grim, the moth Mnemo on his lapel fluttering its stained glass wings. The moment his foot touched the ice, the leviathan wrested free of the last tether and sank into the waves. The last thing Enrique saw was the blue water lapping over its bulging, glass eye.

"You have the wrong person," said Séverin, staring at Ruslan.

"I thought you were unconscious somewhere," said Ruslan curiously. "Wherever did you come from?"

"The belly of the devil," said Séverin.

Ruslan took one step back from Zofia, and Enrique's heart rate eased.

"Sounds spacious," said Ruslan. "And very intriguing, but I'm more curious about why you think I have the wrong person? Laila has a *touch* unlike anyone else. I'm sure you'd agree."

Séverin's face darkened.

"She is a descendant of the Lost Muses—"

"She's not," said Séverin. "*I* am."

Enrique went still. What?

Ruslan stared at him, then started laughing. "*You?*"

"What do you see when you look at that lyre in your hand, Rus-lan?" asked Séverin. "Do you see dull, metal strings? Because I don't. I see a song waiting for my hands. I see the guide to a temple where the lyre must be played if you want its true power. Other-wise, it's useless to you."

A hungry expression flickered across Ruslan's face. "Prove it."

Séverin reached for the Mnemo bug on his lapel and slashed the sharp end of the pin across his palm. Out the corner of Enrique's vi-sion, he saw Laila strain forward, her eyes round with hope. Ruslan held out the lyre, and Séverin smeared his hand across the strings. Enrique held his breath. For a moment, nothing happened. And then, he heard a low sound. He couldn't say where it came from . . . some pocket of his soul or a corner of his mind. But if there had ever been a Music of the Spheres, a hymn that moved celestial bodies, it was *this*. A sound like winter wind shuffling icicles on branches, the mournful song of swans at dusk, the groan of the earth turning. He felt it sear through his bones, expand in his heart . . . a song woven into a thread that wound through his whole being.

But only for an instant.

Near the wall, Laila let out a cry and slumped forward. When she raised her head, blood trickled from her nose. Around them, pieces of the wall broke off, crashing into the ice. Ice sculptures, once moving, now froze. The projectile podiums went from glow-ing to muted and dull.

Everything Forged was failing.

Enrique forced his gaze to the lyre . . . there, the once dull and metallic strings shone iridescent. At least, Enrique *thought* it was iridescence. It was a sheen the likes of which he'd never seen. Something like the cross between a spill of oil on the surface of a pond and the ocean backlit by the sun.

"Amazing," said Ruslan. He tilted his head as he looked at Séverin. *"How?"*

And then he paused.

"Your mother," he said softly. "The woman from Algeria . . . I remember tales of her. And her name . . . *Kahina*. I wonder if the old patriarch of House Vanth knew what a treasure he'd managed to smuggle out of that country." He smiled, and then looked eagerly at the lyre. "Well, don't hold us in suspense any longer! Don't just pluck a string, play the thing!"

Enrique thrashed again on the ice, trying to catch Séverin's attention. *No! Don't do it.*

Laila spoke, her voice breaking. "Please, Séverin . . . please. I need you to play it. I . . . I'm dying—"

"I know," he said, cutting her off.

The ice in his voice would've frozen the room over.

When he said nothing else, Laila flinched. Her mouth opened, closed. Enrique watched the horror settling behind her eyes, and he wanted to tell her . . . no. Not that. He wanted *Séverin* to tell her that the lyre destroyed all that was Forged. That there was a reason behind this pain.

"Please," she said.

"Yes, *please*, Séverin," said Ruslan, like a child. "Play it."

Séverin looked at Laila, his expression utterly blank, and then he turned to Ruslan.

"No."

Laila hung her head, her hair curtaining her face, and Enrique— even as relief surged through him—felt his heart ache.

"I won't play it here and risk my own chance at godhood," said Séverin with a cruel smile. "You need me, so I suggest you follow my rules."

"Play it," insisted Ruslan. "Or . . ." His gaze slid to Enrique and Zofia. "Or I'll kill them."

Enrique's pulse turned jagged. If he played it for them, Laila would die. If he didn't play it, all three of them would die. But however much he struggled with his thoughts, Séverin seemed collected.

"I'll save you the trouble."

Séverin moved swiftly. His face was blank and cold, and Enrique thought he had never seen such empty determination in someone's eyes. Enrique struggled against his bindings as Séverin crossed the room, standing before Zofia. She flinched back as he grabbed the nape of her neck. Something red glinted on his hand. And then, impossibly, Séverin's dagger went to her heart.

Zofia's heart.

The same heart that offered so much without hesitation. A heart full of bravery. Full of fire.

Enrique blinked. He had to be wrong. Maybe he'd lost so much blood, he couldn't see straight . . . but no. Séverin stood so close to Zofia that he might have been whispering in her ear. Not that Zofia would see. Her eyes widened, her body slumping forward as she went utterly still. Séverin's hands were cherry red. Laila let out a scream, just as Séverin turned to him with that same knife. His eyes held no humanity, but something older. Something feral.

Séverin moved closer. Enrique's heartbeat thundered so loud in his ears that he almost didn't realize Séverin was speaking. When he finally heard him, it made no sense.

"I wish my love was more beautiful."

I don't understand, Enrique wanted to say.

But Séverin didn't give him the chance.

35

LAILA

Laila did not trust her body.

It had failed her by not lasting long enough. It had failed her by filling her soul with the wingbeats of false hope. It had failed her now by showing her something that could not be real. Each blink of her eyes, each beat of her heart rendered what she saw more sharply until she could not ignore her own senses.

Séverin had killed Zofia.

Séverin had walked to her, his gait unchanging, purposeful. He looked down at Zofia, and Laila *wished* she had not seen her friend's face. She wished she hadn't seen her blue eyes widening, hope glossing her gaze.

How many times had they done this? How many times had Séverin swept in at the last moment . . . and freed them?

Hope squeezed through the cracks of logic. There was a moment—bright and suspended—where Séverin bent down, as if to whisper in Zofia's ear, and Laila thought all might still be well.

She could not see her hope for what it was, nothing more than a silvered serpent.

"No!" she called out.

But it changed nothing. Zofia slumped to the ground, beside Enrique who squirmed and kicked out against the ice as Séverin turned to him. Then he too went still.

Gone.

They were both *gone*.

And for some reason, she was still here. The wrongness slanted through her heart. She was not supposed to outlive them. She thought about her mother on the day she died. For two days before her death, Laila had clutched her mother's hand so tightly, she was convinced her soul wouldn't be able to find its way out of the body. In that time, her father's grief became a land of exile. One that, perhaps, he never left. Maybe that was why he knelt at his wife's bed when he thought their daughter had gone to sleep. Maybe that was why he said: *I keep praying they will take her instead of you.*

Her mother had shushed him for saying such things: *I would never wish for the pain to outlive the ones I love. Even in this, I can find God's blessing.*

To outlive the ones she loved.

She had not considered such a thing to be a curse until now. Though how long that existence would last, she could not say.

Laila had always wanted her last sight to be beautiful—and he was. He was moving darkness, and he was all she could see. Séverin walked toward her, rubbing his thumb across his mouth. Laila zeroed in on that mouth, the same one that had spoken such truths and whispered her name as if it were an invocation meant to save him. The same one that had just condemned her to death.

I'm dying—

I know.

Such words held all the finality of a thrust blade. He knew. He knew, and he didn't care. Laila wanted to believe she had dreamt up all of the last hours' tenderness—his kiss, his smile, his body curling around hers in sleep. But then, peeking out over the collar of his shirt, Laila glimpsed the evidence of last night: a smudge of her lip rouge. *Wrong wrong wrong.* How could she have been so wrong?

"Laila—" started Eva, looking stricken. "I never . . . I thought—"

Laila tuned her out.

"I take it killing her won't make you play the lyre either, will it?" asked Ruslan.

"No," said Séverin. "She'll die soon anyway, and my knife is too slippery. I'd like to get moving before dark. I am sure we have a ways to travel."

Ruslan nodded. He reached for the lyre on the ground. The strings still shimmered from Séverin's blood, but the light in them had dulled. Laila stared after it. Her body had failed her once more, for while it might look like a member of the Lost Muses . . . that too had been a lie.

"Goodbye, Laila," said Ruslan, waving sadly. "You might not be a true muse, but you will live on as inspiration to me."

He blew her a kiss and then glanced to Eva.

"Knock her out."

HOURS LATER, LAILA WOKE UP sprawled out on the ice.

Beside her, she caught the faintest stirring of colorful wings. She blinked, her senses slowly flowing back into her as she saw what lay beside her head: a Mnemo bug and a single diamond pendant from the necklace Séverin had given her.

Laila touched her throat. The rest of her choker was gone. Maybe Eva had taken it, ripped it off her like some prize. Laila wished her throat didn't feel so bare. She wished she didn't recognize that Mnemo bug lying on the ice. Once, it had been on Séverin's lapel. Laila stared at the thing, her hand twitching to reach for it, but she refused. This had always been the risk. That she should offer her heart, only to be told it wasn't as precious as she had thought it to be. The last thing she wanted to see was the moment when Séverin had come to that realization himself.

Across from her, Laila saw the broken forms of Enrique and Zofia. They almost looked asleep, if it hadn't been for the red seeping into the ice beneath them. And Hypnos . . . where was he? What had Séverin done to him? Laila pinched her nose, feeling sick. When she looked at them, she was reminded of every moment they had spent in L'Eden. Every moment they had sat beside her in the kitchens. When she closed her eyes, she could almost smell those memories, fresh bread and—unmistakable to her wrung out senses—the tang of raspberry jam.

It was this scent, biting and sweet, that made her reach for the Mnemo butterfly. Its colorful wings burned with Séverin's memories. She held that knowledge lightly in her palm for a few seconds. And then, in one swift movement, Laila dashed it against the floor. The images in its wings rose up like smoke. Whatever memories the moth held soaked into the ice and vanished, leaving Laila alone in the frigid Sleeping Palace. Around her, the icicles chimed and the ceiling quivered so that a light snow sifted to the ground, and Laila thought of Snegurochka. She wished she were like her, a girl whose very heart could thaw and unmake her on the spot. Perhaps if she had been a girl made of gathered snow, she would be nothing but a puddle of water. But she was not. She was bones and pelt, and though every part of her felt broken, she wrapped her arms around her knees as if it might hold her together.

36

SÉVERIN

Séverin Montagnet-Alarie knew there was only one difference between monsters and gods. Both inspired fear. Only one inspired worship.

Séverin sympathized with monsters. As he walked out onto the hard ice of Lake Baikal, his heart humming, his body numb . . . he understood that perhaps monsters were misunderstood gods; deities with plans too grand for humans; a phantom of evil that drank from the roots of good.

He should know.

After all, he was a monster.

Ruslan and Eva flanked him on either side. The slow crunch of footsteps behind him reminded Séverin that they weren't alone. The Sphinx of House Dazbog—*no, the Fallen House,* he corrected silently—followed, casting reptilian shadows across the ice. And that was to say nothing of the members spread out and hiding across Europe.

"Séverin, I have no desire to rush you, considering the events that just transpired . . ." said Ruslan. He tapped his chin with the severed hand of the former House Dazbog patriarch. "But . . . when, exactly, do you plan on playing the divine lyre?"

"As soon as we're in the right place," said Séverin.

At the back of his mind, he saw the way the room had begun to fall apart . . . at the mere *touch* of his blood to the strings. He remembered Laila lifting her bloodied face, her wince of pain. Séverin was so lost in thought that he almost didn't hear Eva speak.

"I thought you loved them," said Eva quietly, so quietly that Ruslan—consulting with his Sphinx—did not hear.

"And?" he asked.

"I . . . ," Eva said, before trailing off.

Séverin knew what she would say.

What he had done had not looked like love.

But then again, love did not always wear a face of beauty.

One hour earlier . . .

"I've made my choice," said Séverin.

"And?" asked the matriarch.

"And I like neither option," said Séverin, turning toward the leviathan's entrance back to the ice grotto. "So I will make a third."

"And how will that work?" demanded the matriarch. "You'll give yourself over to them, and then what? Let them become gods and lay waste to the world?"

"I'll figure it out," said Séverin.

Delphine grabbed hold of his sleeve, and he shook her loose.

"If you go up there, the leviathan may not hold!" she said. "It may crumble out from beneath you, and then what?"

Then the reward is still greater than the risk, thought Séverin, even as he said nothing. Ruslan had only given Laila ten minutes. Already, their time dwindled.

"Wait," said the matriarch.

Something in her voice made him stop.

"I know where the lyre will take you," she said. "It will lead you to a temple far away from here . . . There might still be ancient Tezcat routes that lead to it, but I don't know where those are. All I know is the location of this temple activates that lyre. Once its true power is ripe, all the Babel Fragments of the world are at risk of being torn out of the earth and joined once more. It was what the Fallen House always wanted . . . that they might rebuild the Tower of Babel, climb it, and claim God's power for themselves."

Séverin did not turn around.

"How do you know this?" he asked.

Delphine paused and then exhaled. It was a sound full of relief, as if she'd finally shoved off the weight of this secret.

"Your mother told me," she admitted. "Your mother wanted to make sure I would be able to protect you, and that—if you needed— you would know the secret she carried with her."

Your mother. All this time, Kahina and Delphine had known that the cost of protecting him meant harming him. And for the first time, he felt like he could finally *see* inside the choices Tristan had made.

For too long, Séverin had wondered whether Tristan's . . . habits . . . would have turned on them. But what if his habits were his version of mercy? All those demons at Tristan's throat, pushing his hand, warping his thoughts. What if it meant that all he could do was displace his horror onto something else rather than *them*?

Tristan's love had worn the face of horror.

Delphine's love had worn the face of hate.

Kahina's love had worn the face of silence.

No sooner had he thought that then he felt the pressure of his brother's blade against his chest. The knife was all he had left of Tristan. Since he'd died, Séverin had held the knife close like a ghost he could not let go, but now he saw it as something else . . . a gift. A final blessing. What he would do next was no less monstrous than Tristan's actions . . . and yet it held its own version of love. Séverin touched his Mnemo bug and breathed deep. For the first time in a while, he no longer caught the scent of dead roses. He smelled the freshness of fallen snow, the scent of a new beginning.

"Whatever my mo—" Séverin stopped, his mouth still not holding the shape of that word. He swallowed hard. "Whatever Kahina told you about the temple's coordinates, I need you to tell Hypnos, so we can get there before Ruslan. But for now, I have to get to the grotto."

"The leviathan won't hold," retorted Delphine. "Soon, its tether will break, and I need to get us out of this machine in the next few minutes! You might not make it to the top, and if you fall with the machine, you'll drown."

"Then I must move quickly," said Séverin, making his way toward Hypnos.

From his jacket pocket, Séverin pulled out Tristan's knife. He turned it over in his palm, tracing the translucent vein on the blade where Goliath's venom shone in the half-light. One slice from this side of the blade was no different from the blood Forging paralysis plaguing the Order of Babel. For a couple hours, it could make even the living look dead. In Séverin's other hand, he weighed the raspberry-cherry jam that looked so much like blood. His plan crystallized. Against his palm, the hilt of Tristan's blade felt warm and reassuring, and Séverin wondered whether his brother was trying to show him that they had far more in common than once imagined.

Séverin knelt beside Hypnos and shook him awake. Hypnos yawned, stared up at him, and then gradually saw where he was. He jolted upright, skittering backwards and raising himself up on his elbows.

"Wh-what's happening?"

"Do you trust me?" asked Séverin.

Hypnos scowled. "I already hate this conversation."

"No need to participate, then," said Séverin. "Just listen closely . . ."

FIVE MINUTES LATER, he headed up the stairs. He heard Ruslan's voice, the crackle of ice as the leviathan listed from side to side, whipping against the underside of the ice grotto. He grasped the handrails for stability. With every breath, he inhaled the terrible metal of the leviathan's belly and repeated his plan over and over inside his head.

By now, he expected Delphine and Hypnos were safely ensconced inside their pod, waiting in the waters. Near the top of the stairs, he took a deep breath . . .

He was about to step outside when he heard a voice call out to him.

Séverin whirled around, shocked to see Delphine a few paces

behind him. She was out of breath. In one of her hands, she held out his great black coat. Tucked under her arm was a coiled rope and a single Shu Gust helmet.

"You forgot this," she said, shoving the coat into his hands. "And it's very cold."

He stared numbly at it, then quickly recovered.

"What do you think you're doing? If you're not out soon, you'll—"

Delphine waved her hand nonchalantly, then shoved the Shu Gust into his hands. "I know. I couldn't risk something happening to you. I made a promise to keep you safe, and I intend to keep it. If I stay in the pod, I know the leviathan won't run aground."

Séverin stared at her. Without the Shu Gust . . . she would die. She was going to die. For *them*.

"Why?" he asked. "Why not run back up? To the grotto?"

To me, he could not bring himself to say aloud.

Delphine's smile was weary and warm and utterly exasperated. It was an expression that tugged at something behind his chest. It was the face he remembered her making when he had done something mischievous and been caught out. An expression that said she would love him no matter what he did.

"And risk Hypnos? Risk letting them find out all that I truly know and might have told you? No, Séverin. I could not give you more time, then . . . but I can now," she said. "Now go."

"Don't leave," he said, the words felt unfinished on his tongue.

Don't leave me, again.

Delphine kissed him fiercely on both cheeks. Tears glossed her eyes, and her voice broke.

"Love does not always wear the face we wish," she said. "I wish my love had been more beautiful. I wish . . . I wish we had more time."

She held his hands in hers, and for a moment, Séverin was a child again, trusting her enough that he would close his eyes when he held her hand . . . always knowing she'd keep him safe.

"*Tante—*" he croaked.

"I know, child," she soothed. "I know."

Then, she pushed him out of the leviathan's mouth, fleeing back down the stairs without another glance. Séverin watched her disappear, sorrow twisting through him. He forced himself to step out of the entrance to the leviathan's mouth. Though the light glancing off the ice shone harsh and blinding, the shapes of Laila, Zofia, and Enrique were unmistakable. The world moved at a relentless pace, and all he could catch were Delphine's last words. He turned them over and over in his heart.

Delphine was right.

Love did not always wear the face one wished it would.

Sometimes it looked downright monstrous.

Something inside Séverin sagged with relief. He touched the Mnemo moth at his lapel, feeling the faint stirring of the wings, the true secret of all that he planned nestled in its wings. Around him, the leviathan began to thrash. And Séverin bent his head, his hands curled into fists at what he knew he must do.

SÉVERIN HARDLY REMEMBERED what he'd said to Ruslan, far too nervous the other man would see through his falsehoods and straight to the truth of what he was doing, to the raspberry-cherry jam tucked into his pocket, to Tristan's paralyzing dagger. Enrique and

Zofia may not like it. But when they woke up, they would understand.

Turning to Laila, though, was harder.

She would not understand that he was trying his best to save her. If they could find the temple . . . if they could grasp the power of God for themselves, then it would not matter that the divine lyre could kill her. *He* could save her.

Remember what you mean to me, thought Séverin, as he ignored Laila's pleading and walked away from her, the weapon of her destruction tucked under his arm. *Remember that I am your Majnun.*

He watched as Eva's blood Forging touch forced Laila to slump onto the ground. He watched her black hair spill out around her and fumbled an excuse of needing to retrieve something from her person . . . but that was not what he had done. He crouched beside her. One last time, he memorized the poetry of her face, the length of her eyelashes, the searing burn of her presence in the world. He slipped his Mnemo butterfly and all of its truths onto her sleeve. And last, he took her diamond choker, leaving one single diamond pendant behind so that when the time came, she might summon him from the dark.

As Séverin walked away from the grotto, he thought of Delphine. She was right. Love could look monstrous. But if they could find the strength to believe in him just one more time . . . they would see past its visage. They would understand that he could still make good on his promise. That he could still protect them.

That he was not a monster, but a god unformed, one whose plan would soon be deciphered.

EPILOGUE

Hypnos steered the small pod, waiting under the waters of Lake Baikal before he made his move. He could not bring himself to look at the bottom of the lake where the bent and crumpled form of the leviathan lay. And where, now, the matriarch lay too.

His eyes prickled with tears, but he kept his hand steady on the steering apparatus.

"My nephew is next, you know, and I won't have any of your nonsense affecting him," Delphine had said to him, scolding and condescending to her last second.

By "next" she had meant *heir*. Hypnos forced himself to joke and grin.

"And?"

"And he's a *saint*," said Delphine. "So be nice to him."

Hypnos had mustered all his strength not to cry. At the very least, he could make her laugh . . .

"Oh good, I like saints," he said, even as his voice trembled. "They're used to being on their knees."

Delphine had smacked him in the arm, and he interpreted this as a hug, for she merely leaned toward him when he kissed her on both cheeks.

"You are terrible," she said lovingly.

"Je t'aime aussi."

Hypnos thought of this now, his heart sinking. He wanted to be there when Enrique and Zofia woke up. He wanted to be there for Laila, who was probably waiting for him now that she'd read the Mnemo butterfly and understood what Séverin had done. But he would have to wait for the right moment to make his move and breach the small circle of water in the ice grotto. He closed his eyes, thinking of his last moments with Séverin.

"I *still* want to come with you," he'd said.

Séverin had refused.

"But *why*—" Hypnos had started to say, when Séverin had grabbed hold of his hands in an iron grip.

"Because *I protect you*," he said. "Do you understand?"

Hypnos felt the words move through him, like answered prayer. Yes, he thought. Yes, he understood. He pressed his hand to his jacket pocket. There lay the coordinates to the temple . . . the place that could lift the Babel Fragments out of the earth and change the world as they knew it. He thought he could feel the weight of this knowledge like something slowly stirring awake, the mere consequence of knowing it already sending rippling effects through the universe.

Soon, he would be with them. Soon, they would race across the world.

But for the next two minutes, Hypnos had no choice but to wait.

ACKNOWLEDGMENTS

2019 has been one of the best, most vivid, and challenging years of my life. Dream wedding! Two book releases in four months! Tour! Travel! PACK UP AND MOVE! Attempts to bribe a cat who is *furious* about all these new changes in addition to his absence at the wedding!

It's been a lot, and I wouldn't change it for the world. I am so enormously grateful to the people who raised this book out of the muck, instilled me with the confidence to keep going, metaphorically smacked me upside the head when I needed it, and read draft after draft after draft.

First, to my husband (!!), Aman. Thanks so much for marrying me. You've got the best face and the best soul, and I'm ridiculously proud to be your wife and co-cat parent.

Thank you to Lyra Selene, a literal dream of a critique partner; Renée Ahdieh, the nuna I didn't ask for but always needed; Sarah Lemon, word sorceress and possessor of infinite empathy;

snap-out-of-it oracle J. J. Jones; Ryan Graudin, fellow meeper and word witch. Thank you also to friends who have always been so generous with time, wisdom, and experience: Shannon Messenger, Stephanie Garber, Jen Cervantes. Thank you, also, to Holly Black. If I could tell my twelve-year-old self that her favorite writer would one day willingly chat on the phone and help brainstorm and bolster up a book that was more adverb than action, I would've eaten my hat. Mercifully, I cannot time travel, and I do not own hats (For this specific reason? Probably not). A giant hug and thanks to Noa Wheeler, who has helped make me a better writer with every critique, and always calmly leads me out of snarly plot labyrinths.

To my family at Sandra Dijkstra Literary Agency, thank you for championing my work and always having my back. To Thao, agent extraordinaire, every year that passes just makes me more grateful to be #TeamThao. To Andrea, thank you for the book passports and texts that brighten my day! To Jennifer Kim, thank you for your patience and attentiveness.

I am indebted to sales, editorial, audio, production, LITERALLY EVERYONE at Wednesday Books. Eileen, for the sharp insight, invaluable support, and holding my hand while I wade through the dark depths of drafting; DJ, for writing chats, and publishing adventures, and Portland airports playing "A Thousand Years" while we violently lose our chill; Jess, not only do you have exquisite musical taste (WE LOVE YOU, J. COLE), but you're also an amazing publicist, and it's such a dream to see this story all over the place. To Tiffany, Natalie, Dana, and all those who have touched this book in any capacity, thank you, thank you, thank you. Thank you to Christa Desir, for warmly and sharply copy editing this book.

A huge thanks to my superhuman assistant, Sarah Simpson-Weiss, who props up my brain and makes all the things possible. Thank you to Kristin Dwyer, for being an amazing team player and for all the humor and guidance.

To my wonderful friends who make reality more fantastical than fantasy, thank you. I could not do this without you. A thousand hugs to Niv, my favorite artist, who has listened to all my stories since literal infancy; Cara-Joy, who could probably tell the sun it was off schedule and it would revert its course at her demand; Marta, the brilliant human embodiment of a warm, fuzzy blanket; and Bismah, who has neither confirmed nor denied her spy status but always has my back regardless. Love you.

To my families, I love you all so much. Thank you for always being there, always encouraging, and always conveniently forgetting the plot twists I mention so that I get to feel smart when I run the story by you for the thousandth time. To Pog: the most brilliant piggle in all the land and holder of delightful miscellaneous historical anecdotes. To Cookie: who eats my food and steals my clothes, and in return offers exceptional counsel, laughs, and warmth. To Rat: who also eats my food and steals my clothes and in return offers love and free dental care (kthxbye!). To Mom and Dad, thanks for bragging about me on Facebook and randomly telling strangers about your daughter who sits around in pajamas for a living. Couldn't do this without you, and wouldn't want to! To Mocha and Pug, you've felt like family for a long time, but I'm glad it's now official. To Ba, Dadda, and Lalani, the most supportive and loving grandparents in the world. To my Ba, especially, I wouldn't be a storyteller without you.

A huge thank-you to my readers who have been with me on this journey since 2016. You guys are amazing, and you have no idea how much you inspire me every day. Thank you, always, for loving these characters as much as I do.

And last, to Panda and Teddy, who can neither read nor write, but whose furry presence somehow makes all things easier.